REQUIEM
B O O K   2 :   E X P O S E D

REQUIEM

BOOK 2: EXPOSED

TAVEYAH LaSHAY

TAVEYAHLASHAY.COM

Dedication

I dedicate this book to my tribe, my village of support.
This book would not be possible without you.
There was a lot to overcome in the making of this novel.
But, through the pandemic, the anxiety, and all other obstacles,
this gift was birthed for all of you!

Happy Reading!

Exposed *(adj)*– no longer hidden, unprotected, vulnerable

Chapter 1

VERDELL

Verdell sat idle in his father's driveway, captured by the notification that popped up on his smartphone.

Police Investigate Decapitation After Temple Terrace Man Found Dead

Hillsborough County, Florida – A man was found dead, decapitated, with full-body trauma inside an empty warehouse in Temple Terrace on Harney Road on February 28 at 4:55 p.m., according to the Hillsborough County Sheriff's Office. Deputies have ruled this a homicide and believe the horrifying murder was not a random act.

The Hillsborough County Sheriff's Office asks anyone with information about the death to contact (813) 777-9311. Sheriff Dunn said that all information is essential information. No detail is too small to report. Anyone can call in tips anonymously to Crime Stoppers.

Police have not released the victim's identity.

A grin spread across Verdell's face as he skimmed the breaking news story. The news notifications helped him keep an eye on how much information the police were willing to reveal. Verdell laughed again as he read that same story a third time. To most people, laughing at something so horrible would constitute insanity, but for Verdell, it was just business. As he got out of his car and grabbed his belongings, Verdell shook his head. He was privy to something the police were not. No one would be calling the tip line to help solve this one. He made sure of that when he disposed of the body.

*

"Hey, Pops. How your legs feeling today?" Verdell asked as he laid his laundry, pressed and starched, fresh from the cleaners, across the new oversized chair in his father's living room.

Verdell Sr., his father, pushed himself back and swayed forth in an old Rocker and Glider chair.

If Verdell was going to continue to stay there, the house needed an upgrade. And social security sure as hell was not paying for luxuries.

"I'm doing as well as I can be, son. You know this plastic keeps me stiff sometimes. But I won't complain." His father grunted and chuckled lightheartedly, tapping his cane against his prosthetic legs.

Verdell stared at his father blankly before bursting into

laughter, a little harder than he should have. His father's look of disgust let him know that he was a little overzealous with that last chuckle, but Verdell shrugged it off. Living without legs was considered a blessing in his father's situation. The old coot should have lost his life.

"Hell, I don't see what you standing over there, snickering about. You over there with both your legs and ain't got the good sense God gave you to not laugh at those who are suffering."

Verdell watched, lip curled into a scowl, as his father used a cane to balance his weight and get up from the chair. Verdell Sr. slid prosthetic feet into his torn old house shoes and shuffled towards the kitchen, mumbling under his breath.

"I don't know why the hell you would ask me just to make fun of me. Something ain't right with that shit there. Not right at all."

Verdell made a mental note to aim higher, possibly for the neck or the head, the next time he felt the extreme urgency to off his father. Verdell hawked his throat and sucked his teeth before following his old man into the kitchen.

Standing at the door, Verdell already knew the answer but figured he would ask, "Did you eat today?"

"What you ask me that for? You going to laugh at me for starving too?" his father asked, full of sarcasm.

Sorting out pots and pans, Verdell prepared to cook a quick dinner of corned beef, rice, and cabbage before he left for the night. "Pops, why all the sarcasm? I asked because I care. I would think that you would have pulled yourself together by

3

now and realized there are better ways to die than starvation."

If feeling sorry for himself was the only sentiment his father gained after being shot and having both of his legs amputated, it was a hell of an improvement. Who knew it would take having his legs blown off to get a little emotion out of him? Maybe if his father had gained a little perspective after they lost his mother, then they would not be here.

Thoughts about losing his mother made Verdell's blood boil, despite reaching into the cold fridge to grab the cabbage and the celery. Verdell had to get a grip on his anger before he ruined everything again.

*

Eight years ago, Verdell shot his father, not once but twice. No matter how justified his anger, it was not an authorized hit. Verdell's job description had always included maintaining self-control as a priority. It was what separated his class from the mongrels. Therefore, his emotional slip-up, howbeit not murder, was still punishable.

When Verdell shot his father, he thought he had walked away from his childhood home for the last time. He would never have expected to be here now, taking care of a man he once blamed for all of the horrible shit that ever happened to him since his mother passed. Maybe he still held him responsible.

After the emotional drain of leaving his father for dead and the gory nature of his assignments in the days leading up to that heated decision, Verdell wanted to give himself a semi-retirement gift. Somewhere peaceful, he could dress his physical and mental wounds, maybe eat a few tasty meals, and take a few ladies for a wild ride. His search for peace led him to a Craigslist ad for a 2.7 acre property with split level home with three bedrooms, three full baths, a barn, and a natural lake in Thonotosassa. It was the perfect location for him to get away when he was not on assignment. Verdell emailed the contact, making sure to tell them he could pay in cash. Not to his surprise, he received a response within minutes, asking when he would be available to see the property.

Verdell checked with all of his sources to make sure the listing was legit. Verdell waited until his connections in the city's Commissioners' office signed off before happily agreeing to set up his walkthrough for the next evening.

The property was more than he could have ever imagined. The pictures were no match for what stood before him. Verdell declined to see the barn and the rest of the land after viewing the main house. Garden jet tubs, marble in the wet areas and main walkways, and plush carpeting in all the rooms. He had to act fast. He felt like he would lose it to another buyer if he did not make an offer now. Verdell could not believe a place like this was still available. And it was going to be his. He offered fifteen percent below the asking price, and it only took the realtor twenty minutes and one question to get his offer accepted. The owner wanted cash. Who would pass up two hundred seventy five thousand dollars cash? Surely not anyone he knew. There was only one problem. Verdell hid his payouts from each job in different accounts. Sometimes, it was hard for him to recall where his handler routed the funds.

The amount of money he accumulated was always a surprise to him. And as long as it kept growing, there were no issues. Verdell chose to live out of his newly acquired 2008 Dodge Challenger and had spent next to nothing since he started wet working. That was one of the perks of the job he loved. It paid for itself. The premium he received for completing each assignment was more like a bonus.

*

Verdell excused himself from the realtor to go outside and check his balance and make the transfer in private. As soon as his foot hit the driveway, he found himself gasping for air as they bagged him.

Verdell began to panic and fought his attackers. He could tell the bag did not have many holes because he felt himself beginning to pass out from the lack of oxygen coming through the small holes in the sack.

Thoughts quickly ran through his head about who could have grabbed him. Who could have known where he would be and catch him off his game? *Could it have been Donnie Belasco's people?* Verdell ruled them out because he had not heard any fake ass Boston accents or smelled any weird combination of basil and cinnamon men's body spray. *How about the guy that had his side piece and his daughter whacked? No. That guy was a fucking sociopath and definitely would have foolishly announced his plan to bag me before paying his stooges to execute me.*

Thoughts about sparing the daughter after murdering her mother made Verdell's chest tighten. He gasped for air, trying to release the tension, but only found himself closer to unconsciousness. He had to stay focused. Verdell realized if he was not dead, the best thing he could do was sit back and enjoy the ride. Verdell breathed in deep and exhaled. Performing that task alone let him know that there was a chance he would make it out of this snatch and grab alive.

Verdell woke up in what he remembered as the diagnostic room. While inside, they showed him pictures of his father airlifted and arriving at Tampa General Hospital. He had not bled out from his bullet wounds. Verdell did not get a chance to explain his botched attempt at revenge. The Camp had Verdell gagged, bare from his waist up, strung upside down, and dipped his entire trigger arm from shoulder to fingertips in concentrated hydrochloric acid. Verdell had to keep his head craned and tried his best to keep it from flailing, despite the convulsions of agony that rippled through his body. They would have to kill him if they wanted him dead. He was not going to dip his head in the acid for them.

Verdell had never felt that type of debilitating pain in his life. He just knew that he would see the bone when they pulled his arm out of the vat. The smell was unbearable. He threw up twice and caught a crick in his neck from trying to stay stiff enough to avoid the acid that was dangerously close to his skull. Burning hair mixed with the smell of dying flesh had Verdell

7

extremely nauseous. To Verdell's surprise, he did not see the bone, but his skin appeared melted into the muscle. He could not remember if he passed out from the pain or the sight of his arm disintegrating right before his eyes.

They tortured and beat Verdell into a haze for days. When he woke up, the fog was so heavy; he could not recall if his torment lasted days or weeks. He was in a dingy two star motel off Fletcher and Nebraska with his arm wrapped in gauze when he came to. Next to him, the number of an orthodontist to replace missing teeth, a manila envelope, and a briefcase holding five hundred twenty five thousand dollars. On the dirt-smudged mirror was a sticky note that said, "If your simple ass didn't know before, now you know who the hell gives the orders, and it sure as hell ain't you. Lay low. We'll call you when we need you."

It took Verdell three full months to heal from his injuries and the surgery on his mouth. He needed to get a sleeve to cover the scar tissue on his arm. He had learned his lesson. The Camp made it clear their position on unauthorized hits. He understood.

Fortunately for him, when he was out of commission, no one had bought the Thonotosassa property. Verdell knew the realtor had a thing for him when they first met, and sure enough, when he called, she was anxious to meet him and go over the purchase contract. Verdell was more than happy to oblige. When he gave her the two hundred seventy five thousand dollars for the property and another fifteen thousand for herself, she had no problem helping him warm the house up. His only catch, she had to do everything in panties, only. Verdell had finally bought his peace.

*

Closing the refrigerator door, Verdell looked at his arm as a reminder of his lack of discipline. He would not dare risk going down that road again. At the oddest moments, the smell of burnt skin and hair still haunted him. Especially in times like these, when he felt his sorry ass father had many more secrets to be punished for.

Chapter 2

TATIANA

"You all closed off and uptight, girl," Mr. Man breathed heavily into her ear.

The disgusting old dog took out a wad of twenty-dollar bills and waved it in the air before rubbing it slowly across her lips. Even the money smelled like old ass muscle cream. The bile shot up from the pit of her stomach and almost spilled out of her mouth. If she wanted to get this money, she knew her throw up would not be the only thing she would have to swallow this evening.

"You need to loosen up a little bit if you want what I got for you."

Tatiana did not want to know what he had for her at all. What she thought was a quick way to make some money to finish paying for a few past due college expenses turned out to be her first take on what it felt like to sell your soul in the back alley of a movie theater. She felt not one ounce of joy at that moment. With the way Mr. Man was groping her ass, Tatiana knew saving her body would mean damning her soul. Hopefully, God would hear her prayers for redemption later. Right now, she had to figure out how to clear her mind and come up with a plan.

Tatiana could not remember the movie they went to see or anything special about the drive over. A smooth jazz set hummed through the air outside the building, and Tatiana tried to let the music soothe her racing heart. She could not breathe. The wind blew the sweat beading on her neck, but she felt confined in the open space. Claustrophobic. The darkness of the night, the stickiness of the humid air, the crowds of people rushing by, and the nasty old man she knew as Mr. Man, pressed against her. Tatiana felt her phone vibrate in her bra. She faked a sneeze and pushed away Mr. Man's molesting hands so that he would not notice.

"Ahhh, hell now." He said as he scrunched up his nose, giving her the stink face. "Cairo told me you were clean."

Tatiana looked at the man like he was crazy.

"Clean? So, sneezing means I'm not clean? You know what? I ain't got time for this shit."

Tatiana began to walk off before turning back around and spitting off, "Cairo told me you were younger."

The phone vibrated again. There was no need to look at it because Tatiana already knew who it was. Cairo wanted to make sure she followed through on their deal. *All this to pay for a few classes?* Tatiana silenced her phone and adjusted her bra.

"Let's just get this over with," she mumbled to herself as she made up her mind and turned to focus on her target. Tatiana made sure to keep eye contact as she swayed over to him. By the time she reached Mr. Man, she had his full attention. Gripping the back of his neck, she pressed her lips against his. Tatiana held her breath, praying he did not open his mouth for tongue. God knows she could not think too hard about what she was about to do.

She had to just do it. *Just do it and get it over with.* Tatiana nibbled at his lobe and whispered into his ear, "You going to keep talking, old man? Or are you going to show me what you got for me?"

Tatiana lifted her leg and rubbed it softly against Mr. Man's. She then took his hand, sliding it up her thigh. When Mr. Man got fresh and began stroking higher up her skirt, Tatiana slapped it down. When he tried to wrap his arms around Tatiana's waist, she redirected Mr. Man's grasp. She was a bit insecure about the scar on the lower right side of her belly. And even though she often concealed it with makeup, it still made her uncomfortable to be touched there. It was a part of her past that she would like to erase, but unfortunately, cosmetics could only hide so much.

"Oh, come on now. Don't tease me. You got me going now," Mr. Man begged, licking his lips, and gyrating in her direction.

In her mind, Tatiana laughed at him, *swiveling those raggedy-ass hips like a horny dirty dog.* She smirked at Mr. Man. *Soon you going to be as dead as a limp dick dog.* Kissing him seductively on the cheek, she grabbed his hand and led him across Canal street back to his car. Mr. Man pushed her against the town car door and began to pull at her nipples through her silk shirt. He tugged at her skirt. If Tatiana did not know any better, she would have thought that this bastard was going to try and screw her right here in the theater parking lot. *Not while I'm conscious, you won't.*

Tatiana slid her hand in Mr. Man's pocket and massaged his growing bulge before pushing the unlock button on his key fob. *He is pretty blessed for an old man.* She was under the impression that old age shrunk a man's penis. *Go figure.* Tatiana let her hand rest in his pocket, stroking his manhood for a moment. It must have felt great because he forgot all about her breasts, and his head bobbed back toward the hood of the car. Tatiana moved her hand toward the pistol strapped to her thigh. The laughter that echoed behind them jarred her. She could not make her move out here. There were too many eyes.

"Come on here, girl, and get this money. I ain't got all night." Mr. Man said impatiently. He seemed pissed she stopped with the hand job.

To appease him, Tatiana purred, "Okay, daddy, okay. But let's get in the car. It's a little cold out here. I can't warm you up if I'm cold, now can I?"

Mr. Man looked skeptical, but he opened the front passenger door for her anyway.

"Oh no," Tatiana stopped him. "Get in the back. I want to ride."

Mr. Man began to lick down her neck and into her cleavage. As sickened to her core as she was, Tatiana had to let him continue.

"Is that all you want to do is put your tongue on my neck?" Tatiana said seductively. She knew Mr. Man would be surprised at her forwardness, considering how much of a prude he thought she was earlier.

"Let's go somewhere a little more comfortable," Tatiana sung into his ear as she maneuvered her body to put the back door in between herself and the aged predator.

Mr. Man was unbuttoning his pants and had them at his hips before he could get his legs into the car. He had to be fully in the car before she could get in and execute her plan to end this. *Damn, nothing could be simple*, she thought.

Tatiana pressed her body against Mr. Man to push him further into the town car. There might be cameras, and Tatiana did not need any witnesses. Desperate times called for drastic measures. She straddled Mr. Man at his knees and kissed his chest, careful not to get the hairs in her mouth. As she squatted over his lap, Tatiana pulled out the pearl grip .38 snub-nose revolver she had hidden in her garter holster. Before she had time to second guess what she was doing, Tatiana pushed the muzzle into his chest, and sent that dirty dick dog to hell. After emptying close to eighteen hundred dollars from his pockets and socks, Tatiana stripped down to her bra and panties and crawled into the front seat. Her phone vibrated against her skin. Running on adrenaline, she snatched the phone from her bra and was ready to text Cairo a piece of her mind for rushing her, but the call was not from Cairo. They were all missed calls from an 813-area code. *Damn.* Something was wrong at home. She just knew it. Three calls after 10 p.m. from anyone was terrible news. Tatiana wrote down the number to call the person back after she finished dumping the car and her phone at the mouth of the Mississippi. *Shit.* She could only take on so much at one time.

*

"Hello? Yes, someone called me from this number?"

The person on the other line did not even greet Tatiana with a "hello" when she answered the phone.

"Child, you know you should be ashamed of your damn self. Your grandmother is over here poor and dying, and you off at college living the la Vida Loca. You know you need your ass beat."

The snide comments left Tatiana speechless, at first. She usually did not take too kindly to being spoken to in such an aggressive manner. Except, she recognized the caller's deep, raspy, and phlegm-filled voice. Ms. Virginia Fuller was Tatiana's grandmother's 74-year-old nosey ass next-door neighbor. The woman had been around as long as Tatiana could remember. She and the neighborhood kids would whisper about Ms. Virginia's scalp, thin grey ponytails. They would shy away from her hugs for fear of suffocating in her size G breasts. The kids would fall over laughing at the woman's colorful muumuus. Despite

Ms. Virginia Fuller's frail frame, she wore her muumuus very big, and the fabric swallowed her like a circus tent. Nanna had warned her that anytime old "Messy Betsy" Virginia showed up, it was always to tell somebody's business. The last thing Tatiana expected was to find that out on her own.

Tatiana knew Ms. Fuller would have her on the phone all day, going on and on about "having respect for her elders," if she addressed Messy Betsy's absence of a greeting and tone. That woman was cranky as hell. Always had been, and she backed down from nothing or no one. Taking the high road, Tatiana inhaled deeply. She decided to put her energy into finding out what was going on with her grandmother.

"Well, hello to you too, Ms. Fuller."

Tatiana dripped with sarcasm. All her life, Tatiana waited to be grown and considered herself a responsible enough adult. Hell, she was doing better than most 20-year-olds she knew, and she was nowhere living as *la Vida Loca* as Ms. Fuller implied. As bad as she wanted to keep up the cynicism, Tatiana kept her momentum going before Ms. Fuller could respond.

"What do you mean, my grandmother is poor and dying? I just spoke to her…"

Tatiana abruptly ended her sentence because she found herself trying to remember the last time she had spoken to her grandmother. Over the past few months, her Nanna's last few calls were either missed or short because Tatiana was busy juggling a full course load or trying to find ways to make money. Taking five classes this semester did not allow her time to have a real job. Instead, she found people needing mobile advertising and other side jobs to make a little extra cash. The grants only covered so much and the horror stories about student loans were enough to keep her away from them.

Tatiana's heart grew heavy as Ms. Fuller talked about her grandmother's declining health, money problems, and other rumored criminal events in her old neighborhood.

"Tati? Tati? You hear me, girl?"

"Ma'am? I'm sorry. I just, I didn't know things were that bad. She never said anything about it when we talked."

Tatiana's heart broke at the news of her grandmother. She had promised before going to college three years ago that she would often call and visit, and she had not done either.

"Well, you know your Nanna ain't saying nothing to nobody about her business."

The weight of Tatiana's guilt lifted a little at that comment, and a light chuckle slipped from her lips. It was ironic to hear how right her grandmother was about old "Messy Betsy" Virginia. Tatiana knew her grandmother to be a very private person, but here was Ms. Fuller, ready to spill all her poor little beans.

"You know, time passes fast when you're trying to forget, little girl. I think it's time for you to come home."

Tatiana felt defeated. She was not trying to forget her past. How could she? Before turning thirteen, Tatiana escaped death twice and had the scars to prove it. Two of them, in fact. One on her stomach where her kidnappers carved a kidney out before leaving her for dead in a smelly alley. The second over her right breast from being stabbed by her attacker before being made to watch her mother bleed out while she clung to life. No matter how far Tatiana ran to get away from the trauma, her scars would never let her forget. It had been cut out and forever engraved in her memory. No one understood the mental and physical pain she had endured. How could they? In a matter of months, Tatiana had been kidnapped, dissected for her kidney, suffered a concussion, had a punctured lung, and witnessed her mother viciously murdered. Going back home would not be about her. It would be about her Nanna. The only one left in this world that meant anything to her. Tatiana wiped the few tears that spilled from her eyes and simply said, "Yes ma'am," before folding her phone to end the call.

Within an hour of their conversation, Tatiana contacted her professors to let them know she needed to take her midterms early. Preferably within the week, even though they were actually over a month away. After she filled in the last circle on the multiple-choice section of her midterm, Tatiana hopped in Maddie Bee, which she had packed and gassed up the night before and was on the I-10 in no time.

*

"I.N.D.E.P.E.N.D.E.N.T. Do y'all know what that mean? I got my own whip. I got my own place." Tatiana sang off-key, to the top of her lungs, as she jammed and sped on the I-10 from good ol' Nawlins back to not so good ol' memories in Tampa.

She turned the dial on the old radio up to its max setting. Her anthem always livened her up.

Already on the road for six hours and forty-two minutes, the bass from her favorite song might have been booming in her ears, but it did nothing for her drooping eyelids. Driving past the *Welcome to Pensacola* sign, Tatiana breathed a sigh of relief. Only three and a half hours to go, and she would be home. Rolling down her window, Tatiana let the warm night air hit her face. She had already chewed every single piece of the thirty-six pack of sweet mint gum and drank two white chocolate mocha lattes. The overdose of caffeine surging through her veins made her itch. It irritated the crescent shaped scar above her right breast. She had to bite her nails to keep from scratching through it. *Keloids are the devil.*

Bouncing up and down in the grey bucket seats of her purple 1998 Pontiac, Tatiana shouted, "I got to pee," to no one in particular. Even though Maddie Bee's model was over a decade old, it treated her well, and she made sure to return the favor and not to mess on her seats.

*

Tatiana named the car Maddie Bee, after a nickname she heard her Nanna call her mother long ago. Her college roommates thought she was crazy for naming her vehicle. If those heifers knew any better, they would not file their taxes anytime soon because some of their refunds were already in her full gas tank, and the rest was in her pockets. Tatiana planned to have the last laugh. Maddie Bee had a few dings and scratches, but she ran like a champ. A/C still blew ice-cold, which mattered a lot in the South and Central Florida. Tatiana's car was the only big thing her Nanna could give her when she graduated from high school. At the end of her ceremony, Nanna had given her a big hug, a kiss on the cheek, a packed bag, a pearl grip .38 snub-nose revolver, a bible, and a pair of keys.

*

Tatiana pulled up to the gas station, still bouncing up and down in the seat. It was 11 p.m., and she was happy to see the parking lot packed. It made her feel safer for some reason. Running through the sliding doors and up to the clerk's counter, Tatiana squeezed her thighs. It seemed like the closer she got to the restroom, the closer she came to pee streaming down her leg.

"Can you please tell me where your restroom is?"

"You have to buy something," the clerk announced without looking her way. Perturbed and seconds away from urinating on this man's floor in front of several customers, Tatiana tried to hold it together and be as polite as she could. Her Nanna always told her that she could get more with honey than with vinegar.

"Excuse me, sir, I would love to buy something, but I am trying not to piss on your floor at this moment. If you tell me where your restroom is, I'll be sure to buy something as soon as I finish."

The clerk looked at Tatiana like he wanted to say something

smart, but Tatiana's glare made him think twice. Instead, the clerk said casually, "you need the key."

Biting down on her tongue to keep from cursing this man, Tatiana asked, "May I please have the key for the ladies' room?"

"I don't have the key. Someone's in there now."

Tatiana felt her blood boiling. "Well, give me the damn men's bathroom key," she shouted, slamming her fist down on the counter, rattling the small colored mints and other assorted hard candies on display on his side of the glass.

Just as she thought to smash the bulletproof glass that separated her and the rude ass clerk, someone laid a chrome car rim with a pink string tied through one of the holes to a giant key that had the word "women's" written on duct tape. Tatiana did not hesitate to snatch the bathroom key and rush to relieve herself.

Feeling better, threw her shoulders back, pushed her chest out, and walked her best YaYa DaCosta. One foot in front of the other like her Nanna taught her on her prom night when she did not have a date and felt awkward for going by herself.

Strolling up to the clerk's desk, Tatiana made sure to give him intense eye contact as she pulled a pair of eight-dollar shades from the display. She took her time trying them on and admired how good they looked on her face in the little smudged mirror. Before the clerk could even open his mouth to get smart and short with her, Tatiana took out a fifty-dollar bill and a counterfeit pen that was kept handy just for the "you look too poor to have that" smart asses, like the clerk. She drew a long line across the face of Ulysses S Grant and placed the fifty under the glass before smirking at him and sashaying out. She did not even stay to help him pick his mouth off his dirty ass floor. Getting back in her car, Tatiana straightened the rearview mirror. She huffed, "We got some more driving to do, Maddie Bee," before speeding off and throwing the cheap shades out the window into the darkness.

Chapter 3

DHORIAN

Dhorian grabbed the glass of orange juice from the coffee table and walked into his bedroom. He sucked his teeth at seeing the naked redhead still sleeping, sprawled across his bed like she did not have a care in the world.

Unfortunately for her, he did, and Dhorian did not want to leave sleeping beauty in his condo while he was gone. She was not to be trusted. That was a lesson Dhorian learned the hard way.

She stirred before purring, "Thank you for coming to get me."

"Yea, you're welcome, Chris, but I can't keep covering for you," Dhorian said as he sat on the bed, annoyed.

He noticed the pout on her face and knew he had to be careful with her feelings. She could be such an emotionally impulsive creature, not to mention she was the boss' daughter.

"I know. I'm sorry. But I couldn't let daddy find out that I was sobering up when I knew he and mom were waiting up for me last night."

Disgusted, Dhorian turned away before remarking. "Your habit is starting to show."

"Oh, yea?" Chris straddled his lap. "You weren't saying that when you were partying with me." Chris giggled and playfully nibbled at his ear.

Dhorian stood up, flopping Chris back onto the bed.

"Why do you keep bringing that shit up, Chris? That shit is old. It was almost a year ago. And let's get something straight. I only tried that shit with you one time. One time!" Dhorian emphasized with his index finger. "And that was only because you tricked me into thinking it was for some damn medical study your conniving ass couldn't find a guinea pig for. I was doing you a favor. I should have left your ass alone then."

Dhorian walked away from the bed and out of the room, afraid of what he might say next. He heard Chris calling for him, but he did not care. He was too busy trying to figure out how he got himself into this mess.

Dhorian was seven years Chris's senior. He came on as an intern for her dad eight years ago, practically watching Chris grow up. They formed a close platonic bond consisting of him serving as her sometimes babysitter, driver, and tutor. It was not until she hit nineteen that Dhorian found out Chris would be every bit as sneaky and vindictive as her mother. He could still recall overhearing Mrs. Christen in Mr. Christen's study, whispering harsh demands to someone on the other line and then reprimanding and accusing him of snooping. Despite the run-in Dhorian had with her mother, Christina Christen was fine as hell with a Jessica Rabbit sort of vibe. Dhorian had never met a white woman who was so shapely. However, because of his respect for Chris's father, Dhorian would have never touched her. At least not without a little plying.

*

In her senior year, Chris approached Dhorian for a favor. Her thesis was due, and she wanted to try out some miracle vitamin created to improve memory retention. She convinced Dhorian that she could not trust anyone to test out the drug for fear they would steal her formula if it were successful. Dhorian dealt with safeguarding intellectual property every day, so it was easy enough for him to understand. Besides, helping the boss' daughter get her degree sounded like a great way to get a raise.

"Okay, so the pill is soluble and should dissolve under your tongue," Chris instructed while showing Dhorian the small green tablet.

"Are you sure you're not doing someone else's thesis?" Dhorian joked.

He could tell by the elevated eyebrow that Chris was offended. Dhorian held up his hands in surrender before continuing. "I'm just saying if you're working on human trials, don't you think the "*shoulds*" should be worked out by now?"

Chris rolled her eyes, motioned for Dhorian to open his

mouth, and began giving him instructions as she placed the tablet under his tongue.

"You're going to get four of these small green tablets to take in thirty-minute intervals. Twenty-five minutes after each dose, I'll come in to record your vitals, ask you how you're feeling, and observe any subtle side effects."

Dhorian practically jumped out of the chair. "Whoa! Side effects? What the hell do you mean, side effects? Don't you think that would be something to disclose before you gave me the damn pill?"

Pushing him gently back into the chair, Chris cooed, "Don't be such a baby, Dhorian. It's a dissolvable tablet, not a pill. It'll be fine. I promise. You do this for me, and I'll owe you big time. Anything you want. I swear! Annddd" - she dragged- "I'll even put in a good word with daddy."

It did not go unnoticed by Dhorian how handsy Chris was with all her promises. *This shit is strong. Her fingers got my skin all tingly.* Dhorian kept that bit to himself, though.

After the third dose, Dhorian started to sweat in his arms' creases and at the back of his knees. His heart was racing, and his growing erection had to be the hardest it had ever been in his life.

"Shit, it's hot in here," Dhorian said to himself while wiping the sweat off his brow with the back of his hand.

He could not wait for Chris to come back in so he could tell her to turn the damn air down. Dhorian tried controlled breathing exercises to slow down his racing heartbeat. Still, the more air he took in, the harder it was for Dhorian to stop the onset panic attack. Dhorian wondered, briefly, if the discomfort he felt was one of those subtle side effects Chris mentioned. What he was experiencing was anything but minuscule.

Dhorian stood up to adjust his throbbing manhood. The sensation of his hand brushing against it weakened his knees. The immense pleasure surprised Dhorian so much that, while in his kneeled position, he released his bulging penis from his pants and rocked back. It was like a weight had lifted from him. Even though he felt lighter, the hardness of his penis still made him uncomfortable. He took his manhood in his hand and examined it. Veins were popping out that he never knew were there, and if his eyes were not playing tricks on him, he would swear he saw red blood cells flowing through the vessels.

"What the fuck is going on?" Dhorian huffed.

Attempting to gather himself, Dhorian tried to maneuver his shaft back into his pants. Yet, the more he moved it, the more sensitive it became. The room seemed to boil at this point, and Dhorian was stuck on his knees with his penis out. Without knowing what else to do, Dhorian held his shaft in his hand and squeezed it gently. Grabbing his penis had always comforted him, even when he was a young boy. It was like having a friend that you knew would always be there with you, no matter what. And this was one of those, no matter what moments that Dhorian felt he needed a friend. With his other hand, he checked his watch. It would be another twenty minutes before Chris came in to check on him. Dhorian closed his eyes and did some more of his breathing exercises. He inhaled a sharp slow breath, filling his lungs, and then exhaled in three short bursts. It was on his second repetition that he noticed he was stroking his shaft and panting. Dhorian's body trembled as he began to jerk the full length of his penis. The air in the room seemed to pick up and cool the hot sweat on his skin. The faster he stroked, the closer to eruption he became. The diversion appeared to reduce the panic that washed over him only seconds earlier. Even as his body convulsed erratically, Dhorian felt as if he was gaining back a thread of control. His toes dug into the rug, and his stomach clenched from the satisfaction he knew was sure to come.

"Dhorian!"

Dhorian turned to face an open-mouthed Chris, standing in the doorway. In spite of her presence, he was reeling from the sensation that rippled through his body and forgot all about his exposed manhood, throbbing in his hand. It was not until Chris cleared her throat that he realized he had an exploding dick in his grasp. Surprisingly, hungry desire filled Chris's eyes.

"It looks like you could use some help with that," Chris said seductively.

Dhorian backed up to the couch as Chris slowly approached him, unfastening a button on her lab coat with every step. His vision was blurring, and he could not find the word "no" in his speech. As Dhorian put his hands out in front of him to stop her advance, the cum on his hand began inching down his wrist. He quickly tried to wipe it off on his pants.

"You don't have to wipe your hands on your pants, silly. I can take care of that for you." Chris purred.

Dhorian fell back on the couch. He was dizzy, his mouth was dry, and his body was weak. He could not push Chris away even if he wanted to. She smiled mischievously and took each of his fingers and sucked at the sticky juice that he had not yet wiped away. Dhorian gasped at his hypersensitivity, and his dick rocked up again, barely missing Chris' chin. The near miss did not go unnoticed by Chris either. Dhorian closed his eyes to see if that would help him to stop seeing double. Chris's cold hands on his penis opened them back up with a start. She cuffed his pulsing shaft in her hands and began pumping them up and down in a twisting motion. Dhorian could not hold the loud moan that escaped him. Everything in his marrow itched with pleasure. Even his eyeballs felt like they were ejaculating into euphoria. Chris opened her mouth and ran her tongue up and down his shaft, playing with his dick like a joystick to a game console. She repeatedly guided it in and out of her mouth, hitting herself in the face with it while giggling and swallowing him down her throat. While all other limbs were flaccid, there was one that was not, and it was not going down.

One hand expertly gave him a hand job, while the other aided Chris in removing her panties and stuffing them into Dhorian's mouth. He was a slave to her. The questions and objections swirled in his head, but the category seven hurricane swarming throughout his body took precedence. Chris climbed on top of him, pinning Dhorian to the couch with her legs tight at his sides. She began rocking slowly. It was like the water of life had fallen into Dhorian's lap, and he was riding the wave. Chris moaned, and Dhorian's moans followed. She lifted herself using his restrained shoulders and slammed her body into his over and over again. Dhorian's eyes widened, and he saw past Chris's inflamed face. With every slap of their bodies, the room changed colors.

Slap. "Mmm." *Orange.*

Slap. "Mmmm." *Blue.*

Slap. "Oooo." *Green.*

Slap. "Unhhh." *Red.*

Slap. "Ffffuuu…" *White.*

The white was intense. The white was too bright. It hurt for Dhorian to see the white and made him stutter. His ears began ringing, and he heard Chris shout something about "harder and cumming", when his body wretched forward. His stomach emptied itself on the floor. The vomit poured from him so hard that he felt like death was not too far away.

After it was all said and done, Dhorian came out of his lustful stupor mad as hell.

"What the fuck, Chris? Why did you do that? Your father is going to kill me!" He started rushing to gather his clothes. "And what the fuck was that you gave me?"

"Dhorian, wait. It was just a placebo."

"Placebo? You may need to check that formula of yours because what I felt wasn't from no damn placebo."

"Okay, okay, okay." Chris chased after him. "The second one was a placebo."

"Only the second one? What were the others? Fuck, Chris!" Dhorian was beyond enraged.

"Well, it was a synthesis of Ginkgo Biloba Extract and *methylenedioxy*-methamphetamine."

Dhorian hoped he heard wrong. He did not know what that first one was, but he definitely knew the second one sounded familiar.

"Repeat that, Chris. I didn't hear you." Dhorian growled through clenched teeth.

He grabbed Chris's arm before she could shy away.

"Dhorian, you're hurting me." She cried out.

Not moved by her pleas, Dhorian shook her, squeezing her arm a little tighter. He spat each word slowly, like a dart guided to its target.

"I said, repeat that again, Chris."

She sniffled. Dhorian knew crocodile tears when he saw them, and this chick just happened to be the queen of the Nile at that moment. He squeezed her arm one last time for good measure, and Chris winced in pain.

"Fine, Dhorian. Fine." She said as she shook herself loose from his grip.

Dhorian watched her like a hawk as she hurried to the other side of the room. *I'm going to do more than shake her ass if she thinks she is leaving this room without giving me a proper explanation of just what the fuck was going on here.*

"It's a synthesis of Ginkgo Biloba Extract and methylenedioxy-methamphetamine. Look, I'm sorry, Dhorian. I didn't know it would have that effect, I just, maybe I gave the wrong dosage or I…"

Dhorian cut her off. "Methylenedioxy-methamphetamine, Chris? You gave me Mollies? What the fuck is wrong with you? Was your plan to seduce me all this time? Do you even have a thesis due? Who the fuck are you? I mean, I can't believe I let you play me."

"I'm sorry, Dhorian," Chris yelped.

"Your "*I'm sorry,*" don't cut it, Chris. This is some messed up shit. Not only did you drug me, but you practically raped me."

"Whoa! Raped you? Nobody raped you, Dhorian. You thoroughly enjoyed everything I did to you."

Yelling again, Dhorian closed in on her, "Yes, but that doesn't mean it was not rape. Ahhhh! I mean, how stupid can you be, Chris?" He jabbed his index finger into the air around her head with each syllable, "What the hell are you thinking?"

Chris's demeanor changed suddenly, and she slapped Dhorian's hand away from her face.

"Let's get a few things straight, Dhorian. I have a thesis, which was not just a big plot to lure you to me, despite what you may think. I am actually on to something big here. And I'm sorry if I gave you the wrong dose, but that's what these tests are for, to work out the kinks."

"Are you sorry for sucking my dick too?" Dhorian chided.

That mischievous look appeared in Chris' eyes again. Even

though Dhorian stood in the middle of the room, he felt cornered. Chris crossed the room and grabbed his semi-hard erection growing stronger with each second she held it. To his dismay, his penis was still sensitive, and damn near jumped into her hand. Dhorian squeezed his eyes shut and groaned at the betrayal.

Chris grabbed his face with her free hand, whispering into his ear, "I have a video that proves I'm not sorry about a damn thing." She licked the right side of his face before releasing him.

The rage that traveled through Dhorian almost made him vomit again. He was speechless. Not only had she date-raped him, but she taped the whole damn thing too. Sliding his hand down his face, feeling defeated, Dhorian asked, "What is it that you want, Chris?"

He glared at her as Chris sashayed over to the couch. She sat down slowly before staring intensely at Dhorian. She teasingly crossed and then uncrossed her legs, revealing her red curly covered mound to him. She slid her ass to the edge of the couch, "I want you, Dhorian. I want you back inside me."

Without remorse, Dhorian screwed Chris every which way but loose that night. Partially to punish her, and he felt the only way he would get through this was to do what she wanted. Chris had him by the balls. His sexual escapades never came with regrets, but this one would surely be different.

*

Feeling so stupid, Dhorian realized Chris tricked him into taking drugs. After that incident, she spent every day trying to repair their friendship and make the drug experiment their reason for a lasting relationship. But the only things Dhorian understood after that night was he never wanted to do drugs again and how much of a freak the boss' daughter was, and still is. Chris always brought up their drug experiment when she wanted to remind him that he owed her. Dhorian owed her for not ratting on him to her father about his supposed narcotics abuse and their happen-ship. Which involved him and Chris just happening to end up in bed with each other now and again.

After pacing for a few moments, Dhorian went back into his room. "I think you need to put on your fucking clothes and get out, Christina."

Dhorian seethed, making sure to say her entire first name instead of the shortened version to let her know he was not playing games. He tossed whatever clothes of hers he could find her way.

Chris was not going to sucker him into giving her some dick today. Today was too important. He paced the kitchen, eating an English muffin and sipping coffee. Ten minutes later, Dhorian had finished his breakfast, reorganized his bookshelf in alphabetical order by subject, and still no Christina. Now pissed, he only had one hour to get to work in Tampa morning traffic. Dhorian marched into his bedroom and stopped short when he did not see Christina lying in his bed. He quickly walked back to the foyer, where he confirmed she had not yet left with her purse and pumps at his door. Dhorian surveyed the rest of his condo. Lucky for him, he could see every room from the front door, except his room. It was not until then that it occurred to him that Chris could have been taking a shower.

Dhorian checked his watch and huffed, *forty-five minutes? Damn what am I going to do with this chick?* Why she would choose to take such a long shower after he had just kicked her ass out was beyond him. *I'm going to let her ass know that if she keeps up with these immature antics, she won't have to worry about tasting this dick ever again.*

He looked into his bathroom, and surprisingly Chris was not there. There were no signs of steam remnants as evidence she had recently showered. Dhorian made his way to his last resort, the closet. And sure enough, Christina was in there, but she was still butt ass naked. And even worse, she was in a fetal position in the back corner of his closet, eyes glazed and high as hell.

"What a fucking waste!" he murmured briefly, as he covered her limp body with one of his coats and cradled her in his arms. It was so sad that such a beautiful creature reduced herself to the wreck he carried out of his condo and across the hall. Once in the unit, Dhorian laid Chris in the bed and dialed zero on the landline.

"Yes. 321 Terrace needs a monitor, please." Dhorian spoke into the receiver.

The concierge on the other line simply responded, "Yes, sir." and hung up the phone.

Dhorian had created the code and cover system for Christina to hide her habit from her folks when she asked him for help after one of her benders. He did not want her to stay with him after that stunt she pulled in her lab, so Dhorian pulled some strings with the building management to rent the small condo across the hall on an as-needed basis. Being alone in a safe space would give Chris time to recover privately with someone monitoring her. At the same time, she detoxed without her parents knowing. But over the last few months, Dhorian had to use the location way too often. Dhorian hesitated to bring it up to her because he wanted to avoid the confrontation. However, at the rate Chris was going, she would not make it past twenty-five. Dhorian knew he needed to have the "addict" conversation with her at some point. Once he had Chris's belongings moved to her recovery unit, Dhorian took off for work, pissed that he only had thirty minutes to deal with traffic.

*

Four hours and three meetings later, Dhorian strolled into the men's bathroom and stooped to peek under each stall door making sure there was no one else in the men's room before he hop-stepped back to the door and locked it.

"YEAAAAAAA!", Dhorian screamed. Fist pumping and boxing the air, Dhorian jumped around the bathroom like he was the next heavyweight champion of the world. "What did we do?" he asked himself, "We came," he responded in a crowd's whisper. "What did we do," he asked again. "We conquered," he blew out in between jabs and quick steps. "What did we do?" he asked himself for a third and final time while enunciating each following word in a controlled scream. "We got *the* mother-fucking job!" "AHHHHHHHH."

Dhorian wore the brand-new navy blue, Irish linen and cashmere suit that his mentor gifted him, just for this occasion. If anyone walked into the bathroom at that moment, they would have thought Dhorian was preparing for a hundred-mile relay. It was an early celebration for his new position as the first Black partner at the prestigious Reed & Morris Law Group. It took him five long, challenging, and overworked years of sorting and organizing files, paper cuts, coffee, sandwich, and donut runs for him to get noticed. Dhorian spent another three years representing *classified,* high-profile clients and protecting the boss' controlling ass daughter. Finally, the old geezers began to appreciate his talent and what he could bring to the table.

*

Paul Christen, business mogul, community advocate, the current mayor, and Dhorian's mentor, took Dhorian under his wings after his father passed during a botched robbery. Dhorian was present at the time of his father's murder and injured with a concussion and several non-fatal lacerations from what he remembered, but it was all hazy. The nightmares lasted for months. Dreams of his blood covered visage standing over his father, eyes gaping wide with rage, haunted Dhorian. Vivid hallucinations that he killed his father and not some transient robbing the funeral home plagued him on most nights and lingered into restless mornings.

*

Looking at himself in the full-length body mirror, Dhorian sucked in a deep breath, taking it all in. He looked damn good, and he felt even better. All of his hard work finally paid off. And he could not have done it by himself. Dhorian felt so lost after his father passed away. If it was not for his mentor, who gave him purpose by pushing him to go to night school to prep for the LSAT, and paying for his Juris Doctor degree, Dhorian might not have made it. At first, the rigorous courses made him want to quit. But once Dhorian stopped fighting and accepted his path, it got a little easier. Already buried in ethical dilemmas and case law, Dhorian was utterly flabbergasted after Mr. Christen's recommendation for partner. It was unexpected considering the Senior Partner and Founder of Reed & Morris Law Group, Edward Reed, saw him as just an errand boy. Little did Mr. Reed know, *whatever it takes to get the job done* had been his motto, and it was not going to fail him now.

"Mr. Hamilton!"

The knock at the door startled Dhorian. Rushing to open it, Joanie, his assistant, met his face with a smirk.

"Celebrating a little early, aren't we?" she joked as she turned away from the men's room and quickly shuffled back into the main hall of the office.

Following right on her heels, Dhorian straightened his

collar and the cuffs on his jacket and took a minute to check out Joanie's tight curves. He watched her take those long steps, and from looking at her body in the A-line corporate casual dress and fitting blazer, if he had to guess, she was about a size eight. *That was not the package she started with when I hired her two years ago.*

*

Joanie was a college freshman, looking to make some money to pay her tuition and car insurance. She wanted to show her parents she could be a responsible young adult. She had drive, a flexible schedule, reliable transportation, and, most importantly, *the freshman fifteen*. If Dhorian had to be honest, those extra fifteen pounds were more like thirty. And it was one of the reasons he hired her. Dhorian had never been into what his mother called *healthy* women. Joanie was healthy enough to keep him focused on other things than her appearance. Even though she was a fox in the face, his dick could not get past those extra pounds that weighed her hips down. He figured they would get along just fine.

He had already been through three assistants in the last five months, all of whom had banging bodies and better-looking faces. But when his expectation of them went back to filing instead of stooping under his desk for a blowjob, their feelings soured, and they gave him more stress than what he paid them. The trend was getting old and was not helping to lessen the strain of his caseload at all. One after the other, the ultimatum he gave always ended with them out on their asses looking for some other Tom, Dick, or Harry to blow for another paycheck.

*

If Dhorian had known then that Joanie would look this good now, he would not have hired her. She was looking *doable* in that money green and black ensemble. She must have felt Dhorian staring at her, or he must have missed a question that she asked because he bumped right into her.

"Oh shit, excuse me, my bad," Dhorian exclaimed, both caught off guard by the abrupt stop and by his vulgar words in the office. *I need to focus.*

As if knowing his thoughts were up to no good, Joanie did not indulge the glimmer in his eyes. She only turned, smiled, handed him his phone, mail, and messages, and followed with, "Mr. Reed and Mr. Morris are waiting for you in Conference Room One, sir."

Clearing his throat, "Thank you, Joanie," Dhorian responded while taking his paperwork from her petite hand.

Giving him a wink, Joanie mouthed, "Good Luck" before taking off down the hall towards her desk and Dhorian's office. Still staring after her, Dhorian took in a deep breath and exhaled. That is why he liked her. Even when she knew he was vulnerable, she did not take advantage of his weakness. He turned left in the hallway towards the elevator bank. Dhorian then pressed the number ten on the elevator floor panel to head to Conference Room One.

His phone vibrated against his chest and Dhorian reached for the inside of his blazer. He pulled out his phone and placed his thumb on the sensor to unlock it. Dhorian could not count all the ways that fingerprint recognition had saved his ass.

There it was on his home screen. Thirty-eight missed calls. Although he had his phone in his hand, Dhorian looked at his watch to check the time. It was only 10:30 in the morning, and Christina had called him thirty-eight damn times. He would have to handle her sooner or later, but right now was not the time.

Not a second after Dhorian had put the phone back in his pocket, it pulsed again, but this time in spurts. Dhorian groaned at the voicemail. It was better that he put it on silent now so as not to be distracted in the most critical meeting that would determine his future at the firm.

Before he could change his settings, the phone shook again, showing "Chris" in big white letters sitting on top of "incoming call" in smaller characters. The bright white words glowed on the screen. He sent her to voicemail. "What the hell is her problem?" he whispered to himself. A voicemail notification popped up at the top of his phone. It was just one more added to the twelve that were already there. "Shit!" Dhorian mumbled. *I don't give a damn who her daddy is. She can wait. Today is my day.*

The elevator approached the tenth floor, and Dhorian began his breathing exercises to help him concentrate. *Those old geezers, Edward Reed and Dwight Morris, better make sure to come correct on this offer for Partner, or I'm going to have to bring out my Danny Roman - Keith Frazier negotiating skills.* Dhorian stepped out of the elevator, straightened his blazer, and sprayed on extra confidence as he walked towards the double doors of Conference Room One. He was on a mission to prove, once again, that he would do whatever it took to get the job done.

Twenty minutes later, Dhorian was back in his office, legs crossed on his desk, drinking a shot of Macallan 25 as a small salute to himself.

"Mr. Hamilton, you have a visitor?" Joanie buzzed over the intercom.

Dhorian expected his mentor, Mayor Christen, to stop by with congratulations, but not this early. Dhorian buzzed back, "Thank you, Joanie. Let him in."

Dhorian poured himself another shot of the scotch and two for Mr. Christen to play catchup.

"You're drinking already, baby? Aww, and I brought your favorite wine to celebrate."

The sultry voice startled Dhorian and made him drop the wooden box carrying the bottle of Macallan. The brown liquid dripped onto the floor. Dhorian seethed, "Christina, what the hell are you doing here?"

Chapter 4

PAUL

"Christina! Christina!" Paul yelled from the kitchen for the fifth time that morning. If he had not known better, Paul would have thought his daughter was twelve years old. Instead, she was a twenty-one-year-old pharma-D graduate from the University of Florida. Christina was in a leadership op program to fast track her into the Director of Pharmacy at one of the city's biggest pharmaceutical companies, MonClaire Pharma. Yet, she still chose to sleep like she lacked responsibility, like some child.

The top of the stairs were quiet with no response from Christina. Paul shook his head while brooding back to his chair at the kitchen table. *This girl has no idea what kind of strings I had to pull to position her for this scale of an opportunity.* Paul prayed his daughter did not let him down after all the asses he kissed and favors he called in. If she did, he could expect to gain more enemies than the few passed over, more qualified for the job.

Sandra placed a hot plate of turkey bacon, scrambled cage-free egg whites, and gluten-free toast in front of him. Paul gave his wife a weak smile.

"Don't you give me that look, Mr. Christen! You know the doctor said we have to."

We? Who the hell is we? I don't see you eating this crap. Paul did not dare speak his thoughts aloud. Cutting her off in exasperation, "I know. I know what the doctor said. You don't have to remind me. Just because I don't like it doesn't mean I won't eat it."

Paul moved the dry and paper-thin meat across his plate with his fork. He hated the subtle reminders that came along with the delicate state of his health. If the daily horse pills, the nightly treatments, and the weekly doctor visits were not enough to remind him, his wife's cardboard breakfast still managed to bring his health issues front and center. *Damn her for that. Thank goodness Sandra and her health nut reminders aren't always around.* He had enough memories of his own to keep him on the straight and narrow. Paul's last episode created enough fear in him to keep him eating paper meals. He could not chance his body rejecting the donated kidney again.

*

It was a Sunday morning. Christen's family Sunday. Paul promised Sandra he would dedicate family time to his wife and child after Christina was born. A day away from his business investments and community projects, solely focused on how blessed he was to have his family. Christina had just turned seventeen the Sunday before, and in that span of Sundays before then, Paul had not missed one. Until that unusual Sunday. It was common for Paul to get out of bed by 5 a.m. for his morning run, shower, and down to the kitchen to make breakfast before Sandra and Christina were up. Instead, Paul found himself still in bed at 1 p.m. He had chills and a fever that was scorching his body from the inside out. Paul's delirium had to be getting worse. He recalled getting out of bed and going for his morning run but did not remember much after passing his mailbox. Paul felt an ice-cold hand against his forehead.

"Paul? Paul? Are you okay?" his wife, Sandra, asked as she placed her palm flat on his forehead before flipping to the back of her hand. "You look a little clammy, and you're burning up."

Paul remembered hearing his wife in the fog that shrouded him. He had to search his mind for her words because it sounded like she was underwater. Sandra always had a look of mourning in her eyes when she thought something was wrong with him. He hated that look because it made him feel as if death was that much closer to taking him away from everything he worked so hard to gain. Paul did not need his wife to tell him the obvious. His body was rejecting the second renal transplant. A few days before his fever spiked to 102 degrees, a punchbowl was sitting on his bladder, and only droplets piddled the toilet bowl.

Paul immediately increased his water intake, hoping it

was just a snag. Dehydration was nothing to be taken lightly, especially in his state. His worst-case scenario was piss that smelled like pure ammonia, seizures, and hypovolemic shock with dehydration. A good saline drip, and he would be good as new. He would take that over having his kidney fail again, any day. Paul had experienced two chronic renal transplant rejections in the last eight years and was on his third. If he so much as sneezed, Sandra was looking to have him admitted to the ER. Paul considered himself blessed that a daily regimen of meds and check-ins were the least of his worries. Living this life had become like clockwork and Paul knew what to expect. Other things kept him up at night, like his daughter's whereabouts and the entire city of Tampa. These were the things out of his control.

"You would think that child was still in high school the way you have to yell at her to get up and come down downstairs." Sandra sighed.

Before Paul could respond to his wife and stop her from adding more paper bacon to his plate, the news story on the small twenty-four inch flat-screen TV left them both staring and silent.

*

"Hello. I'm Tiffany LaSalle, and behind me is the Gas Kwik quick shop gas station and grocery. The last known location of Candy Ellis, a twenty-three-year-old part-time student, and waitress at the nearby Village Inn. Her

manager says Candy came in for her 8 p.m. shift like normal. Walked out of the diner three hours later for her fifteen-minute break, headed north to the Gas Kwik to purchase a charger for her phone, and never made it back. No one saw Candy leave the Gas Kwik, but her body was found cold and lifeless in the early hours this morning. Bob Rand is on-site with more."

"Thank you, Tiffany. At approximately 3:45 a.m., several cars passed under the on-ramp of I-275 North and Columbus. They called 911 to describe seeing the body of what appeared to be a young woman lying unclothed, bloody, and lifeless in the brush. Witnesses' detail of the brutal scene led TPD officers just two miles away from the Gas Kwik to this area behind the Kingdom Inn motel. The area is known for prostitution and narcotics. It is still unknown how Candy ended up on this side of the tracks, and her cause of death still has not been confirmed. There are rumors and speculations of organs missing from the body, but that has also not been confirmed. We have been told that the medical examiner has no comment at this time. Candy Ellis's death is the eighth one like it in the past two years, and with few leads, it leaves a community hopeless and full of fear. I'm Bob Rand, Channel 8 reporting, back to you, Tiffany."

*

"It's such a shame how they take dignity away from the victim."

"Huh? What did you say?" Paul sat, watching the remaining coverage on the news story, only partially hearing his wife's comment. The killings were getting more frequent, and they still had not found a suspect, or the killer, or a motive, or a correlation in the victims. In a few hours, Paul would meet with Barry, his brother-in-law and legal advisor, and other key members of his staff. He needed a strategy on how to end his second consecutive term as mayor with a bang. Pressuring the police to find the serial killer may be just the thing he needed to push him into his new aspiration as Governor. During his eight years as mayor, Paul had always been a strong community advocate. However, with his health taking an unpredictable turn during the first year of his second term, he had not been as active as he would have liked. The once favorable poll numbers with his constituents were declining. Bringing the murderer to justice was a perfect chance to show the city why he would be very effective as Governor if given the opportunity.

"I said that it was a shame. These women, being objectified even in murder. I mean, for God's sake, they are dead. Let them at least have peace in death."

Paul took his wife's hand and kissed her on the lips. "No need to worry yourself over the dead, huh? It's not you, and it's not Christina, and that's all that matters. I'm sure our police force is doing everything they can to catch the bastard responsible for this. To make sure you feel safe, I'm going to call Police Chief Woodrow this afternoon to tell him to put every available detective on solving these crimes."

Paul saw Sandra's look of concern soften into a look of tenderness.

"See, that's why I love you, Mr. Paul Lee Christen." His wife kissed him gently on his cheek. "This city is not going to know what to do without you."

Paul patted his wife's hand gently before kissing it. He could tell she meant every word and that he had indeed consoled her. Paul, on the other hand, was not quite yet at ease. There was still a lot of work to be done. He had a feeling, things in his city would get worse before they got better.

Chapter 5

VERDELL

Verdell merged onto I-4 West and drifted into the left lane towards I-275 South. His mind was busy tonight. The Gasparilla Sant' Yago Knight parade had Tampa traffic bumper to bumper, and yet, Verdell moved through it unbothered. More sensitive matters vexed his thoughts. Verdell had been thinking of his mother lately. It had been thirteen years since she passed, and most of the time, she was not even a thought. If his father were to mention his mother, Verdell would not dwell on her. Instead, it was moments like this. When he was alone and could see the clear skies with light from the full moon guiding his way, he would reminisce.

Verdell recalled the times, in the dead of night, when he and his mother would stay up and watch the stars together in the backyard while waiting for his father to come home. The memories made his face flush warm and Verdell rolled the window down to feel the cold night air. But at only six mph, the humid and sticky February night was a disappointment. *Damn this Florida weather.*

*

Verdell pulled up to the big brick red house on the corner of Hyde Park and Platt. The wrought iron gates squeaked open and Verdell parked his muscle car in a free space amongst the luxury vehicles in the expansive driveway. He took out his phone and dialed. Verdell announced, "Benji, I'm outside." And as fast as it picked up, the line went dead.

Verdell started his stopwatch and let the countdown begin on how long it took Benji to come outside. They had a recurring game with time. Time and time again, the man upstairs blessed both Benji and Verdell with more hours than fate intended. They made it their business to remind each other of how precious each other's time was. No matter how insignificant the task.

Verdell text Benji after five minutes had passed. *I could have shit, showered, and shaved faster than it takes you to bring yo ass out.*

Shut up, stupid. It's this damn makeup, was the message Verdell received back.

He knew not to push the makeup bit. Verdell knew it was a sensitive subject for her. He cut the ignition and stepped outside the car. He leaned against the driver's door playing an expert game of Sudoku on his phone while he waited.

Verdell met Benji while walking through the Marshall Student Center, looking for a cheap bite to eat after one of his jobs on campus. He took the long way through one of the corridors to put space between him and the heat he knew was coming once they found the body. Verdell crept past the open doors in the hallway stopping at the one where he heard children giggling. That sound on a college campus was a little out of place. Needing to be out of the open to lay low anyway, Verdell stepped into the room. He walked down a few rows and took an end seat in the middle of the room undetected.

Other than the laughter, a voice floated off the walls. Verdell did not see anyone at first. Then he noticed the puppet show to the left of the stage. The story intrigued him. It was about a South African princess who was loved by all. An evil spirit cursed her with white spots on her skin. The village people believed God's wrath plagued her and threw her out of town because of their fear. Long story short, because of her good deeds, her village accepted her back into their arms despite her looks. It was not until the puppeteer came from behind the box that Verdell realized how appropriate the story's character had been.

When Verdell saw the young woman, he thought of cookies and cream. He could not tell if her face was white with chocolate freckles or chocolate with white freckles. A dreadlocked goddess standing at what Verdell gauged to be five foot ten inches with a swimsuit model frame, the woman was utterly intriguing. It only took a few seconds to realize that he was at a function for Vitiligo awareness. Staying longer than he intended, Verdell approached the woman, found out her name, and invited her to coffee off-campus, to find out more about her cause.

Benji was South African. The pigmentation of her skin mentally and physically subjected Benji to social stigmas. At sixteen, Benji was lured away from school, beaten, and left for dead in a well. It took her parents days to find her. They sent her to Miami to be with her mom's brother. From there, she was able to grow and fell into her own space as an IT analyst during the day, a hacker for private firms at night. In her spare time, she was all about social advocacy for Vitiligo.

Overcoming her past and breaking through the mental purgatory of her childhood torture to create someone Benji could be proud of really resonated with Verdell. Even though she was fine as hell, Verdell made an extra effort to show her that he did not want to take advantage of her pain. He wanted to protect whatever innocence she had left like he wished someone had been there to defend his when it still existed. If there were anybody that he considered a friend, it would be Benji.

*

"You ready for a night out on the town?" Verdell asked when he heard Benji try to sneak up on him and slide into the car's passenger front seat.

"Yeah, right, Vee. Will I have to run this time? Because if I do, we need to stop at my house to get my wedges. I'm going to break my ankle in these stilettos messing around with you."

"Aww, stop that! What did I tell you last time? If you had brought that piece out the car I gave you before we went in, you wouldn't have to run."

"Yea. Yea. Yea." Slapping his arm, playfully, "I still owe people for stitching me up that night, too."

"Anybody tell you that you whine too much." Verdell tossed Benji 20 twenty dollar bills waded with a rubber band. "That should shut your mouth."

Sucking her teeth, "For now."

Verdell watched her tuck the money away in her bra. "What? You not even going to count it?"

"Ha, ha, ha. No, I trust you."

"You better. Put your seatbelt on." Verdell skirted away from the curb and made his way onto US 92 towards the wealth of The Avala. He and Benji had a party to crash.

*

Verdell pulled into the rounded driveway in his rented midnight blue Camaro SS. Checking his watch, Verdell was twenty minutes early. *Right on time.* Verdell could have been earlier, but he stopped at the gated entrance about a mile back to make sure he had all of his tools. Slowing to a stop in front of the immaculate mansion, a young valet made it to his window. Verdell did not bother to roll it down. Instead, he pushed a button in his center console that swung the door open like butterfly wings, forcing the valet to back up a few steps.

"Here is fifty dollars to make sure she doesn't get scratched."

Verdell chuckled as the young man visibly gushed over the car. He was so distracted that he fumbled over his words, "Yes, yes, yes, sir. Wow. Your car is amazing."

"And it will stay that way, right?" Verdell waved the fifty in the valet's face, determined not to release it until he received the response he wanted.

Gathering himself before clearing his throat, the valet finally responded, "Yes sir, Mr…"

Verdell noticed how the young man extended the "Mr.," waiting for him to give his surname. But Verdell never gave an alias, and full names were too easy to remember. It gave people a way to identify him and show familiarity. This was just business. So Verdell went with the title the boy gave him.

"Mr. will do," Verdell interjected before handing him the crisp bill. He quickly showed the boy a Franklin and gave the eager valet his next set of instructions before nodding to Benji to get out of the car.

Verdell memorized the grounds and the expansive mansion's layout, including its fifteen bedrooms, three sitting rooms, eight bathrooms, two kitchen entrances, and its main hall. Now it was time for the show. *I hope Benji remembers her part.* Holding Benji's fingertips in the palm of his hand, Verdell escorted her into the party like royalty. His mother had always said that there was nothing more commanding than seeing a couple where the man knew his woman's value and was not afraid to let her take center stage. That story always ended with why his father and uncle would not amount to shit, because they were not in the habit of putting their women first, but Verdell saw through his mother's hurting words and received the general message.

Over time, Verdell learned that his mother left out a vital word of the saying, though. The man had to know *when* to let his woman take center stage. Although he and Benji were not a couple, he needed her presence tonight. She had more than a few assets of value that would give her the spotlight he needed for their diversion.

As they stepped over the threshold, they could hear the whispers.

"Who are they? Don't they look stunning? I wonder what's their net worth?"

Verdell and Benji were in character and refused to acknowledge the stares. Verdell stopped in front of the bartender and told him, "Gin two rocks."

"And for the lady?"

"Make her something sweet." Verdell smiled shamelessly at Benji before whispering into her ear. "Here, he comes."

Verdell swiped his drink from the bar, gulping it down fast before briefly kissing Benji on her neck and walking through the crowd to the opposite side of the ballroom for a better view of the action.

A man approached Benji at the bar. "I hope you don't mind me saying, but you look stunning tonight."

Please don't roll your eyes. Verdell needed her to be subtle tonight even though she was quite the opposite in appearance. The red sequin dress she wore dipped low at her back and plunged teasingly in the front. And if that was not enough, Benji's above the knee split and bright red stilettos exposed enough thigh to make any man risk looking three times in their wife's presence. But tonight, they were going for a little fish. Terrance McDaniel. Local business owner, husband, father of three, chairman of the board for the county's "Yes You Can" weekend STEM program, and rumored scout for an international trafficking ring about to turn rat.

Verdell did not know who Mr. McDaniel had pissed off to get a visit from him, but in his line of work, people always have their reasons. That, and their checks clearing was all that mattered. Which meant Mr. McDaniel was as good as dead. He just did not know it yet.

Verdell usually worked alone. However, he had intel that Mr. McDaniel liked to step out on his wife every once in a while. This flaw was in addition to being a third-party snake. In an event this big, it was better to be quiet when you knew the outcome would be messy. Benji would give him just the cover he needed.

Verdell smiled behind his empty glass when he heard Benji respond. "Why, thank you."

He watched as the mark played with her shoulder strap. He was running his finger underneath the material and over her skin. After a few more words back and forth, they were on their way up the winding stairs.

That's my girl, Verdell grinned. He taught Benji to let the mark lead the way. You never want to be in front when you cannot control what is before you or who is behind you. She was learning well.

Verdell moved seamlessly around the room and shook hands with people he never met, laughing, smiling, and promising to meet up soon. Of course, these people were clueless about who he was, but his presence made them think he was somebody whose hand they should shake or someone they needed to meet.

Making his way to the staircase, Verdell checked his watch. *Benji should be ready in precisely one minute and thirty-two seconds.* Verdell saw a shadow in his peripheral crossing from the main ballroom towards the kitchen as he took the first few steps up the stairway. His eyes followed her. Her bright red curls, full breast, and shapely hips stood out in a crisp white shirt and black A-line skirt. Verdell could tell she was not here to participate in the festivities by the way she dressed, but that was not going to stop him. He had to talk to her. She was gorgeous. For some odd reason, the more he stared at her, the more he felt déjà vu. She looked like someone he once knew.

The alarm on his watch went off. "Shit!" Verdell's outburst caused a few stares. He glanced back through the crowd trying to find the woman that distracted him. *I'll have to find her later.*

As Verdell made his way through the crowd to the top of the staircase landing, he smiled and waved. Verdell slunk around the corridor, whispering Benji's name loudly. *She's never going to forgive me for being late.* Just when he thought Benji might be in trouble, the last door in the hallway exploded open. There was Benji, looking perfect as ever, adjusting her tousled, messy bun at the top of her head.

"Stop screaming. What the hell is wrong with you?" Benji questioned.

"I couldn't find you."

"Don't give me that shit, Vee. You mean, you were running late."

"Naw, whatever. Like I said, I couldn't find you." Verdell reiterated, trying to play things cool.

"Mmm-hmm." She looked at him suspiciously. "You know I'm not letting you live that down, right?"

"Yea, yea, yea." Changing the subject, Verdell added, "Where he at?"

Verdell followed Benji's nonchalant hand wave inside the room. From where he was standing, Benji started the job without him.

"Damn, girl. What you do?" Verdell questioned.

"Don't worry. Mr. McDaniel's still breathing. He nasty, Vee. You don't even want to know some of the mess he was trying to get me to do."

Verdell only chuckled. As good as Benji looked, he had an idea of some of the nasty things Mr. McDaniel could have suggested to her.

"Shit ain't funny." She pouted.

"I know. I know. Let me get a good look at you." Verdell said as he turned her shoulders to face him.

"You good?"

Benji shook her head, yes, once, and then handed Verdell a microchip half the size of a dime.

"Is this it?"

"I took it off his phone. It has all his contacts, messages, even geotagging from the last year." Benji said, almost gushing.

Verdell sometimes forgot that the techy stuff excited her.

"Damn. You saw all that on there?"

"Well, you were late, Vee."

He knew she would not let up on that, so Verdell quickly redirected the subject from his tardiness again. Verdell gave Benji a once over, "You know you look hot tonight, and you did good. Now go. The car is waiting for you under the bathroom window down the hall. I need everything you can pull from this tonight."

"Yea, yea. I know." Benji replied snobbishly.

Verdell handed Benji an envelope and slid the chip inside. He smirked as she kissed his cheek. Before he could walk into the room to finish what he came to do, Verdell whispered in a scream towards Benji, "be easy on my gears."

Verdell shook his head. He knew Benji was not going straight home with his car and that money he just gave her. Stepping into the dimly lit room, the light flickering from the fireplace showed the fear in Mr. McDaniel's eyes.

Verdell addressed him, "Mr. McDaniel. You don't know me,

but I'm here because I have a handler that wants to know what you know. And now that I know what you know, I have to do what I know."

The tears began to flow and mixed with the blood running from his cracked nose, courtesy of Benji. Getting closer, Verdell reached a hand into each pocket and pulled out a blade in one and a syringe in the other.

Mr. McDaniel began to moan against the tape that Benji put across his mouth.

"Shhh. The knife is only for show. It's what is in the syringe that will kill you first. You won't even feel me making you pretty. Handler's orders."

Chapter 6

TIFFANY

Tiffany's eyes darted left and right, navigating the rows filled with cars, vans, and trucks. All of the doors were ajar, in what otherwise would be considered, an abandoned grocery store parking lot. It was unusually still for a place so commonly full of life, full of people rushing in and out. There was not one person in sight. A chill ran deep into Tiffany's bones even though there was no wind.

The greying sky quickly shifted to black, and cherry sized raindrops began to splatter her cheeks. Suddenly, Tiffany felt a hand squeeze her own. Startled, she glanced down into a little round, light-brown face. Terror glazed in the dilated eyes staring back at her. Without warning, the little girl's squeeze turned into the grip of death. Tiffany wanted to pull away, but the oppressive desperation made her hold steady. Tiffany's stomach sank into her bowels. A vicious game of tug of war with an unknown force ensued and Tiffany found herself fighting on the losing end.

The screams that escaped from the little girl's throat caused goosebumps to surface on Tiffany's arms. The invisible blonde hairs on the back of her neck tingled as they stood at attention. The girl's shrill cry sounded as if someone or something was ripping her body in two. Tiffany grabbed the little girl's forearms, straining to pull her back from the darkness that engulfed them. The black sky melted into the tarred pavement swallowing the yellow flashing lights of the cars. Tiffany could feel the tiny hands slipping from her grasp. Digging her heels into the dissolving earth, Tiffany watched in horror as a small flailing body hovered off the ground, being sucked, inch by inch, into the black abyss.

Tiffany could only see the little girl's arms now. Her body, eaten to the crown of her head. Those screams, she still heard the screams. Looking around frantically, Tiffany searched for something that could help her yank the girl out, but only the void was there. All at once, the noise and the silence surrounding her clashed in the night air, frightening her to tears.

There was nothing else Tiffany could do but hold on, even if it meant her getting sucked in too. Without warning a different noise sounded.

Beep. Beep. Beep.

A car horn? Maybe someone found their way through the darkness and is coming to help.

Beep. Beep. Beep.

Tiffany squinted her eyes to peer through the murk and saw headlights coming their way.

"Hold on, Babygirl. Someone is coming to help us. Just hold on. I won't let you go."

Hearing the persistent screams from the other side of the hole let Tiffany know the little girl may be a whole lot of banged up, but she was still among the living. There was hope. The raindrops became fatter as the headlights drew closer. The *beep beep beep* became louder and more frequent. Tiffany threw her hands in the air to flag the car down. Help was on the way.

"We're here!!!" She jumped wildly, waving her arms.

"We're here. Please. Help." She shouted.

Beep. Beep. Beep.

The car grew nearer. Tiffany's tears of relief mixed with the raindrops on her cheeks. Help had come at last.

It was only then Tiffany realized she had not heard the screaming anymore. She had let go of the little girl's hands in her haste to wave down the car for help. Tiffany dropped to her knees and wailed. The little girl was gone, and it was all her fault.

Beep. Beep. Beep.

Beep Beep. Beep.

Beep. Beep. Beep.

Tiffany heard the horn but ignored it. She saw the headlights within feet of her, and instead of moving out of the way, she laid in the fetal position, wishing it was her the darkness had taken away and not the little girl.

*

Beep beep beep beep. Beep beep beep beep. Beep beep beep beep.

Tiffany reached to the left of her, where her alarm would usually be, and it was not there. She felt something else. *A shoe? Why would a shoe be on my nightstand?* Struggling to open her crust leaden eyes, Tiffany realized she was on the floor of her bedroom instead of in her California King. And she had a splitting headache.

Tiffany shakily rose to her feet and stretched. She darted her tongue around the inside of her dry mouth. The tart taste and gritty feel let her know that she would have to search for vomit somewhere between her front door and the bedroom. Despite the throbbing at her temples, Tiffany managed to stumble to the nightstand to turn off the beeping alarm. It was 4:45 a.m.

"Ughh! The sun isn't even up yet," Tiffany sighed.

She took a sip of the half empty water bottle on her dresser and swished the liquid around in her mouth. Spitting the vile brew into the garbage bin, Tiffany spotted the barf trail leading from her bed into the garbage pail. The bed got most of it.

She made a quick call to her cleaning lady for an emergency disinfectant session. Marcia came out twice a month, but Tiffany hoped she would make an exception for this mess.

"Hard night, huh?" The voice on the other side of the phone giggled.

Wishing the pounding at her temples would stop, Tiffany whined, "Not now, Marcia. I need you. I have to leave in a few, but you know where the key is."

Before saying goodbye, Marcia congratulated Tiffany on her Monday night story. Marcia's comment blew away the drunken cloud shrouding Tiffany's memory of the investigative piece she did two nights before.

The police found another victim. A young woman had been taken, beaten, and carved for parts. It was only June and Candy Ellis was the fourth victim this year, the eighth in the last two. Women were being targeted for their organs and the idea of the ghastly murders becoming more frequent scared the shit out of Tiffany. Not knowing if there were more victims frightened her even more.

Tiffany was prey to what she coined as event zero or the first instance of this madness in the city. It spooked her enough to quit her laid-back career as an office assistant and pursue journalism and investigative reporting. Tiffany's father had not made it easy for her to come to him, ready to do something ambitious with her life at thirty. However, when he heard the deep-rooted fear the ordeal left her with, he felt the best thing to do was to help her combat the terror with knowledge. He eventually agreed that a career in journalism and acquiring the skills to research your enemy would be her best offense. Her father not only paid for her education but provided influential references and contacts to jump-start her career after graduation. Tiffany was grateful. Grateful for how far she had come. It was going on her third year as lead correspondent for Channel 8 News. And for a time, life was good. It was so good, in fact, that her painful experience from years ago was wiped out. Almost like something she had read in a newspaper or drama novel, that is until Monday night's story.

In the hot shower, Tiffany hoped to scorch the nightmare from her skin and burn the puke from her hair. She stood under the scalding water as punishment for falling short all those years ago. A little girl was kidnapped and mutilated because she failed to protect her. Tiffany lost a friend, almost lost her life, and lost herself. The frequency of these gruesome murders unnerved her. It could have been her. Nothing was stopping it from being her or maybe even someone else she knew and loved. Tiffany would not lay down on the job this time. She was going to solve this for Madisin, for Tatiana, for herself. Tiffany wanted redemption. She never had the opportunity to make it right for her friend, but she would make damn sure it did not happen to anyone else.

*

Before the plush bath towel could cover her wet and tender skin, Tiffany had her assistant on speed dial.

"Blake? Blake? Get up. Yes, I know it's five in the morning, but I want you to get me an interview with the mayor. What do you mean, how soon? Now, if possible!"

Tiffany snapped the phone shut and shuddered as her wretched bloodshot eyes bore into her reflection. She squeezed her eyes shut to stop the tears from rushing down her face. She would make sure everyone made finding this sick bastard a priority. Maybe then, the little girl in her head would stop screaming.

Chapter 7

TATIANA

Tatiana noticed a woman following her and her grandmother through the produce aisles of the open market. The warehouse-style fresh foods and produce stand were usually packed shoulder to shoulder on Saturdays. It took them nearly twenty minutes just to cross Hillsborough and find parking. Being leery of crowds, Tatiana made sure to keep her eyes open and Nanna close. She suspected someone was following them three aisles ago as they made their way through the bulk household cleaners' and paper products' section towards the freezers of frozen seafood. Finally, buggy bumping their way through the exotic fruits, Tatiana's suspicions were confirmed.

"Greta, old gal, is that you?"

Tatiana had called her grandmother Nanna for so long that she almost forgot her first name was Greta. And then to add "old gal" to it was just disrespectful. Her grandmother was not even sixty-five yet.

"Nanna, you know this lady?" Tatiana asked with attitude as she stepped in between her grandmother and the woman. She was ready to knock her old ass out if it came down to it. Catching Nanna's eye and the *it's okay* look, Tatiana took the hint and the list of items from her grandmother's hand.

"Nanna, I'm going to let you talk, and I'll go finish this list. I'll meet you back here, okay?" Tatiana said slowly, eyebrows raised, and lip turned up at the other woman.

"Little girl, I'm not slow. Gone head and find you some business. I'll be right here."

Tatiana made an "mm-hmm" noise and brushed off her grandmother's indifference. She knew the look Nanna gave her over her glasses. There were a few choice curse words for Tatiana's hovering, and more importantly, the look was supposed to make her not worry. True to form, Tatiana walked backwards out of the produce aisle and even waited, busying herself with nothing in particular for a few seconds, before leaving the aisle altogether. Ever since her mother's murder, Tatiana accepted the responsibility of looking after her grandmother. No one ever gave her the role or told her directly that being her grandmother's caretaker and protector was her job. Still, something about that horrible night made her grandmother grow old quicker. From the ages twelve to seventeen, Tatiana worked overtime to make sure she slowed that aging process down in every way she could.

After Nanna's home burned to the ground, for a while they lived with her grandmother's brother, Uncle Steve. Tatiana recalled meeting him only once before the fire. Uncle Steve was a big burly man. Taller and wider than any man she had ever seen. When Nanna introduced them, Uncle Steve tried to shake her hand, and Tatiana ran and hid out of fear she would disappear in his grasp. He called her *Little Rabbit* after that because she was so small and timid. Tatiana did not remember much before that time, but she remembered the fear. Her mother and her grandmother reeked of it. Nanna still reeked of it now. She and Uncle Steve spoke in whispers whenever Tatiana was around. There was a constant buzzing in the house. Everything was at a busy bee's hush. They assured her it was "for her own good," and that she was "too young for grown up worries". It was a funny thing to feel safe and afraid at the same time.

It took weeks for Tatiana to warm up to Uncle Steve, let alone speak to him. But he never rushed her. The most he ever did was pat her on the head as he came and went, calling her Little Rabbit each time. One day, Tatiana saw him playing with a fish and asked him curiously, "Uncle Steve, what you doing?"

"Little Rabbit speaks," was his hearty response.

Instead of telling her, Uncle Steve motioned for Tatiana to come closer. Helping her to hold the funny shaped pliers in one hand and a stunned catfish in the other, Uncle Steve guided Tatiana in expertly peeling the skin from its flesh. And if Tatiana thought that was disgusting, she was proven wrong when Uncle Steve sliced the belly of the fish from its tail to its gills and let the insides fall to the neatly spread newspaper that covered the wooden table. Uncle Steve insisted Tatiana clean one for herself if she did not want to go to bed hungry. Tatiana felt sad for the catfish. Its open mouth made it look like it was gasping for air. The gaped jaws reminded Tatiana of how her mother's mouth looked when she took her last breaths. Hot tears streamed down her face. Tatiana tried to make her first cut to skin the fish but could not stop stabbing it. She had forgotten Uncle Steve was there until he wrestled the pliers from her hand and wrapped his great big arms around her. She stayed in his embrace until her heaves of grief turned to breathless sobs. When Uncle Steve saw that Tatiana was too exhausted to cry any longer, he dipped a clean rag in boiling water, rung it out, and let the wind cool it before wiping her face spotless. Even though Uncle Steve had not said one word, she felt like he understood her hurt and passed no judgement or expectation as to how she *should* feel or react. It had not been a full month since Tatiana lost her mother. She was still recovering from her own injuries from that fatal night attack. But it took a dying fish for Tatiana to finally come to grips with what happened to her family. She had Nanna, and now Uncle Steve, but her mother would not be here to tell her stories at how to look at the good things in life, despite all the bad. Tatiana stared at the chopped and bloody fish. This is an example of what her life would be now. She had to learn to fend for herself.

Uncle Steve took the damaged fish and gave her a new one

to clean. At dinner later that evening, Uncle Steve, fried fish and plopped that same fish from Tatiana's episode, earlier that day, on her plate with a heaping serving of buttered grits. The fish, though mangled, looked and smelled amazing, but Tatiana tensed when she recognized the stab wounds that she delivered earlier through the crisp batter. The fried mix barely held the fish together. *Did I do that?*

Tatiana's thoughts were broken by Nanna's surprising chuckles, "well what happened to that one?"

Eyes bulged, Tatiana wildly looked back and forth between Nanna and Uncle Steve's awaiting glances. She stammered over her words, praying that Uncle Steve would not tell about her meltdown. Her uncle stepped in to save her from herself for the second time that day.

"It looks like that catfish lost the war with a rabbit," Uncle Steve mused, giving a roar of a laugh.

And just like that, Nanna laughed, and Tatiana was back at ease. It was the first time either of them had laughed in a while. Tatiana vowed on that day that she would do more to make her Nanna smile. Whenever Uncle Steve went fishing or hunting or card playing, Little Rabbit was right there to do her part. Tatiana even got a little silly with her tactics and would throw a towel around her head and body to sing Erykah Badu's *Tyrone,* which was always a hit and a sure way to make her Nanna smile.

Nanna voiced her displeasure at their card playing, even though they always returned with money. The *devil's card* money, she would call it. Uncle Steve never fussed with Nanna about it either. He just left it in a cookie jar on the counter, and when it got low, he and Little Rabbit would go out and get more. Of course, Tatiana did not realize she was gambling and doing illegal things back then. Still, she never regretted the things Uncle Steve taught her. Tatiana even used some of the same tricks to help pay for her college tuition. She only saw Uncle Steve one time after that, five years later, at her graduation, and he still called her Little Rabbit.

*

Tatiana finished the grocery list and walked up to her grandmother just as her conversation was ending.

"What did she want, Nanna?"

"Well, why she gotta want something, child? She was just catching up with an old friend."

Putting her hands on her hips, Tatiana mocked, "Friend? You didn't tell me you had any friends, Nanna?

Frustrated with Tatiana's questioning, her grandmother sucked her teeth and almost popped her hip out of place to face her.

"Well, do I have to tell you everything? I mean, I am grown. And I wasn't always *just* your grandmother. I have friends. You not the only one who has a life, you know."

So, there it was. Tatiana felt she might have read a little too much into it, but her granddaughter sensor knew she had struck a nerve. As happy as her grandmother was to see her, she was still upset that Tatiana stayed away for so long. For a while, they just stood there. Tatiana was too ashamed to look at her grandmother for fear of seeing the pain on her Nanna's face up close. A sorry was not going to cut it. No excuse was going to work, and even the truth would not suffice. Tatiana was gone for a little more than three years and had not been back home once. Now that Tatiana thought about it, she had been very selfish the last few years.

Instead of focusing on her own hurt, Tatiana threw her arms around her Nanna and held her tight. There were no words Tatiana could say to make up for her absence. She hoped her presence, at that moment, would take away the hurt. Before long, her Nanna was swatting her away and patting the tears from her eyes. Tatiana sealed her apology with a kiss to her Nanna's cheek and promised she would cook her Nanna's favorite, liver and onions with grits and gravy. That sealed the deal. Over dinner, Nanna told her all about the job offer the mystery friend wanted to extend their way.

*

Who would have known that a local busybody following them through the grocery store a month ago would ever have her standing in a place as gorgeous as this? Tatiana walked into the kitchen and immediately became dizzy. Her head was on a swivel, spinning around the room in amazement. She had never seen anything like it. Everything in the kitchen was in twos. Double ovens. Two refrigerators. Two farmhouse sinks. It was immaculate. It did not surprise her one bit that it was her

Nanna who was called on, at the last minute, to cater a party in The Avala. Tatiana knew her grandmother was a great cook and personally loved her food. Rich fancy people paying to eat Nanna's food was confirmation. Even though they looked a little bougie for the type of soul her grandmother put into her cooking, nobody could argue that good food was universal.

It did not take her grandmother long to convince Tatiana to help cater the Gasparilla Sant Yago Knight Ball. Tatiana was all too happy to take the lead in making Nanna's impromptu catering company look as professional as possible for the occasion. She even gathered some neighborhood girls to build the prep and hostess' teams needed to help pull it off. Tatiana stood by the kitchen entrance smiling, watching her crew work the floor. *So far, so good.*

"Tatiana!"

Tatiana jumped at the sound of her grandmother screaming her name.

"Yes, ma'am," Tatiana shouted as she made her way through the hustle and bustle of the pots, dishes, and food trays being stacked with appetizers and desserts. The furrowed brows that met her gaze signaled something was not right.

"Nanna, what's wrong?"

With a heavy sigh, Nanna shook her head, "They found Angel slumped over in the bathroom throwing up in the toilet."

"They who? Nanna, please don't tell me one of these uppity folks found that girl doing something nasty…"

"No, no, no." Her grandmother stopped her before she

75

could get worked up. "Tiki found her balled up in one of the bathrooms." Then getting closer to Tatiana's face and lowering her voice, "I think she's pregnant."

Chuckling a little, "Nanna, stop that. You know that girl only fifteen. It's more likely that she was out there sneaking drinks."

Cutting Tatiana off again, this time by grabbing her face in both her hands, Nanna looked her straight in the eye and spoke slowly, "I know what I know."

Just then, Angel and Tiki came through the back entrance of the kitchen. Tatiana said a silent prayer of thanks that it was the entryway the guests could not see because Angel looked terrible. And if she was not mistaken, she thought she saw a hint of a baby bump under the white button-up that Angel wore. *Damn. Nanna was right.*

Tiki broke the awkward silence by speaking first. "Ms. Greta, we're sorry. But I hope you don't mind if I take my cousin home. She is not feeling good, and I don't think she'll be able to get back to work anytime soon."

"Of course not, baby. Here is y'all earnings for the night."

Tatiana's mouth dropped at seeing her grandmother take four hundred-dollar bills from her bra strap to pay them. They had not worked the floor longer than thirty minutes and did not deserve the niceties, let alone compensation for their time.

But Tatiana knew better than to interrupt her grandmother. She let Tiki and Angel whisper their *thank you*'s and head out in the same direction they came in before she spoke again.

"Nanna, why would you pay them lazy heifers anything? They barely did any work! Now, I'm going to have to find someone to come way out here to take their spots, and they may not make it here in time."

"Psshhh. Call someone? Why would you call someone?" her grandmother asked nonchalantly.

Tatiana eyed Nanna like she had just asked her if she was strung out on hard drugs.

"What do you mean, Nanna? We need help. We ain't even laid out the entrees yet. And we still have to finish some of the desserts."

The calmness in her grandmother's eyes exasperated Tatiana.

"See, that's what I mean. Why do you need to waste time calling two inexperienced people when you have everything you need right here?"

Oh no, Tatiana thought. She knew where her Nanna was going with this.

"I'll pay you everything Tiki and Angel would've gotten plus a little extra, because I love you."

The smile Nanna gave her was priceless. Tatiana would have done the job simply because her Nanna asked. But who was she kidding? They both knew Tatiana needed the money. She had been in Tampa for four months and had not found a job yet.

Tatiana kissed Nanna on the cheek. "Whatever you need, Nanna. You know it's not about the money. I'm doing this because I love *you.*"

77

"I know, child," her grandmother mocked before popping her on her butt and throwing her an apron.

Tatiana playfully slapped at her grandmother's hand. She crossed her eyes and licked out her tongue before grabbing the appetizer tray of homemade mini cinnamon apple donuts and strutted into the main ballroom.

Thank God this night is almost over. Tatiana's feet, nose, ears, and eyes had enough. The black pumps were killing her feet. The different colognes and perfumes mixed with food, alcohol, and stogies were enough to make a permanently stuffy nose smell again. The humming of conversations and music had her ears at a consistent ring. And she did not even want to get into the fashion nightmares.

Kelis' *My Milkshake* began to fill the air. It was a contrast to the jazz set that was playing on the stage of the main ballroom. A few people stared at Tatiana, and before she could check them, she realized that her phone was the source of the music. Tatiana steadied the tray of empty glasses with one arm while rushing to shut off her phone with the other. Her grandmother would kill her if she found out Tatiana had brought a phone with her on the floor. Tatiana glanced at the screen, hoping it was a call from one of the job interviews earlier that week. But as she thought about it, *no one from a job would call this late in the evening.* Her disappointment slowly turned into fear as she read the short message that flashed across her screen. It simply said, "This Cairo, you know what time it is." And Tatiana knew *exactly* what time it was. Time to pay up. She never gave Cairo her number. *Shit! How did she find me?* The call was not one that Tatiana wanted to return, so she decided to ignore the text. If Cairo was trying to scare her, she would have to do more than send threats via text message.

*

Cairo was a lady pimp from New Orleans who disguised her illegal activities as a modeling agency. She would lure young girls in with a nice five figure signing bonus and a contract full of legal jargon that they would not understand unless they paid a lawyer. Cairo made sure the girls were young, broke, and naive. Once she paid them their signing bonus, she owned them until the "fine print advancement" was paid off by pimping them out to the highest bidder. Tatiana met Cairo when she had a lot of needs and hustling her dorm mates out of their book stipends was not paying nearly enough to cover her tuition. It was happenstance that Cairo approached her in the mall, complementing her skin, her smile, and her shape. She cheerfully presented the benefits of being a model with *Cairo's Exotics*. If her circumstances had not been so dire, Tatiana might have questioned the name. But the ten thousand dollar signing bonus, monthly wardrobe allowance, and promise of continuously booked gigs with one hundred percent tips sounded like the perfect solution.

It was not until she was fighting off her first trick before Tatiana realized Cairo pimped her out. When she went to Cairo to correct the misunderstanding, Tatiana had no money left from the signing bonus to bargain with. She used her schoolwork as an excuse to stay away until Cairo introduced her to Mr. Man. He was a rich old man who always carried a ridiculous amount of cash. Cairo offered Tatiana the deal of a lifetime. *Fuck him, kill him, rob him, and bring me back the loot and the car.* In the past, Tatiana had only done one of the things that Cairo asked. Hopefully, nasty ass Mr. Man was still resting in his Cadillac in hell at the bottom of the Mississippi River where Tatiana left him. Her nerves were so bad that she only grabbed the few dollars he had from his pocket before driving his car into the black waters. She forgot to check the rest of the vehicle for his stash. Now Cairo had found her and, no doubt wanted her money.

*

Tatiana was frozen in place and had forgotten all about the party. Distracted, someone bump into her, and the empty long stem glasses spilled to the floor.

"Dammit!" She managed to shout before she remembered where she was and met eyes with her assailant.

"You look like a waitress. You act like a waitress. But I bet you all the bills in my pocket that you are not a waitress."

As worked up as she was, Tatiana could not help but be drawn in by her assaulter's good looks.

Temporarily forgetting about the broken glass and the unwelcome text, Tatiana grinned and put out her hand, palm up, for her prize.

Suddenly, there was a scream from upstairs. The text message immediately jumped back to the forefront of Tatiana's mind. *Was Cairo here?* When Tatiana turned her head around to ask the man if he heard it too, she found him closer to her face than he had been seconds ago. Tatiana took a step back.

"If you're looking for something that's not as dry as this crowd, give me a call."

Before she could speak, the man placed a clip of money in her hand with a business card and disappeared into the crowd.

Tatiana slipped the money and the card into her bra and picked up the broken glass off the floor.

Damn, he smelled good, she thought as she adjusted her bra and walked the tray back into the kitchen.

"Tatiana. Tatiana."

Hearing Nanna call her name with such urgency sent a chill up Tatiana's spine. She walked faster to get to her grandmother. When she finally made it into the kitchen, Nanna was on the floor hanging on to the small doorknob. Sweet potato pie filling and dozens of mini crusts spilled on and around her. The laugh that came from her grandmother's mouth looked misplaced because it did not mirror the empty stare in her eyes.

Dropping the tray on the nearest counter and running to her grandmother's side, "Nanna, what happened? Are you okay? I was only gone for a minute, and I come back to you flipping pies over?" Tatiana tried to jest.

Picking up her grandmother slowly from the floor, making sure not to injure her further, "Let's get you to a chair so I can have a look at you." Tatiana gently took Nanna's head and looked into her eyes, then at her head, around her neck, at her back, down to her wrists… "Oops," she heard her Nanna wince.

"They are just a little sore. But only a little."

Tatiana knew it had to be worse than what Nanna was saying because she barely touched her wrists.

"Okay, Nanna, let me check if there is a doctor out there that can help us."

"Okay, Babygirl, but what about the dessert?"

Tatiana smiled because she had not been anyone's Babygirl in over eight years, and it was always like her grandmother to put everyone else before herself.

"Let them eat cobbler instead," Tatiana whispered as they both laughed lightly.

As she went into the main hall searching for help, the worry of the night's events finally took over Tatiana's face once out of her grandmother's sight.

Chapter 8

PAUL

Paul woke up feeling well rested. It was the first time in months that his sleep was not troubled by nightmares. The dark green slop his daughter concocted for a nighttime cocktail had Paul skeptical at first, but it went to work better than Christina described. After he got past the slimy film and the initial bitterness, there was a sweet aftertaste that let Paul get a solid six hours of shut eye. Paul grabbed a sticky note from his nightstand to write a reminder to ask Christina to make him another cocktail tonight.

Rolling out of bed, Paul pulled his tablet from the drawer to check the calendar for today's schedule. Before he could tap on the app's icon, an email notification from a name he had not recognized appeared on the screen. *Peggy O'Neale?* Paul was sure his personal email address was private and heavily protected. *Who could have gotten past the safeguards?* Paul scanned the subject line and the email's preview pane, looking for grammatical errors and other signs of phishing. *I have to tell Barry to tighten my email security.* Paul clicked on the email.

Pressure can turn coal into diamonds. Only time will tell what it turns you into. Your clock is running out and your cloak of deceit is burning. Tell me, who are you?

Paul's face went flat, skin turning pale. His throat dry, hands trembling. The words would not have carried much weight by themselves, but the picture that popped onto his screen was enough to send ice-cold fear snaking down his spine. The image was an old polaroid of a brown-skinned man and woman standing with a pale younger version of himself. Paul stared blankly at the photograph. If he had not lived it, Paul would have been in denial. *It can't be! Who in the hell could have this photo? How?* Paul distinctly recalled watching the last surviving copy, burst into flames, at his own hands, years earlier.

Paul threw his tablet to the floor and paced the room. His mind raced, searching his brain for the names of the possible people having access to this photo. Whoever it was, undoubtedly, wanted to ruin him. Or at the least, extort him, but they had not asked for anything, yet. "Shit," Paul whispered. In his agitation, the curses spilled louder from his lips, "Shit. Shit. Shit. Shit. Shit."

There were only a few people Paul could think of that had this photo. I burned the copy *Madisin gave me. It can't be her because she's been dead for years now.* Paul did not know how Madisin acquired the photo but was pretty positive that when she died, his secrets died with her. And this was one secret that needed to stay buried. Suddenly struck with grief at the memory of his late lover and their daughter, Paul's throat tightened. It had been ages since he allowed himself to think about them freely. Paul's political career aspirations murdered his secretary and soul mate of thirteen years. They had been on the outs when she passed, but he never wanted to see her hurt and most definitely not murdered. The pain and guilt from his daughter's cold case was almost enough to make Paul confess his indiscretions to Sandra. Almost. It was deemed a necessary evil for Paul and his family to succeed without the hindrance of buried "skeletons in the closet." Collateral damage was the only explanation he received for their deaths.

Paul pegged his wife, Sandra, as a possibility, but she had not shown any signs of knowing his truth. This secret was big enough to tear their family apart. If Sandra knew, Paul was certain he would not have woken up this morning. *That was for damn sure.* He would be dead just like Madisin and their daughter.

*

All his life, because of Paul's skin color, he was assumed to be white. Even though Paul was perfectly fit and an average healthy child, by any standard, he was diagnosed with Albinism at birth. His parents were as dark as milk chocolate, and he was born of their DNA but white as milk. After a rough childhood of being teased and ostracized because of his unusually pale skin, it was the kindness and oversight of a college buddy, Barry Mellow, that started him down this path of deception. The fear of being cast away was the reason he stayed quiet for the past twenty-two years. Only God knew what he had to fear now.

Paul benefitted from this mistaken identity by being placed into social circles and provided opportunities that would otherwise not have been made available. If caught now, the public, political, and social scandals would mangle his reputation. Not to mention the seething hate, disgust, and utter disappointment that would radiate from his wife and her family. After all the commotion Paul made during the family debates about assimilation, invisible ceilings, and affirmative action, they would certainly throw him into exile. They would maybe even pay for his head on a wooden stake. By all accounts, he was living his life as a privileged white man.

*

Paul's pacing was interrupted by the sound of approaching footsteps. He quickly tapped out of the email just in time to see Sandra walking through the bedroom door.

"Paul, can we talk?"

Trying to smooth out his curly red locks, composing himself as best he could, "Umm, sure, Sandra. Give me a sec to get showered, won't you?"

"Is everything all right, Paul?" Sandra asked, sounding suspicious, eyeing him cautiously.

"Yes, just another one of those nightmares again." Paul

scoffed out a laugh as he walked around the room, gathering nothing in particular for his shower. He knew if he did not grab his undergarments or something quick, Sandra would never leave him alone.

"Well, we will just have to ask Christina to change up that cocktail now, won't we?" Sandra muttered, walking across the room to put her hand on his forehead. "You know I worry about you, dearest?"

Paul took his wife's hand and kissed it before pecking her quickly on the lips. "Yes, I know, dear. But I promise I'm okay. I just need to wash the dream away, and I'll be downstairs for breakfast."

"Well, okay. No, wait. I knew there was something. Barry wants you. He said something about a reporter calling." Sandra hesitated as Paul rushed her to the door.

"All right, dear. Tell Barry I'll be right down."

Paul quickly shut the door behind Sandra, walked to the bathroom, and ran the shower, full steam. Barry was usually his "go-to" guy in situations like this. Be that as it may, there was no way Paul was going to request his help on this one. Barry would kill him with his bare hands. Paul had to find a way to handle this himself, or at least with someone who could be more acceptable and understanding of his plight. He made a mental note to see if Dhorian could lend a hand in identifying the enigma and what the hell they wanted.

*

"It's the eighth call from Ms. Tiffany LaSalle's assistant Blake Andrews."

"Who?" Paul asked as he squinted, trying to match faces with the names.

Barry repeated, "Ms. Tiffany LaSalle. You know the Channel 8 News correspondent?"

Paul remembered her. He gave out a short chortle, "Oh yea, the blonde with the great legs."

Barry rolled his eyes, "Yes, that one, sir."

"Well, what does she want?" Paul asked as he corrected his stance to address the ball on his indoor, putting green.

Barry leaned against the desk in the office, "She says she wants to speak with you about the organ trade in Tampa."

Scoffing, Paul looked at Barry disgustedly. "Organ trade? What organ trade in Tampa?"

"Paul, she just did a piece on the women who were murdered and gutted, for lack of better words," Barry responded exasperatedly.

"Yes, yes, yes. The murders I'm aware of, but who gave it the moniker of organ trade?" Paul made quotations with his hands loosely flailing in the air. "The last thing I want to do is give the people in the city of Tampa the wrong impression about what's going on here. Murders we can handle, but when you start using words like *trade*, it implies a more sinister spectrum of evil and know-how. And then to compound the word by adding organs to it…well now that's just irresponsible, don't you think?"

"Well, yes, I do, sir, but it wasn't me that came up with it.

And if we don't get in front of it, I'm sure your constituents will find some way to make you the irresponsible one."

Paul stared at Barry thoughtfully for a few seconds. "Fine, well, get her on the line. I would love to have dinner with her to discuss the care she should use with her words when reporting on the tragedy that has befallen on the people of this city."

Barry pulled out his tablet to search the calendar for available time slots.

"Good, it looks like Mrs. Christen is available for dinner on Thursday night at 7 p.m. this week? Should I add you and Ms. LaSalle to the calendar with her? Let's say, Maggiano's at Westshore Plaza?"

"Don't get ahead of yourself. This situation will have to be taken care of with white gloves. Scratch the Mrs. and see if Ms. LaSalle is available on Wednesday at 6 p.m. for dinner at Ocean Prime in International Plaza."

If Ms. LaSalle also happened to be his mystery emailer, Peggy O'Neale, Paul did not want his wife anywhere near this meeting. He and Barry would be better at handling this one alone. Paul had a mind to tell Barry to sit this one out too. But, with Barry as his best friend, brother-in-law, political advisor, and all-around right-hand man, Paul could not say that without Barry getting suspicious. Paul ignored the scrutiny in Barry's gaze as he put the ball down the green into a bronze waste bin lying on its side. He took that as a small sign. Things would fall in place soon enough.

Releasing a deep sigh, Paul looked at Barry, "Okay, now what else is on the agenda?"

Chapter 9

TATIANA

Tatiana stared somberly into the mirror and rubbed smushed aspirin paste on the scar tissues above her right pelvic bone and over her right breast. The damaged skin began to keloid ever since her road trip back home and it had not stopped since her return. The lesions used to only itch when she was anxious. Now, there was an uneasy feeling that seemed to follow Tatiana around all the time, which would explain the constant flareups she was experiencing. She picked up the phone and prayed that the job offer from her mystery guy at the Avala party was legit. Maybe if she found a job Tatiana would be less tense. With her Nanna sick, she would have to pick up the slack, and the small criminal gigs she did to make it by in college would not cut it. Tatiana wanted to stay away from any illegal activity, if at all possible. The last thing she needed was her Nanna worrying about her when she should focus on getting better.

*

Appointment after appointment, second and third opinions, all the doctors gave the same diagnosis. In addition to a fractured wrist, Greta Elaine Foster had severe chronic obstructive pulmonary disease, otherwise known as COPD. Every day Tatiana watched stage three progress on the fast track to stage four. Her Nanna was short of breath, restless, and had a decreased appetite. It was like she was witnessing a murder in progress; only there was no one to blame. No one to feel the brunt of her anger. No one to share the pain. There was nothing she could do but watch as her grandmother came to terms with the disease exploiting her body. Tatiana tried her best to clean, cook, feed, medicate, and entertain her grandmother as much as possible. But what good was it to clean house for someone who stayed in bed; to cook for and try to feed someone who took no pleasure in the smells of food or the taste of it. Tatiana's mother and grandmother raised her to be a foodie. Her grandmother would always tease that it was passed down in their blood to love and enjoy food. To know the great cook her grandmother was and to now see her turn her face up at Shepard's pie was overly depressing. It was one of her Nanna's favorites. Tatiana even took her time and let the meat and veggies stew for a few hours to make it flavorful and not ooze out of the layers when she baked it. The medication dulled her grandmother's bronchitis symptoms for hours at a time. However, she still had other side effects like dry mouth, shuddering tremors, nervousness, and terrible headaches.

Once filled with laughter, the house was now eerily silent. Tatiana was regretfully reminded of her childhood all over again. She was living helplessly while things just happened to her and around her. She had not come home for this. And waiting around for things to get better was not an option. She refused to be a bystander this time while they happened to her grandmother, the only soul she had left in this world who loved her. Nanna was at home with her for the time being, but she needed better care than Tatiana could give her. She deserved better. In just three months, her grandmother's medical costs and living expenses depleted the money Tatiana hustled up before coming home. Her reserve was now at the lower end of three figures. Tatiana barely had enough to get groceries, her Nanna's refills, keep the lights on, and put gas in her car. If she had to tell one more bill collector to "go to hell," she was afraid God was going to come to Earth and throw her down there himself.

*

Tatiana sat on the edge of her bed and looked down at the black business card. She needed some steady income, and she needed it now. Picking up her cell phone, Tatiana slowly pushed each sparkly number into her phone.

Ring. Ring. Ring.

Ring. Ring. Ring.

Ring. Ring. Ring.

Tatiana was getting ready to hang up, but she heard the line pick up. It sounded like elevator music in the background. "Hello. Hello," she shouted.

A smooth and deep baritone voice responded, "Yep. Yell-o. This is the Top Hat. May I ask who's speaking?"

Tatiana could hardly hear the person with the noise in the background. Glancing at the clock, she noticed it was only two o'clock in the afternoon. What kind of place had music bumping like that mid-day? When she Googled *Top Hat, Tampa, FL*, the search returned as a sports bar and gentlemen's club from 8 p.m. to 2 a.m. She had no idea what to expect from this type of club.

Putting her finger in one of her ears, Tatiana cleared her throat and shouted into the phone again, "I'm having a hard time hearing you. I was given this card by someone who works there."

"Does the card have a name on it?"

Tatiana flipped the card over and over, examining it for a name. "No. Just the business name and number."

"Turn the bass down."

"Excuse me," she said.

"Not you, give me one sec."

Tatiana heard the phone drop and a loud voice in the background. When the person came back on the line, the music had not stopped, but it was damn sure softer than it had been.

"Yea. Hello? You said the card ain't got no name on it, right?"

Tatiana was almost nervous to answer. "Right."

"Okay, cool. That's Vee. He's the only one here who got a card with no name on it. Dude thinks it makes him mysterious or something. So, are you calling for the man or a job?"

The question caught Tatiana off guard because the man gave her the card and just said call. Tatiana did not know if she needed *Vee* to get her the job, or if she just told this guy she needed a job, would he be able to hire her.

"Yo. You still there? I don't have all day. I got a band that's waiting to turn their bass back up."

"Yes, yes. I'm still here." Tatiana stammered. "I'm looking for a job. I need a job." She corrected. Tatiana did not have time for a job search, and she needed him to know that she was not looking past this one.

"A'ight. Cool then. Can you be here by five?"

"Five as at five o'clock p.m., today?"

The man sucked his teeth. "Yes, 5 p.m. today. You said you needed a job, right?"

Putting more certainty behind her voice, Tatiana glanced at the clock before responding, "Yes, five is good. I'll be there."

"Cool." And the line went dead.

Tatiana looked at the phone. He did not give her a chance to ask any questions about how she should dress or who she was meeting. She did not even get his name. Tatiana fell back on the bed and blew out her anxiety. She had never been to a gentlemen's club, let alone worked in one. Tatiana made sure to prepare for all the unknowns. She took her time getting dressed, rubbing mango Shea butter lotion on her peanut butter-colored skin as she got out of the tub. Tatiana outlined her big, light brown, slanted eyes with a dark brown pencil. She placed a new crystal stud in her nose and put on her favorite matte cranberry lipstick that helped accentuate her thick lips. Tatiana did not like to wear much makeup because she always seemed to sweat and got almost immediate breakouts at the worst times, so just a little was enough for her. Tatiana jammed to one of her dancehall favorites by AfroB and wined her body back and forth in her full-length mirror. She pinned her naturally curly Twizzler red hair up, letting some of the curls fall in her face. Tatiana danced seductively while putting her bra and panties on. She hoped dancing was not a requirement for the interview but wanted to be ready in case it was. Tatiana donned her grey "My Black is Beautiful" crop top and her favorite pair of high-waist destroyed denim jeans. She kissed her Nanna on the forehead and walked out the door with prayers on her lips. Simple prayers for her grandmother to be alive when she got back and for this "interview" to not end up being a terrible idea.

*

The front entrance to the Top Hat was on the corners of Main and Albany. The GPS led her around the back, but she circled and parked next to the nearby barbeque joint instead.

"Hey. Hey. You. Lil momma. You fine as hell, but you can't park there."

Tatiana chuckled at his accent. He sounded like he was from the South but not from Tampa. Not to mention he looked like a 1999 Billy Sparks. Shades and all.

"Oh, my bad. I couldn't find any parking. I'm just here for an interview."

"You are? Are you?"

The Billy Sparks look-alike eyed her up and down and was on her faster than she could blink. He almost pushed her off the sidewalk into the busy street. She quickly sidestepped and took a few steps back.

"Don't be scared, sweetheart. If you here for an interview, then you here to see me. Money *Maan* Manny. I handle all the interviews."

The sight of him flicking his tongue at her gave her the willies. Tatiana gave him a once-over before rolling her eyes. *Damn.* She forgot her pearl handle at home. The only place he looked like he possibly had money was in his mouth. The entire bottom row looked like aluminum foil had been super glued to it. All she could think was, *dear God, what have I gotten myself into.* She was starting to have second thoughts and had not stepped into the building yet.

"Manny, is it?" Tatiana asked like she had not caught the ridiculous name he threw at her.

"Yes, Lil momma? It's Money *Maan* Manny."

"Okay. Money *Maan* Manny. I'm going to move my car. I'll be back."

He was still staring her down like he could gobble her up at any moment, "Well a'ight then. Don't make me wait too long. I can't wait to get your fine ass on that table. Mmmm."

The emphasis on *wait* and the disgusting noise he made caused Tatiana's stomach to turn. She said, "all right then," as she hurriedly walked away.

Tatiana could not seem to make it to the driver's seat of her car fast enough. Tatiana could feel his eyes squeezing her ass as she walked. *Why did I have to wear these tight-ass jeans with so many damn holes in them?* Tatiana thought. She was second-guessing not only her attire but her decision to work here. Finally, making it to the car, Tatiana's head immediately hit the steering wheel. Tears were at the corners of her eyes. She pulled a napkin out of her glove compartment and quickly dabbed at her eyes. Tatiana did not want to mess up her makeup if she did decide to go back and go through with this. She thanked God her grandmother was at home, sick. Tatiana knew that if her Nanna caught her in a place like this, she would whoop her ass right off the stage before dragging her out. *Dammit.* She whispered. Too bad tax time had already passed. Her mind ran through several tables, card spots, and hustles. She could try her luck to make some quick money, but all of them put her in too much danger. She did not have her Uncle Steve to watch over her. She was home, but it had changed so much that she did not know who or where to turn. Tatiana felt an anxiety attack coming on. She put her keys in the ignition and jumped when she heard a loud knock at her window.

The look she gave must have said it all because the man

jumped back from the window. Tatiana could only imagine how her face looked mushed tightly against her purple bling studded steering wheel. *Damn, he caught me slipping.* She checked her face in the mirror before looking at the man. She recognized him immediately and was embarrassed. It was the good looker from the party, the one who gave her the card.

Vee, she remembered the guy calling him. She quickly rolled her window down.

"Ay. I didn't mean to scare you." He put his hands up in surrender. "I just wanted to come out here and make sure you hadn't left yet."

He seemed to recognize her too, which made her blush. She had almost forgotten how fine this man was. He was an impressive-looking specimen. It took her a few seconds to find her words.

"Ummm. Yea. I just needed some air. I was going to come in, and …"

"Oh, no need to explain. I saw Manny working you over on the office cameras. He can be a bit much, especially if dancing isn't your kind of work. By the way, I'm Vee. I manage the bar."

Tatiana shook his hand through her window. She noticed he had a few scars under all the ink on his arm.

"Look, speaking of dancing. I don't think dancing is what I want to do. I don't have time for men to be ogling me and trying to touch…"

"Aht! Say no more. I didn't give you the card because I thought you were a dancer."

"You remember giving me the card?"

"Hell yea. How could I forget a face like yours?"

Tatiana blushed at the compliment and averted her eyes. This man was fine as shit. Clearing the nervousness from her throat, "Well, why did you give me the card?"

The man stared at her so long she thought she had missed something he said.

"I'm sorry, did I miss something?" she asked hesitantly.

"Well, are you going to make me interview you while you are sitting in the car?"

Tatiana guffawed and then covered her mouth. She did not mean to laugh that loud or that wildly.

"Nah, don't cover up that pretty smile now. I already heard it. Come on. Get out the car, and I'll give you the grand tour and the interview. I'll also show you what other job openings we have here besides *dancing*."

Tatiana grinned at the air quotes he put up around "dancing." She checked her face in the mirror again.

"Okay, give me a sec to get myself together, and I'll be there."

He eyed her skeptically. "You keep me waiting, and Im'ma send Manny back out here to get you. From the way he talks about you, I know he would be more than happy to do that for me."

"Don't you mean Money *Maan* Manny," she scolded.

They both laughed.

"I'm serious. I'm coming." Tatiana had already checked herself in the mirror. She only needed a slight touchup on her lips, but Tatiana could have done that in the dark. What she did not want is to have him watching her stroll in front of him. Tatiana just knew her legs would disappoint her and give way. The last thing she needed was to be further embarrassed. Just her luck, her ankles would suddenly forget how to stand firm in heels.

"Cool. See you in a few."

She let him get a few feet in front of her before she got out of the car. Tatiana could not believe his physique matched his face. Her eyes were open so wide, watching him walk towards the club entrance that they began to burn a little. He was wearing the TB hat, jersey, and same color, orange, red, and pewter Retros on his feet to match. *Damn. He fly as hell.* Tatiana knew she would have to watch herself with this one. She took a deep breath. Feeling a little more at ease, she was ready to get this steady cash.

Chapter 10

DHORIAN

Dhorian stood in his ceiling to floor window, looking at the sunset on the Hillsborough River. He had worked so hard over the years to be able to see his life from this place. It felt good just to enjoy the warmth of the sun on his face as he took it all in. Dhorian had to put in a bit more work than he liked, but he had no regrets. There was some unfinished business, though. Mr. Christen made him start a to-do list years ago to keep him focused when Dhorian wanted to quit his studies. It was that same list that sat on his desk now. It helped to focus him. At first, Dhorian had his doubts that a list would work. But now, Partner at the prestigious Reed & Morris Law Group, Dhorian smiled because he knew different. Overlooking the water and the hustle and bustle of Tampa Riverwalk, Dhorian felt like he got in when the market was good. A lot of construction was underway to refine and redevelop the area. He could not wait to seize the opportunities.

Happy with himself, Dhorian looked around his office and sat at his desk to look over his list. Finish school – Check. Make lots of money – Check. Make Partner – Check. Pay Mr. Christen back the two hundred seventy-five thousand dollars for room, board, and tuition – Dhorian sighed and laughed to himself, partially checking; only one hundred twenty-five thousand left to go. He paused his checklist for a moment. Dhorian always dreamed he would have that kind of money when he was younger. He told his father he needed *BIG* money for the rich and famous lifestyle he imagined for himself, and college would not get him that life. At age eighteen, Dhorian saw no point in spending money he did not have to learn how to make the kind of money a college education could not guarantee him.

His professors and Mr. Paul Lee Christen helped him prove that he could be successful without a traditional education. Dhorian laughed out loud. He shook his head at his ability to entertain himself and then grabbed a protein shake from his mini fridge. As he gulped and enjoyed the smooth sizzle of the beverage in his throat, he thought about his father. *You died too soon, Pops.* It took him back to his to-do list, where he wrote in capital letters FIND OUT THE TRUTH at the very bottom. It was something he meant to do but was afraid of what he would find. Dhorian patted the cover of his mother's diary, which he kept with him at all times to keep her near him. The book held so much truth and yet so much mystery.

Dhorian recalled bits and pieces of his parents arguing and

snippets of his mother's depression before she passed, but it was like one day he woke up, and she was gone. He was away at a four-week basketball camp when word of his mother's death had reached him. Dhorian never knew how it came to be until his father's confession during an argument they were having four years later. The heated exchange echoed through his mind, and Dhorian re-lived it like it was yesterday.

*

"Are you, my father?"

"Yes. Of course, I'm your father. What would make you ask me such a stupid question like that?

"Isn't that the same stupid question you asked?" Dhorian quipped.

His father stammered, "Now, now you hold on there. You don't know anything about what your mother and I went through. I loved..." Dhorian watched him gulp those words down hard, "I love your mother, son."

"Don't call me that!"

"What the hell you mean, don't call you that. I raised your ungrateful ass. And I don't give a damn what you found. I am your father, and you will respect *me*."

"What happened to my mother? Why did she write all this stuff about secrets and needing peace and shit? Why are you lying to me?"

"Boy, I'm not going to tell you again to watch how you talk to me!"

"Tell me what the hell happened to her!" Dhorian screamed.

"Boy, I'll show you to respect *me*. How dare you talk to me like that? Your mother tried to talk to me like that. She tried to take you away from me. I had to show that whore who she was talking to. Like mother, like son. Huh? That's how I know for sure your ass ain't mine. Too bad it took all this time for me to see it…"

*

The voices in his head trailed off when the intercom beeped.

"Mr. Hamilton."

Clearing his throat and his mind, Dhorian responded to his executive assistant.

"Yes, Joanie."

"Mr. Reed wants to know if you are still on for your 6 p.m. dinner celebration."

Dhorian looked at his watch and then his calendar. *Shit, I'm going to be late.*

"Uhhh, yes, tell him I am finishing with a client meeting, and I will be a few minutes late. Actually, where is this place, Joanie? Did he say?"

"Umm, yes, sir. I have the address here."

"Okay. Great. Text me the location."

"Yes, sir, Mr. Hamilton. Also, Ms. Christen called again. She's on line two."

Dhorian sighed hard. He forgot all about the rendezvous Christina planned for them later that evening. It was the fourth time in the last two weeks that she tried to meet up with him, and he would have to reschedule. She was not going to let him live this down. They were unofficially dating and officially screwing. Christina wanted more, but Dhorian refused to risk her thinking he had more to give. She would just have to wait.

"Tell her I've left the office and will call her back as soon as I get a chance." And then a thought came to him, "Joanie?"

"Yes, sir?"

"Would the firm happen to have any PIs that you could recommend? I need a personal matter looked into."

"I am not sure, but I can ask around and find one, sir."

"Okay, make sure it's someone who is highly recommended and also bill them on my dime, not the firm's, please. I mean that, Joanie."

It was not that Joanie specifically had done anything wrong before. Dhorian believed in keeping his business and personal life separate, especially since he had no idea what he would find.

He heard Joanie's exasperation accompanied by a heavy sigh through the phone, "Yes, Mr. Hamilton. I will be extra careful with your request."

"Thank you, Joanie. After that, you can go home for the night."

"Thank you, Mr. Hamilton. I text the address to your phone. You should be there on time if you leave now. You enjoy and have a good night."

Dhorian grabbed his blazer from the back of his chair and ran to the elevator. He repeatedly pushed the button even though it did not make the elevator arrive faster. Still, it did not stop him from pressing the down button over and over again. For a brief moment, Dhorian thought to call Joanie and tell her to cancel the PI. But he knew that if he wanted to move forward in his life, finding the truth was something he needed to scratch off his to-do list.

*

Dhorian pulled up to the building five minutes before six o'clock. Top Hat Sports Bar & Gentlemen's Club. Dhorian checked the address on his GPS just to make sure it was what Joanie had sent him. He could see a valet, and the building did not look bad. The neighborhood was not exactly where he expected someone of Reed & Morris' caliber to mingle. Especially not at the request of the senior partner Mr. Reed himself. Dhorian knew he could not sit at the corner contemplating his boss' choice of venue much longer. The old men sitting at the chess table were starting to look at him and his BMW 328i suspiciously. Dhorian made it through the valet and entered the club precisely at 6 p.m.

When Dhorian opened the heavy mirrored glass door, a set of dark-skinned, blond, and busty twins stood in front of two sets of French doors. Dhorian wanted to laugh. Instead of Top Hat, the establishment should have been called Top Heavy. He managed to hold it in because he did not want to seem rude to the pretty ladies. It was not their fault he kept himself entertained.

"I'm here to meet with Mr. Edward Reed."

"Oh yes, Mr. Hamilton, right?" the busty blond on the left asked.

The hostess's baby doll voice did not come as a surprise, whereas her expecting him did. Mr. Reed must have been a regular here. Busty blonde on the right said, "Mr. Reed wanted to let you know that he got caught up in a last-minute meeting, and he is running a little behind schedule. But he wanted you to go in without him and enjoy a few drinks. On him, of course."

Damnit, Reed. Dhorian thought. He could have been knee-deep in Christina instead of some hole-in-the-wall gentlemen's club.

"All right then, ladies. Lead the way."

Each of the ladies grabbed a handle to the French doors and opened them, waving him inside. In unison, they said, "Welcome to Top Hat Sports Bar & Gentlemen's Club. Enjoy."

Dhorian was reluctant to say, but so far, he was impressed. The welcome service exceeded expectations. Sexy and classy, not slutty or too eager. Entering the room, it looked bigger than he thought could fit into the building walls. The luxury decor was not at all what he expected. The colors were vibrant and coordinated. There was a live band on the stage, and three dancers, swinging suspended in the air in blinged-out cages. The booths scattered throughout the room had high-back velvet trim with leather seating. There were a few high boy chairs and then the bar. *Nice*, he finally concluded.

After taking in the room, Dhorian decided to take a booth

in front of the band. He could unwind and have a drink unbothered until Reed arrived.

"Welcome to Top Hats, where the drinks and the show will certainly TOP you off."

The sultry voice he heard approach him from behind, grabbed at the crotch of his pants. Dhorian was speechless when he came face to face with the most breathtaking woman he had ever seen. Her natural red curls, big eyes, and pouty lips mesmerized him. She was beautiful. Dhorian did not remember giving the woman his order, but the cognac she brought back was right on point.

Transfixed by her, Dhorian never drank so much in his life. With every drink order, he tipped her a freshly ironed Benjamin to get her attention. After the fifth order of Louis XIII on the rocks, the stunning redhead finally spoke again. Although she had sass in her delivery, she was still sexy as hell.

"Sir, I understand this establishment I'm working in will lead you to believe that you can purchase what you see, but I do not dance, and I am not for sale. You cannot put this kitty kat on layaway, nor do I accept coupons or rainchecks. Now my shift is ending. Thank you for your generosity. Have a good night."

Dhorian watched her sashay away and groaned at the thought of her lying naked in his bed. His lust-filled and drunken haze almost made him mistake the four hundred dollar bills she returned to him for dirty napkins. Looking around, Dhorian realized a DJ replaced the live band. The loss of time did not register until Dhorian saw the note about Mr. Reed needing to reschedule but could not recall when someone left it at his table. With all the little details missed around him, Dhorian did notice the exact moment when the redhead left the room. Then a text came to his phone. It was a picture of Christina wearing one of his hats and white button-up shirts while sitting on the stairs, legs spread wide open, exposing her bare-naked self to him. Dhorian heard the redhead say "kitty kat" in his head, and he smiled like a Cheshire. He would settle for this kitty kat tonight, but he would be back to get the one he wanted.

Chapter 11

JUNE 28, 2001– THIRTEEN YEARS EARLIER

Annemarie sat in her car, anxious. Her leg bouncing so hard the car rocked. She immediately scooched down in the driver's seat to hide, not wanting to draw any attention to herself. Annemarie waited. She had to be sure no one else was home. She needed answers and hated sneaking around to get them, but what other choice was there? Annemarie counted backward from one hundred to gather her wits before peeking out the window to make sure her cousin-in-law, Dhorian Senior, was gone.

It had been months since she heard from or seen her cousin, McKenzie, and she was starting to worry. Annemarie's husband, Verdell Senior, and her cousin McKenzie's husband were brothers. Fraternal twins, in fact. The men would have poker night, and Verdell went every Tuesday and Saturday, faithfully.

Every time he returned; her question was the same. "How is McKenzie?" And he would only grunt, tell her to *spread 'em*, and end it with an unconcerned "You know damn well I don't get in married folks' business" right before entering her.

For the most part, Annemarie agreed. Married folks' business had its own set of rules that outsiders would not understand. However, when it involved her blood, who in the last few months fell off the face of the Earth, the term married folks' business was about to get another rule: *Thou shall not fuck with my kin.* If it had not been for the few words about his mother that she pulled from Dhorian Jr., Annemarie would have thought her cousin was dead.

Annemarie crept up the driveway and around the back of the house. She did not know what she would find, but anything was better than waiting on answers to magically appear. Annemarie only had to jiggle the doorknob before it gave and opened into the kitchen. The smell of burning hair and spices made her gag. The stench turned her attention to the pot on the stove. Annemarie cautiously looked around the kitchen. A fine brown powder covered the countertop and the floor near the stove. It only took a few more glances for her to see the nearly empty bottle of nutmeg on the counter. *Nutmeg. Who uses that much nutmeg for anything?* Annemarie thought. She covered her nose with her shirt and made her way to the next room. She had to get out of the kitchen because the smell was making her feel dizzy and sick.

Annemarie continued looking around. She walked into the

clean and freshly dusted living room. Her eyes wandered to a wall full of family photos, but only one of them caught her eye. It was a picture of the boys at their first birthday party. Their resemblance was strong at that age. Their fathers were brothers, and fraternal twins themselves only made onlookers comment on how much all four of them looked alike. For the first few years, the only thing that helped people tell the cousins apart was who they were with. Annemarie always had Verdell Jr., and McKenzie always had Dhorian Jr. That and Verdell's slightly darker shade. Annemarie ran her fingers over Dhorian Jr's face. For all intent and purpose, he was McKenzie's son. She would never take that from her.

Bang. Annemarie jumped. She heard something heavy crash to the floor behind her. Annemarie ran to the window to make sure Dhorian Senior had not come back home. Her hand clutched her racing heart as she breathed a sigh of relief.

She crept toward the back of the house to investigate the noise. Annemarie passed a door that led to a newly added portion of the home. She remembered McKenzie complaining about Senior doing some personal work and talking crazy about wanting to double their house's size as a funeral home. His brother thought he was mad for it too. Annemarie thought it was good that her brother-in-law wanted to do more for his family and put action behind it. However, what would not be so good for him was if Annemarie found out Senior did something to her cousin. Wife or not, she was not playing about her blood. The knot that grew in her stomach kept her from opening the door.

Annemarie realized, at that moment, her greatest fear would be to find her cousin lifeless behind that door. Chills slithered up her spine, releasing a shiver throughout her body. Annemarie took in a deep breath to calm herself. The smell that swarmed her when she first entered the house was still encircling her. It was almost intolerable. She could only imagine what the scent would have done to Dhorian Jr. if he was there. She was glad he was at basketball camp with Verdell Jr. Annemarie slid her scarf from around her head and tied it around her face, covering her nose and mouth. *Bang. Crash.* This time when Annemarie jumped, she bit her tongue on the way down.

"Dammit," she tried to whisper as she held her mouth, attempting to quell the pain.

"Who's out there?"

The small voice was almost unfamiliar. Then it came a little stronger. "I said, who is there? I'm strapped, and I know how to use it."

Annemarie gulped. She did not realize how dry her throat was until the terror made her swallow. It had been three months since she saw her cousin that Annemarie would not put it past McKenzie to shoot her.

Inching along the wall, Annemarie made her way towards the voice. Although the bedroom door was open, Annemarie still lightly tapped on the door with her fist.

She called out, "Kenzie, it's me."

Annemarie heard shuffling and waited a few seconds to see if she could make out the sound of a cocking shotgun, but there was nothing. She slid her body around the corner of the bedroom door and was stilled. McKenzie sat on the edge of her bed, eyes sunken and bugged, clothes swallowing her body, face visibly thinner than Annemarie last remembered. It was unlike McKenzie to look this out of sorts. Even her hair was an absolute hot ass mess. Her room looked like a fabric store exploded. Shreds hung from the footboard, the headboard, on the rocking chair by the window, the dresser, and more pieces flung across the body-length mirror that stood in the corner. There were old dishes, cups, and bowls with half-consumed portions still in them. Annemarie winced in disgust when she spotted maggots and mold growing in some of the bowls.

Her hand flew to her mouth to stifle the nausea. Annemarie was at a loss for words. She almost forgot that her cousin was in the room. When their eyes met, Annemarie took in the shell before her. McKenzie's face was puffy but hollow, and the rest of her appeared frail as if she had not eaten in days. The circles around her eyes gathered and sat heavily atop of her cheeks, making McKenzie look like a bruised raccoon.

Annemarie felt helpless as her cousin's eyes shifted all over the room, not stopping to look at anything in particular. The wind blew into the room from the open window. McKenzie flinched at the shadows made by the light through the curtains. It was like McKenzie did not even know she was there. Annemarie's first thought was that her cousin had lost her damn mind. She shook her head at what was in front of her, but Annemarie edged slowly towards McKenzie, determined to break the ice and get her sister-cousin back.

"Kenzie, don't tell me that you've been letting Senior put his hands on you? Look at them bruises 'round your eyes!"

At first, Annemarie thought McKenzie did not hear her. There were no visual cues, given her once lucent eyes were now dull.

"McKenzie Yvette Anderson II!" Annemarie called her by whole government and maiden name. "I know you hear me talking to you!"

That got her cousin's attention. Even though she was not fully alert, she was at least looking at her now.

There was a lazy, slurred response back. "Girl, that ain't nothing but lack of sleep."

"Lack of sleep, my ass." Annemarie shot back.

Was she on drugs? She had to be on drugs or a damn fool if she thinks I am stupid enough to believe lack of sleep would make her look like that, Annemarie thought.

"Look, Annie, you worry too much. You know damn well I ain't letting no man put his hands on me. Not even Senior."

McKenzie's voice had a little more spunk in it, but she still sounded out of it. Skeptical and hands on her hips, Annemarie got right down to it.

"Mmm-hmm. Well, how do you explain me not seeing you for the past three months? I mean, I've had get-togethers, card night, hell I even had the boys' birthday party at the house, and only your husband and Dhorian Jr. showed up. And you know I'm a proud woman, and I usually would leave it alone, but you not being there hurt me, Kenzie. And you know that asshole of a husband of yours ain't give me no damn reason for you to be MIA."

"Stop making everything about you, Annie. Maybe I just couldn't make it."

Annemarie huffed. "Make it about me? Why do you think I'm here?"

"Why are you here, Annemarie?" McKenzie asked, sounding exasperated with the dramatics.

Annemarie placed her fingers to her temples, kneading deep and slowly to calm her nerves. Putting her finger under McKenzie's chin, Annemarie turned her cousin to face her. And to both of their surprise, tears were rolling down their cheeks. Even though they both were self-reliant, Annemarie could always sense when something was wrong with her cousin and when she needed her help. She always thought of them more like sisters. Anything McKenzie needed, she would give. Annemarie would even give her womb if her cousin required it. And there was a time when she did just that.

Slowly, Annemarie choked back her tears and spoke. "I'm here to check on my sister. Now, either you gonna tell me what's going on, or Im'ma shoot Senior in his ass for what I think he's done."

The two stared at each other, waiting for the other to break. Just as Annemarie nodded and started to leave the room, McKenzie grabbed her wrist and spilled everything.

"He knows Annie. Senior knows. I don't know what made

him ask me, but he did. I didn't answer, but I couldn't lie to him. Somehow, he knows, and I know he is going to do something crazy."

"Slow down, Kenzie. What do you mean, he knows? What does Senior know? What happened?"

Annemarie feared where this conversation was leading. From what she knew of her cousin, she was a good mother and a faithful wife, leaving only one major thing that Senior could have found out. Annemarie's heart began to race.

"He knows about the boys," McKenzie said softly.

Annemarie's worst fear manifested from McKenzie's mouth.

"McKenzie. I need you to speak in complete sentences here. What exactly does he know about the boys?"

Looking sadly at her cousin, McKenzie began to sob. "He knows Dhorian Jr. isn't his."

Annemarie gasped. "What do you mean, not his? Did he tell his brother?"

Before she could respond, McKenzie began to cry hysterically. So much so that Annemarie forgot her own onset of delirium and tried to calm her. The harder she hugged McKenzie, the more McKenzie wailed and screamed. Annemarie did not know what the hell to do. She figured something was wrong when she had not heard from McKenzie, but insanity never crossed her mind.

"McKenzie, please. Please. Dear God, help me."

"He knows. He knows. He knows." McKenzie's delirious laughter made Annemarie's blood curl.

"What the hell is all that noise you making?" Senior's voice boomed into the house.

"What the hell you got going on in here, Kenzie? I leave you alone for not even an hour, and you already tearing the place up."

Oh shit. Senior was back. Annemarie and McKenzie's eyes locked. McKenzie motioned for her to hide in the closet. That was the last place Annemarie wanted to be, but there was no other way out of the room without passing him, and there was no time for the window. She opened the closet, just a crack. Annemarie felt claustrophobic with all of the clothing, shoes, and other knick-knacks surrounding her. She watched McKenzie go back to her place on the bed and pick up a notebook and scribble in it feverishly. Her cousin, who was usually so quick with her comebacks, was silent. She just kept writing in the book. Annemarie almost spoke her thoughts out loud. *What the fuck is going on here?*

"I keep having these headaches and hearing voices." McKenzie grabbed at her temples. "You said it would stop Dhorian. You said they would stop."

"And they will, Kenzie. Drink this, and the headaches and the voices will go away. You have my word."

Annemarie's lip curled, and her face frowned as she got a whiff of the disgusting smell that accompanied Senior when he entered the room. She watched as he forced the cup to McKenzie's mouth and held her nose to make her swallow the liquid. It had to be that vile brew from the stove. McKenzie wretched. Annemarie was speechless. She had a hunch that Senior was using nutmeg to drug her cousin. *Where in the hell would he get an idea to do something like that? And to make her drink it, of all things?* Just the smell alone gave her blurred vision, dizzy spells, and a throbbing headache. She could only imagine what the side effects of drinking it would have on her cousin. *Damn him!*

McKenzie kicked both feet, flailing at Senior while she choked down the drink. Sputtering through a coughing fit, droplets of liquid flying from her mouth as she tried to speak.

Shouting as she gulped for air, "You're trying to kill me." McKenzie slapped Senior and pushed the cup away.

"Trying to kill you. Why would I try to kill you? It's not like you've done anything for me to want to kill you for. Now, have you?"

Annemarie was not the only one who picked up on the deep sarcasm in Senior's questioning tone. McKenzie shrunk back onto the bed.

"Answer me, whore!" Senior roared.

"I know you're trying to kill me, Senior." McKenzie screeched back.

Annemarie watched in horror as Senior pounced on the bed pinning McKenzie against the headboard. She could not believe her eyes. The raised voices in the room thundered and echoed in her ears. McKenzie shrieked.

Senior slung his body over McKenzie and forced his tongue into her mouth, kissing her deeply. He screamed out in pain when McKenzie bit his lip. Only a split second passed before Senior grabbed McKenzie and squeezed her throat mercilessly. Annemarie thought her cousin was dead until she heard her weakened voice pleading out to her husband.

"Dhorian, as God is my witness, I never cheated on you. I never had a reason to. You gave me everything a woman could want. My only sin was giving you what God had denied me."

"What the hell do you mean, woman? You not making any sense. You sound crazy." Senior challenged.

"You're making me crazy," McKenzie shot back.

Senior shook his wife like he was shaking a purse for loose change. Annemarie cringed as she thought about the damage that their shared secret could do to her own family. She prayed silently, "please don't say it, Kenzie."

McKenzie's face turned grey as Senior choked the life from her. Annemarie could not just sit by and watch. She burst out of the closet and jumped on Senior's back. Scratching his arms and biting at his neck, forcing him to let her cousin go. McKenzie gasped for air. Annemarie grabbed Senior around his neck and held on tight. She dug her nails into his shoulders, and he growled in pain. Annemarie did not know how long she could hold on. Senior spun her around the room, and Annemarie crashed hard into the dresser. She felt her body getting weak, and she could not see McKenzie anymore. The pain was so intense that it caused Annemarie to go in and out of consciousness.

"McKenzie, put that knife down." Senior demanded.

"You put your hands on the wrong woman Senior. I don't know how you did it, but I know it's been you making me sick. All these years, I ain't never did nothing but love you. Why would you do this to me?

"Baby, put the knife down. You're going to make me hurt you." Senior pleaded.

"Oh, now I'm baby?" McKenzie asked while inching closer to Senior. She continued, "Make you hurt me? Make you hurt me? Look at my damn throat and face, Senior. Look at me! I trusted you, and I didn't want to believe you could be so evil and so cowardly that you would rather kill me than to ask me, than to know the truth."

"McKenzie, no!" Annemarie screamed.

"Annemarie, get out of here. Go now! What me and my husband has going on has nothing to do with you. This is married folks' business." McKenzie hollered.

"But, please, Kenzie, just come with me. Come cool down, and we can deal with Senior later." Annemarie tried to reason.

"Shut your ass up, Annemarie," Senior interjected.

"No, you shut up, jackass!" McKenzie shifted the focus back to her husband, the tip of the blade pointed at his throat.

"Woman, I done told you about talking to me like you crazy." Senior sputtered.

"Motherfucker, haven't you been listening? I am crazy!" McKenzie hollered back in a surprisingly controlled voice.

In the next instant, Senior tried to grab the knife from McKenzie's trembling hand. They were struggling to gain hold of the hilt, and the blade slipped and sliced through McKenzie's hand. She howled in pain as blood spurted everywhere. Senior kicked the fallen knife by Annemarie, but he tumbled to the ground and beat her to it.

When he came back up, he had Annemarie facing him, staring into his cold dark eyes, her shirt collar jacked-up in one hand and the knife to her throat in the other.

Annemarie began to pray harder than she ever had before. All she wanted to do was check on her cousin, and now she was fighting for her life. How could an innocent act of love turn into a secret buried so deep that the only cure was death?

Annemarie saw McKenzie walking toward her and Senior with a lamp in her hand. She thought she gave it away by staring too hard, but Senior did not get suspicious until it was too late. *Bam.* McKenzie slammed the ceramic lamp against Senior's head. He let Annemarie go to grab his aching skull, but in a fit of rage, he swung the knife and stabbed McKenzie in the stomach. It took him only a second to realize what he had done, and he immediately snatched the knife from her wound. McKenzie grabbed at the hole in her stomach and cried out as she dropped to the ground and hurried toward the bed. Annemarie choked back her horror. Senior stood over McKenzie with regret on his face. Annemarie wanted to check on her cousin, but she could not move. The fear of what was to come next had her glued to the floor.

McKenzie surprised them both when she gave out a sore chuckle that quickly turned into delirium. A small all-black revolver appeared in her blood-soaked hand out of nowhere, and she pointed it right at Senior's head. Annemarie could not recognize her cousin at all, no matter which way she arched her head to look. McKenzie had indeed lost her mind.

"No, McKenzie, no," Annemarie begged.

She crawled over to McKenzie and tried to take the gun from her hand, but McKenzie would not let go. Annemarie turned to McKenzie's wounds and tried to find something to stop the bleeding. She whispered words of consolation, trying to convince her cousin and herself that everything would be all right. However, the look in her cousin's eyes let her know that this was going to end up everything except all right. When their eyes locked for the second time that evening, McKenzie wrapped her arms around Annemarie and hugged her deep and long. When McKenzie finally pulled back, she gave Annemarie a bleak smile. She whispered, "I can keep a secret," before kissing her on her cheek and pushing Annemarie away. Then, McKenzie pointed the gun at her cousin. Annemarie wanted nothing more than to get out of there. Her cousin pulled the trigger, and the bullet zipped past her, hitting the wall.

"Run, Annemarie, and don't look back. If you ever loved me, run."

Terror had gripped Annemarie in a way that she never thought possible. She scrambled to her feet and struggled to make her way through the chaos in the room.

"Ruuuunnnn, Annie. Run!" was the last thing Annemarie heard as she ran for the door.

Tears slowly streamed down McKenzie's face as the gun slid from her grip. She winced as the pain from the fatal stab wound began to overtake her. McKenzie's mind flashed to her son. She was dying, and the bastard responsible for her death would live to raise her son, her secret. Life was not fair. God took her only child, gifted her another one, and now would not let her live to see him grow up. McKenzie took in a shallow breath and closed her eyes. She could not remember if she wrote enough in her journal for Dhorian Jr. to find out the truth. She took her last breath, praying she did.

Chapter 12

TIFFANY

Tiffany walked toward the waterfront restaurant, nervous. For some reason, this felt more like a date to her than an interview. She did not know why Mr. Christen would invite her to a place so lavish. She had been to Ocean Prime before, but it was always on her dime. Tiffany knew firsthand how expensive the night could be. Of course, she brought her own money, but if she profiled Mr. Paul Christen correctly, he was trying to put on a show. And if it got her dinner, who was she to stop him?

It took her two hours just to get ready. Usually, she just threw on nice jeans, a cami, a blazer, and some three-inch pointed toes for her interviews. However, this time, she found herself checking how she looked several times in the mirror to make sure she was presentable. Who was she kidding? She wanted to look attractive. Tiffany did not know if it was meeting the mayor for dinner or if she wanted to impress him, but whatever it was, she knew she had to be on her "A" game.

Tiffany called an Uber. She took five minutes to look over the notes her research assistant, Blake, handed her earlier that day. Mr. Christen was a fascinating read. Tiffany memorized the highlights. Right out of college, he started a venture capital firm, Christen Funding LLP, which became very successful within the first year of its investments. The firm received its startup and continual commitment funds from private investors and wealthy individuals, including his now father-in-law, William Mellow III. *Hmmmmm.* Tiffany made a note to put a thumbtack in that tidbit. It may come in handy later. After more years of gains, wealth, and achievements, blazay, blazay, etc., the City of Tampa and the Chamber of Commerce recognized Mr. Christen for various community improvement projects. Tiffany paused. She made a mental note to ask Blake for details on the woman with Mr. Christen in the "Backpacks for Jills and Jacks" community drive photo. She looked very familiar. Almost eerily familiar.

Bzzzz. Bzzzz. Bzzzz. Bzzzz. Her phone vibrated with a text from the Uber driver to let her know he had arrived. Tiffany took one last glance through the discovery documents. *Kidney failure?* Now, how ironic was that? In his tenure as mayor, Mr. Christen needed several kidney transplants and has had eight women in his city brutally attacked and murdered for their organs. All unsolved murders. That was going to make for excellent dinner talk, she jested to herself.

*

The Uber driver flirted with Tiffany when she got into the sleek black Lincoln Town car until he opened the door for her in front of Ocean Prime. If she did not know it before she got in the car, Tiffany knew it when she got out of the vehicle that her ensemble was doing its job. She hoped her striking and beautiful appearance, a direct compliment from her driver, Salvatore, would take the bite off of her line of questioning. Tiffany had not dressed up like this since corporate America years ago. She was glad to know she still had it. Just thinking of those days was bittersweet. It made her remember a friend, a friend who she had lost. A friend who made her realize why this interview was so important helped her refocus more on the task at hand than on looks.

Walking up to the entrance, Tiffany noticed her name written in black marker on a wooden plaque, *Ms. Tiffany LaSalle*. Fancy. It was not like she was some celebrity arriving into Tampa International Airport. Immediately, her brain went into overdrive. This was different. It felt more like a date than an interview. Impressions were being attempted and made. Tiffany appreciated a good first impression like any woman would, but Paul Christen was the mayor. There was no need for theatrics. It was too early to make assumptions of what the evening would bring, but she had her eyes wide open now for the subtleties of the night.

Instead of giving the concierge a reaction to report back to his boss, Tiffany pulled herself together. She smirked slightly, standing tall at five foot eight inches, and strolled forward. The city needed answers. She needed answers, and she would get them tonight.

Walking up to the valet, Tiffany handed him her business card. It was always good to make time for business.

"Hi, I'm here for Mayor Paul Christen."

Simply enough, the valet grinned and said, "Yes, ma'am. This way."

Tiffany found nothing outstanding about the man as she followed him through the crowded restaurant. She nodded to some of the patrons that recognized her face as they passed the maître'd. The valet guided her to a room in the back with a view of the water. The room was big enough for at least six different party groups to have their separate tables and eat, but there was only one. One table and two people sitting. One face she identified as the mayor, but she had never seen the other before. Not even in any of the photos that Blake had given her. She did not like to be blind-sided and would have to remind Blake of that later.

Arm outstretched, "Mayor Christen, it's nice to meet you finally. Thank you for making the time. I hope this wasn't an inconvenience for you."

"Oh? No. No. No. I'm sorry. My schedule has been so busy lately with all of the... well, you know. The news and planning for my next venture?

"Oh, yes! Your next venture. Do you care if I get information on that too?"

Tiffany was perplexed as to why Mayor Christen would brush over the news about the violent string of murders. She thought that would have been at the height of his discussion, for sure. Not whatever else it was he planned to do with his already successful career. *Narcissistic, for sure.* Tiffany chided herself for the thought.

Nonchalantly Paul muttered, "Well, it is your interview."

"Perfect! I hope you don't mind if we eat and talk?"

"Sure."

Tiffany took her recorder out of her clutch and placed it on the table. She noticed the other man with the mayor still had not spoken yet. Was he like a bodyguard or something?

"Not now, but whenever you're ready to start the interview, I hope you don't mind if we record?"

"No. Not at all."

Tiffany noticed Mayor Christen pass a glance to the other end of the table. It was the first time he had done so since she got there. Tiffany glanced at him too. She moved uncomfortably in her seat to try and warrant an introduction. And it worked.

"Oh, excuse me. How could I be so rude? Please, Mr. Barry Mellow, meet Ms. Tiffany LaSalle, Channel 8 News."

Tiffany shook his hand and smiled. It was not sweaty and was cold to the touch. Usually, when most people meet a reporter, they are often nervous. Even the mayor's hand was a little clammy. However, this man's hands held no moisture at all. As a matter of fact, his hands were not even soft. They were rough, even though he was dressed as if he had never seen a rough day in his life.

Paul finished the introduction.

"Barry, Ms. LaSalle works as the lead correspondent for Channel 8 News. She made time in her busy schedule to meet with us today to do a poli-social piece on me and discuss all the work put into the campaign trail and my time as mayor."

A few moments passed before Tiffany cleared her throat and smirked at Mr. Mellow, who was staring at her hungrily and still holding her hand.

Tiffany watched the mayor laugh uncomfortably. This must have been out of character for Mr. Mellow.

"Are you all right?" Mr. Christen asked Barry.

Releasing Tiffany's hand, Mr. Mellow replied, "Yeah, sure, sure, sure. I'm good."

Mr. Mellow turned towards Tiffany. "Why don't you have a seat, Ms. LaSalle?"

When they were all seated, Mr. Christen snapped his fingers, and a maitre'd appeared.

"Would you like to choose a wine, Ms. LaSalle?"

"Oh, no. None for me. I hope you don't mind. I like to keep a clear head while I interview." Tiffany politely waved away the beverage menu.

Turning to the maître'd, she said, "I would like to have a cranberry, pineapple, and ginger-ale spritzer, please. Light ice."

Both of the men looked at her and chuckled. While Mr.

Christen's laughter held a bit of taunting in it, Mr. Mellow's was more of intrigue.

"A woman that knows what she wants." Mr. Mellow added before taking a sip of his own drink.

Tiffany smirked at the way he ignored the seething look from Paul. She was almost tempted to ask Mr. Mellow if he saw something he liked, but she did not want to tease him. Not this time anyway.

*

After they finished their meals, Tiffany was ready to begin her line of questioning.

"So, Paul, tell me a little bit about yourself."

He chuckled and clapped his hands eagerly, "Okay, great. We're gonna start with the easy stuff."

She led with the pleasantries regarding his educational and political background, corporate career, and family life. But now, Tiffany was ready to do her job and ask the hard questions.

"You are known for surrounding yourself with a young and talented entourage who go on to do great things in the community."

Tiffany showed him the photo with the familiar face in it that she was beginning to recognize more and more.

"Do you keep up with all of them?"

The question was asked only as a way to gauge Mr. Christen's reaction when he saw her face. The beautiful brown skin in the photo. Tiffany's oldest and best friend, who had been dead a little over eight years now. Just as she suspected, Mr. Christen's face froze. If she was not mistaken, Barry's eyes sparked an inkling of recognition as well. Or maybe not. Tiffany knew she may be crossing a line, but she decided to go with her instinct.

Although Mr. Christen tried to play it cool, Tiffany could tell he was starting to sweat. He fidgeted using his napkin to wipe his mouth, pushing his plate to the side, adjusting his collar, uncrossing and re-crossing his legs. Mayor Christen was nervous.

"I try to keep up with all of my interns and proteges, but we all know life sometimes gets in the way...and so does running a city..."

He gave the dry chuckle that made him sound more like an asshole than a caring mentor. Tiffany decided at that moment, she did not like the mayor too much. Thank God he could not run for mayor again because she was definitely voting for the other candidate.

"Let's switch gears. What are your plans to catch the psychopath terrorizing our city with the string of heinous murders?"

A blank look took over his face, and Tiffany knew it was a cover-up for an awkward surprise. Mayor Christen was not expecting questions about anything other than his upcoming campaign trail. But no worries. Tiffany would tie that in all right. Before Mr. Christen could pull himself together to answer, Tiffany continued.

"At least eight innocent young women we know of have

been brutally killed, mutilated, and had one or more organs removed over the past two years. There have been no suspects or persons of interest named. Do you have a response to those in the community losing trust, not only in the Tampa Police Department but also in you, sir?"

Tiffany waited a little longer for the mayor to recover and respond this time.

"Well, the people of this city will be happy to know that I and Chief Law Enforcement Officer, Sheriff Dunn, have put together a special task force. They're working on getting the answers that this city so desperately needs and to put a stop to this unnecessary violence."

Tiffany's face had a smile on it, but her brain was having a hard time computing the bullshit that just spewed out of this man's mouth. He did not address her question at all. Fine. If he wanted to play hardball, then she had a curveball of her own.

"Thank you for that. I know I'm looking forward to seeing what this task force can do." Before Mr. Christen could get too smug, Tiffany shot off with her next question.

"Now, I know that a few years back, you were hit with your own medical crisis where you needed a kidney transplant. It's known in the medical industry that the waiting process can be very lengthy for those seeking a transplant. How do you respond to your supporters that have sided against the heartless individuals participating and benefitting from this illegal organ trading?"

If looks could kill, the mayor had just committed homicide,

and Tiffany was six feet under. The vibrating phone in her purse broke the awkward silence.

"Oh, that's me." Looking between the stone-faced Mr. Mellow and at the seething Mr. Christen, Tiffany asked innocently, "Um, neither of you mind if I get this, do you?"

"No, of course not." They both conceded.

She heard Blake's rushed voice on the other line. "There's been another one. Where do you want me to pick you up?"

Tiffany gave him the address and turned back to her host.

"I'm sorry. I have a live story. You don't mind if we continue this interview at another time, do you?"

"No, of course not. Please let me know if there is anything I can do to help. Leave your card with Mr. Mellow, and he will reach out with my availability to reschedule."

"Oh, that sounds perfect. Thank you."

She tried to ignore the hungry look in Mr. Mellow's eyes and the flirtatious smirk he gave her when she handed him her card. She made sure not to touch his hand this time. She chose to ignore their electricity last time but did not know if she could play it off again. She had been denying herself for twelve months and fourteen days and did not want to ruin her streak. Mr. Mellow was intriguing enough to pique her curiosity. But she could not lose focus now.

Tiffany quickly gathered her things and raced to the front of the restaurant. Blake said he was not far from her, and she wanted to make it to the scene before the other hounds started sniffing around.

If Tiffany was honest, she was grateful for the interruption as well. The interview was getting tense. She usually had someone there to assist with diverting and help her play good reporter/ bad reporter, but not this time.

She knew Paul was lying about something, but not sure what. She would have Blake fact-check the recording before she went live with the story.

Chapter 13

TATIANA

Tatiana waited impatiently at the nurses' station for the black Betty White look-alike to tell her where they moved her grandmother and, most importantly, why? Her Nanna had been in the hospital for over a month, and she had not gotten any better. However, to her knowledge, Nanna had not become sicker, either. Tatiana slapped the desk hard with both palms and made the nurse jump as she fumbled through logbooks.

"The damn computer is right there. I don't understand why you can't find her. My grandmother was in room 1218 just yesterday. How do you lose a whole person in one day? I mean, *DAMN*, is this a hospital or not?"

Tatiana saw the terrified look on the woman's face and paused her tirade to take a breath. She figured a moment of silence would give black Betty time to vindicate herself by providing some relevant information. No luck. It was as if an angel sat on her shoulder next to the devil. Tatiana heard her mother's tiny voice. "You can catch more flies with honey than you can with vinegar."

The voice was bittersweet, but Tatiana understood she needed to try a different tactic with the now terrified and mute nurse.

"Ma'am. I apologize for yelling. It's just that I am really worried about my Nanna. I was here to visit her yesterday, but when I arrived, she was asleep in room 1218, and I was told to come back tomorrow during visiting hours. Today is tomorrow, and I took off work to be here and check on my grandmother. I am the only person in the world that she has, and I would love it if I could just see her."

The empathy Tatiana was looking for finally appeared on black Betty's face. "Let me page the night nurse and see if she can help us."

Us? Tatiana thought. Being nice got me an "us." We are in this together. A tight smile spread across Tatiana's face. Tatiana was so happy her calmed approach worked because dragging the incompetent nurse across the counter would have sent her to jail. Within minutes the night nurse explained that her grandmother's insurance only covered a single room for five consecutive days, so they had to "downgrade" her to a sharing space. This news almost pissed Tatiana off more than the idiot nurse. But, as soon as she laid eyes on her grandmother, she forgot all of that.

Tatiana caught her Nanna up on her new job and all the drama at the front desk. They avoided conversations about Nanna's health and Tatiana's plans for school. Tatiana only wanted to talk about happy things with her Nanna. Not being able to find her earlier reminded her of how short life was. So, the moments they were alive should not be focused on death. But death was all that Tatiana could think about lately. They laughed and cried and ate hospital jello and graham crackers together. The duo was even shushed by Nanna's roommate a few times, but Tatiana did not care. She actually felt bad for the frail woman, the sourpuss roomy who did not have any family to visit her and make her laugh through her pain. That would never be her Nanna. She even made her Nanna laugh harder on some occasions to emphasize to the old grouch that her Nanna was not alone in this world, and someone would fight for her if she went missing.

The minutes quickly turned into hours, and sadly it was time for Tatiana to go home. She wanted to call out from work again, but she knew they would give her a hard time. Besides, she needed as much money as she could get to either get Nanna better insurance or self-pay her way into a single room. Tatiana kissed her grandmother on her forehead before saying goodnight. She held back tears as her grandmother's sunken visage was glowing but visibly weakened.

"Next time I come, Nanna, I'm going to give you some braids. We can't have you looking a mess in front of folks," Tatiana teased.

"A mess? Child, I'm sick. What's your excuse for the way

your head looks? Ain't nobody worried about me, and I am not worried about nobody." Nanna shot back.

They both laughed hard and consequently got another shush from the roommate. Tatiana was about to walk out the door before her grandmother called, "Babygirl, I almost forgot. I know your birthday is coming up."

Tatiana squeezed Nanna's hand. She had forgotten her own birthday, but her sick grandmother remembered. Was not that something?

"Aww, thank you, Nanna. You don't have to..."

"Hush, child, and let me finish. I feel a coughing fit coming on. You know it gets worse at night."

Tatiana rushed to pour her grandmother some water from her bedside pitcher and held the cup while she took a few sips.

"Your mother left a box for you to open on your eighteenth birthday, but you never made it home."

Tatiana cringed at yet another reminder of her abandonment. Before she could apologize again, her grandmother held up her hand to silence her.

"It's on the top shelf of my closet, underneath my church hats."

Tatiana held in her laugh at Nanna's mention of church hats. Her grandmother had not been to church since she came back home. They used to go regularly, like eating breakfast. That is how often Tatiana could remember them being at church. Breakfast then church. It went on like that for years until her mother died.

"Visitor hours are over, honey. Let's give your grandmother some time to rest," a nurse came and interrupted her thoughts.

After a few more moments of silent reminiscing, Tatiana kissed her Nanna. To her surprise, she was met with the rising and falling of her grandmother's chest. Nanna was already sound asleep.

*

Tatiana's mind was so preoccupied with thoughts about the box her grandmother mentioned that she could not remember the drive home as she parked in front of the house. She noticed the sway of nosey Ms. Fuller's blinds when she shut the car door. *Nosey ass. She ain't even called to check on Nanna,* Tatiana thought. Tatiana opened the door, and her curiosity burst into action as she ran to her grandmother's room. It took only a few minutes of moving shoe boxes, hat boxes, and books around before Tatiana spotted a rose gold box with Madisin scrawled across the side in gold type. Tatiana gently grabbed the chest at its sides and held it that way until she made it into her room. It was all so surreal. Tatiana always fed herself excuses not to come back home. All that time running, and her mother was waiting for her right here. Tatiana fingered the gold letters on the box. It took her a moment to open it and rustle through the contents.

She found young photos of her mother, pictures of her and her mother, and a small manila envelope. Tatiana shook the yellow sleeve. Out came a folded piece of paper, an ATM card, and a key, all with Tatiana's name written or stamped on them. Tatiana inhaled deeply to calm her nerves and steady her shaking hands. If there was an ATM card, money had to be involved, but what about the paper and the key? Tatiana unfolded the paper and noticed her mother's handwriting. She heard her mother's voice as she read.

Hey Babygirl,

If you're reading this, it means that I missed your 18th birthday and I am so very sorry, my heart. You are probably hurting from my absence, but I know your Nanna is taking good care of you. She is one strong bird. She tells me that I've been hovering too close since they found you out on the street, hurting, just thrown away like someone's trash. They caught me with my guard down once, but they won't get me again.

In the manila envelope are a few safeguards that I put in place. The police think your kidnapping was a one-off, but something tells me it was more. When I worked for your father, I put some money aside on the ATM card. I have your name on it, and it's tied to an account that belongs to you. There should be a little over $275,000 in the bank. Please use it wisely.

And yes, you heard me right. I said I worked for your father. It's hard for me to talk about him because our relationship was tense. But the key holds secrets to your father's and my relationship that I buried for a long time now. I have to warn you, what's in the lockbox will reveal who your father is. But it will also tell you things about your father that could damage him and possibly ruin his career and get him killed. It is up to you to decide what to do with that information. If you need help

choosing what to do, find Tiffany LaSalle. She should be able to help make the picture a little bit clearer. I never told her who your father was, but somehow during our friendship, I think she could piece together how much power he had and never questioned me.

Right now, I know you must be confused and trying to make sense of it all, but soon everything will be made clear.

Love you, Babygirl - Your Mother

All this time, Tatiana spent running from her past, trying to find herself, when the answers she sought were here all along. She thought maybe her mother left her a few hundred dollars for a birthday gift, not a few hundred thousand dollars. And her father? Who was he, and who in the hell was Tiffany LaSalle? Now she had to go on a search for a needle in a haystack. There was so much to take in.

Tatiana left items from the box on her bed and walked dazedly into the bathroom to turn on the water. She absently stood in the shower and let the hot water run through her hair and trickle over the rest of her body. It was not until the water began to go cold that she realized her body had been tense. The cool water jolted all her emotions together all at once. Tatiana trembled uncontrollably, wrecked with sadness and joy all at the same time. Once she calmed herself, she did not want the soothing waters to end. She plugged the tub while the water still ran from the showerhead and laid down in the tub on her side. As the water rose past her chin and began to caress her face, Tatiana let the tears flow quietly into the water. Once again, her mother was there to save her. She was drowning in debt, working as hard as she could to help her grandmother stay on her feet, and at some point, she wanted to go back to school. Before now, Tatiana had not seen a way to make it all happen. She did not know what she would find in the lockbox, but Tatiana could not wait to tell Nanna what was in the box.

Chapter 14

VERDELL

Verdell Hamilton was no stranger to dirty work. It was what he had become accustomed to in the last decade. Over time, Verdell developed a stomach for the gore and bile. But assignments involving those of the cloth made him pull his torture from a separate bag. The supposed leaders of lost sheep were no more than lost sheep themselves. It was his duty to bring those most strayed closer to their maker for atonement.

While awaiting trial for selling off his young, naive sheep to the highest bidder under the guise of sending them to an all-expenses-paid purity camp, a local preacher was allowed to attend and lead services. Someone's child came home with more than just stories of campfires and saving themselves until marriage. The tale frightened and upset the parents so badly they pressed charges against the staff who supervised the trip, the church's treasurer for allocating funds to the trip, and the pastor who organized and advertised the trip. According to the reports, the children were lured into separate quarters, stripped, and made to play dress up for a silent auction. As the highest bids rolled in, camp leaders left the children with their benevolent donors for the first seven days of camp. During that time, they were abused, chained, starved, and forced to do unthinkable acts. When the time with their donors ended, the camp counselors spoiled them with all of the food, snacks, and games a child could ever want. The attempt to wash the sour from their soiled innocence would work on most occasions, but on this one, it did not.

Verdell's contribution to society consisted of sending sick bastards to stand in front of one before being judged by twelve. He was more than happy to rid the world of the wolves in sheep's clothing, starting with the Alpha wolf. Verdell watched as the saints marched in and out of the spinning glass door. The vision was full of irony for him—the revolving door of saints hurrying to ask for prayers from the devil. Verdell sat through the comings and goings of three services. It was dusk by the time he spotted his opportunity.

"Excuse me, Pastor Mason? Can I trouble you for prayer?" Verdell asked as he jogged up behind the pastor, leaving the church for his car.

Pastor Mason slowed and eyed Verdell, "Son, I don't remember seeing your face at the altar when we called for prayer."

Verdell chortled, "You right, pastor. I missed the call. I had to work, but I am here now. Can you make time for me?"

The pastor looked at his imitation, glass bezel, Swiss made watch. Verdell could tell it was a knockoff. He sighed at the wolf, contemplating the time. Little did Pastor Mason know, he did not have much time left.

Asking again, with a little more earnestness, Verdell said, "Please, Pastor Mason. Spare a little of your time for a sinner. I promise this won't take long."

Verdell noticed the pastor's eyes soften and knew now was the time to make his move. He allowed Pastor Mason one last look at his fancy timepiece before lights out. Verdell sent a current of thirty milliamps at twelve hundred volts right into his neck. He then fished the pastor's keys from the inside of the clergy's coat pocket. The headlights of the luxury charcoal grey Mercedes AMG S65 lit up the parking lot when Verdell pressed the unlock button on the expensive looking key fob. He was not surprised. Of course, it would not have been the brown Subaru Forester, the only other car in the parking lot. That would have been asking for too much humility.

Verdell slapped the stunned man across the back of his freshly shaven head and tased him again for good measure. Just thinking about how many children he had to sell and how many lies he told to afford the six-figure car made Verdell's blood run cold. Verdell threw Pastor Mason over his shoulder and into the passenger seat. He tried to make sure the pastor was as uncomfortable as possible, but that was nearly impossible in the luxury vehicle. Verdell left him inverted on the passenger side floor. He had been in a lot of nice cars, but this one took the cake. Too bad, he was going to burn it. After starting the car, adjusting his seat and mirrors, and playing with a few features, Verdell stumbled on the seat warming massage function. His body settled into the gentle vibrations, and he changed the radio station to Smooth Jazz WSJT 94.1. Verdell pulled out of the parking lot and relished the cold night air, and Kenny G's, *The Way You Move.* He took the back streets from Temple Terrace to Tampa International Airport. He could not risk someone seeing the pastor's car before he arrived at its destination.

"Hey Benji, meet me at Economy Yellow B365."

Verdell had already arranged for Benji to meet him with a chopped vehicle and clean plates; she only needed to know where to park it. Verdell pulled off toward the Air Cargo exit and drove past the cell phone waiting parking lot.

The drive to the Tropicana would not be as comfortable as the ride to the airport. Then again, this was when his job was anything but relaxed. It was necessary. Verdell took out his special gloves and snapped them at his wrists. Putting them on sent a charge through Verdell that made him want for lethal exploration. There was a time when gloves similar to the ones he wore now were his lifeline. They were the only thing that stood between death and hunger, death and the bitter cold. He would have never imagined that gloves, something so simple, would be his salvation. Verdell's appreciation of being among the living gave him that much more disdain for those who did not. He would be the gloves of salvation that sent them to their maker.

*

"Ahhhh. Jesus Lord! Dear God!"

"I wouldn't look down if I were you, pastor."

Verdell calmly grabbed the ropes that held Pastor Mason upside down. He swung one of the cords, and the tension from the pulley stretched the man's limbs further apart. Verdell imagined the pain running from the pastor's throat as a purging of the sickness that ran deep within him. He had to be sick to think that it was okay to sell another human being, let alone innocent children.

"Pastor Mason, you are closer to your Lord than you have ever been," Verdell stated matter of fact after the screams died down.

"My God, son! Are you crazy? You came to me for prayer. I am a pastor! How can you do this to me? Do you know who I am? I know some connected people! You don't know who you are messing with, boy! I am a child of God. Don't do this."

The pastor's rambling went on and on from idle threats to utter despair, but this did not sway Verdell one way or the other. The stoic look on his face did not waiver.

Voice flat, Verdell began, "Right now wouldn't be the time for you to tell me what I should or shouldn't do. And listen, before we get too deep in this, I just want you to know that I'm still going to need that prayer from you because what I'm about to do is going to get messy."

"Help me! Help me! Somebody, please. Anybody, please help me."

"You can scream all you like, but on a night like tonight, your calls for saving are going to go unheard."

"Please just tell me what you want. I'll give you anything."

"Pastor, you are already begging, and you don't even know why you are here."

Verdell unrolled his canvas pocket tool belt and took out a pair of sharp-tip Westcott Tenotomy Scissors. The surgical shears were less than five inches long from handle to tip and were commonly used for eyelid surgery. However, Verdell would let the pastor keep his sight for now. He had other means of torture on his mind.

"What do you say, Benny? A snip for every kid?"

Verdell pushed the spring handle on the tiny scissors and clipped at the skin between Benny Mason's toes. Before Pastor Mason could finish his wail of agony, Verdell cut at the tender skin between his toes on the other foot.

"Eight slits for eight kids. Only two hundred and thirty-one left to go, Pastor Mason."

The contents of Verdell's lower intestine almost made it into his mouth. Not because of the blood rushing down his victim's body or the gurgling sounds of pain spilling from his mouth. It was blasphemous to continue to think of or reference this sexual predator, who exploited children and cashed in on stealing their innocence, as a pastor. Two hundred and thirty-nine children. Verdell refused to believe the number when he first heard it. Then an unforgiving soul out for vengeance delivered irrefutable evidence to him with a note that read, *make him pay*. And that, he would have no problem doing.

"Please. Please don't kill me. I have some information that could prove very valuable to you." Benny Mason pleaded, squinting rapidly as the stress sweat dripped from his neck into his eyes.

"I already know of the snakes in your bush. Don't worry. I'll shake them out, and they'll have to deal with me before meeting their maker too."

It was something about the dry chuckle and sarcasm from the pastor that made Verdell perk up and listen.

"Do you think my bush is the only one full of snakes? There are others worse than me. Be sober, be vigilant because your adversary the devil, as a roaring lion, walks about, seeking whom he may devour."

Verdell was not surprised that the man started quoting scripture. Not that he could recall which chapter and verse it was, but he did not think it would take him this long to do it. Verdell pulled the rope tighter, stretching the tightly wound threads of muscle tissue between Benny Mason's limbs and torso.

"You better start talking straight, or you might as well take whatever it is you're trying to say to the grave."

"Oh, no... wait, wait, wait, wait. Okay, wait, please just listen."

"I'm listening." Verdell motioned to the pastor's timepiece to signal how much time he was wasting.

"Okay. There has been a string of murders in the city lately."

"So, what? I probably committed them." Verdell said, irritated. He was uninterested in where the conversation was going.

"No. I'm not talking about regular street crime. I'm talking about the ones where the women are found dead with their organs missing."

Verdell perked up and motioned his hand for the pastor to continue. This bit of detail might be interesting enough to defer Benny's final moments a few more minutes.

"Okay, so it's not just one person behind it. It's an organization."

Skeptical of the information, "An organization? What would an organization want with young women? Young black women who couldn't possibly have anything to offer them."

"It's not what the women offered them. It's what they offered the women."

Verdell slapped the inverted man in the face with the back of his hand. "Do I look like I have time to sort through your word games?"

Verdell began to walk back and forth. "Do you know that those called to teach will be judged harsher for their crimes? Unless you tell me this organization is full of wolf preaching snakes like you, I don't see what this has to do with me or why I would find this relevant to the *hows* and *whys* we are here.

Now I am getting paid to do a job, and by God, I will finish my work tonight, Mr. Mason. With or without this important information, you're hesitant to leak."

Verdell watched as Benny Mason gathered his wits and cleared his throat.

"There is a medical company that did some top-secret trials on a memory drug a few years back. All of the participants in the study came out of the trials with no side effects. But they started getting sick—all of the patients exhibiting deterioration in the lungs, liver, and kidney organ tissues. Like any sane person who felt unwell, they visited their doctor, who ran tests that came back negative for the common diseases. But one doctor. An umm..."

Verdell watched as Benny Mason struggled to provide him with the only bit of information he spouted out that may have mattered.

"An umm... Dr. Weiss. That's his name. Dr. Weiss knew a specialist who..."

Verdell froze at the mention of Dr. Weiss. There was only one doctor in the city he knew by that name. Simultaneously Verdell also noticed a bright red dot centered in the middle of the rambling pastor's forehead. Before he could act, shots rang out and echoed throughout the stadium. Verdell ducked in the bridge of the scoreboard, and when the smoke cleared, Pastor Benny Mason hung limply, streams of bright red blood draining from his chest, neck, and head. Verdell peeked past the metal railing to see if he could pinpoint where the shots came from or if the shooter was still there, but nothing. He waited only a few more seconds before he shimmied down the ladder and ran back to where he parked the car. His mind was racing. *Who the hell knew where he was? Who the hell knew where he took the pastor? Did the owner of the brown car follow him? Did the bullets hit the intended target, or was he still in danger?*

Verdell rode eighty miles an hour on I-275, occasionally checking for trailing lights in his rearview mirror. He had to make a few calls to figure out what the hell was going on. Someone made him.

"Yo, Benji. Benji! Where the fuck are you?"

"Whoa, Vee. What's up with all the yelling. It's like three in the morning. You know a girl got to get her beauty sleep."

"Benji, I'm not for your shit right now. Were you on a job just now? Did somebody send you to off me? Huh?"

Verdell could hear her shifting in the background. He turned the Bluetooth up louder to see if he could listen to signs of her betrayal.

His line beeped. Verdell glanced at his caller id and saw it was his father. He did not believe in coincidences, especially at 3:00 a.m. Why would his father be calling?

"Benji. I'll call you back." Verdell abruptly hung up, not answering her question. His tone was short when he responded to his other line, "yea, what up. I'm kind of in the middle of something."

"Your mother came by and wanted me to tell you that she loves you and she'll be back later."

Verdell could not have been more annoyed. His mother had been dead for years. "Are you drinking again?

His father continued, "she told me to tell you that your lunch is in the fridge."

Got dammit! This senile old man. Verdell could not even remember the last time his father mentioned his mother.

The last time he heard a reference to his mother had to be years ago when he and his cousin DJ walked in on a conversation.

*

His mother left home without warning or an explanation. When Verdell asked his father where she was, he was always short, saying that she needed a vacation but would be back soon. That was his initial response, but the more Verdell asked, the more irritated his father became. Verdell Sr. slapped his son and threatened to do worse if he asked for his mother again. When she did not show up at his aunt's funeral, even at fifteen, Verdell thought it strange. What was even stranger was that his uncle was the funeral director. DJ never mentioned that his dad was an undertaker.

His uncle was distraught at the funeral. His whispers of "please forgive me" did not go unnoticed by those in attendance. There was some argument that led her to kill herself, and his uncle felt guilty. Verdell's first funeral and he could not rationalize how you could get so mad that you would want to kill yourself. It did not make sense to him at all.

Weeks went by before he saw his uncle or his cousin DJ again. Then one day, his uncle and cousin came over. His uncle's eyes bugged but empty. Verdell took DJ to the backyard to play a game of ball. The game of basketball came to an abrupt stop when they overheard their fathers' raised voices. Verdell and DJ ran to the house's back door and snuck into the kitchen entrance to listen in on all the fuss.

"How long were you sleeping with McKenzie behind my back?" his uncle asked his father.

Verdell and DJ's mouths dropped open, and their gazes grew wide. They hesitantly looked at each other before crouching behind the kitchen wall to put their ear to the door to listen harder.

"I'm not sure where you would get a fool's idea like that. For you to think that I would continue sleeping with Kenzie after y'all got married. Not only did I love her, but I respected her enough not to disrespect her decision. Kenzie was a good woman, and if she was out there, it was because your unfaithful ass pushed her."

"Be careful of your words, brother. I was never unfaithful to MY wife," Dhorian Sr. growled, putting the emphasis on *MY* and pointing to his chest to make himself clear.

"McKenzie knew her husband dug holes, hid bones, and covered them. She didn't need me or no one else to tell her that he was a dog too." Verdell, Sr. spat back.

Verdell watched his uncle hurl a drinking glass into the wall, making him and DJ jump out of their hiding spot. They caught

Verdell's father's eye first, who cleared his throat to get Dhorian Sr.'s attention.

"Dhorian... I'm sorry you are hurting." Verdell Sr. gulped hard before continuing, "I love you, brother."

Dhorian Sr. shrunk away from his twin brother's touch and bit back tears as he spouted, "Even your wife knows the kind of bastard you are. I wouldn't be surprised if she killed herself just to get away from you!"

"What the hell do you know about my wife? Get the fuck out of my house Dhorian."

"Let's go, DJ. You're no better than me, brother. You'll find that out one day soon, I hope."

His uncle then turned and walked out, grabbing the statue that was DJ. At age fifteen, both of them knew that something about what they just heard was not right. The furrowed brows and look of uncertainty mirrored on their faces. The next time Verdell heard anything about his mother was a few months later at her closed casket funeral.

*

For only a moment, Verdell had a foolish hope that his mother was back from the dead. As mad as he was at his father, he was even madder at himself for having hope. Sure enough, when Verdell arrived at his father's house, the pungent smell of alcohol and the drunk as a skunk Verdell Sr. met him in the hallway as he came in the front door. Too emotionally drained to shoot him, this time, Verdell helped his father to the couch. He went into the kitchen, made himself a strong cup of coffee, and watched the sunrise through the kitchen window as he pondered what to do next about the mess he was in.

Chapter 15

PAUL

"Is it your intent to make me look bad?"

Silence echoed off the concrete walls in the room.

Paul asked again, louder, straining each word.

"I said, is it your intent to make me look bad, Sheriff Dunn? The question was not rhetorical."

Paul was seething. There had been two more murders. He had to overhear the news during an interview with someone who was quite possibly trying to railroad him, and the information should have come to him first. The crimes did not register until after Ms. LaSalle rushed out of their meeting, and Paul's phone began to ring. Several families, all donors to his campaign, screamed into his ear, wanting to know the same thing. Could it be the bodies of the women found maimed and murdered on the doorstep of the private Catholic school were their missing wives, daughters, or family members?

Before, all of the murders were committed in the underdeveloped parts of Tampa. Now, this psycho was making a statement by literally piling the bodies up at the affluent's front door. If Paul did not get this under control soon, he could forget his future in politics.

Paul stared daggers through Sheriff Dunn as he stammered through the weak apology.

"Mr. Mayor. I am so sorry. I don't know how intel could have gotten out to the media. I will do my best to make sure we stop the leak and deal with it, sir."

"Deal with, huh? I would like to hear more about how, exactly, you can plug a leak and catch a killer that has been under your damn nose for the last two years!"

Even though Paul was hovering over him, the police chief stood his ground.

"Mr. Mayor, the two are not the same thing. We have Internal Affairs to assist us with finding and stopping corruption on the force."

"Ah, ah," Paul interrupted. "Who said anything about corruption?"

This Paul had to hear. He had been on edge ever since that damn email came to him, and he was not about to be baited into anything. He still did not know who sent him the photos, but could it have come from the police chief?

"If someone on my police force is leaking confidential information to the media, Mr. Mayor, that individual is an enemy of the department. Any person causing civil unrest, providing misinformation or propaganda during a widely known high-profile, ongoing investigation is corrupt and a threat to order. And quite frankly, not fit to be on my police force."

It only took a moment for Paul to digest this and nod in agreement. Rolling his wrist, he urged the conversation forward.

"Continue. The killer. How do you intend to get the killer? Would you like some assistance with that as well?"

"Sir?" Sheriff Dunn asked, confused.

"Keep up, Sheriff. If Internal Affairs has to help you catch the leak, your detectives are obviously not sharp enough to catch the killer. Would you like my assistance?"

Before Sheriff Dunn could respond, there was a knock at the interrogation room door. It was the only place they could control their privacy. There were no two-way mirrors, cameras, or buried mics. Just an eight by ten concrete room, furnished with a steel table and two steel chairs. One way in and one way out. The room intimidated persons of interest, making them *touchable*. Sheriff Dunn went to answer the door, no doubt grateful for the interruption. Paul stayed seated, entangled in his thoughts, while Sheriff Dunn spoke in quick whispers at the door. Returning to the table, Sheriff Dunn slid a manila envelope his way.

"This just arrived for you by courier."

Paul scoffed, "Me?"

No one knew he was there except Barry, and why would he

need to send him anything. Paul hesitated for only a second before unwinding the string and bending the clasps on the envelope to open it. His stomach took a sudden leap into his mouth. The nasty taste of bile must have reflected on Paul's face because Sheriff Dunn asked, "Are you all right, Mr. Mayor?"

Paul quickly stuffed the papers back in the envelope and got up to leave.

"I only offer my assistance once, George. I will not offer it again, and it will come with a price."

A look of clarity washed over the sheriff as he opened the door for Paul's exit.

"Understood, Mr. Mayor."

*

Charming but arrogant; Is Tampa Mayor on our side?
Once a multi-million start-up mogul, is it possible that Paul Christen has used his corporate popularity to play mayor all these years? His most significant achievement was the beautification project in his first term, expanding the Boys and Girls Club in West Tampa. The expansion displaced hundreds of families. It gave children a facility their parents could not afford to send them to and cost the city millions of dollars in relocation fees and subsidized vouchers.

"That bitch!" Paul screamed as he rushed home. "How could she write these lies about me? Get me the head of Channel 8 on the phone! I can't even read the rest. The words are making me sick. Get Dhorian in here! What the hell am I paying him for if I can't use him to stop these lies?"

Tiffany LaSalle made him look like a complete fool in the print version of the interview. Paul was now sure that she was the one behind the personal attacks on him.

"Honey, you must calm down. You're worrying me. We don't want your pressure going…"

Before his wife could finish, Paul exploded. "What the hell are you talking about, Sandra? My pressure? Who gives a shit about my pressure when some fake news harlot is practically railroading me? Fuck my pressure. Fuck calming down. Fuck her and everyone who agrees with her. I've done too much for this damn city to treat me like some punk-ass politician."

"Paul, this is just one journalist. By the time we get through with her, no one will even remember her name. She's dead to us as of this very moment. As a matter of fact, I'm going to call Barry right now to get on this, and I'm going to run you a nice hot chamomile bath to help you relax," Sandra promised.

This time, Paul let her words soothe him, if only for the moment. He stopped pacing long enough for her to kiss his temple before patting his hands and leaving the room. Now that she was gone, he could finally think. How dare anyone question his loyalty to the city. Tiffany LaSalle might as well have accused him of being on the killer's payroll. And where in the hell was

Barry? Paul had to chase Dhorian down these days, but Barry was his right-hand man. It should have been Barry calming him down and promising to rectify the situation, not his wife.

Paul took several quick swigs of cognac from the crystal decanter to calm his nerves. He relished the burn as it flowed from his throat to his chest. He then proceeded to take out the other articles that were sent to him in the manila envelope, in addition to the trash newspaper clipping. There was a copy of his *pre-college* driver's license. The license said he was a red-haired, light brown-eyed, five-foot nine-inch tall, *Black* male. Then there was a picture of his birth certificate, which would not have been damaging enough by itself. However, when it came with pictures of his brown skin mother and father taped next to his birth certificate's parental information sections, it was a lit stick of dynamite.

Paul Christen is a Black man who is passing for White. He has lived this lifestyle for almost three decades and would not have made it as far as he had in life if he were not White.

Reading his most sacred thoughts in the handwriting of his blackmailer chilled Paul to his bones. He believed these words whole heartedly. Paul knew the secret was damning and had not confided this information to a single soul. Except for Madisin. When she died, all of his secrets went with her, including their love child. The solace initially felt became booming and sudden anxiety. Losing his job or being removed from office was not his greatest fear. This secret collapsing in on him like a volcanic explosive black hole that gained its energy from consuming his successes and shitting out the emptiness that remained was his fit of terror.

Paul had to protect Sandra from melanin-intolerant neo-racists. His left-wing in-laws supported affirmative action but were not progressive enough to be ecstatic when he married into their family. And then there was Christina. She was grown now, but would she be cast out from her family, her friends, her achievements? Protecting himself and his family from the self-destructing enigma that was his past life was now at a level one priority for Paul. If Ms. LaSalle wanted to play hardball, he would kill two birds with one stone.

It was ironic that he survived kidney failure, twice, only to end up in an early grave from the stress of posing. There was a time when this secret pushed him to withdraw and isolate himself, but he was no longer that man. He refused to be bullied by the truth. Over the years, Paul created his own reality and mapped his destiny. Who was anyone to tell him who he was? Paul picked up the phone and dialed Dhorian's number. Surprisingly, he answered on the first attempt.

"Mayor Christen, good to hear from you. To what do I owe this pleasure?"

"Stop with the pleasantries, Dhorian. I was hoping there would not be a need for me to remind you of your obligations."

Paul listened as the rustling in Dhorian's background stilled. He knew he had Dhorian's full attention now.

"What can I do for you, sir," Dhorian said despondently.

"I need you to get all you can on Tiffany LaSalle?"

"Tiffany LaSalle? Why does that name sound familiar?" Dhorian inquired.

Having to repeatedly hear and say her name left Paul with a sour taste in his mouth.

He fumed, "Yes, you've heard of her. She is the lead correspondent on Channel 8 News."

"Oh, yea. The one who does freelance work for the Tribune."

Dhorian's light chuckle of familiarity annoyed Paul. This is not a laughing matter.

"I'm glad you recall who she is," Paul said, irritated before continuing. "I'm not sure if you've seen today's paper, but I'm thinking of bringing a libel suit against that cow of a media farce for the embarrassment and possible harm and defamation to my reputation."

There was hesitation on Dhorian's side of the phone.

"Sir, if I'm not overstepping, I read the article, and after the first paragraph, the rest was all about the search that needs to happen for this psychopath on the loose. Besides, you know how much time and effort goes into a lawsuit, and we may not even find enough facts to support the claim."

"It's not about facts. It's about what we can prove!" Paul screamed through his teeth.

The silence between them permeated their cellular space.

Paul was relieved when Dhorian began to speak first, so he did not have to think of a way to recover from his outburst.

"Sir, is there anything else going on that I need to know about before I get someone to help me look into this?"

Paul hesitated. *Could this have been Dhorian instead of the reporter?* Paul quickly dismissed the thought. Dhorian was intelligent, but he was not a genius.

"No, why do you ask?" Paul inquired.

"I'm just asking because it sounds like a lot of work to put in over a newspaper article that didn't even make the front page. I bet this will go away in no time, sir. She's probably just trying to get her next big break off your name. Why give her the satisfaction?" Dhorian asked.

Paul gritted his teeth. He was beginning to get the feeling Dhorian was dismissing his request and brushing him off. He needed to remind him that was NEVER a good idea.

"I'm sorry, Attorney Hamilton. Did I catch you at a busy time? I didn't realize they kept you loaded with so many cases over there at Edward, Reed, and Morris. Maybe I should call up old Reed and let him know your talents would be better elsewhere."

Dhorian's dry gulp came through the phone loud and clear. Paul knew they had an understanding.

"I would like all information you can find on Ms. Tiffany LaSalle on my desk by the end of this week. Two days should be long enough for you to wrap up what you currently have on your plate and focus on my request."

"Yes, sir. What about the libel, sir?

"Just get me what I asked. I'll figure out how to handle it once I know what I'm dealing with." Paul declared.

"Yes, sir."

"And Dhorian. Don't disappoint me."

Chapter 16

DHORIAN

After his last conversation with Mayor Paul Christen, Dhorian had no doubt good old Paul was strong-arming him, but what could he do? Dhorian practically owed his life to the man. So, he would place any personal endeavors or other high-profile cases on hold.

Dhorian stared at the files and photos spread across his desk. Joanie's investigative connections dug up everything they could find on Channel 8 News' Tiffany LaSalle.

"Joanie, I don't know who you're using these days, but this is good stuff. How did he find all these pictures?"

In a sing-song voice, Joanie responded, "Now you know I cannot give you my sources. And how do you know it's not a *she*?"

Dhorian chuckled, "Touché. Well, tell her I said thank you. She really came through this time."

"Will do. Will there be anything else before I leave for the day, Mr. Hamilton?" Joanie asked on her way out of his office.

Dhorian fought the urge to respond with a cheap come-on line like, "yea Joanie, there is something else. You butt ass naked on top of my desk on all fours."

Over the years, Joanie proved to be way too classy to fall for that line anyway. Dhorian cleared his throat and pushed the image from his mind before continuing, "No. No. That'll be all. Thank you for your hard work today. You've been doing great."

"When doing great means a raise, you let me know," she blasted in the same melodic tone as she closed his office door behind her.

Now that he thought about it, Joanie was due for a raise. Dhorian would see what could be done about a pay increase or bonus once things slowed down. But if he brought it up now, Dhorian knew Joanie would not shut up about it until he made it happen. He liked to save himself from unnecessary headaches whenever possible, especially with this new request on his plate. Dhorian separated the photos and the files on his desk while perusing through the information he came across.

"Birth certificate. Forty-one years old. Hmm, she looks younger. Mom and dad own some land, properties and hit it big foreign trades back in the seventies. No broken leases, no evictions, no foreclosures, two medical bills in collections paid in full, student loans never late. Phone number and address changes, three area codes and states in twenty years. Nothing extraordinary there."

Dhorian was used to finding secrets in people's past. He came across hidden babies, side pieces, houses, cars, entire estates, millions in foreign accounts, trusts, and even an undisclosed island. Everyone had skeletons in their closet, but from what he could see, Ms. Tiffany LaSalle was an enigma. There were a few semi-famous boyfriends back in her early twenties. Still, she was able to leave those without scandal or making the gossip column headlines from the looks of it. And then he saw it. Dhorian picked up the photo and held it closer to his face to make sure his eyes were not playing tricks on him. Tiffany LaSalle was in a picture with Madisin Foster? How did Tiffany know Madisin? The way they smiled at the camera, cheeks touching, capturing the good times, made Dhorian see they were more than acquaintances. They looked to be close friends.

From what Dhorian could recall, Madisin worked as Paul's secretary for over a decade. She was only around for a month or so when Dhorian started his internship. Be that as it may, Madisin's name was still whispered around the office, even after she left. Madisin had it rough after she stopped working for Paul. Her daughter had been kidnapped and found with one of her kidneys missing. Shortly thereafter, Madisin's body was discovered in the charred remains of her home. No sign of her daughter or mother, who lived there also.

Dhorian gasped, "Oh shit." *Madness. I'm thinking complete madness.*

A lot of detail surrounding the kidnapping and the murder

was buried at the time. The headlines were concise and to the point. *Little girl kidnapped and found with organ missing.* And then, *Woman found murdered in a house fire.* However, the headlines did not connect the two incidents back then, nor was there a word or promise of an investigation. Maybe Ms. LaSalle was trying to fill in the gaps. And Paul just happened to find a successful kidney donor at the same time Madisin's daughter went missing. Shortly after authorities found the little girl, Paul was on the road back to recovery. That would insinuate a biological connection between Madisin's daughter and Paul. Yet, Dhorian's brain could not handle how plausible it all sounded.

What the hell is Paul Christen pulling me into? First, his crazy-ass drug and sex-crazed daughter has me hiding her habit and our quasi-existent relationship. And now her father has me on some revenge espionage shit to tie up loose ends. That is at least what Dhorian assumed initially. Of course, there were a million possibilities. Maybe neither Paul nor Tiffany knew who their joining link was. Dhorian stayed with that theory for a while. If he was the only one that knew of the connection between Paul and Tiffany, maybe he could use it to his advantage. Dhorian smelled an opportunity to gain the reins back over his life from his mentor. He did not mind stepping in and helping Paul, but he did not want to continue to be spoken to like a flunky every time the man found himself losing control. There was a possible networking opportunity with Ms. LaSalle, as well. Most of his clients ended up in the tabloids and on the news before he got a chance to do damage control and spin the narrative. This bit of information could prove to be a very profitable advancement in his career.

By the time Dhorian pieced together Ms. LaSalle's client profile, his brain felt like it would explode. He tried to relax the racing musings of his imagination to process all the data collected. He needed facts. Instead of finding a sports bar to unwind, Dhorian headed home to find his peace of mind.

*

Knock. Knock. Knock. Knock. Knock.

Dhorian checked his watch for the time. It was 11:00 p.m., and someone was knocking at his door like they were the police. He was not expecting anyone and had no intentions of getting up to answer the door until he heard, "Dhorian, it's me, Chris. Please open up. I have to talk to you."

Dhorian dragged his hand down his face. Good pussy was not an excuse for crazy and at that moment, Dhorian did not care how good Christina Christen was in bed. Tonight was the last night that she would be allowed to invade and control his space.

When he came home tonight, all Dhorian wanted to do was meditate in his Japanese Washitsu room so he could find his peace and Zen. When he was in this room, he created positive and thought-provoking energy that helped him think through his problems and confusion. He was not up for Christina's bullshit tonight, and he was going to let her know as much.

Dhorian unfolded his legs and stood up from the tataki mat where he sat. He tied a robe around himself to cover his thin pajama bottoms and bare chest. On many occasions, Christina came over with only a trench coat and her birthday suit, trying to seduce her way into his bed. Like a fool, it worked every time. Well, he would not let his dick run the show tonight. At the least, he would cover himself, so his manhood was not easily accessible.

He peeked out the peephole and whispered a short *Thank you* to the man above because there was no trench coat. No sooner than he turned the doorknob, Christina pushed the door in on him and spouted, "I'm Black, Dhorian!"

The force of her entry and the absurdity of her words threw Dhorian into a choking hysteria. He was coughing so hard that he left Chris at the open door. She found him in the kitchen, mouth under the faucet, gulping down water to moisten the dryness in his throat. Dhorian felt her eyes drilling holes into him. Chris was impatient as she waited for his attention. Despite knowing this, Dhorian took his time. There was a point where he stopped drinking the water and just let it run over his opened lips. But Christina never moved from her spot. She just leaned against the island, watching him.

Even though he was annoyed that Chris barged her way into his place, her words piqued his curiosity.

Dhorian dried his mouth with a hand towel and faced Chris. He made sure to project all of the irritation he felt into his words.

"What? What are you talking about, Christina?"

His directness and *"are you stupid"* tone must have staggered Chris because she could not form any words that made sense. Dhorian grew more frustrated as she tried to find her words. Patience wearing thin, Dhorian cut off her stammering, "You know what? Never mind. I've been meaning to talk to you anyway. I think you need to go into rehab."

Before she could respond, Dhorian began to escort Chris out of the kitchen with his hand at her back. They were almost to the front door when Chris found her voice and started again.

"Rehab? Are you serious, Dhorian? I'm not even high. You haven't even looked at my face once since I got here."

"And you know why? Because I am not doing this with you anymore. I am done enabling your habit." Dhorian shouted and then composed himself before calmly saying, "And we're done. I can't keep hiding from your father. It's starting to affect my work. Making me all paranoid and shit. And I worked too damn hard to get here." Pointing a strong finger in her direction, "I won't let even you fuck this up for me."

Wiping the tears forming in the corners of her eyes, Chris sniffled, "Well, I'm glad to know that I mean so much to you."

She grabbed her purse and her coat off the loveseat and started towards the door. "If nothing else, I thought we were friends. Or at least you would be someone I could count on when I was in trouble."

Dhorian knew Christina was trying to give him the guilt

trip, but just hearing the word *trouble* come from her mouth made the hairs stand up on his arms. Chris was not one to scare or stir without reason. Then again, he never knew when Chris was up to her shenanigans. Dhorian decided that hearing what kind of trouble she was hinting at may have been worth stopping her from walking out the door.

"Okay, Chris. Okay. But I need to check your eyes first. I swear if your ass is high, I'm calling your father myself. This shit has got to stop."

Dhorian motioned for Christina to come to him. He grabbed his keys from the bowl by the door and clicked the button on his keychain flashlight to test her pupil dilation. He had to admit this was the best he had seen her look in a while.

Attitude on display and hands at her hips, Christina asked, sarcastically, "Are you happy now?"

Dhorian moved the light from her face and threw the keys back in the bowl. He started walking towards his living room, with Chris trailing not far behind.

"Well, you know you can't just make statements like "I'm Black" without a very detailed explanation."

"Okay. Okay. Okay. Let me back up," Christina said, waving her hands excitedly.

"Last year, I was in school in Gainesville, and we had this project where we had to do a study on genealogical diseases in our family tree. You know my mother and father aren't big talkers when it comes to their health. I mean, I had to overhear Uncle Barry talk about daddy's kidney failure before he would even mention it to me. So, I knew I had to do the research on my own."

"Okay, I'm following so far," Dhorian said stoically.

"There was this DNA company offering genetic testing, but all I could give them was my blood sample and hair samples from my parents. Before I could get the test results back, dad calls and tells me about the leadership op program for MonClaire Pharmaceuticals. And you know I couldn't pass that up."

Dhorian ran his hand down his face and sighed. "You're losing me, Chris."

"Okay. Long story short, I got the results back today."

"Okay, and?" Dhorian rolled his hand impatiently. Urging Chris to get to the part where she tells how her lily-white skin, baby blue eyes, and burnt orange hair equals Black.

Christina riffled through her purse before placing folded papers on the table in front of him. Dhorian waited a moment for Chris to continue with the story. But when she remained silent, Dhorian picked up the papers and began looking them over.

"Are you serious, Chris?"

"Of course, I'm serious, Dhorian!" Christina said indignantly.

"What kind of game are you playing? This report isn't a genetic test result. It's an ethnicity estimate. You know that, right?"

Dhorian glared at Christina. She was shifting uncomfortably under his gaze. He knew she was full of shit. Dhorian flung the paperback results booklet across the table.

"Look, I know you're mad." Christina tried to walk in front of Dhorian to cut him off.

"You don't know shit, Chris. Because if you did, you would know that you didn't have to spin a fucking web of lies to get me to listen to you." Dhorian chided and pushed past Chris as he continued to the door. It was time she left.

"But this isn't a lie. This paper proves that I'm Black. I am not lying about that."

"Chris, you're a brilliant girl, so I'm going to try to say this in a way that doesn't make you feel stupid. It's an ethnicity estimate, Chris. Estimate. That means someone's best guess. There's no science to this. It could be all wrong. This stuff is based on the available pool of people that they have to compare your samples to. Which means those numbers, your percentages, and your ethnic makeup could change at any time based on their sample size."

"Dhorian, how much can a nationality of thirty-five percent Cameroon, Congo, and Southern Bantu change with an increased sample size? It would only make it the truth, right?"

"And what truth would that be? I mean, I just don't understand why you would even do a genetic test like this?"

Before Chris could answer, Dhorian threw up his hands in frustration. "No. Don't tell me. I don't want to know. It's time for you to leave. And if you don't go, I'm going to call your father."

"Fine, Dhorian. I'll leave. And I'll find out the truth on my own."

Dhorian did not take the bait. "You do that, Chris. Have a good night while you're at it." Slamming the door behind her.

Dhorian did not know what scared him more, that Christina could be right or that someone else could learn the truth before he got a chance to use it to his advantage. Either way, Dhorian knew he had some quick truth-finding of his own to do.

Chapter 17

VERDELL

Verdell sat, racking his brain on who was on his tail until he saw Tatiana walk in. "What you doing here on a Thursday night, girl?"

"Same thing you doing here, I guess."

"Manny!" Both Verdell and Tatiana said in sync and chuckled as Tatiana sat down at the bar.

"Can I get a cranberry, pineapple, and vodka?" Tatiana asked.

"You look like you need more of a sex on the beach. What's up with you? And don't start by saying nothing cause then I'll be offended that you bold enough to lie to me in my face," Verdell smirked.

He watched Tatiana blush and gave a sarcastic chuckle before downing a third of the drink he placed in front of her just seconds before. She licked the droplets of alcohol that sat heavily on her pouty mocha-tinted lips. Even though all she really did was lick her lips, but what Verdell saw was her sucking and biting them.

"This is tasty." Tatiana raised her glass and nodded in Verdell's direction.

"Shit, it looks like it. I need to make me one the way you gulping down yours. Just guzzling."

They both laughed. Tatiana was the most beautiful lady he had ever seen. Yet her face looked so familiar. Any opportunities Verdell had to make Tatiana smile, he had to take. Her smile warmed the room and swallowed him in her vibe. Verdell caught himself staring at her lips and into her big brown eyes long after their joking died off. The last few weeks since that debacle was crazy for Verdell. It had him thinking about simpler living, settling down, and doing little things like sharing a laugh with someone special. It had been a while since he cared enough to want to make anyone smile. There was Benji, but she was more like a little sister. He would never try to flirt with her, and he knew that she would not want him to do so for whatever reason. They respected each other's space.

Verdell allowed himself to care for Tatiana, even though doing so made him nervous. His life was dangerous. Verdell knew all too well what it felt like to have love and then have his heart snatched right out of his chest. He was in no rush to go back to that dark place.

"So, you gonna tell me what's wrong, or do I have to make you start paying for your own drinks?"

"What? I pay for my drinks!" Tatiana said face frowned up, faking offense.

"When? Please let me know when. Cause I'm always at this bar, and you know I keep my tabs straight."

"Hmm," Tatiana shrugged and nodded in agreement.

"Shit, if I didn't, I'd have a case on me for whooping Manny's shit-talking ass." Verdell snickered.

Tatiana finally met his eyes for the first time since sitting down. "You really want to know what's up." She asked shyly.

"Woman, why else would I have asked you?"

"I know, I'm just saying, you know how people ask, but they, you know, being friendly and don't really want to know.

"Do I look like I like being nice?" Verdell put on his sternest face and puffed out his broad chest.

"Okay, okay. But this doesn't leave this bar." Tatiana whispered.

Looking around the barren club, Verdell made an exaggerated scene of searching for someone. "Ain't nobody here but me, you, and Lafayette, and you know how he gets absorbed whenever he has a chance to play some Miles Davis."

They both looked in the corner where Manny kept the redwood baby grand piano and where the New Orleans born, middle-aged Lafayette always sat. Verdell met Lafayette what felt like forever ago while serving time in prison, just like him, for a crime he did not commit. Lafayette looked out for him. When Verdell got out and had a few dollars in his pocket, he tracked Lafayette down and gave him a business offer he could not refuse. Lafayette was quiet and did not get close to too many people, but Verdell liked that about him. It meant that he cherished his privacy and relied on trust to form relationships. Verdell knew the kind of loyalty he could garner from a business partner with those traits, so like his own. Even though Manny only let Lafayette play for an hour before the night crowd arrived for the adult entertainment at 10 p.m., he never missed a night or a chance to finger those ivory keys.

"So, are you going to tell me or what?" Verdell feigned his impatience. He watched Tatiana look around the club, from one side and then to the other, seemingly satisfied that the Thursday night crowd was dead enough.

"I don't know Verdell. I'm just tired. Usually, my birthday is a big day for me, but since coming back home, I haven't been able to sleep through the night. I wake up in cold sweats, worrying about my grandmother and thinking about my mother and me. I just can't get back to sleep."

Tatiana downing the rest of her drink, bouncing her foot rapidly, now chilled from the goose bumps present on her chest and arms made it more than clear how shaken she was.

Reaching out to touch her unsteady hand, Verdell asked, "Are your peoples okay? I'm sure if they are anything like you, they'll make it through whatever it is."

Tatiana met his eyes for a second time that night as she moved her hand from under his. Exhaling slowly, she started, "My grandmother's in the hospital. She's recovering. It's just a little slower than I thought." She fidgeted before continuing, "and my mother passed away a long time ago when I was a little girl."

Feeling like an ass, Verdell rushed to get his foot out of his mouth, "Aww damn. Look, I'm so sorry. I didn't know. Well, I didn't mean to umm open that wound for you."

Shaking her head, "It's okay, you wouldn't have known. I don't get a chance to talk about myself often. Especially working in a place like this. Talking ain't what they pay me for."

She chuckled with tears appearing at the corner of her eyes.

"Girl, please, I think they tip your ass extra to talk. I hear you over there sweet-talking those old heads out of their hard-earned ones."

Tatiana's face flushed red until she heard ones.

"Ones??" Tatiana questioned with a wrinkled nose. "You tried me, and I don't get anything less than Bubbas."

"Well, excuse me." Verdell's hand went to his chest in mock defense. "My bad, Missy poo."

*

Damn. Bad play on words. Verdell thought. Saying the name, Missy, out loud was not planned. It just came out. He had not spoken his first love's name out loud since she appeared to him on the only job he regretted. The only job he never finished. The targets were a woman and her twelve-year-old daughter. But there was an older woman he was not expecting, and the women were fighters. They fought him harder than most men. And then it happened. Right as he watched the life draining from the mother's eyes, he saw Missy's face. He heard Missy's voice calling out to him. It was so clear that he even spoke back to her. The event shook him so bad that he let the daughter and the grandmother go.

Verdell knew he imagined the ghostly encounter with Missy because she and his unborn child died in a freak accident in which he was charged and convicted. At the time, Verdell convinced himself losing his baby and fiancé so close to a sensitive assignment like that was the reason for his emotional breakdown and unusual compassion for his targets.

After years of dealing with undiplomatic affairs, Verdell came to believe that nothing happened by coincidence. Even if the cue this time was only a reminder that he needed to catch up with Missy's father, Dr. Weiss, to find out more about his supposed involvement with a killer organization. He did not know what it had to do with Tatiana at this point, but Verdell knew that in time, all would reveal itself and become crystal clear.

*

Continuing his teasing, Verdell said, exaggeratedly, "Dang. I did not know what a few words from you were worth. Should I pay you starting now? Or are you going to bill me for the last hour?"

"Shut up, Verdell," Tatiana screamed flirtatiously before laughing and popping his shoulder over the bar.

Her hand did not slide right off, though, and Verdell noticed. Looking at his watch, Verdell realized they still had three hours before the club closed, so there was plenty of time to kill, and he knew just the thing.

"You like playing cards?"

"Playing cards like what? Like bid whist or Jim rummy?" Tatiana said, cackling.

"So, you just gonna keep throwing shots all night, huh? You tryna say I'm old?"

"Nah, I'm not saying that, even though I know you older than me. I'm just asking what kinda cards you like to play."

Verdell pulled his shirt up, exposing an exquisite set of six cocoa brown perfect rectangles stacked two by two and divided by a thin line of fine dark hair. Verdell asked, "I'm talking about this deck! Does this deck look old to you?"

Noticing Tatiana did not have a clever comeback, Verdell looked up to a slack-jawed Tatiana. Her head tilting a little to the left like she was trying to get a better look at something.

"What? Something on my face?" Dropping his shirt and touching his face, Verdell looked questioningly at Tatiana as she giggled and asked him for a refill.

"You got something on your face, all right. Now were you serious about the cards, or were you just trying to get me to look at your *deck*?" Tatiana asked as she took another sip of her drink and pointed towards his groin.

Looking down, Verdell shook his head, "Man, get your head out of the gutter. I showed you all I wanted you to see. Now are you up for getting your ass whooped on your birthday in spades or what?"

"Whatever, Verdell, I never get my ass whooped. And spades with two people? That game ain't real."

"It's as real as you and me, baby girl." Verdell retorted.

Tatiana stared at Verdell so long without blinking that he started to think that maybe she fell asleep with her eyes open.

"What's up? Tati, hey, girl. You good?" Verdell waved his hand in front of her face.

Blinking rapidly, Tatiana came to and winced from embarrassment, "I'm sorry, Verdell. I think I need to go. I'm not feeling well."

She started to get off the barstool. Verdell rushed from behind the bar door. He had to make his move before she got away.

"Nah, you not sick. You just need a little bit of fun and a soundboard to help you get back to you. Now you gonna come with me and play these cards or what?"

Looking around the empty club, "where are we going to play cards, Verdell? Huh? Besides, you can't leave the bar. Manny'll kick your ass."

"Kick my ass? Ain't you supposed to be working tonight too?"

"Yeah, but ain't nobody to bring drinks to, so technically I'm off the clock."

"You can bring drinks to me," Verdell growled seductively.

Tatiana turned and fully faced him. "Boy, you play too damn much with your fresh self. We can play this whack ass two-person spades as long as you don't try no mess."

"Why would I try any mess? Come on, girl." Verdell took Tatiana's hand as he rushed over to the bar to grab a fresh pack of cards and put them in his back pocket. Tatiana smiled when he reached for the pitcher with the rest of the vodka, cranberry, and pineapple mix she had been drinking too.

"What? I'm saying we might get thirsty." Verdell shrugged.

"Yeah, like there wasn't any water to drink," Tatiana mumbled sarcastically.

Chapter 18

TATIANA

With her hand still in his, Tatiana followed Verdell towards Lafayette, who he asked to watch the bar for him. Lafayette nodded. Verdell then led her past the baby grand and into the main hallway of the club. He made a sharp left turn before they reached the club's entrance and down a long hallway towards a lone ruby red door at the end of the hallway.

With everything Tatiana had going on in her life, the call from Manny to work on her birthday was almost a relief. She went hoping the change in scenery might perk her up and take her mind off Nanna. Verdell was an unexpected twist in her night.

As Verdell put in the code to open the door, Tatiana squeezed his hand, "I've never been on this side of the building before. Just promise me you not going to kill me."

Taken aback at her request, Verdell pushed the door open. "Kill you? Baby girl, please believe me when I say that killing you is not even a thought in my mind."

Something about how he licked his lips distracted her from being called by her childhood name again.

"Well, come on. Don't be scared now."

Pushing the door open further, Verdell released Tatiana's hand and walked into the room. Despite her initial hesitation, the room appeared well furnished. There was a full-size pool table, a wet bar, several lounge chairs in front of a large flat-screen TV, a poker table, a roulette table, and a card table.

"Oh my God, Verdell. What is this?"

"This is where Manny holds his monthly poker night, and his celebrity friends get to relax and have fun away from prying eyes."

"Well, damn, it sure looks like he and you know how to have a good time."

"Hell, I plan on it. You sitting down to play or what?"

Tatiana looked over at the purple velvet-lined card table and the chair Verdell was holding out for her and thought, *what the hell*!

Verdell poured both of them drinks and started to explain the rules of the game. Feeling cheated because she had already had a drink and a half to his one, she made him chug one in front of her, so they could be on even playing ground. Content now that they were on the same intoxication level and feeling a little more comfortable in her new element,

Tatiana asked slyly, "so what do I get if I win?"

Shuffling the cards, Verdell asked, "what do you want?"

Tatiana spoke up quickly, although a little too fast, the words were already out of her mouth. "I don't know the last time I had a good massage. If I win, I want a foot massage."

Tatiana giggled while unsheathing her feet from her strappy white and gold heels and pointing her toes in Verdell's direction. Verdell immediately scrunched up his face.

"Rub nasty feet? Not bad. Not ideal, but doable."

"Damn right, it's doable. Cause I'm spanking that ass." Tatiana roared while slapping the table with feigned aggression.

Verdell laughed. "You funny, you know that, right?"

"Yeah, yeah, just deal the cards."

"Deal? You pull your own cards."

"See, I knew this game was lame."

"Hush and pull your card, woman. You got to pull one to keep and pull one to drop in the throw-away pile. If you go with your first card, you can't keep the second one."

"Okay, okay. I got it. I got it."

"You sounding too eager to get beat." Verdell chimed, and they both fell into an easy laugh.

*

Four rounds of two-person spades later, with Verdell winning all but the last one. It was not until the last game was over that Tatiana realized Verdell never said what he wanted if he won.

"Why you never said what you wanted if you won?" Tatiana

asked as she sipped the remainder of their drink.

"What you mean?" Verdell shrugged his shoulders. "You never asked me."

"Are you serious? I thought the only game you wanted me to play was spades?"

"Nah, I didn't want anything. Getting you down here to let loose with me was winning enough." Sitting back in his chair, Verdell rocked and continued, "But I do owe you that massage, though."

"I thought you said my feet were nasty?" Tatiana quipped.

"You must have misheard me. I said your feet were doable."

Choking on her laugh, Tatiana recovered from his pun and said, "Yes. Yes, you did. But since you tricked me into spending time with you, I think I deserve a full-body massage. But I don't want no funny business."

"You can get your full-service massage, and I promise nothing will be funny about how I handle my business."

Standing up from the table, Verdell walked next to the wet bar and opened a coal-black folding closet door that she had not noticed before. If nothing else, tonight was her clue to pay more attention to her surroundings. She made a mental note for herself. Verdell placed a fancy navy blue plastic-wrapped package on the card table.

"I'm going to go and check on Lafayette and make sure we still good on time. When I get back, I want you changed and laying down on the long chaise lounge," Verdell pointed, "over there in the corner by the roulette table."

Following his finger, Tatiana looked at the long couch. Verdell must have sensed Tatiana's hesitation because he turned her head gently toward him with his index finger.

"I promise you I won't do anything other than what you ask me to. Besides, you really do look like you need this massage. Go ahead, get comfortable. You can leave on your undergarments, and I'll be right back."

As smooth as Verdell was, Tatiana almost expected a kiss. Before he walked out the door, Verdell gave her a wink, hit a switch on the wall, and turned on Ordinary Love by her favorite female artist, Sade. Tatiana felt her face flush and her body heat up. It was surreal how Verdell knew little things about her that made her feel like she had known him for years. Despite the walls Tatiana built around herself, Verdell was slowly making himself a door. Tatiana had never seen or heard Verdell be so forward. Especially not with her. She trusted him because he had been nothing but a gentleman since meeting him, but just the idea of Verdell putting his strong hands on her skin made her weak. She silently prayed her melted juices would not embarrass her by trickling down her thighs.

Looking around at the immaculately decorated and put-together room, Tatiana decided to trust fate and started taking off her silk blouse and Levi jeans. There was a chill in the room that rubbed across her nipples through her lace bra, and she felt the skin around them tighten. Tatiana covered herself and ran to the Navy-blue package Verdell left behind. She unwrapped it and found an oversize plush cotton robe, matching belt, and a sleep mask. There was also a pair of fluffy white slippers in there that looked too big, but she knew she would not need those because, if nothing else, Verdell was damn sure rubbing her feet.

Feeling a little lightheaded after all that drinking and quick-moving, Tatiana was relieved when she laid down on the long couch. She dozed off for five minutes, but what felt like at least an hour before the feeling of warm hands and tingling saturated her feet. When she finally shook the daze from her eyes, Tatiana opened them to see Verdell smiling at her and rubbing oil on his hands and through her toes.

"I thought my feet were nasty?"

"How many times we got to go through this? I said they were doable."

They both chuckled.

"Close your eyes and relax. I promise you I got you. Now let me be."

Tatiana wanted to come back with something witty to say, but the way Verdell was rubbing her feet felt so damn good. She did not want to chance a moan slipping out as she opened her mouth, so she decided to let him have that one and laid back. Sade serenaded her through the best thirty-minute massage Tatiana ever had in her twenty-one years of living. In the past, she and her college roommates paid out a hundred dollars per session for worse massages. This one may have been shorter than those, but it took the cake, the icing, and the ice cream. And to top it all off, Verdell was a perfect gentleman through it all. She was sad their little session was ending and almost a bit disappointed that he did not try anything.

"You mind if I massage your upper thigh?"

Tatiana glanced over her shoulder. Verdell looked like a man gifted at his craft. There was nothing in his eyes or body language that would suggest mannish intent, so she replied, "Yeah, sure."

Verdell's touch made her thighs betray her. His strong hands kneaded her muscle and caused her legs to tremble. Tatiana could not control the moan that escaped her lips. "Oh my God, Verdell. What are you rubbing on me?" Tatiana purred.

Verdell chuckled, "I'm not rubbing anything but oil on you. See?" He showed her the coconut and shea oil gel. Her legs were still trembling as his strong hands worked their way up her thighs.

"Damn," Tatiana growled into the sleeve of the cotton robe as she tried to drown out her sounds of ecstasy.

"See. I told you it looked like you needed a sex on the beach instead of that vodka and cranberry mess you had me drinking. You want me to stop?"

Still attempting to work through her own sexual tug of war, Tatiana said a little louder than necessary, "to be honest, I don't know what l want right now, Verdell. But I do know that I can't think straight with you rubbing my thighs like that. It makes me feel weird."

Chuckling, Verdell said sarcastically, "I didn't know that weird is what they called it these days."

Tatiana pulled herself away from his touch and turned and sat Indian style to face him. "I don't know what you talking about."

Tatiana averted her eyes when she caught Verdell licking his lips.

"I know what I finally want for winning."

Drawn into his eyes, Tatiana asked measuredly, "and that is???"

"I want to taste you. Will you let me?"

Thrown back by his forward statement, Tatiana tried to piece together her next sentence. But, before she had a chance to recover, Verdell started again.

"I promise I'll only taste you, and I'll go as slow as you want me to."

Her words caught up with her thoughts, "Verdell, you know I'm not a virgin, right? Like I've had other encounters."

"I hear you on that, but you never had me."

If Tatiana had not known it before, she sure knew it now. Verdell was one sexy motherfucker. Drinking in everything about him, Tatiana leaned back on the long couch and slightly spread her legs open. Verdell did not rush right in. He took his time massaging her feet and then her ankles and then her inner thighs. *Damn those inner thighs.* They let her down every time he touched her there. Rubbing his hands closer toward her heat, Tatiana knew he would soon find out her secret; that she had been wet for him all this time. And with him being so close to her moist treasure, she wanted him to find her truth. Wanted him to taste her nectar. He blew on her mound through her lace panties, and Tatiana gasped with excitement.

"Oh shit." Trying to push herself up to her elbows. "You said you wanted to taste me, not that we were still going to play games."

Verdell moved her panties aside without acknowledging her statement, pushed his finger into her folds, and blew on Tatiana again.

"Shhhhhhh!"

Verdell dove his face into Tatiana's wet center with reckless abandonment. She squirmed and wiggled as Verdell sucked and slurped on her pearl. He hooked his strong arms under her ass and through her legs and pulled her closer to his face. His hot and wet tongue left no stone unturned. He licked her folds, stiffened his tongue, plunging it deep inside her, and trailed kisses from the top of her mound to the small sensitive area of skin that bridged her heaven and her earth. The feeling was a first-class out-of-body experience. Tatiana had earned her wings on this one. The sensation between her quivering thighs quickly changed from a mild tickle to a warm throbbing tingle. The shock pulsed from the pit of her moistness, up through her spine, and into her hair follicles.

Tatiana did not know if she was catching a fever or if something was going wrong between the chills and the lightheadedness. Nothing in her whole life had ever made her feel like this before. She loved every minute of it. Her screams were spewing from her lips and sounded more like low gut growls than moans. As embarrassed as Tatiana wanted to be, the pleasure of it all would not let her. That is until the ecstasy became as great as the pressure on her bladder, and Tatiana jumped up, snatching herself away from Verdell.

Looking confused and breathless, Verdell asked, "What's wrong with you? Did I do something wrong? Did I bite you?"

Shyly shaking her head, "No…. I mean, I think at this point, if you would have bitten me, I might have loved it."

"Sooo…" shrugging his shoulders and looking stumped, Verdell asked, "well, what's the problem then?"

Still shaking her head, Tatiana responded, "I think that's enough. I can't take any more."

Verdell crawled closer to Tatiana on the chaise lounge.

"Like hell, you can't.

Interrupting him, Tatiana scooted further back towards the arm of the plush couch, "Exactly, like hell, I can't. I can't take any more."

"What is it that you're so afraid of? You said I didn't bite you. I'm not going to hurt you, Tati. I just want to make you feel better and take your mind off of things."

"Well, you definitely get a five out of five-star rating on that."

Verdell chuckled, "well, let me finish and see if I can get a ten out of ten."

Chapter 19

DHORIAN

"So, why you don't know how to call anyone back?" Christina chided.

Dhorian sighed, aggravated with the lack of common courtesy and the exaggerated snippiness.

"Christina, you can stop it with this sister girl, acting Black Ebonics stuff. It's not funny, and it's not you."

Dhorian was still bothered by the "I'm Black" stunt she pulled at his place a few weeks ago. She needed some serious help.

"Well, apparently, I'm not the only one who is experiencing an identity crisis."

Dhorian wanted to be done with this conversation but went for the bait anyway. "And what does that mean?"

"It means you don't take me or our relationship seriously."

Growing more perturbed by the moment, Dhorian felt the

need to remind Christina, "Chris, we are not in a relationship. What in the hell are you talking about?"

"I'm pregnant, Dhorian. *That* relationship."

Dhorian laughed hard. *This chick really is crazy.* "So now you're pregnant and Black? Don't be so quick to join a statistic!"

"I'm not laughing, Dhorian. I'm pregnant with your child, so deal with it. And I am telling my father about the baby. And how you were at some raunchy strip club, making our family look bad." Christina goaded.

Deal with it? Who in the hell does she think she is, telling me to deal with it? Dhorian decided to ignore the comment about the baby. That was not an idea he was entertaining.

"What? What strip club? Are you having me followed?" Dhorian asked as he mentally scrolled through his memory bank to recall the last time he was in a strip club.

"You think I'm stupid? I've been calling you for two days straight with no response. I bet you were with some whore. What kind of double life are you living? My father put a lot on the line for you, and this is how you choose to repay him? By wasting your time with some nasty ass dick sucking whore. For our baby's sake, you better hope she doesn't have any STDs." Christina nagged relentlessly.

Dhorian suddenly had the biggest migraine conceivable park itself at the T of his forehead. *Why does she keep bringing up this baby? She must have her wires crossed. The only dick sucking whore I know is you!*

"I'm not sure if you're on another bender. I don't know how

much oxy you've digested, but your brain is fried. I haven't been to a strip club in years. Now I have been to the gentlemen's club, a time or two. But I don't see why that would be any of your fucking concern."

Christina let out a huge sigh and, in a low voice, spoke up. "My addiction is funny to you?

Dhorian heard the gasp. All that he said, and his drug accusation was the only thing Christina heard. Hurt feelings or not, Dhorian was not taking it back. Hell, someone had to be honest with her.

"Addiction is not funny. But you are. What Chris? What the hell do you want from me? I'm in the middle of something very important." Dhorian chided, dismissing the conversation and Christina entirely.

"Oh, I bet you are, jackass. You are in the middle of some deep shit, alright."

The line clicked, and there was silence.

"Did she just hang up on me?" Dhorian asked the empty room.

Thoroughly annoyed, Dhorian stared at his cell phone and threw it on his desk. Before Christina called, he was going over the Private Investigator's report, which he asked his assistant for months ago. All those years of wanting answers about his mother and even with the information he was given, Dhorian had more questions than answers and no closure.

It was all too much: Paul's stupid vendetta with Tiffany LaSalle, then Christina's childish need for constant attention, the information he needed to dig up on her father linking him to a nine-year-old murder, the cases at the firm, and now this shit. Dhorian felt himself approaching the dawn of a mental breakdown despite increasing his meditation sessions.

For now, he had to throw distractions to the wind and try to wrap up at least one of the problems on his plate, with the most pressing issue being the truth about his mother. He needed to have closure on this to help him move forward. Sometimes he was so unsure of himself and who his father was that he missed out on more significant opportunities because of the insecurities. It did not take expensive sessions with a therapist for Dhorian to realize that he would never feel complete until he closed this chapter in his life.

Medical records for McKenzie Yvette Anderson II show nothing about a live birth around the time he was born. In fact, there was a single entry about a stillborn made in the margins. *Am I the stillborn?* Dhorian questioned. The investigator made sure to mention that a deep stomach wound was the cause of death. Still, an autopsy was not performed before his mother's burial. For as long as he could remember, Dhorian was told his mother committed suicide. Deep down, Dhorian knew she would have never killed herself, but he had nothing else to help state otherwise. Now, he finally did. Too bad his father died before he could get the truth out of him. *My entire life has been a total and complete lie.* Dhorian thought these words over and over until they manifested into rage and burst from his lips.

"Ahhhhhhh!!" Dhorian screamed as he pushed the papers off his desk in rage.

His life felt like it was spiraling down, and there was nothing for him to grab onto to regain control. *Am I adopted?* Dhorian worked on a few severely complicated adoption cases before, and none of them carried weight like this. Even with all the lies wrapped up in a dilemma to tell or not to tell the child that they were not raised by their birth parents, this betrayal felt darker and more profound. *If my mom isn't my mom and my dad isn't my dad, what's the big deal?* All at once, the questions kept coming, increasing the pressure that was building at the bridge of his nose.

Dhorian needed a drink and he needed to call Chris back for some oxy and some ass. Maybe that would calm him and put him to sleep. At least for a little while. After a few swigs of Paul Mason, straight from the bottle, Dhorian decided he preferred a long hot shower over *Act Two* of Christina's dramatics.

First thing in the morning, Dhorian would call that sorry ass PI and cuss him out for giving him a half-ass report. *Why would they tell me who my mother was not and not who she was? Just asinine.*

Chapter 20

TATIANA

Tatiana threw her phone into her purse. It was the twelfth call today from a private number. She had no doubts that Cairo wanted to collect. Tatiana had not received a text or call from Cairo in months, but she became suspicious of the silence. Over the past week, unknown numbers were calling her and because she did not have them saved in her phone, Tatiana refused to answer. There were even a few threatening texts that went ignored. Tatiana did not know where to turn or even how to begin to settle things with Cairo. She could not go to the police. In her experience and from watching crime shows, no one ever believed the victim until it was too late, especially one who had a pimp after her. And paying up was out of the question. By her calculations, Tatiana only owed Cairo fifteen grand. Ten from her initial investment and the other five that Tatiana forgot to take from the john she killed. No matter if she could repay the debt, Cairo would be out for blood.

Tatiana thought about telling Verdell or her grandmother about her problem but thought it too embarrassing. It only made her feel gullible, naïve, and thirsty to relive and think about spending ten grand without stopping to think Cairo wanted something in return. Tatiana would have to deal with Cairo on her own. Tatiana peered in her purse to make sure her pistol was still there.

"Yo, Tati! Table seven needs drinks."

Tatiana jumped. Verdell knew she hated when he yelled at her from across the room, but he used any reason to get under her skin these days since that full body massage four months ago. Refocusing her energy on work, Tatiana bobbed her head and hummed to the new Russ joint, *Loson Control.* Tatiana did not think it was a song anyone could dance to, but the hottest dancer at the Top Hat, Amber Embers, never failed to prove her wrong. She was more than an exotic dancer. Amber Embers was a performer. Seeing her in action was like watching the Nutcracker ballet. Amber treated her 10 p.m. to 2 a.m. like an art class. Men and women alike paid top dollar for private shows. Amber was a genuine Picasso on the pole. This girl was bad. Tatiana tried not to stare too hard at the production as she passed the stage with two bottles of Belle Air Rosé and weaved through the crowded booths until she made it to table seven.

"Welcome to the Top Hat, where the drinks and the show will definitely TOP you off." Tatiana hated the provocative adage, but it came with the job. Besides, the patrons always seemed eager to tip more when she was enthusiastic and sultry.

"Yo, Tati. Table twelve needs drinks."

This time Verdell shouted into the microphone. *Ooo, that boy knows he play too much.* Tatiana thought as she cringed at Verdell's obnoxiousness.

When she stopped at the bar, she had a mind to give Verdell the business for calling her name out like that. But she knew he would not care about her sharp tongue. That did not stop her from mentioning it to him, though.

"Listen, that mic is for MCs and hype-men. And the last time I checked, you were a bartender."

Verdell chuckled and slapped her on the butt. Tatiana giggled.

"That mouth so slick." He teased. "Why I can't be your hype-man?" Verdell asked her with a shrug.

Tatiana sucked her teeth and twisted her face into a "boy please" scowl. She tried to play hard, but Verdell had her heart. He always knew what to say and what to do. He was a perfect gentleman. Almost too perfect, but he had not shown her anything but love and loyalty, and until he showed her different, she would give him the same.

Verdell motioned to her from behind the bar, "Give me kisses."

Tatiana leaned in and flicked her tongue across Verdell's lips. She then pressed full lips against his. Verdell's moan vibrated in Tatiana's chest and was on its way down to her spot before a commotion behind them stole the moment.

"Aye thickness, give me a dance," the table seven patron hollered at Amber Embers as she was stepping off the stage.

The intoxicated man grabbed the hem of Amber's shorts as she passed. It looked a little too close to the girl's pocketbook for Tatiana. She watched as Amber smiled politely and removed the patron's hand from her skimpy shorts.

"I'm sorry, love, but the club has a strict no-touch policy. Not to mention, I'm not available for that type of entertainment tonight, but if you like, I can find you one of our best."

Tatiana smiled wryly. It was just like Amber to let them down with such class. Tatiana made a mental note to tell Amber that when she saw her before their shift ended. Tatiana's smile instantly faded into a look of aggravation. She recognized the drunkard's face. He was the same Friday night table seven patron who got pissy drunk every week he came in. She hoped he did not have anyone at home to answer to because he left Top Hat his paycheck each time he came.

"I 'on want none of them hoes," he slurred and snatched Amber's arm. "I want you."

"Please let go of my arm, or I'll have security come help you," Amber's voice cracked a little.

That slight rise in panic was all Tatiana needed to set her off. She moved out of Verdell's grasp and across the room before he could protest.

Mr. Table Seven's face frowned up, "Trick ain't nobody thinking 'bout no fucking security. I been here three weeks straight tipping your bougie ass. And you ain't giving me shit in return but a hard dick. I think you betta start paying me some personal DAMN attention!" By this time, his six foot four frame towered over Amber's petite five foot three, and his free hand now clutched over the crotch of his pants.

Tatiana was used to patrons with beer muscles and boisterous behavior. She shook Amber's arm loose from the man's grip.

"The only thing your broke ass needs is to have someone pay attention to your rabid ass mind. If you think those sorry ass ones you throwing around here makes it okay to put your raggedy-ass hands on her," Tatiana's rant was cut off by Verdell's presence and booming voice.

"Is there a problem here?"

Before Mr. Table Seven could respond, he recognized Verdell's shadow darkening the space around him. A six foot seven mixed martial arts frame tended to induce speechlessness sometimes.

"Vee, I didn't know you were working tonight," the man stammered.

"What the fuck you mean? I work every night," Verdell's nose wrinkled in response.

Tatiana saw how frightened the guy was and started to feel sorry for him. As long as she had been working there, Verdell always let club security take out the trash. Tatiana assumed her involvement made it personal for him.

Amber looked a little weary. Tatiana took that as her cue to get Amber out of there. Tatiana looked at Verdell, "You got this handled?"

Verdell nodded without looking her way and said in his baritone voice, "Yep, baby girl, we good here."

"Cool, I'm on break anyway, "Amber mumbled as she walked away, speaking for the first time since Tatiana came over. *So much for me getting her out of here*, Tatiana thought. Tatiana was due for a break herself. She made eye contact with Verdell again and then followed Amber towards the club's side door to get some fresh air.

*

"Amber? Amber?" Tatiana whispered loudly.

Amber slipped through the side door maybe a few minutes before she did, but Tatiana saw no sign of her anywhere in the alley. There was a low fog that drenched the darkness. The lone streetlight illuminated a portion of the wide sidewalk outside. Tatiana was hesitant to step out of the light. She grabbed her phone before she left out of the building. Tatiana expected a call from her grandmother, but there was nothing but more private numbers as she scrolled through the missed calls. Tatiana refused to listen to the voicemails. She scrolled through her contacts, looking for different variations that she could have saved Amber Embers' cell number under. Tatiana typed in Embers Amber, Amber - Top Hat, Top Hat- Amber, and came up with nothing. Just as she was giving up and going back inside the club, Tatiana's phone rang. Without checking the caller ID, she picked it up and said, "Hello?"

"I thought I was going to have to come in there and cause a scene for you to come out here."

"What? Who is this?" Tatiana replied breathlessly. She already had an idea. But Tatiana had to hear her caller say her name.

"You know who this is, don't you? Of course, you do, or you wouldn't be over there shaking like booty meat. I mean, that is what you do in there at the Top Hat, ain't it? It's just sad you had to steal from me and cut me out of the deal. All you hoes is just alike."

Tatiana felt her body stiffen and her blood run cold. Cairo found her and was watching her at that very moment. Tatiana tried to peer into the dark alley, but she would not walk any further than the light's edge.

"Where are you?" The fear that gripped Tatiana made her reach for the pistol in her purse. Then she realized that she left her bag and gun in the club.

"You don't worry about that. You just focus on how many lap dances it'll take for you to get me my ten grand and how many tricks you'll have to turn until you come up with either the money or the body from that Mr. Man job."

Tatiana audibly gasped.

Cairo continued, "Yeah. That's right. I know you killed and ran off with his money. I'm sure the police back home would love that bit of information too."

That was all Tatiana could take. She dropped her phone and turned to run back into the club, and something or someone ran into her at the same time. Tatiana screamed so hard her throat felt scorched. This was it. Cairo had rushed her and stabbed her. *I'm dying,* Tatiana thought. Erratically she grabbed at the gravel and scratched at the tar, looking for her phone. She needed to see if she was wounded.

Tatiana finally found the phone, turned on the flashlight, and began scanning the light over her body, looking for wounds. There was so much blood, yet Tatiana felt no pain. Tatiana wondered for a moment if she was already dead. Then, she heard it. There was a groan, sniffle, and a small cry for help. Tatiana shakily took her phone and slowly flashed the light on the heap close to her feet. She had to know who it was. Tatiana counted backward from ten to block out the terror that was beginning to overtake her. With every second, the light moved closer to the face. Tatiana shuddered and moaned, *Amber*.

Chapter 21

VERDELL

"Yo, Tati! Table seven needs drinks."

Verdell chuckled from behind the bar as Tatiana practically jumped out of her skin. He knew she hated being yelled at from across the room. Still, Verdell did anything he could to make eye contact with her and see that sexy ass smirk. He observed Tatiana as she eyed her purse again before rushing over to the bar to get the drink order from him. She refused to look his way when he placed the bottles of Belle Aire Rosé on her tray. He liked it when she played hard to get. If Tatiana thought she would be able to ignore him, she better think again. Verdell held onto the last bottle of Rosé for a few moments longer than the others before placing it on the tray. Tatiana looked at him perturbed, and Verdell grinned like a happy cat. Tatiana scoffed and then stuck her tongue out at him before delivering the order to table seven.

The little games of cat and mouse he and Tatiana played gave Verdell a restored existence of his youth. Since age nineteen, he experienced a life of death and violence, most of which he inflicted. But now, at age twenty-eight, he was beginning to hope for a life that was less savage than the one he lived currently.

The more time he spent with her, the more Verdell began to believe that Tatiana came into his life at a time when they needed each other. About four months ago, a stolen moment had now grown into a mutual fondness and maturity that they had not put a label on yet.

Verdell still did not know who was trailing him, but he knew he had to be careful. He would not forgive himself if anything ever happened to Tatiana or her grandmother because of him. He knew those who were after him would do everything in their power to get to him. On countless occasions, he had resorted to the same tactics.

Since the Tropicana mystery hit, Verdell let his hair grow out on his head and face. He stopped staying at his father's house in West Tampa and rented an efficiency in Bradenton. He smashed his sim card and got himself a few burner phones. Verdell kept cash on him to make sure there were no card trails. He had Benji set him up with a new ride. Something not too flashy but nice and stylish in the city. Verdell had not stopped at his place in Thonotosassa. He only recently got insurance on the spot and would not dare risk his dream home on the whim that war was coming his way.

Nevertheless, with all that Verdell had against him, he had

to have her, despite the danger. What he and Tatiana shared reminded Verdell of his first love, Missy. It was what he imagined, what he had planned for before she and his child were snatched away from him. But he was young then. Life had a way of using naivety to steal innocence and callous a man, if not careful. Now Verdell was older. More mature. He understood the fragility of life and love and how lucky he was to have someone like Tatiana to experience it with.

Except lately, she has been distracted. Tatiana thought he would not notice her being extra attentive to her phone or purse. Verdell was positive it was not another man. But he was convinced Tatiana had more going on than just caring for her sick grandmother. There was something else bothering her. Verdell dealt with enough people hiding secrets to know that Tatiana was hiding something. Yet, he was torn. He could not risk breaking the fragile state of her trust by prodding or snooping. He wanted Tatiana to feel comfortable enough to tell him. He knew it might be too soon for them to be at that level, so he tried not to sweat it or her. Verdell held on to his ghosts to keep Tatiana safe. However, he did not know what ghosts Tatiana had and what he would need to be kept safe from. For now, he would stay strapped and continue to watch her back and his own.

Verdell noticed the change in music and the spotlight on the stage. But he had his own spotlight on Tatiana. He eyed her hips as she subtlety changed her walk to be in rhythm with the music. Everything about her made him tingle. Verdell began wiping down the bar as he bobbed his head to the new Russ joint, *Losin Control*. Verdell grinned at the song's lyrics and how they may be mirroring his sentiments of the moment. Another drink order buzzed in on the electronic printer.

"Yo, Tati. Table twelve needs drinks." Verdell shouted into the microphone.

When Tatiana stopped back at the bar to pick up the new order, Verdell readied himself for all her attitude to come with her. He could care less about her attitude, though. Verdell actually thought it was a little sexy. It was a means to an end.

"Listen, that mic is for MCs and hype-men. And the last time I checked, you were a bartender." Tatiana snapped.

Verdell only grinned and slapped her on the butt. Tatiana did not even flinch. Instead, she only giggled. Verdell felt his manhood thump against his jeans.

"Ooo, that mouth so slick," he teased. "Why I can't be your hype-man?" Verdell asked her with a shrug.

Tatiana sucked her teeth and twisted her face. Verdell saw past her facade. He knew he was slowly winning her heart. Verdell motioned to her from behind the bar and said, "Give me kisses," before poking out his lips. Tatiana obliged by leaning in and quickly flicking her tongue across his closed mouth before pressing her full lips against his. Verdell moaned, now desperate for Tatiana's body to be close to his, until a commotion behind them stole the moment.

"Aye thickness, give me a dance," the table seven patron hollered at the club's premier dancer, Amber Embers, as she was stepping off the stage. Verdell tensed when the inebriated man grabbed the hem of Amber's shorts. He quickly assessed the room and the looks on Amber and Tatiana's face and knew it was only a matter of time before things got funky.

Amber smiled politely and removed the patron's hand from her skimpy shorts. Verdell recognized the guy as the same Friday night table seven patron who got pissy drunk every week he came in. He literally signed his paycheck over every time he came. Verdell would know because Top Hat also cashed payroll and personal checks for their loyal customers.

"I 'on want none of them hoes," the man slurred and snatched Amber's arm. "I want you."

"Please let go of my arm, or I'll have security come help you," Amber's voice cracked a little.

That was what Verdell interpreted as the last straw for Tatiana. She was out of Verdell's grasp and across the room before he could protest. *Damn, she moves fast,* Verdell thought. He quickly unfastened his pistol from the holster under the bar and tucked it into the waist of his jeans.

Mr. Table Seven's face frowned up, "Trick ain't nobody thinking 'bout no fucking security. I been here three weeks straight tipping your bougie ass. And you ain't giving me shit in return but a hard dick. I think you betta start paying me some personal DAMN attention!" The man stood up. His six foot four frame towered over Amber's petite five foot three, and his free hand now clutched over the crotch of his pants.

Verdell watched the men and his crew closely as Tatiana

approached the table. Verdell was ready to put a bullet in anyone's ass who moved to hurt her. He knew when she snatched Amber's arm from the man's grasp, it was going down. Verdell signaled Lafayette, who made eye contact with him from across the room, and they both began to enclose on the action. Tatiana was just getting into her tirade when Verdell cut her off.

"Is there a problem here?"

The man turned to face Verdell, but that was before he recognized who had approached. Verdell knew his stature was intimidating. The *don't fuck with me* stare on his face was added weight.

"Vee, I didn't know you were working tonight," the man stammered.

"What the fuck you mean? I work every night," Verdell's nose wrinkled in response.

Verdell usually let Lafayette and club security deal with the troublemakers, but Tatiana getting involved made it a little more personal for him. It did not cross his mind that this could be a trust-building moment for them. At least not right away.

Amber looked a little shaken. Verdell caught Tatiana's gaze, "You got this handled?"

Verdell nodded without looking her way and said, "Yep, baby girl, we good here."

The intoxicated man and table seven stayed quiet while the women gathered themselves and walked away from the table. It was a sharp contrast to the scene that took place moments earlier, but Verdell was not surprised. His presence came with certain civilities that did not have to be said out loud. Once Tatiana and Amber were away from the drama, Verdell motioned across the club to Lafayette. He looked at their digital host machine and saw that their tab of four hundred ninety four dollars had not been taken care of yet.

"I'm going to need y'all to pay in full, cash, mandatory thirty percent tip." Verdell directed, making eye contact with each of the five men to let them know he was not bullshitting.

Two of the men at the table jumped up with their hands at their waist in protest. However, with his newfound sobriety, the overly inebriated man put his hands up to stop them. He dropped seven crisp hundred dollar bills from his wallet and backed away from the table.

"We don't want no problems, Vee. Tell the ladies, we apologize, and we'll be on our way," the man conceded.

"Get these disrespectful motherfuckers out of here, Lafayette. Get back with me if you have problems." Verdell growled.

"I got you, Vee," Lafayette confirmed as he and two other bouncers escorted the five men from Table 7 to the exit.

Verdell walked to the bathroom to cool down. The cold water felt good on his face, but his thoughts still burned. He locked the door to the single employee's restroom, turned the lights off, and began to pace back and forth in the open space between the sink and the stall. Past experiences showed him that he thought best in the dark. Verdell was the basketball prospect who got fucked over by the city and did time in prison for those who knew him from his younger days. He came home with a prison body, a little money, a sick father to take care of, a little street cred, and some respect. There were rumors of how the murder of his baby momma led him to prison. If people were not sympathizers, they were conspiracy theorists and chose to stay away. Either way, it all worked for his image. Only a few knew his power was built on being a man of mystery with mediocre means. And only Lafayette knew he was the true owner of Top Hat, not Manny. The Top Hat was only one of Verdell's silent ventures. And Verdell wanted to keep it that way. Having to flex his muscles too often would get people talking and possibly blow his low profile. Losing focus and acting out of character was becoming too familiar for Verdell. Tatiana made him too emotional. Verdell would let Lafayette handle the light scraps next time. While dealing with Tatiana's situation, there was no telling how many angles his unknown stalker was getting on him. Verdell concluded that he and Tatiana needed to break off whatever it was they had going on. At least until he knew who stepped into his territory and made his hit.

Verdell hit the switch on the wall, took one last glance at his face to level himself, and walked out the bathroom searching for Tatiana. They were through. She would be pissed, and he didn't know what reason he would give her, but Verdell's mind was made up. He walked back out to the floor in search of Tatiana but did not see her. Verdell checked for her purse by the bar and saw that she had not left because her bag and keys were still there. It only took a little nudge to the outside of her purse for it to open wider. Tatiana's phone was gone. *That girl and her damn phone.* Tatiana and her phone would not be a worry of his much longer. Verdell asked a few of the girls standing outside the women's restroom if they had seen her.

He received every answer, except no. Verdell huffed at their caddy lines and pettiness. *Women.* He said to himself.

Verdell continued searching the remainder of the club but could not find her. Any other time she would pop up and just be there. Maybe it was his sign that tonight was not the night to end it. He did not believe in coincidence. He had one last place to check. Sometimes the girls would go to the alley exit door to smoke. From what he knew, Tatiana did not smoke, but it was worth a shot.

As he approached the heavy steel door, he heard a loud thud and what he could only make out as a scream. It was hard to hear clearly with the loud music pulsing behind him. But Verdell touched his pistol and forced the heavy door open. Seeing Tatiana covered in blood, fumbling to push numbers on her phone, and mumbling to herself was not what he was prepared for. A panic attack began to set in so deep that Verdell could hear his heartbeat bursting through his chest. He could not speak, and he could not move. For only a second, he saw Missy's charred face, eyes blazing, staring back into his.

Noise by the dumpster under the streetlight made him reach for his pistol and aim it in that direction.

There was only an alley cat, but it sounded like something bigger. Verdell stepped forward to investigate the noise, and he stumbled over something soft. *Oh, shit, Tatiana.* Verdell had momentarily forgotten about her being there, but once he laid eyes on her again, he sprang into action. And she was not alone.

Verdell grabbed Tatiana's stupefied face in his hands. He grabbed at her shirt and her arms.

"Tatiana? Tatiana? What happened? What happened to Amber? Are you hurt?" Verdell asked frantically.

Verdell continued using the light from his phone and his hands to check for Tatiana's open wounds. There was so much blood on her that he was confused when he found none.

"Whose blood is this?" Verdell pleaded for Tatiana to tell him.

"Amber's," Tatiana whispered solemnly.

It was like she had just woken up. Verdell switched his attention over to Amber, balled up in Tatiana's lap. However, unlike Tatiana, he could tell she was injured, bad.

"Who was it? Did you see the son of a bitch?"

Tatiana began stammering, trying to find her words. Verdell wanted to be annoyed at her breaking under pressure, but he remembered his first run-in with blood. He wrapped his arms around her and counted the seconds until she stopped shaking in his grasp. *One one-thousand, two one-thousand, three one-thousand, four one-thousand, five one-thousand Verdell counted.* When her body gave way to the emotional tension of the moment, Tatiana fell limp in Verdell's arms, sobbing. Now that her cry was softening, he took Tatiana by her shoulders,

"What happened?"

"I don't fucking know, okay?" Tatiana said hysterically.

Verdell did not even flinch at her tone or response. "I need you to know something because Amber might not make it, and when we call the police, you knowing nothing is not going to help them or you or Amber. So, I need you to take a deep breath and tell me what happened."

Tatiana sniffled, wiping blood across her nose, and began, "I came out here to check on Amber, but then I didn't see her. I called her name a few times, but she did not answer. I heard something over by the dumpster."

They both looked in that direction. Verdell thought he saw something moving in the shadows. Keeping his eye on the open space under the streetlight and his peripheral on Tatiana and Amber.

"Okay, what happened next?" he urged.

"Umm, and then, and then, I got a call."

Verdell noticed Tatiana's hesitancy to mention the call. He would not dwell on that now. He needed to help her get her story together.

"I was on my way back in the building, and then she ran into me out of nowhere. I thought I was hurt. Dear God, not again."

Tatiana went from a fully seated position to kneeling. She pushed Amber's dying body off her lap and began to scratch at the keloids on her chest. Whatever she was going through, Verdell knew it was real. Verdell recognized a panic attack when he saw one, and he did not have time to get sucked into it with her.

Verdell shook her vigorously, "T? T? Tatiana? What are you doing? We don't have time for you to lose your shit. We need to call the police."

Tatiana stared at him wildly with fear in her eyes. For a moment, he knew that look of terror on her face, but it was from someone much younger. Each one of his victims had their own unique stare when faced with death. No one's death stare was ever the same as anyone else's.

Verdell tenderly stroked her face. Speaking to her slow and steady until she was responsive.

"Tatiana, you good?"

Even though she nodded, Verdell saw the fear and shame on her face. This situation exposed her weakness. If there was nothing else he was sure of about Tatiana, he knew for sure that she was not weak.

"You sure?" Verdell repeated.

Tatiana nodded again, more fervently this time.

Verdell asked gently, "Are you okay enough to call the police? It looks like Amber needs help as soon as possible."

"Yea, I got it. I can do it."

She took deep breaths. Verdell heard a noise over by the dumpster again, and this time he did not look away. He pulled out his pistol and yelled, "I suggest you come out because if I have to come over there, you're dead."

Verdell and Tatiana rose from the gravel together. He shoved her phone back into her hands after hitting 911 on the dial pad and making sure the line was connected. Verdell then took a step towards the streetlight, and someone took off running. Tatiana gasped.

"No, you worry about getting Amber some help. I'll meet you back at your place to check on you." Verdell said assuredly as he kissed her forehead before taking off into the night behind the person.

He had to find out what in the hell was going on. If they were not here for him this time, who knows about the next. Verdell always made sure to be so careful, and he could not continue to live like this and put those around him in danger. Whoever it was, Verdell knew they would be coming after him again.

Chapter 22

TIFFANY

Tiffany stepped out of the warehouse elevator into the modest hallway. A tiny bright red light caught her attention, compelling her to look up into a plainly visible camera. Thinking about how many cameras could be on her at that moment put her on edge. To the left of the camera was a small mirror allowing Tiffany to see the cage elevator behind her. The added line of sight in the cramped area made her claustrophobic. In her line of work, it was the minute details that said a lot about a person. To a regular individual, the camera and mirror appear as protection from the outside world. But that is not what Tiffany saw. She saw a possible Type A personality with a need to control the environment and dominate it; a borderline narcissistic sociopath. It was only an assumption using basic concepts from what little background she had on the Mellow family. From what her assistant, Blake, could dig up, the Mellows were a very wealthy and well-to-do family. All living members had careers spanning from ESQ, Ph.D., MD, SEN, CEO, COO, and CFO. Not one family member fell into the median income range or made less than four hundred seventy-five thousand a year. There had to be a bit of grand delusion in there somewhere, Tiffany gathered. No matter her gut feeling or her novice experience in psychoanalysis regarding this family, Tiffany had to scale back her desire to investigate. She was here for more personal reasons.

Blowing out a few breaths of nervous energy, Tiffany balled up her fist, ready to knock on the oversized door in front of her. However, it opened before her knuckles hit the steel.

"Come on in," said Barry, waving her through the threshold.

Walking past him and into his lavish home, Tiffany smiled. Not only did he smell like heaven, but whatever was on the menu smelled great too. Just a few feet into his condo, Tiffany froze in place. The rusted metal, peeling paint, and overall worn-down appearance of the warehouse building gave no hint of the renovations that were inside the condo. Barry's place had an open space concept with only a few support beams to separate the pink pearl granite and stainless-steel kitchen from the projector theater room. The double-sized office library opened to his recreational space and then his bedroom. She was impressed. The man had taste.

Barry zipped past her to tend to a boiling pot in the kitchen. "Make yourself at home. Dinner is almost ready."

"This is a really nice place you have here. You would never

know by the outside that it looks like a photo shoot for Best Homes and Gardens magazine in here." Tiffany gushed.

"Sit. Sit. Sit. I hope you like lamb, smashed potatoes, and brussels sprouts."

Tiffany scrunched up her nose and quickly attempted to save face when Barry caught her look of disgust.

"Well, I haven't exactly had Brussels sprouts or lamb, but it smells delicious."

To Tiffany's surprise, Barry laughed it off. "Are you vegan? Allergic?"

"No to both. And I don't mind trying new things," Tiffany said, as a matter of fact, flipping the napkin onto her lap.

"Great. That's what I like to hear." Barry placed the well-arranged dinner plate in front of her.

The food really did look and smell amazing. Tiffany unintentionally looked around for glowing red lights and any other indication that she was under surveillance. When her eyes shifted back to the table, Barry's penetrating gaze was the only thing watching her.

Cutting into the lamb on his plate, Barry asked, "Do you pray before you eat?"

Tiffany smirked, "I can say my own thanks if that's what you're asking."

"Good!" Barry responded impatiently, mouth full of smashed potatoes and brussels sprouts.

Tiffany tried to push the word *barbarian* from her mind as she watched Barry indulge.

"So, tell me. Why did it take so long for you to accept my invitation?"

Tiffany was not surprised at his forwardness. Ever since their meeting at Ocean Prime a couple of months ago, Barry had been very persistent and blunt regarding his intentions with her. In short, he wanted her bad. Instead of addressing his question, she redirected the conversation.

"How did Mayor Christen take being called out?"

"Not too well, but it comes with the job. Paul will be all right."

"How long have you known Paul?" She questioned.

Barry raised his hands in surrender. "I invited you here to get to know you, not to be interrogated or to talk about damn Paul."

"Don't you mean interviewed? I'm an investigative journalist, not the police."

"What's the difference? It all leads to the same place, right?" He sighed.

"And where is that?"

Barry wiped his mouth with his napkin. It was the first time during dinner that she saw him do something civil.

"It's somewhere between the truth and your version of justice." He hissed.

"Well, that's a vague and defeatist take on the police force, the news, and justice." She declared.

Barry guffawed, "if you think that's defeatist, wait until you hear my take on the electoral college."

That one made Tiffany laugh. She could get used to his dry humor.

Barry cleared his throat and rose from his seat with a wild glare in his eyes, making Tiffany slightly uncomfortable. They played with this flirtatious dance before. However, they were surrounded by a restaurant of people at that time, giving Tiffany a sense of security. Now, there was nothing between them but a hot plate and table space. And with Barry slowly closing in on her, licking his lips, even that collateral personal space dwindled.

Seductively, Barry disclosed, "There is something that I've wanted since I first laid eyes on you."

Playing it cool, Tiffany asked, "and that is?"

"You on my face," Barry said seriously.

Tiffany choked on a Brussels sprout. She did not know what turned her on more: Barry's direct approach to getting laid or his refusal to hide his craving for her.

"Excuse me?"

"I know you've felt our energy too. And I must say, I'm not interested in discussing much else until I get this off my chest."

Tiffany rose from the chair to put some space between them, but it did the exact opposite. Barry swooped in like a hungry lion on an unsuspecting prey. She barely had a moment to inhale before he was on his knees in front of her. Her back pinned against the island counter; he began placing wet kisses at her ankles. It tickled until Barry's lips reached mid-thigh when his wet kisses transitioned to suckling on her skin. Tiffany never had a man worship her before. It embarrassed her to look down at him and she was too curious at what he would do next to stop him. Tiffany forced herself to relax as Barry lifted her leg and placed it on his shoulder. Her eyes shut tightly when his strong hands reached under her dress and pulled at her panties. *Why is he going so slow? Is he giving me time to say no? Am I really going to go through with this? Ooo, his hands feel so damn good.*

"Look at me."

"Huh?" Tiffany came out of her thoughts.

"I want you to look at me." Barry insisted.

His fingers teased the lace lining of her panties. Tiffany's eyes squeezed tighter when his thumb entered her while the other played with her clitoris. Tiffany moaned involuntarily, "Mmmmmm."

"I asked you nicely to look at me. If I have to ask a third time, it won't be this satisfying."

Despite Barry's voice seeming gentle enough, Tiffany had no history with him to call his bluff. So, she blinked her eyes until they were open and fixated on his.

"Good girl." Barry crooned.

With his thumb still inside of her, Barry kissed her clit through her lace panties. The growing wetness between her thighs was shameful. *Damn, how long has it been?* Tiffany tried to remember but was coming up empty. She did not know if that was because her last time had not felt this good or if it had really been that long. Barry licked on her through the netting.

"Oooo, my God." Tiffany stuttered.

Barry had her standing up like a flamingo, Tiffany's grounded leg giving way. Without luck, she tried to push up on the counter to steady herself. Her arms shook uncontrollably under the unbalanced weight and the immense pleasure that came from Barry sucking on her jellybean. She knew her panties would be ruined after this experience. Tiffany toyed with the idea of letting Barry keep them, depending on how the evening finished. So far, she had no complaints.

Tiffany let her head fall back as she climaxed into Barry's open palm. She had never endured anything so roughly seductive and gratifying. Barry did not have to ask her to pay attention again. After that second orgasm, Tiffany hoped he saw her eyes begging him to continue ravaging her more.

*

Tiffany bit down on the twelve hundred thread count sheets. The rich cotton tasted sweet as she pulled the material through her teeth and across her tongue. The act made her already dry mouth even more parched, but she was unconcerned because Tiffany was in paradise. No plane ticket, no luggage, no exotic destination needed. Tiffany counted this as the fifth time Barry lapped the wetness from in between her thighs, and she felt like a blackout was coming soon. It would be a first for her; to pass out without the aid of alcohol. To regain control, Tiffany jumped up, trying to shake off the haze of aphrodisia that seemed to paralyze her. She made a weak attempt to pull away from him, but the lingering numbness in her legs made her fall back. Tiffany gasped in surprise when Barry grabbed her, his left hand wrapped around her waist and his right forearm across her breasts. He bent her forward over the side of the bed and began to thrust rhythmically into her from behind.

"Spread that ass open for me," Barry instructed.

Without hesitation, Tiffany backed up a little and steadied her knees on the bed, and reached behind her, opening herself for Barry to see it all.

"Good girl," Barry cooed, smacking her butt for good measure.

Everything in Tiffany seized as she embraced the orgasm that rose from her toes. Chilled sweat covered Tiffany's numb body as the tingling sensation washed over her in an explosive shutter. Sheets still clenched in her mouth; Tiffany purred a long "Mmmmm" as she released. Her juices surging out of her like river rapids and down Barry's rock-hard shaft.

"Shhhiiiit. Damn girl!" Barry stammered.

Sweat trickled from the tip of his nose down Tiffany's back. Barry picked her up and laid her gently on the bed as he slid out of her. Tiffany shivered as his warm breath fell on the nape of her neck. Barry planted kiss trails from each shoulder down to her hips, making Tiffany arch her back more with each touch. Tiffany caught the predatory gaze in Barry's eyes when she turned on her back. She knew Barry had more in store for her. The man was dangerous.

She never experienced lovemaking like this ever in her

life. If Tiffany had not known her lover count, she would have considered herself a virgin before this instance. It was like having sex with a karma sutra master. *Damn.* She never thought she would be attracted to someone like Barry. When he was not around Paul Christen, he was a different animal. Not the stoic and bland *yes man* Tiffany made him out to be.

Tiffany lay in bed, staring blankly at the ceiling, her mind racing. She accepted Barry's invitation with the intent of getting more information on Paul. Yet, at some point during the night, Tiffany abandoned that plan and let Barry's rock-hard shaft work her body over like rapid fire on a speed bag. The kinky shit he whispered in her ear gave her mind orgasms. She did not need to convince herself that the climax was necessary and worth it. Barry's arms wrapped around her as he snored softly into her neck. She would need to get extremely creative to get out of this one.

*

Tiffany woke up to the bright light of her phone screen on her face. She did not know when the sex-induced coma fell upon her, but Tiffany felt like a Mack truck hit her now.

"Tiffany. Get up. Your phone has been ringing for ten minutes. I suppose it's important if they keep calling back."

Ten minutes? Back-to-back calls? That couldn't be good.

"Oh shit." Tiffany got up and gathered her clothes.

"You're leaving?" Barry asked, disappointed.

"Uh. Yes. This is probably a story I got to catch. I really

enjoyed myself, though." Tiffany pecked Barry on the lips.

Barry kissed on the revealed parts of Tiffany's body until she was fully dressed.

"Well, at least let me walk you to the door."

When they arrived at the front door, Tiffany slipped her panties into Barry's pocket.

"Don't you need those?" Barry smirked.

"Don't you worry about that. I have more." Tiffany said seductively.

Their phones rang at the same time.

"I need to get this." They said simultaneously.

Barry embraced Tiffany for a long and deep kiss. It took everything in her to pull away. She still had tingling remnants from their earlier escapades. Tiffany waved goodbye as she stepped into the elevator, and Barry closed the lift gate behind her. *Short and sweet.* Tiffany pulled her thoughts from the reality of all that transpired and was trying to figure out what it meant for them going forward. This was a means to an end, and unfortunately, she underestimated where the end would be. Tiffany checked her phone. It was later than she realized. It was 12:42 a.m. and her assistant, Blake, called her six times in ten minutes. With this many missed calls, she knew this story had to be good.

Tiffany ruffled through her purse to find her keys. She would hate to be in a dark, unfamiliar place, looking lost and vulnerable. But Tiffany could not find them. *They must be in Barry's condo,* she concluded. Tiffany pushed the emergency stop button on the elevator and sent it back up to Barry's floor. When she stepped into the vestibule, Tiffany called Barry's phone and hung up when there was a busy signal. *Damn.* She forgot he had a call too. *Wait, he had a call too after midnight— what a coincidence.*

Tiffany knocked on the steel door, and it opened with little effort. She began the search for her keys on the floor underneath the kitchen table. Nothing. She heard a raised voice as she walked closer to the bedroom, silently retracing her steps.

"You fucked up, Barry," a woman's voice screeched through the speaker.

Tiffany did not see Barry in the bedroom at first. Then he came in from the bathroom, towel wrapped around his waist, his body still moist from the quick shower he must have taken. Tiffany ducked behind the support beam that separated Barry's office from his kitchen.

"Fucked up?" Barry chuckled sarcastically. "I don't fuck up. What are you talking about?"

"Did you see the news? Turn to Channel 8 News."

"I'm turning it on right now."

Barry watched the news story, silent. Tiffany could only hear bits and pieces of it. From the sound of it, there was a double homicide at a local gentleman's club. *Shit. I should be there. If I could just find my damn keys.* Tiffany needed to get closer. She had a feeling her keys were in the bedroom, but she could not just waltz in there. He would know that she was listening in on his conversation.

234

"Did you see her? Did you see that? That little bitch is still alive!" Sandra yelled.

Barry paused the screen. Tiffany attempted to look at the TV but could not make out the face of the woman. But whoever she was, she was important. And she should have been dead.

"How do you know that's her?"

"Oh! So now I'm stupid, Barry? I know what the fuck my husband's bastard love child looks like!"

"Sandra, it's been nine years."

"It could have been thirty-nine years, and I would still know that face." Sniffling, she continued, "Hell, she looks just like him."

"She does not look just like him, Sandra. You're exaggerating. Have you had anything to drink tonight?"

"Are you serious, Barry? While you're over there twiddling your passive ass thumbs, this thing could blow up in our faces. Do you want to explain to father why the plan didn't go as he instructed?"

Barry huffed loudly. "Fine. Let me do some digging, and I'll let you know what I find. Give me a week. Stay by your phone."

"You have forty-eight hours." Sandra threatened.

They hung up, and Barry walked back into the bathroom and turned on the shower. Tiffany waited until she heard the shower door slide close before moving from her hiding spot.

So, Barry's sister had a husband who cheated on her and created a love child. She could not forget that Barry was the one who was supposed to kill that said bastard child. The only things she needed to know now were: Number one: Who is Barry's sister Sandra married to? And two: Who was this child?

Tiffany found her keys on the floor under the foot of Barry's bed. And not a moment too soon because the water shut off in the bathroom. Quickly, Tiffany ran to the front door and was down the cage elevator and in her car in minutes.

Tiffany called Blake back.

"Where have you been? I've been calling you. Please tell me you've listened to my message and you're close. You're missing the story." Blake whined.

"Yea. I'm on my way but forget about that. I think I have an even bigger story. An exclusive." Tiffany said hesitantly but excited.

"Oh, yea? I should have known you were busy working on something. What is it?"

"Well, I got to check with some sources first. But think grand on a cosmological scale."

"Whoa, really? I mean, that's huge, Tiff. Do you need me to sit in on this one for you while you work on the cosmos? It sounds career-changing."

"I would like to think of it more along the lines of life-altering. Anyway, I'm almost to you now. Don't worry. I'll be working on both stories."

"Wait. There's something you're not telling me, isn't it?" Blake probed.

"Dammit, nosey. I'll tell you more when I have more. For

now, just sit tight, and make sure my mic is ready when I get there."

Tiffany hung up the phone. Despite her hands trembling on the steering wheel, she was driving in a straight line. She had an odd feeling that what she overheard was not any old run-of-the-mill crime. It felt a lot closer to home. And if Barry was in on it, Tiffany had no doubt that Paul Christen was somehow involved too. Tiffany pushed her foot down hard on the gas and prayed that her instincts were not wrong on this one.

Chapter 23

PAUL

Paul sauntered past Barry, holding open his condo door, and headed straight for the dry bar. He could feel Barry staring daggers into his back but refused to speak first. *Hell, he called me over here.* Hearing from Barry at all surprised Paul. They usually saw each other several times a day to touch base on crucial city issues like major crimes, political threats, partisan ties of the nouveau riche, and media surveillance. However, Barry had been missing in action these last few months, leaving he and Sandra to brainstorm countermeasures and solutions to his most pressing issues. And with Sandra being his wife, there was no way he could privy her to all of the sordid details of his affairs. That was usually Barry's job.

Most of the high-profile events in the city were canceled until further notice or until the police chief found the maniac responsible for the city's recent surge of homicides. *There is a possible serial killer on the loose, someone is trying to blackmail me, and that brazen dog of a TV reporter is raging a libel war with me. Where in the hell is Barry during any of it when I needed him most? And that little shit Dhorian is doing the bare minimum.* The more Paul thought about it all, the more perturbed he became. Paul's phone rang. He looked at it, scoffed, and sent the caller to voicemail.

Barry cleared his throat, "Boss, we have a problem."

Back still turned, Paul rolled his eyes and grumbled, "Tell me something I don't know."

"Sir?" Barry questioned.

Paul faced Barry and tried to quell the smug asshole trait he carried when he was in one of his passive-aggressive moods.

He shrugged. "I was in the middle of a Swedish massage, Barry. You're going to have to be more specific."

Paul emptied his drink all the way to the ice. Before Barry had a chance to respond, Paul guffawed to himself. He plopped the olive from his dirty martini into his mouth and cleared the space between him and Barry in seconds. He wanted Barry to feel the hot aggravation and disappointment that radiated from his skin.

"With everything I have going on, what problem could I have that's bigger than any other problem on my plate. Not that I would expect you to know anything about what I'm dealing with because you haven't been present for any of it."

Paul wanted Barry to know that a line had been drawn in the sand, and today he was going to be held accountable for his absence. Barry's face remained unemotional. Paul gritted his teeth. *Maybe Barry takes me for a joke. Time for me to stop beating around the bush.* "Barry, I have enough problems, and I'm starting to think that you're one of them."

"Excuse me?" Barry asked indignantly.

"I pay you to come to me with solutions and to fix things for me. But as of late, you are either absent or relaying an issue. Now, what is it this time?" He seethed.

Paul noticed Barry's eye twitch and his fingers coil into fists. *You better gauge your next actions carefully if you know what's good for you,* Paul thought as he matched Barry's resentful stare.

"This problem is one of a more personal nature." Barry gritted, visibly holding back any other sentiments he may have had regarding Paul's outburst.

Personal? Chills quivered their way down Paul's spine. Paul shoved his hands in the pants pocket of his suit and glanced at Barry to see if his brief moment of panic was noticed, but there was no reaction. Nothing. Barry was detached and his demeanor gave Paul pause. *If the news was so bad, why is Barry so cool about it? It must be terrible.* Paul instantly feared the worst. *Was Barry the blackmailer?*

The shrill ringing of Paul's phone broke through his mulling. He took it out of his pocket and put the ringer on silent. He and Barry were dealing with business matters. Sandra would have to wait. Paul placed his phone face down on the kitchen counter and then turned back to face an unbothered Barry.

"If you're done with your little temper tantrum. I can

show you why I called you here."

Barry's sedated tone and composed disposition made Paul hesitant to follow. Paul had never been afraid of Barry before. Despite all of the sinister things he knew Barry was capable of and had done during their twenty-two year friendship, he had never been in fear of his life. Not until now.

It was a short walk from the kitchen to the sitting room, but Paul had already identified three different ways to get to the front door if attacked and his weapon of choice if he needed to fight back. For the very first time, Paul sized Barry up. He was considerably more fit than Paul but not much taller. Paul could take him, but he would not win if it turned into a dog fight. In the sitting room, Barry turned on the TV and pressed play on the remote.

Paul stood away from Barry on the other side of the sofa. *I'll be damned if I'm going to be a sitting duck. I won't go out like that.* He remained tense, arms folded at his chest. But all that changed when he saw what was on the television. The scarred and rugged face of a dark-skinned man, who looked very much like a young Dhorian, was on the screen.

The search is still on for the person of interest, Verdell Hamilton, in tonight's double homicide. At 11:35 p.m. on Monday, witnesses say a woman came running into the club screaming for help...

The broadcast continued however, Paul no longer heard the reporter. His focus was on the name and face of the woman speaking to the reporter. Paul let his body sink as he fell back on the couch. The color drained from his face and water slipped from the corners of his eyes. Paul's mouth dropped open and his shock turned into rage.

"What??? How in the hell is *she* still alive? You have to be fucking kidding me? How could you screw up so damn bad, Barry? Not only do I want the arrogant son of a bitch that didn't finish the job, but I want her dead too. I don't care how you do it. I don't care who does it. But I want it done, and I want it done right!"

On second thought, "Barry, let's get Ms. LaSalle in here and see what she knows."

Barry's silent hesitation irritated Paul. "Is there another personal problem that I should be worried about?"

Paul gestured wildly with air quotes around the word *personal*. Barry moved his toothpick from one side of his mouth to the other while he grumbled nonchalantly and closed his office door.

Barry began, "For as long as we've known each other, I have attended every single one of…"

Paul cut him off, "Are you going to whine like some pussy or are you going to listen to what I have to say?"

"Well, it's actually two problems," Barry said with a drawl.

Barry's cell phone interrupted the brewing storm. "Hey, Sandy. Yes, he is here." Barry handed Paul the receiver.

"What, Sandra?" Paul said impatiently. "I'm in the middle of…" Paul went silent and hung up the phone.

The tension of the moment was forgotten. Paul looked at Barry with desperation. "Barry, I need you to drive me to

Tampa General Hospital. Something's wrong with Chris."

Barry grabbed his keys, donned his coat, and began walking to the front door. Clearly pissed, "This is your fault. You and all your damn secrets."

Paul scoffed, "My fault? Barry, I know we are not on the best of terms right now. But you don't know what you're talking about."

"Like hell, I don't. You're so busy trying to cover your shit with dirt that you left the holes for your family to fall in."

Paul sucked his teeth. "What? What the hell are you talking about? Just shut up and get me to my daughter."

Paul knew this situation could turn bad quickly, but he was over Barry's complaining. *He left me high and dry, not the other way around, and I refuse to kiss his ass."*

"You think you're better than me?" Barry asked heatedly.

Paul only gave Barry the side-eye as he followed him into the elevator cage.

*

When they exited the garage to the main street, Paul's mind was an explosion of bright lights, the smell of toasted bread and spices, the colorful blur of hurried passersby, and cause-and-effect scenarios. His city was filled with it all. And to think that his hand in its greatness would all be reduced to his mistakes and few indiscretions. He plastered a grin on his face, waving and nodding at all who noticed him in case the moment happened to be his last sighting. Paul wanted his people to see him as strong, not the coward he was feeling like in that instance.

Although the town car was roomy, Paul would rather be anywhere else than in the same space with Barry. Paul pulled at his collar to loosen his tie and rolled up his sleeves. If he thought Barry's apartment made him claustrophobic, then the car was his coffin.

Paul stared blankly out of the tinted window. Despite how long he lived in Tampa, Paul never got used to how different life looked on 8th street and when turning the corner onto 15th. Part of his mission as mayor was to rid the city of some of those disparities, but the reality was that making a change in politics was an uphill battle.

The right turn on Adamo Drive transformed brick cigar warehouses doubling as luxury lofts into commercial buildings, used car lots, and a string of gentlemen's clubs. The sight of them made Paul think back to the news story Barry played for him a half-hour earlier. *That man was the spitting image of Dhorian.* And then there was Tatiana. Paul's head fell into his hands. She was stunning and looked a little like Christina. *My daughter is a stripper. She would have been better off dead.* His parents were probably rolling over in their graves. Paul knew Madisin would never forgive him.

Barry's voice tracked him down in his apprehension. "You know what your prob is, Paul?"

If it was possible for Paul to fold himself into the seat, he would have. Barry's tone let him know that he was about to make an uncomfortable fifteen-minute ride infinitely unbearable. Paul released his reddened face from his palms.

"I am not in the mood for your shit, Barry. I just want to focus on my daughter right now. If that's fine with you."

"Don't be like that, Paul. She's my niece. I care about her too. But until we get to her, it looks like you could use some advice. Friend to friend."

Paul bristled at Barry's seemingly chummy nudge. Instead of responding, Paul gave Barry an examining glare and prepared himself for the *smarter than thou* soapbox experience.

"You know what your problem is? You care too much about what people think. That's why your lies catch up with you. See me, I tell everyone how it is and either you like it, or you don't. That way, there are no misunderstandings or hard feelings if you find out I'm something I'm not."

Is he serious? Something I'm not? So, Barry is the blackmailer. I wish he would just tell me what he knew so we could get this shit over with instead of stringing me along while he gets off playing Dr. Jekyll and Mr. Hyde.

"For instance, you and your little side piece. You couldn't pull out or make her swallow like a real man. Oh no, you just had to get the bitch pregnant. Well, I hope that the pu…"

Before Barry could get the rest of his sentence out, Paul swung a tight left that connected deep and quick. The blow caught Barry in the rib cage, making the car swerve, almost hitting the center island of the Channelside roundabout.

Paul grabbed at the *oh-shit* handle above his window in

case the car went spinning out of control but let go to grab his stinging face after Barry retaliated with a right.

"What the fuck is wrong with you, Paul? I'm driving! Almost a decade and you're still sensitive about dead pussy when your black ass should be concerned with more present matters."

That is it! Paul reached over and interlocked his fingers around Barry's throat, squeezing for dear life. The scenery outside of the car whizzed past them in a blur as Barry tried to regain control of the car and fight Paul off of him.

That's it. I'm going to jail for the rest of my life. Paul acknowledged the thought as clear as day. The voice that birthed the idea was calm and resolute. It would be a fact. He knew the consequences of his actions. Even so, Paul could not let go of Barry's neck.

That is until the *chirp chirp* of the police siren, and the red and blue flashing lights cleared his vision and softened his resolve. Reality rushed back to their current situation. Barry grasped his neck, coughing and gasping for air. Paul was surprised Barry managed to safely get the car pulled over. Despite the boiling tension between them, both Paul and Barry stared blankly ahead, breathing deeply, awaiting the officer. Barry pushed the button to roll down the window.

"Mr. Mellow. Mr. Mayor." - the sheriff tipped his brown suede wide-brimmed hat – "I saw the car swerve and noticed the tag was one of your cars, Mr. Mayor. I thought I'd check to make sure everything was all right."

The shit-eating grin on Sheriff Dunn's face made Paul's chest tighten. There was a silent game of chess between the politicians and policemen of the city. Mayor Paul Christen had just been checked.

Paul leaned over into the driver's seat, avoiding Barry's clenched fist. Paul had no doubt that if given the opportunity, Barry would try to sneak another lick in.

"Hi there, Sheriff Dunn. Nice day we have here, isn't it? Barry and I got a call that Chris was in the hospital, and we are in a bit of a hurry to get there. Please accept my apologies for Barry's speeding."

Paul ignored Barry's frown and quickly added, "You know Chris is like a daughter to him."

Barry's sharp elbow jugged him in his diaphragm.

"Oompf," Paul winced.

"Are you sure everything is alright, Mr. Mayor? It looks like you may need a hospital yourself. You got a nasty shiner starting to form there." The sheriff inquired pointedly.

Paul and Barry exchanged uneasy glances. Paul's eyebrow shot up, and his mouth dropped as if he had not already felt the skin tightening around his eye. He pulled down at the visor to look at the ugly red, discoloration that he could already feel overtaking the left side of his face.

Paul saw the sheriff slowly moving for his utility belt. As bad as Paul wanted to see Barry tased at this moment, he did not want him dead. At least not yet. Paul coughed before starting again.

"Oh yes. The swerving. There was a nasty-looking tree

spider on the dash, and it gave Barry and me a run before Barry here swerved and knocked it out the window. I wasn't prepared, and my head hit the window. But you are right. It looks really bad and will be the second thing I look into when we get to the hospital."

"Must've been one hell of a tree spider." The sheriff slow drawled, trying to get a better look into the car.

Barry's fingers flexed on the steering wheel; his jaw tight.

Paul leaned across the car again towards the open driver window.

Sensing Barry's agitation, "As you can see, Sheriff Dunn. Everything is fine unless for some odd reason you'd want to arrest Barry and me to keep us from getting to my Chris."

A nervous laugh thundered from the sheriff. "Oh no, Mr. Mayor, I wouldn't dare. I'm glad to hear everything is alright, and I hope Chris is okay too."

"Why, thank you, Reginald. If it's all the same to you, we'll be on our way now."

"Yes, sir. Drive safe."

Barry's finger turned from pink to red as he pressed the button for the automatic window to go up.

"You know this isn't over, right?" Barry growled as he put the car in drive.

"Just get me to the damn hospital." Paul sneered.

Knock. Knock. Knock.

They both were startled by Sheriff Reginald Dunn's eager face at the driver window again.

Knock. Knock. Knock.

Barry reluctantly let down the window. "Yes, officer."

"Hey there. I was thinking I could escort you all over to the hospital. You know, to make up for the time lost here."

Barry tried to reject the offer, but Paul instantly spoke up. "That'll be nice. We'll follow you."

Chapter 24

DHORIAN

After another wasted night of binge drinking, the hot water soothed Dhorian's angst. The pulse setting massaged the tension in Dhorian's shoulders and back. The steam seemed to clear his sinus pressure and ease his migraine. All of that changed when he stepped out of the shower, and the warm mist choked his calm. Dhorian rushed to open the bathroom door and let in a bit of cool air when something on the television caught his ear.

Authorities have now identified Verdell Hamilton as a person of interest in relation to this past Monday's double homicide at the Top Hat Gentlemen's Club in West Tampa. Tampa PD is asking for the public's assistance in locating Verdell. Sources say that Verdell Hamilton has prior run-ins with the law and a previous charge of first-degree murder. If anyone sees this person, please do not

engage. He should be considered armed and dangerous.
Anyone with information about this individual is asked
to call or text the TPD confidential tip line at (813) 777-
9311.

Dhorian sprinted from the bathroom and sat on his bed, grabbing the remote to rewind the live feed. It began to playback, and there was the picture of his cousin Verdell's mug plastered across the entire TV screen. Dhorian watched the news story again.

Now we turn it over to Tiffany LaSalle with more of the
story.

Thank you, Bob.

He rewound the live feed again and paused it on Verdell's face.

"My God," Dhorian whispered.

If he had not known any better, the man's picture on the television was him. He stepped down from the bed and crawled in disbelief toward the TV.

"What in the hell?" Dhorian asked himself.

The face on the TV had a scar above the right cheek. It was not Dhorian's face. *Am I going crazy?* Dhorian never thought he and Verdell looked much alike when they were growing up. But sure enough, he saw it tonight. He was not as dark as Verdell, but the similarities were there. He may have been hungover, but not out of his mind.

What the hell was Verdell doing here? I thought he was locked up. I went to the Top Hat, and I never saw him there. Dhorian's mind ran ahead of him. He stepped over the broken glass from the night before to pour himself a drunk.

Dhorian found a pen and began to scribble his and Verdell's name in the middle of a blank sheet of paper. Around them, he wrote his mother and father's name and his aunt and uncle's name. He wrote down his and Verdell's birthday under their names. Somehow, he forgot they were on the same day. This only made Dhorian write more fervently. He circled him and his dad because he knew his mother could not have given birth to him. Then he circled Verdell, his aunt, and his uncle. *Was there a possibility that his dad was not his biological father?* Dhorian's pen dropped.

It can't be. There was only one way to know for sure if his speculation was correct, and Dhorian's inhibitions were just low enough to make the request. He picked up the phone.

"Yea, it's me. Get me everything you can on Annemarie Anderson Hamilton.

Dhorian stumbled a bit before hanging up the phone, and he reacted too late to keep himself from toppling to the ground. The tears came and fell in line with the shards of glass that dressed his floor. Like that glass, he had finally broken.

*

"Mr. Hamilton. Mr. Hamilton!"

Dhorian heard Joanie hog calling his name as soon as he stepped foot into the main lobby. He had a mind to walk right past the receptionist desk pretending to be fascinated by whatever new thing was on his phone. Nonetheless, his assistant Joanie was not letting him off that easily. She met him with a hot cup of coffee, made just how he liked it and was back to her station just as quick. *Damn you, Joanie,* Dhorian thought. *Haven't you ever heard of an inside voice?*

Dhorian could not stay mad at Joanie long. She was what his mother called 'sweet as pie'. *And she comes bearing gifts.* Dhorian savored the hot toddy libation.

"Mr. Hamilton, I'm glad I caught you." *More like cornered and trapped me.* Dhorian paused to sip his drink before giving Joanie his full attention.

"Mayor Christen has called twice for you this morning. It sounded pretty urgent. Would you like for me to call him back for you?"

Her normally youthful and bright face was now overshadowed by perfectly arched and deeply furrowed brows. Dhorian checked his watch. *Two calls before 8 a.m. is not a good thing.* He leaned onto the welcome desk and asked in hushed tones, "did he say what was wrong?"

"Only that I send you to Tampa General Hospital and you come over there urgently. Would you like for me to call a car?"

"No, Joanie. I'll leave in a second. I only need to pick up a few files, and I'll be on my way."

"Great. I'll give him a call and let him know you'll be there shortly."

Dhorian saw Joanie's lips moving, but an eerie spirit gathered in the space surrounding him, smothering the room in silence.

The heaviness sat at the joints of his knees, rooting his body to the needle felt carpet. Staring at nothing, in particular, Dhorian's subconscious contemplated the series of events that would require his presence at a hospital before 8:00 a.m. He kept coming back to the same conclusion—*nothing good at all.*

"Mr. Hamilton!"

Dhorian practically leaped out of his skin. Joanie's shrill voice screeched for his attention. Paperwork spilled from his briefcase to the floor along with his coveted fresh cup of brew. Dhorian mirrored an owl in the way he turned his head, checking the office to see if anyone saw him make a fool of himself. But that only made him feel even more ridiculous when he remembered that his was the only occupied office suite on the floor.

"Let me help you with that," Joanie sighed, always willing to assist.

Dhorian reluctantly joined her on the floor to collect his things. And he did it just in the nick of time. *Oh no. She can't see that.* Dhorian almost ripped the documents, snatching them from Joanie's unsuspecting hands.

He snapped, "Don't worry about these. Can you please just go make yourself useful and find something to get this coffee up with?" shooing Joanie away.

"Hmmph." Joanie was to her feet in an instant, hands firmly at her hips.

Dhorian felt bad. He really did. She was on her hands and knees in her best business dress, helping him clean up his mess, as she tended to do in one way or another, and here he was being an ass. Her eyes drilled into him, waiting, almost demanding an apology, but Dhorian could not meet them to give one. His behavior had even embarrassed him this morning. There was no explanation for it, other than his shit of a life. Now Paul Christen's ambiguous hospital call was adding to the pile.

Fortunately for him, Joanie did not speak on his cantankerous disposition. Instead, she simply headed in the direction of the common area for something to clean up the spilled brew.

Why can't everyone in my life be no drama like Joanie? Dhorian gathered all the scattered papers and stuffed them into his briefcase, with the exception of the document Joanie almost saw. How he obtained it and why he had a copy of Paul Christen's birth certificate and medical records would not be a hard thing to explain at the surface. However, he would not be able to hide his deviant intentions if he were asked.

Dhorian doubled his steps toward his office, leaving Joanie to deal with his clutter. *Why would Paul Christen need to meet me at the hospital? Does he know I had him investigated?* He had to get to his office to make sure the files were still there. If anyone found out what he knew before he had a chance to use the information, he would be done for, and there would be no coming back. No sooner than Dhorian's briefcase hit the desk, his cell phone rang. The brightly lit screen flashed several times with the strangely familiar number before he finally decided to pick it up.

"Dhorian Hamilton speaking."

Squabbling voices greeted him.

"Call him."

"I am calling him." Paul shouted.

"Yes, but you said you called him already."

"I called his work phone but not his cell phone. I'm calling that now."

"Well, did he pick up?"

"I can't tell Sandra; you won't hush up long enough for me to hear."

Sandra? What did she want? Dhorian pondered.

"Hello?" Dhorian said into the phone.

"Ah. Yes. Hello Dhorian. We have an emergency... Umm... Over here at Tampa General, and we need you to come as soon as possible."

"Will someone tell me what the hell is going on? Is everything alright?" Dhorian asked.

Sandra's voice came through the background again, "What did he say? Is he coming?"

Dhorian removed the phone from his ear to look into the chaos he heard coming from the receiver.

"Uh. It's not. But it will be." - there was a long pause on both sides of the phone – "Listen. The sooner you get here, the better. Do you understand?"

"Understood."

"Good. We're in room 2123."

Dhorian dropped his phone into his satchel along with the other papers he needed and was out the door.

*

Ten minutes later, Dhorian was speeding up the emergency entrance ramp and emptying his pockets at security.

"Yes, I'm looking for a patient by the name of Paul Christen."

"Yes, sir. Just one second."

Several seconds passed, and the woman was still typing on her computer. Dhorian fidgeted, looking back and forth between his watch and the noisy clock on the hospital wall. He walked in short circles, wandering away from the desk and slowly making his way back.

"Sir. No one by that name is a patient here."

"What? Are you sure?"

"Yes, sir. I checked several times."

Dhorian slid his hand down his face and growled in frustration.

"Was there anything else you needed, sir?"

Dhorian was ready to take the sign as his omen to leave. But then he remembered the room number.

"Umm. Yes. Actually, he gave me a room number."

He fumbled through his phone, looking for the note where he wrote down the room number.

"Yes, found it. I'm looking for Room 2132."

Dhorian watched as the nurse keyed in more information in the computer, glancing between his license, her screen, and his face. He noticed the security guard to his right watching them intently. Dhorian nodded his way, and the officer returned the nod, but it did not ease the growing tension.

"Room 2132. Christina Christian. They've been expecting you..." the nurse said plainly as she placed his license on the counter. "Behind me to your left is the West bank of elevators. You'll want to take it to the Rehab bridge on the second floor and then follow the signs to room 2132."

Dhorian felt the heaviness in his chest coming on again.

Christina's here? And in rehab? What was so urgent about Chris' rehab that Paul would want me here? It's about time they dealt with her issue as a family anyway.

Dhorian was certain his reasoning would propel his leaden feet to the elevator. Yet his logic was no match for his gut. Dhorian pressed the up button on the West Bank wall. Waiting for an elevator to arrive, Dhorian overheard harsh whispers and his instincts told him to move out of the line of sight. Listening to other people's drama always took the stress away from his own. He surmised it was one of the biggest benefits of being a lawyer. From the few words he could hear, someone was in hot water.

The elevator dinged, and the doors opened. Dhorian stepped in and five other passengers, who appeared out of nowhere, boarded the elevator behind him, including the angry whisperers. They all bustled in, pushing him to the back. Dhorian shrunk into the corner and buried his head in his phone as he recognized the side profile of one of the mumblers, Barry Mellow. Right hand and brother-in-law to Mayor Paul Christen. *Barry's here too?* Dhorian squinted, unsuccessfully pinpointing where he knew the other guy from. He kept drawing blanks even though Dhorian knew he had seen that face somewhere before. The elevator arrived on the second level, rehab bridge. Dhorian watched cautiously as everyone spilled out of the elevator, keeping a few feet in between him and everyone else.

"What choice does he have? The guy on TV looks a lot like him. It would be easy to add him into the mix and get charges brought up for conspiracy, collusion, even murder." Barry mumbled.

"But that's only if he doesn't what? Marry the mayor's daughter?"

The duo stopped abruptly, and Dhorian ducked behind a supply cart.

"Marry the mayor's daughter? If only it were so simple. You don't get how big this is, do you? You think this is some game? Let me help lessen your ignorance."

"I, I, I wasn't saying that, Bar. I was just thinking that..." Captain Stewart stammered.

Cutting him off, Barry mushed the man's forehead with his index and middle fingers as he enunciated each word. "But that's just it. We don't pay you to think. We pay you to act. And you told us you were keeping close tabs on the schmuck."

"Frank is handling him. You have my word?"

"Are you sure you have enough to cover those kinds of bets? Because if Frank had it handled, we would not be in this hospital with the mayor's suicidal and pregnant daughter." Barry gritted.

Dhorian watched breathlessly.

Barry continued, "So let me break it down for you. And if I ever fucking hear what I'm about to tell you again, you can kiss your new wife and baby goodbye. And you, my friend, won't get another chance to start over this time."

From his viewpoint behind the mile-high pile of bedsheets and single-ply rolls of tissue paper, Dhorian could see the man slumped over, sweat beads running down his face. He truly felt sorry for the man. Dhorian heard rumors of Barry being the muscle but never witnessed it for himself.

Barry slapped the man heartily on the shoulder before asking him, "We clear?"

The poor guy, who reminded Dhorian of a slim Ashton Kutcher from *That '70s Show*, except with glasses, jumped at the weight of Barry's hand before nodding his understanding.

"Good. So, my sister is married to the washed-out, lying-ass mayor. The same mayor that you and I are going to frame for the guttings that have been happening in this city. The same mayor who has past connections to bribery and murder with the guy on TV. The only guy that may be able to clear him is this weasel ass protege lawyer, Dhorian Hamilton, who looks like the guy on TV. I mean, is any of this connecting for you, Captain Stewart?"

Captain Stewart? Good, the man has a name and a title. Shouldn't be too hard to look up. Dhorian ignored the weasel-ass lawyer description of himself. Barry was becoming a more violent and treacherous version of the well-put-together "yes" man that Dhorian knew. Captain Stewart only dipped his head.

"Good. That bastard got all he needed from Chris, enough to get her pregnant, and then threw her away like she was some floozy when she tried to tell him."

"Damn, that's cold, Bar."

"No, that's worse than cold Stewart. It's a nasty little trait that he and his sleaze of a mentor have in common. Weaseling their way into places they don't belong. And sticking their dicks in women that are out of their league."

"So why not kill him?"

Barry's laughter unnerved Dhorian.

"No. Killing him would be elementary. He has debts to pay that he doesn't even know exist. He could prove useful to the family for a while. Then and only then would we toss his ass out on the streets. But right now, we need to give him something worth losing. We need him in our pockets and loyal to the family."

"Yea. That sounds really good, Bar," Captain Stewart chuckled hesitantly as he and Barry started on their way to Christina's room, Dhorian assumed.

Dhorian, on the other hand, took the end of their conversation as his cue to be anywhere but room 2132. Anywhere but the hospital. Anywhere but in the city. Dhorian pulled out his phone and sent Joanie a text to cancel his meetings for the rest of the week and to book him a flight to Grenada. He needed a vacation.

Dhorian tucked his phone and slowly made his way back to the elevator bank, looking to make sure no one was watching him. As he was stepping on the elevator, he heard…"Dhorian! Dhorian!"

Dhorian stopped suddenly in his tracks. His bladder instantly felt heavy as urine pushed to find its own escape.

"Where have you been? We've been waiting on you, and Chris won't stop asking about you."

Dhorian did not know if the recognizable voice put him at ease or made him too afraid to run away. Uncertain about what to do next, Dhorian did the only thing he could think to do. He slowly turned around to face Sandra Christen.

Chapter 25

TATIANA

"So, tell me how you met my mother again?"

Tiffany made a habit of coming around after interviewing Tatiana on the night of the shooting. The news reporter's request for a follow up only two days after the fatal event had Tatiana contemplating escape plans. Not even the police questioned her about the second body. Tatiana thought it strange, but a blessing. She had no idea if one of those bodies were Cairo's, or not, however she had not received any threatening texts or calls since that night either. In fact, neither the police nor the news stations had released information on the second victim. The thought of a second meeting with the Channel 8 journalist made Tatiana want to run except she was much more curious as to what she could find out from her. *Maybe it was Cairo. Were there going to be more questions about Verdell's involvement?* She had not heard a peep from him either. *Was he the second victim? Couldn't be?* Tatiana remembered him running into the alley. She saw that with her own eyes. Or did she? Tatiana's uncertainty is why she needed to show up to the meeting.

"How is your grandmother? Are you in school? You look so much like your mother."

What started as a follow up lunch at a jerk joint downtown shifted into an awkwardly familial hour of interrogation about her personal life. Turned out her long-forgotten play auntie and deceased mother's best friend was no other than, Tiffany LaSalle.

In the last nine months Tatiana ran into all kinds of people; classmates from elementary school; teachers, old neighbors, deacons and pastors. There were not many people who recognized her or knew her past. Not many people who were born in Tampa left Tampa. Tatiana would smile politely, even stare long enough to catch their attention, but they all looked at her like she was a ghost. Like she was out of place. Now here was this woman who clearly knew who Tatiana was, knew of her past, and had no problem barging herself into Tatiana's present. She felt naked and bulldozed. The interview about Amber's murder turned into a reunion that Tatiana was not at all emotionally prepared for. Despite Tatiana's reservations about good old Auntie Tiffany, Nanna had convinced her to accept all the love she could. Everyone needs someone to look out for them when it's genuine. So here they were in Nanna's kitchen playing twenty questions reminiscing over half eaten plates of eggs and bacon.

"So, tell me how you know my mother?" Tatiana asked again.

"What? Seriously? I've already told you at least twenty times over the past two days."

Silence. Tatiana had to stop herself from rolling her eyes. She had not invited Tiffany over as a guest. Today nor the past two days. She just kept showing up and always knew what time to catch her. So, any sarcasm, attitude, or just plain meanness Tiffany had to endure, she brought on herself.

Tiffany sucked her teeth at the wide eyed and inquisitive Tatiana who with folded arms was not giving an inch.

"You don't believe me? These pictures aren't real enough for you?" Tiffany pointed to the opened photo book.

Hearing stories about Madisin Foster made Tatiana feel like she was listening to a life that was not connected to her own. Tiffany's flamboyant hand gestures and fast-talking, matter of fact southern accent embellished the narrative and enhanced the unbelievability of it all. Tatiana always thought her mother was the greatest; close to superhuman even. Yet, hearing about her mother's brokenness, need for healing, and self-love journey during the time Tiffany was in their lives made Tatiana see her mother in a different light. Not as weak, but as courageous. Tatiana always wondered what shattered her mother in the first place. So yes, she was serious. Tatiana could care less if she had been told the same story one thousand times. To Tatiana, Madisin Foster was only her mother, but Tiffany's stories made her a woman. Not much different from herself.

Tatiana slid the photo book closer to her side of the countertop. Her eyes lit up at the smiling images of her mother. "I don't think I ever got a chance to see momma this happy."

"Oh, you did. You were so spoiled and selfish that you only wanted her to be that happy with you." Tiffany stated, matter-of-factly, while playfully tapping Tatiana on her shoulder.

"I was not that bad," Tatiana pouted. She did not find the statement funny one bit.

"Oh yes, you were. Your momma had you rotten. I told her three years was too long to breastfeed a child."

Tatiana and Tiffany both broke out into laughter. Surprised to see Nanna up from bed.

Tatiana rushed to her grandmother's side to help her to a stool at the high round kitchen table.

"Now Nanna you know you are not supposed to be out of bed. You should be taking it easy."

"Mmm mmm", Nanna rebuked. I heard y'all laughing and talking about my baby. Them doctors don't know nothing. They done ran all their tests, now I'll let God and some smiling do the rest. I'll be fine. Stop fussing over me." Nanna swatted Tatiana away with her hand towel and waved at Tiffany, "Keep talking. Don't mind me."

Tatiana sighed. She knew there was no winning. Especially when Nanna got to rhyming. Her mother used to do the same thing. It was nostalgic to see where she picked it up from.

Before Tiffany could start again, Nanna swiped the book and flipped through the pages. "Ooooo, I remember this one."

"Where?" Tatiana pushed off her seat to peek across the table at the photo in question. She caught a quick glance at her mother dressed in a pretty money green Empire waistline dress with a tan shawl draped over her shoulders while she looked into the wind. The trees and the shelter by the rocky shore in the background reminded her of a park her mother used to take her to when she was little. The name of the park seemed to escape her though. *It was Cypress something.*

Tiffany grabbed the book and held it close to her chest for a second, screaming out a high pitch of recollection.

"Oooo! This was the time your mother had a terrible day at work. I mean everything that could go wrong, went wrong." Tiffany used her fingers to count off the incidents. "She spilled coffee on the boss' wife, her printer ran out of paper and then when she found some paper, the printer ran out of ink. You would not believe how hard it is to run up and down three floors of an office with five-inch stilettos!"

Stilettos? Tatiana questioned. She had never seen her mother with so much as a wedge on. *Maybe she changed from her comfortable flats into stilettos when she got to work?* Madisin Foster had become an enigma over a span of days.

"Oh yeah! And then to make matters worse, Madisin went to the ladies room during a break between meetings. We only had like five-minute breaks, so we knew how to go in like two... three minutes max. So, when I didn't see her, I knew something was wrong. I go into the ladies room to find her and she is at the sink using foam soap and paper towels just scrubbing the hem off her cardigan. I called her name and couldn't get her to look at me right away, but I read the room. There was a trail of liquid from one of the stalls to the sink. I could only assume the worst."

"Are you telling me that my mother had pee on her clothes? Like piss?"

"Alright now little girl," Nanna berated her.

Nanna I am twenty-one years old, Tatiana thought, but she did not dare say what she was thinking. No matter how grown Tatiana thought she was, she knew she would always be a little girl in Nanna's eyes.

"Sorry, Nanna. But in pee?" Tatiana repeated for Tiffany, not losing a step.

"Yes, I assumed, I mean the floor was wet."

"What did she do? I mean, was it even her pee?" Tatiana was horrified. She hated public restrooms, but for your clothes to fall in the toilet of a public restroom was beyond comprehension. Even though she found herself disgusted at the idea of it, the image of her mother's scrunched up and mortified face made Tatiana laugh so hard she felt her side would split. The look on her grandmother's and Tiffany's faces were even more comical. Tatiana slid off her stool onto the floor hit with the sudden urge to use the restroom.

"Ooop, let me go before I mess myself up." Tatiana grabbed at the crotch of her pants, as if it would hold back her bladder, and ran into the hallway bathroom. She relieved herself and coughed to clear the built up giggles from her chest.

"Woo, that was good stuff. I haven't laughed like that in forever."

Tatiana washed her hands and face in the sink and stilled. *It couldn't be.* Had she misread the room? *Is somebody crying?* She turned the doorknob slowly. She hesitated at what would await her in the kitchen that was only moments earlier, filled with happiness. *How could the energy change that quickly? What did I miss?*

Tatiana rounded the corner on pins. Sure enough, Tiffany was crying, head buried deep in her hands. No, not crying. More like bawling uncontrollably. Tatiana glanced at Nanna who had Tiffany coddled in her arms, stroking her hair to quiet her. "Shhh now."

Tatiana cleared her throat. "Ummm what did I miss? I'm sorry if I was ru..."

Nanna didn't let her finish. "Shush child and put some tea on. Give her a minute to gather herself."

Tatiana did as she was told and came back to the kitchen table with three steaming cups of decaffeinated green tea and sweetened milk. By this time, Tiffany's eyes were dry but red as a tomato.

"Thank you, Babygirl," Tiffany managed to say past the knot of emotions still lodged in her throat.

Tatiana shifted in her seat at the mention of the pet name her mother gave her. It felt like being called by a ghost. The name did not go unnoticed by Nanna either. Silence rushed in and held the room hostage for the next few minutes. The women sipping their tea, looking off into their own bits of space. Tatiana was just about to excuse herself when Tiffany grabbed her hand so swiftly it stunned her in place.

"I want to apologize for my reaction. It was inappropriate and I am so embarrassed." - Tiffany sniffed, wiping away her tears with the tips of her free hand. - "I'm all over the place. You'll have to excuse my bluntness, but I don't know any other way to say this other than to just get it out. I can try to fill in the holes later if you need me to. But I've been carrying this guilt in me for close to a decade and I never thought I'd have the opportunity to, well to" - Tiffany hesitated - "to get it right." She squeezed Tatiana's and Nanna's hands.

The stern look on Nanna's face is the only thing that settled Tatiana. Both of them acting up right now would not be good. She had a feeling whatever Auntie Tiffany had to say might get her jabbed in the damn throat, which is why she held everyone's hands so tightly at that moment.

Instead of pulling away, Tatiana stared blankly and nodded. Nanna simply continued sipping her tea. *Maybe Nanna already knows what this was about.*

Pointing at the picture Tiffany began explaining, "This is the day your mother told me that she felt like she was being followed."

"Followed?" Nanna and Tatiana yelled at the same time.

"Yes, followed." Tiffany sniffled.

Whatever hardness Tiffany had found was lost with the hard penetrating glances that bore through her from the other side of the table. Her next words spilled from her lips like running water.

"The garage lights were already acting funny and she said she heard footsteps behind her when she was walking to the car. I told her she was paranoid. And then you were taken a few days before your twelfth birthday. It all went downhill after that." Tiffany stared at nothing in particular before turning her eyes back to Tatiana.

"I think your mother thought I had something to do with it, at the time. I mean I couldn't blame her cause the last thing I told her was that I had you. And she trusted me," Tiffany's voice cracked.

"Maybe if I would have listened to her, she would still be here. You would have never been taken…"

Tears, regret, it all came too late. For her abduction and torture to be reduced to "being taken". Tatiana could not stand to hear one more word. She never told anyone what she went through and swore to never relive it again. It was all too much.

"Taken? Taken? Is that what you think happened? That I was taken?" Tatiana's outburst had the room's full attention.

"Well, I was not taken. I was abducted. I was tortured. They cut me open." She lifted her shirt to expose the scar above her hip. "They told me they would kill me if I didn't stop screaming. Kill everybody I cared about if I asked for my mother again. They cut me. They stole from me and left me for dead in a funky ass alley." Tatiana cried out.

"You know what's worse than dying? Actually, thinking

you're going to die and then being expected to trust people like you and to be normal after that shit. That's what's worse!"

Tatiana's tirade took her around the room in a storm and it was only the dampness she witnessed falling from Nanna's eyes that brought her back to the present and out of her solitary darkness.

Through clenched teeth, Tatiana seethed, "Your fault or not, I hope the bastards that did this to me and killed my mother are dead. Cause if not Imma…"

Nanna cut in… "You know God has a way of dealing with these things baby."

Tatiana pulled away from her grandmother's soothing hands.

"I hear you Nanna. But he ain't getting the job done quick enough," Tatiana chuckled cynically through her pain.

"It's been nine damn years and everybody wants me to act like all is well and like nothing ever happened, but I can't Nanna. They killed your daughter, your only child, in your face. Now maybe you have found your peace and can walk away, but the older I get, the more in my face" - she pointed angrily at Tiffany - "the damage is. I've tried to push it all down and forget, but my past keeps finding me and catching me off guard. I wasn't ready for this," making sure Tiffany caught her meaning, "and I didn't ask for any of it."

Tiffany spoke up again. "After I heard about the explosion, I looked for you. I swear I did. The police report said three bodies were found but only one arrived at the Medical Examiner's office and the rest was buried. I didn't know what to think. But I know there is a reason for us finding each other now."

Tatiana's face read *bitch please*. But her mind was still racing. Playing with the key dangling from her necklace, Tatiana had an idea.

"Maybe there is a reason for it all."

"Huh?" Tiffany questioned.

"My mother gave me this key for my birthday. She said it would tell me everything I needed to know, even things about my dad."

Tatiana dodged Tiffany's curious hands when she reached for the necklace.

"I've been meaning to check out the safety deposit box at the bank. But with Nanna recovering," Tatiana looked at her grandmother and hesitated, "I didn't want to pull her from bed to come with me."

Tiffany quickly spoke up, "you don't even have to ask. Let me grab my purse. We can take my car. Nanna do you need to eat before we go? Do you have everything you need for a few hours until we get back?"

Nanna looked irritated. Glancing back and forth between Tatiana and Tiffany. "I am not a child and I refuse to be a burden. She tried to get up from the table and stumbled a little". Tatiana caught her arm before she went down.

"Nanna, no one thinks you're a child. And you're definitely not a burden. I. Well...," Tatiana tilted her head Tiffany's way, "We just want to make sure that you are okay and healing."

Her grandmother looked at her solemnly, "You know I did the best I could by you, don't you?"

"Yes, Nanna. I do." Tatiana kissed her grandmother gently on the cheek before leading her back upstairs to bed.

*

The drive to the credit union was quiet and thankfully short. No words were spoken between the two women as they exited the car and entered the bank. They both understood the mission and were hesitant to speak from fear of jinxing the answers they hoped to find. It took everything in her to come today and she did not know if her stomach was up for the trip again. She fought back the nausea and exchanged a hopeful glance with Tiffany.

Tiffany took her cue to step in and flagged down the first bank employee she saw. "Excuse me, can we please see the bank manager. It's an important family matter, if you will."

The banker looked both women over. Nervousness reeking from only one of them. He nodded and left without a word. Tatiana was sure he was going to do as they asked despite the line of waiting people. The five minutes ticked to ten, and Tatiana grew unsure. Just as she was ready to go outside for air, or leave, she had not decided which yet, someone called her name.

"Ms. Foster. Ms. Foster. F.O.S.T.E.R? Is there anyone here by that name?"

"Uh, yes. That's us." Tiffany jumped in front of Tatiana to announce.

The bank manager looked skeptically at them.

Tatiana tried to hold back her flustered look of irritation at Tiffany's eagerness to be overly involved in her life. *She probably can't wait to get a good story out of this. Damn reporters.*

Tatiana stepped forward to speak up, giving Tiffany the side eye. She quickly shrunk back after getting the hint.

"Yes, I'm Ms. Foster."

"Great. Ms. Foster, I'm the branch manager, Ms. Moorely. Would you like to speak in my office regarding your matter?"

Tatiana cleared her throat to answer, but her nerves caught her words before they could escape.

"Ms. Foster? Are you all right?"

Tatiana jumped when she felt Tiffany grab her hand. She did not mind so much when Tiffany spoke for her this time.

"Yes, I think that's best." Tiffany stated.

"And you are?" Ms. Moorely asked.

Tatiana gained the use of her tongue back, "she's a family friend."

Tiffany smiled appreciatively.

As overbearing and dramatic as Auntie Tiffany was, Tatiana knew that she would not have walked through the doors of that bank without someone as assertive as the news reporter by her side.

"Fine. This way please," Ms. Moorely said sharply as her heels clicked across the linoleum bank floor to her office where they were seated.

The clacking sound of the heels made Tatiana think

of her mother. She had never seen her in heels before and briefly wondered if she walked as good in her heels as Ms. Moorely did. It was a childish thought, but it only added to the building list of unknowns surrounding Madisin Foster. The items in the safe deposit box might as well have belonged to Pandora.

"So, what can I help you with, Ms. Foster?"

"Well, umm," she cleared her throat, "my mother passed away a few years ago and I recently found a letter from her with a safe deposit box asking me to open it."

Ms. Moorely looked over her bright red cat eye glasses and simply responded, "I see."

The woman's brevity made Tatiana and Tiffany glance at each other.

Talking about her mother was not an easy thing for Tatiana. And being brushed off about it was not going to do.

Tiffany must have sensed her agitation because she began to speak, but Ms. Moorely raised her hand to cut her off.

"I have the account here." She stated matter of fact as she eyed her computer. The screen reflecting blurred images off her lenses. She scribbled a note on a post-it and rose from her desk.

"Are you ready?" Ms. Moorely asked while motioning for the door with her hand.

"Ready for?" Tiffany questioned.

"Ready to be shown the safe deposit box." Ms. Moorely answered Tiffany's question but directed the response to Tatiana.

The same confusion showed across Tatiana's face too. *What? That was too easy!*

"To be clear, are you saying that my mother did have a box here and just like that," - Tatiana snapped her fingers, - "I can access it?"

Ms. Moorely chuckled lightly, "Nothing happens just like that, Ms. Foster." She snapped her fingers. "That last name is not very common in Tampa and definitely not here in this bank. When your mother came to us years ago, I had just been promoted to team lead and was assigned to handle her appointment. There was a man accompanying her and they wanted to open an account."

"Well, nothing sounds out of the ordinary about that. Why would you remember something like that?" *Damn did everyone in the city of Tampa know more about my mother than me?*

"Well, the man for one. He had bright red hair. He was handsome, but something looked off about him. I couldn't put a finger on exactly what though."

"Was he mean to her? Rude? Disrespectful? Pushy?" Tatiana continued digging.

"No, he was none of those things. He was a complete gentleman to her and overly generous. It was clear that he was funding the account. But there was another thing that struck me as odd."

Tatiana's heart drummed in an un-syncopated rhythm. She was trying to process the information as it was being given to her, but her stomach had a hard time digesting the anxiety.

"After the account was opened, they walked to the door. She let him leave and made her way to the restroom. When she came out, she slipped me a note with specific instructions on how she wanted the safety deposit box opened and how much, in cash, she wanted transferred from her newly opened checking account, at weekly intervals. At first, I wasn't going to do it because I needed signatures, you know there is a protocol for these things."

Tatiana listened intently and prayed that Tiffany did not interrupt either.

"I kept the note in my desk for weeks. I don't know why. When I could have just thrown it away. But it bothered me that a woman who looked so put together with a man that nice would need to sneak for anything. Sure enough, about a month later, I received a package with a power of attorney in the contents giving me the power to open the safe deposit box for her. The power of attorney was only temporary, and I honestly have no idea how your mother got my information to put on there."

"What else was in the package?" Tiffany asked.

"Some loose pictures and a manila envelope."

"Did you look inside?"

Ms. Moorely raised her hands on the defense. "I did not."

"Why would you do all this for a woman you didn't know? I mean you could've gotten fired for breaking protocol," Tiffany inquired.

"And I can still get fired so I would appreciate your discretion. Look, I only wanted to help a woman who was in need. She looked like she had it all together but there was something in her eyes that said help me. Initially, I did feel bad like I should've turned myself in. But when I saw the news story a few months later that she had been murdered, I knew I did the right thing."

Damnit. All roads led to that bitter truth, didn't it? No matter how much she found out about her mother, she would still be dead.

Tiffany must have noticed Tatiana's change of emotion.

"Thank you. We're ready now."

Ms. Moorely nodded her head and led the way to the safe deposit boxes.

Tiffany and Ms. Moorely entered the stone-grey room enclosed with spaced steel bars and Tatiana solemnly trailed behind them.

"Can you give her a minute? It's just a little emotional for her." Tiffany whispered.

"Sure thing. Just ring the bell when you're done." Ms. Moorely said as she pointed to the small school bell that hung on the inside of the barred vault door. The bars clanged shut as she exited.

When the room was clear, Tatiana let out a heavy sigh. She thought she would be excited to open the box that could be holding the biggest secret to her convoluted life. However, it was the shaking of her hands not allowing the tightly gripped key to fit exactly in the keyhole that made her know otherwise. She was terrified. *What if I really don't want to know what's in this box? I mean momma had her reasons for hiding it. Maybe I shouldn't open it in front of Tiffany in case it's something embarrassing.*

Tatiana turned to glance back slightly over her shoulder. Tiffany must have been watching her every move because she walked right up as if on cue.

"Don't over think it. If you want some privacy, I'll go. But if you want me to stay, I'm here. I promise as long as Auntie Tiffany is back in your life, you don't have to worry. You hear me?"

Tiffany's wet eyes and soothing hand that sat atop of her own said a lot for her sincerity. Tatiana was glad Auntie Tiffany was there with her. Whatever she would find, they would work through it together. She did need to give the news reporter a disclaimer though.

"Ok then. No matter what we find here, it is off the record. I don't want to see my life plastered all over some blog or in a newspaper or on television."

Tiffany threw her hands up on defense. "I would never..."

"Fine. That's all. I just had to hear you say it." Tatiana steadied her hand enough to slide the key in the lockbox and enter the code written on the post-it that Ms. Moorely slipped her before she left.

Like Ms. Moorely claimed, there were bank statements showing monthly deposits into the safe. Despite not seeing any actual cash in the box itself, Tatiana felt she could trust that Ms. Moorely had set it aside if the paperwork was there. She went for the manila envelope to see what was inside when she heard a harsh gasp escape from Tiffany.

Tatiana was almost afraid to ask with the intense glare and mixed look of shock and anger that came radiated across Tiffany's face, but the photo she held in her hand made her ask.

"What is it? What's wrong?"

"I don't know why I never put the two together. Stupid. Stupid. Stupid." Tiffany slapped her forehead repeatedly.

"Hey! As much as I like hearing you admit your wrongs, you gone tell me what's up?"

Tatiana winced at Tiffany's deadpan stare. "I know who your father is. And the things I think I know about him, you are not going to like."

Tatiana glanced at the picture and covered her mouth with her hand. "I'm going to be sick."

Chapter 26

VERDELL

Verdell opened the safe house door, flashing the QR code from his phone over the flushed wall scanner. The lightly furnished space smelled of concentrated bleach and strong antiseptics. The flat white and grey color scheme added to the location's blandness. At this point, Verdell was unfazed by smells and bad decorating. His only concern was being able to sleep at a 180-degree angle, even if only for an hour. The last few hideouts all involved him resting with his eyes open, sitting upright in a car. All except the first spot, which almost became his final resting place.

*

After the shooting at the Top Hat, Verdell contacted his handler and requested a lease. The word "lease" was code for a fully furnished and grocery stocked place to lay low because odds were the requestor would be there for an undisclosed period. Verdell followed the labyrinth of instructions to an upscale one-bedroom loft off the main drag in South Tampa. The luxuriousness of the space did not stop Verdell from noticing the dark grey Honda with the Lightning tag following him on his twilight runs. The first three days, Verdell brushed it off as paranoia. There were dozens of small businesses and hundreds of families in the neighborhood. It could have easily been entrepreneurs looking to get an early start or cheating spouses burning that midnight oil that could keep the people of the intimate Soho community up at all times of the night. On the fourth occasion, when Verdell saw the same exact car, he jogged a different route and circled back through Hyde Park to his loft on Bay St sooner than his usual two-hour regimen. He waited in the alley of the restaurant next door, and sure enough, the vehicle came speeding around Bayshore, slowing as it approached his building. The bathroom light in Verdell's unit was visible from the street. He strategically left it on to give the appearance that someone was home. Verdell could see a figure through the windshield glancing up, possibly at his bathroom window. The likelihood was enough for him to stay put in his loft until he decided his next move.

The truth of the matter was that Verdell was a wanted man. So, it was only a matter of time before someone stepped outside of his usual hangouts in West Tampa to widen the search for an alleged murderer with priors. But which "someone" was it this time?

Verdell's hardened teenage mugshot from nine years ago is what the news outlets and police were using to ask for the public's help in identifying him. Luckily for Verdell, hand-rolled twists, facial hair, and an unkempt beard kept him incognito. But for how long? Verdell thought as he ran his fingers through the tangled tresses covering his chin. For the past few weeks, every news station within a fifty-mile radius of the city broadcasted the murders, fishing for clues during urgent news breaks, on radio stations, and on live social media feeds. Verdell only had one tip for them. *Get your facts right.*

Blood was on his hands for only one of those vics. Unfortunately, Amber was already dead by the time he got there.

The floor-to-ceiling windows on both the long walls of Verdell's unit gave a clear view of the streets surrounding him. The car with the Lightning tag parked on the corner of Magnolia and Bay and sat for hours before pulling off. No one ever got out of the vehicle. It was the only thing out of place. The other cars zipped in and out of traffic through pedestrian crossings to get parking spaces close to the restaurants in the heavily foot trafficked area.

Verdell's speculation about being trailed was realized almost too late. If it were not for a car alarm jarring him from sleep, he would have missed the broad shadow creeping on three of the five security camera screens positioned over the inside of the bedroom doorway. Camera number five hung in the hallway outside his room. He had to act quickly.

Verdell grabbed his burner and sent an encrypted text to a contact labeled "dry cleaning" while thinking of the hundreds of ways to kill a man. As Verdell stalked his stalker, he relaxed at the sight of the silencer on the Saturday night special sitting at the intruder's waist. He doesn't even have the gun in his hand, ready to use. Verdell knew whoever sent this rookie intended to kill him. Verdell had his own message to send. I am NOT to be fucked with. He doubled back through the middle of the loft and clutched the Damascus steel hunting knife hidden under the pillow. Verdell crotched low to the ground, waiting. It did not take long before his attacker stood in front of him, Verdell hidden by the shadows. Even with the moonlight peeking through the windows, scattering light into the room, Verdell could not make out the man's features. Not having another face to answer for at the pearly gates, Verdell considered a blessing.

He controlled his breathing, preparing to strike and timing his attack. Verdell sprang forward and jammed the tip of the knife into the assailant's foot. As the unsuspecting man unleashed a blood-curdling scream, Verdell balanced his weight on the balls of his feet as he rose to meet face to face, dragging the blade up and through the flesh along the way. Lacerated tissue and muscle gushed out from the splitting skin. The intruder was dead before Verdell regained his balance, and just to be sure, Verdell swung his blade in four swift motions, leaving an unidentifiable corpse before it hit the ground.

Verdell stripped and showered using a peroxide-based lather he created himself. He left the shower curtain and bathroom door open so he would not be caught off guard again. Verdell intended to take a quick shower, but the heat felt good on his skin. He caught a glance of his scarlet-stained face in the mirror. *I look like a fucking wild man.* Snippets of the violence he committed played in his mind like a movie trailer as he stared at his reflection. "I'm an animal. They turned me into a motherfucking animal. And now they want me dead!" Verdell screamed, slamming his fist into the shower wall until tile chips fell at his feet. Verdell looked at his hands. They did not shake. *How could anyone love a monster like me? Under normal circumstances, he would be considered a serial killer.* Verdell chuckled softly, and it grew into a maniacal cackle. *His only saving grace was that he did not live under normal circumstances. And that shit was funny.*

It was not often that Verdell lost himself in introspection and pity, but the tables were turning, and he was running out of people to trust. Verdell finished scouring his flesh, washing the blood out of his beard, and drying off to throw on a sweatsuit and nitrile surgical gloves.

He bagged the hands and head of the deceased, dousing the inside and outside of the bag with bleach. He threw it in the tub along with his blood-soaked clothing, the sheets, pillow, drinking glasses, plates, and any other knick-knacks that he touched and set it ablaze. Verdell wiped down the remaining surfaces and grabbed his things to leave. He took one last glance at the loft before he walked out the door. Just in case dry cleaning was in on plotting his demise, Verdell was determined not to leave an easy trail.

He had no plans to call The Camp back after the attempt on his life. He had zero contact with anyone, especially regarding his whereabouts, which meant the only people who knew where he would be to target him had to come from The Camp's top.

Verdell found the dark grey Honda Civic sports car with the Lightning tag at its usual corner. After jimmying the lock and disabling the alarm, Verdell drove the vehicle into the underground garage and began to rifle through its contents. There were a few sticks of gum, a phone charger, an opened case of Coke with crushed empty cans everywhere, recent pages of the Tampa Bay Times, the Tampa Tribune, and the Florida Sentinel. Verdell grew frustrated. It was all things he would expect from someone on a stakeout but nothing that would identify who may have hired him. He could get a few fingerprints, but without access to his home or The Camp's resources, there would be no running them.

Verdell continued sweeping the car. Checking under and between the seats, in the glove compartment, under the visors, and the trunk. There was no registration or paperwork on the car, but Verdell did find industrial garbage bags, towels, bottles of bleach, and peroxide, which were all, no doubt, to clean up his body postmortem. There was also a black storage box with a few hand blades, a dagger, and a high-grade rifle that Verdell would surely keep for himself after scrubbing them thoroughly. He chuckled to himself as he toyed with the throwing stars admiring the weight and size. There's no way these stars belonged to that lame-ass. Verdell made a mental note to get some practice with the shuriken soon. Before closing the trunk, Verdell heard the distinct ring of a Motorola phone. "Hello Moto..." the techno beat started.

Verdell began tossing the items in the trunk, searching for the phone. It rang twice more before he located it, tucked away in the cloth lining. "Now, this is something I can use."

Verdell scrolled through the phone's contacts and noted names that repeatedly appeared on the call log. He was copying the data and its sim contents onto his burner when a few recognizable images zipped by on the screen. Verdell wanted to pause the transfer to investigate further, but time was of the essence. The missed call would indicate that something went wrong with the hit, and backup would be on the way.

Verdell stepped out of the garage just as the data hit one hundred percent and was barely missed by what he could only assume was backup. Three darker grey Hondas, sports editions all pulled up to the south entrance of the building facing Bayshore.

Verdell waited for the goons to leave their vehicles before tossing the crushed phone and walking into the night, deliberating his next moves. First things first, he needed to see those images again. Verdell kept moving until he was at the bus station on Cass. His initial thought was to hitch a ride on one of the trains going any direction to sit things out until the heat calmed down a little. His plans to lay low outside of town changed when he saw the pictures of himself and Tatiana. There were at least thirty of them, both individually and together. Pictures of him leaving the Sant Yago ball at the club, dragging the Pastor Mason's body from the visitor's dugout at the Trop, at Pops' house. How long have these people been following me? Instead of boarding the next train, Verdell snatched a phone off a sleeping old man's newspaper to text Benji. He would have used his own but did not want to chance it. Somebody was following him. Benji would help him find out who and hopefully why.

"2grand g@22." Verdell gave Benji his code red. Shit was getting serious. Verdell circled back around to where the old man was sitting and dropped the phone back on the newspaper, grabbed the keys, and quickly made his exit. Verdell brushed past security, giving him a slight nod. The chirp alarm on the keychain made the old Volvo easy to find. Tatiana and his father could be in danger, and Verdell needed Benji to look at the transferred files to help him figure out what in the hell was going on.

*

It had been forty-seven days since the double homicide at the Top Hat. Forty-seven days since he went into hiding. Forty-seven days since he last saw Tatiana. Forty-seven days since his unconventional but comfortable lifestyle turned into a full-on shit storm.

As a "cleaner," it was common for Verdell to be the concentrated force behind scrubbing other people's dirt; at a hefty cost. His job description was to eradicate targets and destroy all evidence of involvement. It had been the objective of all his jobs before. However, Verdell had to admit things had been different since the night of the Sant Yago ball. His marks, usually individuals sharing no relation to the other, seemed connected. The Intel that Benji spread out in front of him seemed to confirm the same.

"From what I was able to gather from Mr. Terrance McDaniel, the Pastor, the vic from the Top Hat, and your intruder's phone, only these four have something in common," Benji said as she pushed the discovery packets towards Verdell.

Verdell nodded, looking at the 8x10 premortem photos, each clipped to its own manila folder. He took note of the guy from the Top Hat as he was not present in the current lineup.

"OK, so this is a good start, but are you going to tell me the rest?" Verdell asked, wondering why Benji was dragging her feet with the information.

"So, do you want the bad news or the bad news?"

"What, Benji? That shit don't make sense. Bad news is bad news so just give it to me." Verdell said, becoming frustrated. He was ready to lay back down on the hard ass cot for a few hours before going to check up on his dad, and Benji wanted to play.

Taking the information packets back, Benji sighed. "You know what? I'll do you a favor. I'll give you the regular bad news first."

"Fine, Benji. Give me the regular. Give me something."

Verdell ran his hands down his face in exasperation.

"It's a line jump scam."

"What? What you mean by a line jump scam? What the hell is a line jump scam?"

"It's where people pay to jump the line, but this happens to be the transplant waiting list line. The high-profile people involved in these things all need some type of transplant: a kidney, a lung, a heart. And they are willing to do anything to get it. Anything. And they aren't paying in cash anymore."

"What do you mean they aren't paying in cash? Organ transplants have to be a billion-dollar industry. Of course, they're paying cash."

"Well, not exactly. They aren't paying cash, but someone is. I haven't found out who yet, but I'm working on that."

"So, what are they doing to get on this list?"

"You're looking at it. The recipients are the middlemen, scouts, and promoters for international and child trafficking rings. They bring in the money, and it pays for their service."

"Hmm, so the people with the money are getting the people with trafficking backgrounds to help them get the organs. But what about the victims?"

"ALL eight victims took part in MonClaire Pharma research studies. First, they pass it off as sleep studies or some other low-profile study to identify donors. Then, they give them placebos for a few days, do a couple of tests to find out if they are compatible donors, and pay them what would be considered a small fortune for a few days of their time."

"But this shit ain't worth their life."

"Of course, they don't know that." Benji took a breath before continuing, "Each victim cashed checks ranging from a thousand to twenty-five hundred dollars in the weeks before they were murdered. All of the checks signed by Christina Christen."

"Why does that name sound familiar?"

"It's Mayor Paul Christen's daughter."

"You got to be fucking kidding me. This family doesn't stop, do they?"

"I take it you've done some work for them?" Benji asked, intrigued.

Verdell brushed off her question. "Long story. Stop being nosey and keep talking."

Benji smirked. "You're right. For another time. The only cash transactions that can be found are from the insurance companies and the hospitals. AND to the middlemen on their payroll, which are the idiots you were assigned to merc. I'm assuming to keep them from talking".

"And let me guess who is signing the payroll checks? Christina Christen?"

Benji nodded her confirmation.

"Damn."

Verdell grabbed a bottle of water from the fridge and shook it. Once the water settled clear, and there was no presence of cloudiness, Verdell opened the water bottle and poured a third of it into a glass vial taken from his bag. He placed a tightly balled knot of cotton into his right nostril and sniffed at the vial. Satisfied with the smell of the liquid, he switched nostrils with a new nose plug and sniffed again. The water did not smell tainted, but he dropped a pea-sized tablet in the vial just to be sure. Dissolving on contact, the water remained clear and without odor. Now satisfied that he would not be poisoned once he drank it, Verdell downed the remainder of the bottle in one long gulp. Verdell had done this with every bottle of water he opened since entering the safe house. He could never be too careful, and to say he was on edge would be an understatement.

A thought came through too clear for Verdell to disregard.

"You think whoever is at the top put a kill order in? You know, like a clean-up?" Verdell questioned.

Benji took a sip of her open glass of water, and Verdell winced. *Damn girl! Got way too much trust.*

"It wouldn't surprise me. They are putting a hit out on their own people."

Verdell rubbed his chin, "You right, me neither."

"It sounds familiar, though, right?" Benji whispered.

"Yea, way too familiar. I don't know what this shit got to do with me, but I got to find out who is behind this because I refuse to live in fear."

"Verdell and fear don't even sound right in the same sentence. You, Mr. BILLY BADASS. Mr. Grimm Reaper. Mr. You don't know who you fucking with. Mr. I ain't scared of shit." Benji motioned exaggeratedly with her arms.

"Yo, shut the hell up, Benji." Verdell chuckled lightly. "You got a name for me or what?"

"You know I do." Benji slid Verdell a flip phone, and he nodded when he opened it.

Verdell felt rejuvenated and ready for his mission. *Kill them before they kill me.* Sitting idle and waiting six weeks for Benji to dig all of that information up was worth it but Verdell hated sitting idle. Especially when it was not by choice.

Verdell rose from the folding card table, grabbed a pre-packed bag, and headed for the door.

"Wait? Don't you want to hear the other bad news?"

"Aww damn, you right. I don't see how bad it could be compared to the other shit but shoot.

"Your girl's a hoe."

"Wait, what?" Verdell's brain began to race. *What girl? My girl?*

"Yes, your girl. Tatiana Foster."

Can I still consider her mine?

"The guy you killed at the Top Hat works for a pimp in New Orleans named Cairo. She deals in women. And word is, your girl owes Cairo for a body and some cash."

Verdell kept his eyes to the ground. On the one hand, he did not care about her past, but on the other hand, *she could have told me.* Verdell knew better than to question Benji's intel. She was always on point when it came to accurate information.

Verdell picked up his bag and headed for the door without a word.

"Oh yeah, and she's pregnant," Benji shouted after him.

Verdell thought he would fall flat on his face before he shut the door behind him, but he did not want to seem weak or emotional in front of Benji. Especially when there were other more important matters to handle. As much as he tried to stay away from Tatiana, the last bit of information Benji gave him might have just won his girl a visit.

Chapter 27

TIFFANY

"That bastard. That deceptive, murdering, son of a bitch," Tiffany beat her steering wheel and screamed.

The cool night air whisking into the Jeep convertible did nothing to calm her rage. Tiffany whipped the SUV through the after seven o'clock traffic and maneuvered east on Dr. Martin Luther King Drive towards the I-275 North on-ramp. Even though the lanes were barely visible on the dimly lit road, Tiffany sped fifteen miles over the limit on two hours of sleep towards the mayor's mansion.

It pained her to leave Tatiana at the hospital, but the girl needed rest. Finding out you were twenty-six weeks pregnant, missing all the signs, and the possibility of your father being a prominent public figure and responsible for the murder of your mother was a lot of information to digest for anyone, let alone Tatiana.

Tiffany would otherwise feel helpless in this situation, but her sleuthing skills were in overdrive. If nothing else, Tiffany could give Tatiana the truth. Not just of who her father was, but all of it; her kidnapping, Madisin's murder, the whole shebang.

Tiffany had an inclination of who could want Tatiana and her mother dead, and she would bury him. *Paul Christen; mayor, philanthropist, businessman, liar, adulterer, murderer, deserter...* the list could go on and on. Tiffany had a lot of experience exposing the ugly side of the truth in the city but never thought it would hit so close to home.

The thought of Paul being Tatiana's father twisted Tiffany's stomach into knots. Her chest tightened as she weighed the consequences of the choices before her. Revealing this secret could be the perfect follow-up to her original exposé on the mayor. And it would also reaffirm his lack of credibility and trust, leaving the city's people with no choice but to forfeit their support for any future political plans he may pursue. However, on the downside, it would undoubtedly push Tatiana into the spotlight, and that might not be something Tatiana was mentally or emotionally ready for.

She had already been through more than any one person should have to endure. She deserved a degree of normalcy between losing her mother and nearly losing her own life without her father's notoriety suffocating her already intense situation.

Tiffany's last words to Madisin rushed back to her. *Why don't you let me take her to the car? I can sit with her. Don't worry. I got her. I got her....* A tear fell from Tiffany's cheek onto her lap as she reminisced about her best friend. No matter how beneficial exposing the truth of Tatiana's father would be for her career, Tiffany could not afford to lose Tatiana after reconnecting all these years later. Tatiana meant far more to Tiffany than any story. Madisin entrusted her with her daughter, her most prized possession, and she would not take that for granted. Besides, it was not her truth to tell. Tiffany knew that karma would eventually catch up to an evil son of a bitch like Paul.

Bzzzt. Bzzzt. Bzzzt.

Bzzzt. Bzzzt. Bzzzt.

Tiffany repeatedly pressed the intercom button at the gated entrance of Mayor Paul Christen's home. Usually, she would have Blake call ahead to announce her intent for an interview, but this was personal.

"Come on, you dirty bastard. Open the damn gate," Tiffany said through gritted teeth.

Tiffany had no forethought on how she would approach Paul regarding abandoning, hiding the attempted killing of his daughter, and his involvement in her mother's death. Yet, she was dead set on not leaving until she got some answers.

Bzzzt. Bzzzt. Bzzzt.

Bzzzt. Bzzzt. Bzzzt.

Bzzzt. Bzzzt. Bzzzt.

"Hello! Heeelllooo!" Tiffany shouted as she simultaneously pressed the button.

She stuck her head out of the car window and tried to peek into the property. She saw eight cars lining the rounded driveway, but no one emerged from the home. As a journalist, Tiffany was used to receiving the cold shoulder. However, this was the mayor's mansion. Tiffany was convinced at least one person in the residence had to be aware of her presence. *Where is security?*

She backed her car out of the entrance and drove a few yards down the road making an illegal U-turn to park on the side covered by overgrown ferns. Tiffany would wait all night if it was required. Finally, after twenty minutes of sitting, a car she noticed as Barry Mellow's came turning slowly into the same entrance she just pulled out of. Tiffany wanted to flash her lights to get Barry's attention, but something told her to sit still and wait.

Tiffany watched Barry get out of his car and walk around to his trunk. When it popped open, Tiffany gasped. *Was that a leg?* Her gut began to bubble as Barry started pummeling the leg's owner. Tiffany swore she saw blood splattering the shirt and coat Barry wore. The air around her grew thin. Barry switched his soiled clothing for a crisp new set from the back seat and glanced Tiffany's way before closing the trunk and back passenger door. Tiffany ducked low. *Thank God this is a rental.*

Tiffany heard the gate beep open and remained hidden until Barry's car was entirely on the property with the gate closed behind him. She finally let go of the air she was holding. Tiffany had to play this smart. She might have thought Barry was Paul's handyman before, but this situation confirmed he was dangerous.

"Boy, I sure know how to pick them." Tiffany sighed.

The mayor's compound appeared lively even though there was hardly any movement outside. *I better text Blake to let him know I'm going in.*

No one's answering at the gate. Time for plan B. Tiffany texted Blake, and he replied immediately. *Good luck! I packed your extra shoes underneath your seat.* Tiffany smiled, pressing the phone against her chest. She was glad to have Blake as an assistant. He always thought of everything. Tiffany searched under the driver's seat for her sneakers. She had not planned on sneaking into the mayor's mansion, but desperate times called for desperate measures.

After switching out her boots for sneakers, Tiffany headed toward the mansion gate. She wiped the sweat from her palms onto her jeans so she would not slip as she climbed.

"Uggh!" Tiffany groaned as she grabbed the jagged stones to pull herself up the perimeter wall.

When her feet hit the paved driveway, Tiffany took a moment to catch her breath. Her eyes scanned the compound, noting every visible surveillance camera. She maneuvered past the one facing the gate and dodged the others recording the driveway. Tiffany crept along the stone wall opposite the mansion until she reached the side of the house.

"Great, it's cracked!" Tiffany whispered to herself when she found a slightly opened door.

As she reached for the handle, a feminine voice cackled, talking loudly nearby. Tiffany gasped, looking behind her. It was one of the mayor's maids, taking her smoke break. She was talking on the phone, chatting with someone about how much she hated her job and the mayor.

"I'm just here long enough to save up so I can leave this dump. Besides, it doesn't even come with benefits. What kind of job like this doesn't include benefits? Hello! I've got kids to feed! Cheapskate. That's why I didn't vote for him," the maid said, scoffing.

Tiffany snickered at the woman and proceeded to the door, slipping in the gap. She observed the "Caution, wet floor" sign on the checkered linoleum floors. Tiffany wiped her shoes on the doormat and tiptoed toward the stairs to avoid leaving footprints. Tiffany hunched, holding the railing, as she approached the second level. She looked to the left and right of her, ensuring there was no one else wandering the hallways.

Looks like it's clear. Tiffany glanced at her watch again. With all those cars outside, she would have thought more people would be present in the house, but it was strangely silent. *What is going on? It's not even eight o' clock p.m. Everyone can't be sleeping. I've never known a politician to go down this early.* Tiffany shrugged her shoulders, thanked God for the distraction, and stood up to begin her search of the premises.

Ding! Ding! Ding!

Tiffany jumped, startled by the grandfather clock across from her. *It's just a clock, Tiffany. Calm down,* she told herself.

Tiffany noticed the luxury pieces decorating the mansion, from the replica of a Picasso, a blue velvet embroidered bench with matching cushioned chairs, to a picture of Dr. Martin Luther King Jr. during his *I Have a Dream* speech. Tiffany rolled her eyes at the irony of the image. Paul was the last person she thought worthy of standing for a great cause. As Tiffany approached the next set of stairs, mumbling came from the top of the staircase. Tiffany sauntered up the stairs until she reached the top of the landing.

"Ugh, I told you I'm fine, Carrie," a young voice moaned.

Tiffany noticed the half-opened door to her right and walked close enough to hear the conversation and see the people on the other side.

"You won't be fine until you're cleared by the doctors, Christina. Don't worry, honey. You'll be back to your normal self in no time. But, you know, you gave us a scare," the nurse said, wiping Christina's brow with a damp cloth.

Christina? Isn't that Paul's daughter? What's wrong with her? Tiffany took out her pocket mirror to get a better view.

Christina looked dull and limp, lying in her canopy bed. She continued to moan as her nurse smashed a medicine pill and sprinkled it into a cup of applesauce.

Applesauce? Now you know that is too much. That is a grown-ass woman in there. She can swallow a damn pill. Good thing Tatiana had Nanna, or there'd be no telling how she would have turned out.

Just then, Tiffany heard Paul's voice, drawing nearer toward where she snooped. She searched for the nearest hiding space, finding a closet next to Christina's room. Tiffany scampered inside and cracked it wide enough to see the nurse close Christina's bedroom door.

"Ouch!" Tiffany grunted, tripping over a bag of golf clubs, taking up half the room in the closet. She saw Paul and his wife walking out of the room across the hall.

"Listen, sweetheart, I told you, this is going to work," Paul said, lowering his voice. "We're almost at the finish line. You just have to be patient."

"I've been patient for years, Paul. Literally decades. Even in death, your whore and your bastard are haunting us. Our daughter is a drug addict and knocked up by your damn intern. And I still haven't found the words to describe your deceitful and pathetic ass."

Damn. She's really tearing into him. Tiffany snickered quietly.

Paul tried to grab his wife's shoulders and calm her down, but Sandra pulled away, and her rant only became louder. "Speaking of which, Dhorian better be happy I'm not calling the FBI on him for pedophilia."

Paul gasped and looked at Sandra like she had lost her damn mind. "Pedophilia? Sandra, you can't be serious? You speak about Dhorian like he's some kind of Chester the Molester", Paul air quoted the words exaggeratedly.

"I'm glad you think this is funny, Paul. But we need this finished in order to talk to my father about getting you into the governor's seat. If daddy knew who you really were…If something goes wrong…."

"Nothing will go wrong. We've talked about this. Barry has already planted the bait for this Verdell character. If he speaks to anyone about what we've done, we will expose him for the shameless, high-paid hitman that he is." Paul cuffed his wife's face in his hands. "Besides, it'll be much more believable to blame the murders on Verdell. No one will ever believe that your prestigious family or I had any involvement. The story of a hometown hoodlum with nothing to lose causing havoc and committing murder for revenge's sake makes for a much better 20/20 episode," Paul advised as he plopped a mint into his mouth and laughed heartily.

A look of acceptance washed over Sandra's face as she finally yielded to her husband and took his hand.

"Good. Now let's go to our meeting. We can't keep our clients waiting, now, can we?" Paul urged and kissed Sandra lightly.

Tiffany watched Paul and his wife disappear down the staircase. Tiffany's mouth dropped at overhearing Paul's confession. Exactly what he confessed to was in the air, but it sounded to her like the mayor was up to no good. *And clients? What clients? I didn't know he still practiced. Maybe it's investments?* Tiffany questioned. Paul being a narcissist was not new to her, but hearing the man reveal his part in multiple murders and a cover-up sent chills down Tiffany's spine. She was now dealing with a psychopath.

"Hey, is everything set up?" a deep voice echoed through the stairwell.

Tiffany recognized the voice as Barry's. He and Paul made inaudible small talk before he proceeded upstairs. Barry knocked on Christina's door to check on her before reaching in his pocket to pull out his phone and make a call.

Who could he be calling? Tiffany wondered, feeling a tinge of jealousy.

Bzzzt! Bzzzt! Tiffany's phone vibrated in her pocket. *Shit!* She thought as she fumbled with the device to quiet it. Barry was calling her. She peeped through the crack to see Barry looking for the noise. Tiffany's heart thumped out of her chest as she prepared to be caught and meet the same fate as the guy in the trunk. Barry slowly paced the grand hallway, searching for the sound. Before he approached the closet door, Paul called him downstairs. Barry hesitated, taking one last glance around the landing before trotting downstairs. Tiffany hurried out of the closet and looked for the closest exit out. She tiptoed past Christina's room, trying to get out the way she came in, except that would be impossible with the fury of voices buzzing toward her. *Damn.* Tiffany tiptoed in the opposite direction and crept down the stairs as fast as she could. She spotted an open back door and took off towards the kitchen. Luckily for her, it was empty. However, more voices were coming from a lower room that sat off to the right of the back door. There were sounds of *Oohs* and *Ahhs*.

"I now have full function of my lungs and can even go running again," a voice said proudly.

Light applause echoed up the stairs. *What's going on down there? A demonstration?* Although tempted to sneak down and find out what all the fuss was about, Tiffany did not want to try her luck. Instead, she jogged back to her car unseen and jumped in, relieved at not having been caught.

As Barry rang her for the second time, Tiffany slowed her breathing and answered welcomingly, "Hello?"

"Hey doll, what are you doing tonight?" Barry asked in a deep, mellowed tone.

"Um…nothing, really. Why? What did you have in mind?" Tiffany masked her disinterest, wiping her sweaty face with her shirt.

"I have a new bottle of champagne I need help drinking. Want to help me out?" Barry asked seductively.

Tiffany paused. She was unsure if she wanted to spend time with Barry, given the bloody pulp that may still be in his trunk and the information she had just found out about Paul. However, there were no doubts in her mind that Barry had helped him. Tiffany only needed more information. However, as much as she hated to admit it, she kind of enjoyed Barry's company.

"Sure. Be there in twenty," Tiffany said.

"Great. That's what I like to hear," Barry responded excitedly before hanging up the phone.

*

Tiffany got off the caged elevator and remembered the camera Barry had positioned at the entrance of his condo. It suddenly made her subconscious about the quick wash-up and wardrobe change she did with the travel wipes and extra clothes Blake packed for her. She would not have made it in the twenty minutes she promised Barry without them. Tiffany made a mental note to thank Blake with a large bonus soon.

Before Tiffany could knock on the door, it opened to a partially dressed and expectant Barry. His open floor-length robe and sculpted bare chest coupled with very thin lounge pants left nothing to the imagination. The swelling and curving shaft that pulsed at the top of Barry's thigh let Tiffany know precisely what was on his mind. *Well, doesn't he look like something good to eat?* Tiffany rebuked the thought. *This is the same man that beat someone possibly to death and helped the mayor cover up God knows what. Yes, he looks good as hell, yes you want him to take you right now, and yes, you will enjoy every second of it. But remember, he is NOT to be trusted.*

"Well, are you going to just stand there and eye fuck me, or do you want to try the real thing?" Barry asked, gyrating his manhood in her direction. Even though he lightly poked his hips at her, Tiffany envisioned him thrusting his package at her face.

The smile stretching Barry's lips invited Tiffany into his domain. The long stem glass of bubbly he handed her did not hurt either.

Tiffany downed her glass before both feet crossed the threshold. *Whew. Tastes a little funny, but it's good. One more glass of that, and maybe my thoughts will stop shouting.*

As soon as the door shut, Barry greeted Tiffany's lips first, sucking the remainder of the champagne from them. Tiffany moaned as his tongue caressed hers. Barry's heat and intensity sent tingles through the most private parts of her body. His strong hands interchangeably squeezed her thighs and gripped her back. Tiffany's mind objected, but her body begged for what she knew came next. Separating the man from the monster became easier to do, especially when Barry wrapped her legs through his muscular arms. Tiffany's head swam as Barry lifted her into the air. Tiffany LaSalle was in heaven. The rugged killer turned dominating romantic knew just how to excite and satiate her. And Tiffany was impatient for the latter. Barry carried Tiffany all the way to the bedroom while alternating kissing her lips and sucking the top of her breasts.

Barry lay Tiffany on the bed and stripped her of the blouse and skirt she wore in seconds. Tiffany said another silent thank you for wet wipes as Barry trailed his juicy wet tongue down to her belly button and removed her panties with his teeth.

What is up with the teasing? Put something in me already! Tiffany whined inside.

Chills rippled through Tiffany's body. Her clit felt engorged even though only the air coming through the AC vent had its way with it. Tiffany's arousal seemed heightened with thoughts of what Barry would do to her. And when his fingers entered her,

Tiffany thought she would go mad. The pleasure was nothing she had ever experienced before. Barry rubbed against her g spot, and Tiffany clenched her walls, encouraging her vagina to swallow his hand whole. She folded her thighs around him as her body writhed.

Breathless, Tiffany shuddered through moans of indulgence. She tried to speak, but her mind was blank. She had no idea if Barry was digging for treasure or if he was trying to fit his entire hand inside her, but she grabbed his forearm, moving his fingers in and out of her wetness to aid him in his quest. The heated pleasure took over, and even though her eyes were open, all Tiffany could see were bright white bursts of energy around her. She blinked rapidly out of fear of going blind, yet that terror could not stop the orgasm from spilling out of her. Tiffany gasped and choked on the dry air. Barry chuckled and removed his fingers from her wet center.

"Oh, you like that, huh? Barry asked with an excited glare.

Tiffany pulled herself up to her elbows. Luckily for her, once she closed her mouth, the saliva flowed freely, allowing her to get back in the groove of things.

Tiffany bit her bottom lip and nodded.

Barry pulled Tiffany's ankles to the edge of the bed, hooked his forearms under her thighs, and dug his tongue deep inside her. Tiffany cried out as his tongue rubbed against her walls. Barry stiffened it like a phallus and plunged it in repeatedly. Tiffany thought she would die. It was almost certain to happen until Barry surfaced for air. Only a second passed before he dove back in but this time focusing on her clit. He sucked and slurped at it like it was sure to make him billionaire-rich.

"Look at me."

Tiffany thought she imagined the voice, but when she removed her hand from over her eyes, she saw Barry's lips move.

"Look at me." He demanded.

Tiffany understood the command but did not understand why anyone would ever want to watch such a thing being done to them until she glanced for herself.

Barry's intense and hungry gaze met hers. At first, seeing his mouth devour her womanhood made her shy away. Tiffany closed her eyes, but Barry suckling at the fleshy piece of her prepuce forced them open again.

"Ahhhhh. Mmmmm. Mmmmm. Ahhhhh. Ahhhhh." *That damn Barry knows what he is doing. Shit.*

Tiffany squealed, kicking her legs, squeezing her toes, and shutting her eyes. Her body bucked as the climax itched her hair follicles, hardened her nipples, leaked from her center, and shot out from her toes. Then, the burst of colors came again, this time in reds and purples, oranges and blues, and the white; the white was iridescent.

"Oh, my absolute GAWD." Tiffany managed to mumble. She successfully pushed Barry off her, and her blood chilled even though her skin felt aflame.

"Are you cold?" Barry asked, sounding genuinely concerned.

Cold? Cold is the least of my worries. That is what she wanted to say. *I'm never having sex again. I have peaked, and I want to be done.* Tiffany thought, laughing to herself. Instead, Tiffany settled on asking for water.

Winded, she asked, "May I have some water, please?"

Barry went into the personal fridge disguised as a part of his bedroom wall and pulled out a bottle of spring water.

Tiffany took a few big gulps and handed it back to Barry.

They both laughed.

"Are you good now?" Barry questioned after a minute of laughter.

Tiffany, hands to her chest, replied, "Yes, I'm good now."

"Good, because we're not done yet." Barry smiled.

Tiffany faked a tired plop back onto the bed. Nevertheless, she was ready for more.

Barry flipped her over, smacked Tiffany on her bare cheeks, and said gruffly, "I want your ass in the air."

And Tiffany anxiously obliged.

*

Tiffany rose from the bed with one of the biggest migraine headaches she had ever endured. It felt more like an extreme hangover. Her mouth was dry, her skin was clammy, and her head was hazy. *I don't remember having that much to drink,* she thought, grabbing her throbbing head and running her fingers through her matted hair.

"I got a story for you. You like stories?" Barry asked as he reappeared in the room, frightening Tiffany.

She took a moment to regain her composure and shifted her weight on the bed, covering herself with the sheets. "Yeah, I'm always up for a good story."

"Well, it's more or less a hypothetical scenario than a story."

Tiffany moved uncomfortably. *What is he talking about?* "Okay, hypotheticals work too. Let me hear it."

"Good, I thought you would be interested, you being a reporter and all."

What's that about? He never mentioned that before. Tiffany examined. The energy shift in the room made her look for her clothes, her phone, her purse, and the nearest exit.

"So, let's say a man and a woman meet. They fall in love. But you know how it is. The honeymoon phase only lasts for so long. The woman always wants more. She wants to tell his wife! Can you believe that? I mean, who can really keep a woman happy these days anyway, right?" Barry leaned forward, inching close to Tiffany's face.

"Uh-huh," Tiffany said, moving back.

"Anyway, so let's suggest that there's trouble in paradise for the adulterous couple. And the man does all he can to keep this woman happy. I mean, he is really doing all he can. And I'm not talking about just flowers and dinner. I mean, the guy is buying a car, paying for college, fathering bastard children, paying all the household bills. I mean doing everything he can to keep this broad happy. But unfortunately for her, nothing seems to work."

Barry paused, looking at Tiffany like he was conversing with one of the guys and expected her to chime in.

Tiffany hoped the fear rising in her stomach did not show on her face. *Barry knows something.*

"So, you know what he did? Do you? Go ahead and guess. I'll give you a free guess."

Tiffany stammered, "Well, this is hypothetical, right? So, there are a lot of things that he could do."

Barry pounced and angrily grabbed her face in between his large fingers in an instant. "Don't play with me, Tiff," Barry growled. "Go ahead and guess."

"I don't want to guess!" Tiffany cried out.

Barry roughly threw her face away from him. "You are ruining my story. And since you are forcing me to tell you, the man ends up loving this lady sooo much that he loves her to death." Barry cackled.

"I missed the joke." Tiffany sighed as she touched her aching jaw.

Barry looked hurt. "Well, you would. She asked for it. Kind of like someone else I know." Barry stated plainly as he eyed Tiffany fidgeting on the bed.

"Well, I know when my presence is no longer wanted," Tiffany said, feigning offense and gathering her items quickly.

"What? You don't like the story? It's just a hypothetical, remember?" Barry pressed.

Buttoning her blouse, Tiffany felt more in control. Even though her head still rang, she was more confident in her getaway and read through Barry's context clues. Tiffany got the feeling that this hypothetical of Barry's was anything but. He had an idea of what she was searching for.

Tiffany decided to play along in his little cat and mouse game and exclaimed, "Are you serious, Barry? What is this some sort of intimidation effort? Do you know in some countries they would fine him and put him under the jail for that little hypothetical he committed?"

"In biblical times, they would stone him to death for what I know he's done. All that means nothing now," Barry responded, tossing back a drink of a strong-smelling brown liquor.

Now Tiffany was pissed. She came to get the truth for Tatiana but fell into an unnecessary lust trap. She had an idea of the kind of work Barry did and expected violence, but the mind games were that of a sociopath. *Good thing I have Blake on standby.* His assignment was to call the police if he did not hear from her by morning.

"Fuck it! Let's stop bullshitting each other and playing games here, Barry."

"Fine, let's," Barry said nonchalantly, keeping a few feet in between himself and Tiffany as he followed her around the room.

"Did you know a woman named Madisin? Madisin Foster? I have solid info that she and Paul dated and had a kid together some years back." Tiffany questioned.

"Yeah, I heard the rumors about my brother-in-law having a mistress and their pickaninny. But you know how stuff can be when you're a politician. People make up shit just because it's Sunday. So, don't believe the lies," Barry said, getting dressed.

This lying dog. I can't believe I let him touch me, Tiffany thought. *Barry fucking Mellow.* Between him and Paul, she could not figure out who was worse. *I cannot wait to get a shower to scrub this bastard off me when I get out of here. If I get out of here,* came as a second thought.

"Well, I have all of the information I need. I better head home. I have an early day tomorrow. Thanks for tonight. I had fun," Tiffany said, grabbing her belongings and heading out of the bedroom towards the cage elevator.

Barry grabbed her arm before Tiffany could hit the elevator button, squeezing it. Tiffany jumped, turning to stare directly into Barry's reddened face.

"Hey, before you go, I got one more hypothetical for you."

Tiffany gulped, lowering her eyes to her arm. "Oh-okay, what is it?"

"A cute journalist is really good at her job. And she has made a good living at finding out things she shouldn't. First, she stumbles on a story that is better left dead. Then, when she goes to report it, the story never makes it to the news. You want to know why?"

Tiffany tried to snatch her arm away, but Barry's grip was too tight. "Are you threatening me?" she asked.

"Do you want to know why?" Barry asked slowly.

Tiffany only glared in response.

"Because the cute journalist did not make it home. HA!"

Barry guffawed. "She can't report on something if she isn't alive to report."

Tiffany finally pulled away from Barry and backed into the elevator pressing the door for it to close. She thought she had gotten away when the elevator stopped, and Barry's booming voice followed down the shaft.

"If you didn't know, breaking and entering is a crime. Next time you may want to wear a mask." And then, as a second thought, Barry, still laughing, shouted, "Oh, I would get a detox if I were you. Compliments of my niece, the effects of those X pills don't just wash off, you know. And I would leave that part out of your investigation. You never know who may be lying in wait to shut you up."

The elevator started again, and Barry's cackle hitched a ride down with Tiffany. She clutched her chest, taking deep breaths to calm her increasing anxiety. But the heart palpitations worsened. Her skin crawled. Now it all made sense, the heat flashes, the extreme sensitivity, the cottonmouth. She had been drugged.

Tiffany rushed through the garage to her car, hurrying inside before locking it. Barry had done a number on her tonight. Tiffany was not so sure she would make it to the car. She could still hear Barry's laugh taunting her. Once inside, she scolded herself while beating the steering wheel, stupid, stupid, and stupid. Tiffany hit the gas out of the complex onto the brightly lit street, found the nearest place to pull over, and turned on her hazard lights.

"Oh my God, oh my God, oh my Goooood!" Tiffany screamed out loud.

Trembling, she worked her fingers loose from the steering wheel. She curled her aching hands back and forth, praying for a release of tension. Tears streamed down her face as she dry heaved. Tiffany had never been this scared in her life, and she had been in some terrifying undercover trafficking reconnaissance missions before. But this was different. Everything was too close. There was too much exposure, and Tiffany did not know her next move. It took a few more minutes for her body to normalize before continuing her drive home. Finally, Tiffany pulled into her driveway and saw Blake standing outside his car, seemingly waiting on her. She could barely put the car in park before hopping out and into Blake's frail arms.

"Tiffany! What is it? Are you okay? What's wrong? What happened?" Blake shot off each question in rapid succession.

Tiffany only wanted to be close to someone she could trust. She was at a loss for words and could only wail in response. *Yes, Barry Mellow did a damn number on me!*

Chapter 28

DHORIAN

Dhorian stormed out of the hospital's revolving doors fuming, glancing back nervously at the security guards who shoved him towards the exit only seconds ago. Dhorian did not plan on getting kicked out of the hospital. However, Paul Christen had threatened him for the last time. That man and his God complex way of thinking could bring out the worst in even the most patient person. As Dhorian slammed the door to his car, thoughts of his brawl with Paul in the hospital enraged him.

*

"You've got two choices, son. One: Marry my daughter or Two: I ruin you and everything you've ever worked for. I suggest you choose wisely because, with the way I'm feeling, option number two has a bullet with your name on it. Don't forget that

I practically made you, and I can end you. So, you'd do wise to make the right choice."

"I don't know what your daughter told you, but she clearly has a problem and her being pregnant is the least of it. So, I would appreciate you taking a step back out of my face and lowering your voice," Dhorian replied to Paul's threat, conscious of the crowded but quiet hall.

"Don't you take that tone with me." Paul seethed. "All I know is that my little girl is sitting in that room," he pointed, "with tubes down her throat because of you! She could've died tonight. And if she would've boy, I would've...."

"Would've what?" Dhorian asked with a sarcastic chuckle and continued, "We are not here because of me. Christina is in this mess because of Christina. Your precious little girl is nothing but a drug-addicted, sex-crazed, manipulative child who trapped me into sleeping with her crazy ass. Hell, all of you are crazy. But if you're not careful, crazy won't be the only name the world will know you by.

"What did you just say?" Paul asked, grabbing Dhorian by the collar and jacking him against the nearest wall. Before Dhorian could react, Paul's fist connected with his jaw. After he stumbled a few steps back, Dhorian charged. He rammed Paul's back into the patient monitor and pummeled him with strategic blows to the head. Dhorian ignored the screams and gasps from onlookers as he beat Paul. Then, right before Dhorian felt himself give in to madness, security pulled him off of Paul and roughed him up a bit before escorting him out of the hospital.

"We are not done here. You'll wish you never put your hands on me, boy!" Paul growled as he scuffled to get past the other security guards.

*

Dhorian heard Paul's ultimatum and ominous threat echoing in his head. There had been a time when Dhorian admired the mayor and even envied his life, but over the years, he grew to see that Paul Christen was a slave to his possessions and his titles. The only choice Dhorian was ready to make was not to follow the same path.

Seething as he pictured Paul's devious grin taunting him, Dhorian hated the notion of Paul thinking he had him by the balls. But little did Paul know, Dhorian was working on a plot of his own. *Nothing like a little exposé to get the shoe on the other foot.*

Ever since Christina came to Dhorian with her pregnancy bit, his life had been a damn rabbit's hole. He fell deeper and deeper into a frenzy trying to define his reality. There were questions about his parents, career, and whether to marry a conniving piece of work like Christina. Even if he was ready to be a father, the Christen family were the last people he wanted to be tied to for the remainder of his days. A life with Christina meant a life spent under the authority of Paul. And Dhorian could not surrender himself to being Paul's stooge any longer.

Dhorian called Joanie, "I'm going to be off-grid for a while.

Cancel all meetings and get the high-profile cases reassigned. And if Paul calls…"

"Paul, sir?" Joanie asked curiously.

At that moment, Dhorian realized he was at a place of no return. He had always kept the utmost respect for his mentor, even in their time of disagreement. But now, Paul Christen was not his mentor, not the mayor, and damn sure not his father-in-law. Paul Christen was just a man. Dhorian had to consider that Joanie, unaware that he had arrived at this conclusion, needed more clarification on the Paul he referred to.

"I'm sorry, Joanie. I'm referring to Paul Christen, the mayor. If he calls, tell him I'm on sabbatical."

"Oh. Yes, sir." Joanie retorted, pausing briefly before ending the call.

This is why I love you, Joanie. Dhorian could tell his comment regarding the mayor took Joanie by surprise, and her short response was riddled with questions that she would never ask. And for that, Dhorian was grateful.

Arriving home without remembering one bit of scenery or traffic along the way, Dhorian tried to shake the agonizing migraine from the days' events. Throwing his keys on the couch, Dhorian headed to the kitchen to grab an ice pack from the freezer. Collapsing on the sofa, he hissed from the pain rippling through his body. Knowing that it would only be a matter of time before Paul came for him, Dhorian could not sit idle. He had to prepare and make provisions for his safety, if he made it through the night.

Paranoia finally set in. Dhorian had not left his place for the last seventy-two hours and had no intentions of doing so anytime soon. The security cameras were delivered overnight and installed within hours. Video feeds from outside his front door, and the elevators played on a constant loop on his living room TV and were available on his phone with the press of a button. Watching his back and being on the lookout for Paul, Barry, and anyone else they would probably send had been a full-time job without a lot of rest. Pacing his apartment like a madman, pistol attached to his waist, Dhorian rang the bellman with instructions to alert him of any new faces coming to his floor. There were twenty condos spread across ten floors in his building. Only fifteen units were occupied. So, Dhorian figured the foot traffic should not be too heavy to monitor.

Over the last few days, Dhorian ignored all communication while concocting a plan to get from under Paul's thumb. He turned his phone off Do Not Disturb for the first time since arriving home.

At the hospital, on his way up to see Christina in the rehab ward, Dhorian overheard Barry plotting to frame the mayor for the recent string of murders in the city. Unsurprisingly, Mayor Christen was also involved in bribery and conspiracy to commit murder, with his cousin, Verdell, no less. Those were a lot of secrets to keep from the public. However, that was not the worst of it. Dhorian found proof that Paul Christen suffered from a rare form of albinism and had been passing as a White man. Back in the mid-1900s leaking this information would have ended in bloodshed, but it was not uncommon in this millennia. It sounded like Barry Mellow and his family already had wind of the betrayal. Nevertheless, Dhorian hoped his exposing this little detail to Mayor Christen's constituents would result in a Twitter or TMZ scandal at the least. Thanks to Barry getting sloppy with discretion, Dhorian knew the other dirty details would break Pandora's box.

Searching through his contacts, Dhorian pulled up Tiffany LaSalle. He never had a reason to call Tiffany before, but if anyone could get the information out faster and better than a viral TikTok video, it would be her.

"Hi, you've reached Tiffany LaSalle with Channel 8 News. I'm sorry I can't get to the phone…."

Dhorian waited for the beep to leave Tiffany a voicemail.

In his most professional voice, he began, "Hello Ms. LaSalle, this is Dhorian Hamilton. I'm one of the partners at Reed & Morris Law Group. I had the opportunity to work closely for the Mayor and have intel I think you'd find interesting. Hopefully, it's something that can benefit us both. So when you get a chance, call…." Dhorian paused mid-sentence, glancing down at a copy of the family tree he'd been scribbling on a few weeks ago.

"Yeah, call me back when you can. Thanks," Dhorian continued before hanging up.

He pushed through the stack of papers on his desk until he reached the diagram peeping out from under the rest. Looking over the details he added to the tree, Dhorian noticed Verdell's birthday: January 12th, 1988. *Why had I never considered our birthdates being on the same day before*? Dhorian had always thought sharing a birthday with his cousin was an inconvenience. Just one more thing he had to compete with. And when they got older, Dhorian had been estranged from his cousin for so long he could not remember when his birthday was. But now, the dates seemed to be glowing off the page, and Dhorian sensed that their having the same birthday could not be a coincidence. Dhorian needed answers, and he had an idea of where he could get them; his uncle, Verdell Senior. A simple phone call would not suffice for a conversation this sensitive. Dhorian wanted to handle this in person. He hated the idea of driving all the way to West Tampa, but Dhorian was desperate for clarity, and he needed something to work out in his favor. He felt so close to resolving this conundrum he could taste it. After guzzling down a few drinks for a little liquid courage, Dhorian grabbed his keys off the counter and headed out the door.

*

Arriving at his uncle's house, Dhorian banged on the door like the police. After no answer, Dhorian knocked again, observing the window curtains moving. As Dhorian moved close to the window, he noticed his uncle's face peeping in between the curtains. So Dhorian knocked again, persistent in getting in. Because of his father's and uncle's relationships, Dhorian knew his uncle did not carry a fondness for him, and Dhorian shared the same sentiments. Nevertheless, Dhorian remained determined to clean house and get what he came for.

Growing tired of waiting for his uncle to open the door after ten minutes of knocking and playing peek-a-boo with the curtains, Dhorian trotted back to his car to figure out his next move. Evidently, the answers he wanted would not come today. If it was not for Verdell Senior's stubbornness, Dhorian would have questioned if they were related. He was the only other person more stubborn than Dhorian.

After spending another ten minutes sulking in the car, unable to focus his thoughts, Dhorian turned over the engine and headed to his next stop. The strip club, The Top Hat. *I need a drink.* At least if he was out in the open and in public, Paul would have a more challenging time getting to him. Or so he had hoped.

*

Walking in the club, Dhorian grinned at the sexy women passing by, taking in their beautiful, voluptuous bodies. *This is definitely the change of scenery I need to get my mind off things.* Of all the familiar faces, Dhorian noticed his favorite girl working across the room. Although a little thicker than he last remembered, in Dhorian's eyes, she was still fine as hell. Biting his bottom lip and rubbing his hands together as if he was about to enjoy a seven-course meal, Dhorian moved to sit in her section.

Dhorian noticed the attractive woman spotting him as she called out, "Verdell! Verdell!"

What did she say? Dhorian heard her say something, but he could not quite make it out over the loud music.

Dhorian watched the woman approach him, and her smile faded as she apologized, "Oh! I'm so sorry! You look like someone I know."

"Oh yeah? What's his name?" Dhorian asked, maintaining his grin, thinking that she only wanted a reason to engage in conversation.

"Actually, his name is Verdell."

Scrunching up his face, Dhorian went through his mental library. *Verdell? I only know one Verdell, and that's my cousin. I thought that convict asshole was still in jail.* The waitress must have seen the confusion on his face because she tried to fix her earlier statement, "Oh, I'm sorry. Verdell isn't bad-looking or anything. Hopefully, you didn't take that as an insult. Actually, you two could pass for twins."

Twins? I know I look way better than that lame-ass. In reality, the only major differences were Dhorian's slightly lighter and less scarred skin. Dhorian never thought much about their similarities before, always wanting to set himself apart from the competition. But, before he could dwell too much on the idea, his phone rang. Seeing Christina's name made him cringe.

"Excuse me, sweetheart, let me take this."

"The name is Tatiana, handsome. Just flag me down when you're ready to order."

Dhorian let the phone ring just a bit longer while watching the red-headed beauty work the rest of the room.

"What is it, Christina?" Dhorian asked dryly.

"Dhorian, where are you? I made reservations for us tonight at the Centro Asturiano. It smells a little like cigars, but Daddy said it's nothing they can't fix. But the place is gorgeous. They have different levels, and it's..."

"Christina? Stop. Just stop!" Dhorian growled through clenched teeth.

"Well, somebody is in a bad mood," Christina responded playfully. "Look I…. I miss you, Dhorian. And…."

Instead of playing the *how could you* game, Dhorian hung up and ordered a round of drinks. Getting the attention of one of the entertainers, Dhorian asked caressing her arm, "So, you going to give me a dance or what, beautiful?"

"Sure. This way, sweetie…" she purred. Throwing back another drink, Dhorian followed her back to a private room. His phone vibrated again, and Dhorian put his phone on silent.

The only female voice he wanted to hear for the rest of the night was the sexy stripper who was about to get all the cash in his pocket.

*

Stumbling through the hallway to his condo, Dhorian almost passed out at the sight of Christina sitting wide-legged on the ground outside his door. Clearly under the influence of something, slumped over, and visibly pregnant, Dhorian's

327

concern outweighed his irritation, "Christina? What the hell are you doing here? What's going on? Are you okay?"

Breathing in labored spurts, Christina reached in her purse and took out a folder, handing it to Dhorian. "I can help you find the truth about your family and get my dad off your back, but before I do, I need something in return."

Chapter 29

VERDELL

Verdell stared at the natural redhead posing in front of the colorful mural on the corners of Albany and Main, the image glowing on his screen. She wore forest green leather thigh-high boots and a matching midi dress. He remembered taking the picture on the second day Tatiana started working at the Top Hat. *For promotional material* is what he recalled telling her. Tatiana's curvaceous silhouette made her look like a goddess with the sunset at her back and the light peeking over the sides and top of the surrounding buildings. Verdell could tell from the post date of the photo that it had been a while since Tatiana had been on her Instagram page. He logged into one of the dummy accounts Benji set up to research his targets. Verdell never thought he would be using it for any other purpose. Still, Tatiana's voice and face were imprinted in his memory, and scrolling through her pictures made her and their time together seem real.

The last time Verdell saw Tatiana, he contemplated ending their relationship. Even with Benji's most recent intel about her, Verdell still found himself longing for this woman. Everybody had a past, and being a working girl was not the worst thing he had ever heard of. The majority of the women Verdell dealt with were escorts. It kept him from catching feelings and getting caught up in remedial things that would only complicate his life further. Verdell felt he should have been more angered by the news because it did not come from Tatiana. Yet another pressing issue kept his emotions bottled. Tatiana could possibly be pregnant with his child. Unsure if the baby could be his, Verdell knew he had to find that bit of truth before forming a definite opinion on how mad to be about Tatiana's past or deciding their future.

Unfortunately, Verdell still had bigger fish to fry at the moment. First, he needed to figure out who had been following him and why they wanted to frame him. Tatiana, his father, and his own life would be in jeopardy until he had those questions answered.

Verdell closed the Instagram app and opened a file folder on his tablet. He wanted to look through the documents and photos Benji had gathered so far. It seemed all too convenient for two bodies, killed outside of a hole in the wall gentlemen's club, to be more newsworthy than the organized organ trading ring silently moving through the city. The encrypted data Benji pulled from the trafficking scout's and the pastor's phones confirmed Verdell's suspicions. Not only had they received multiple payouts from MonClaire Pharma. But in the months and days leading up to the victims' deaths, they were both in constant communication with a man named Stewart Logan. Benji backed into the money trail and found a personal holding company that functioned as a financing vehicle funding offshore shell company. These shell companies, in turn, washed money for pharmaceutical companies and research labs, in particular, MonClaire Pharma. It did not take long for Benji to find out that Stewart Logan owned the holding company and that he and Captain Stewart Logan of the Tampa Police Department were one and the same. That fact alone made the idea of a coverup that much more probable. The captain could not possibly make his salary and six and seven-figure wire transfers without help from someone higher, pulling the strings. Verdell mentally jotted down his questions while waiting in the parking lot across from the police station where Captain Logan would finish his shift in fifteen minutes. *Time to find out what you've been hiding, Captain.*

He's heading down to the parking lot now, Benji text Verdell.

Bet, Verdell text back.

Verdell hid behind a black SUV truck just three spots down from where Captain Logan's car was parked. The evening sky helped to conceal his shadows. The lock chirped as Captain Logan strolled within feet of his car. Verdell appeared behind the SUV and paced behind the captain in the darkness.

"Ahem," Verdell cleared his throat, startling the man.

"Evening, Captain Logan. I didn't know you moonlighted as an officer of the law."

Captain Logan jumped, "Who the fuck are you?"

Verdell disregarded the captain's question. Continuing to provoke as he walked towards the man, "Tell me how is it that a second-year captain making only seventy-five thousand three hundred seventy-five dollars and forty-two cents after taxes can make several million-dollar offshore transfers?"

Captain Logan tried to speak, but Verdell interrupted before he could utter his first sound, "Now I want you to think long and hard before you lie to me or ask another stupid question, like who am I? Or who sent me? If I'm here, I know enough. And because I know what I know, let's just skip the small talk."

The Captain fumbled with his keys as he scrambled to get into his car and hit the push to start. Before Verdell could grab him, Stewart Logan jumped in his car, flooring it out of the parking lot and onto the street, the door still open and swinging. Verdell chuckled to himself, knowing that Captain Logan would not make it very far. After sneaking through the parking lot gate, Verdell tagged Stewart's car with a GPS kill switch. He would catch up with him in a mile or so.

Verdell hustled across the street to his waiting vehicle and turned on Sade as his choice of chase music while following the GPS signal. Captain Logan weaved through traffic, swerving, switching lanes, and running three red lights with Verdell trailing not too far behind. Verdell waited for the Captain to turn off E Jackson St near a dead-end before enabling the kill switch. Captain Logan jerked the wheel, and Verdell watched in amusement as the Captain's face smashed into the steering wheel at the abrupt halt of the vehicle. He hung back and waited for the Captain's next move. Stewart Logan jumped out of the car just as fast as he hopped in it, cursing loudly, kicking the wheels of his car while holding his aching nose.

The Captain pulled out his phone and began yelling, "I'm being stalked. I don't know, the son of a bitch-".

That was the cue Verdell was waiting for. *I need to know who is on that phone.*

Verdell quickly tiptoed across the street and surprised Captain Logan. *BOP! BOP!* Punching him twice in the face.

"Ah, shit! Hell! My nose, man," Captain Logan stammered while holding his bleeding nose. He continued shouting, "Dammit. If this is about the Hamilton kid, tell Barry I got Frank to handle it!"

Verdell's head leaned to one side as he looked curiously at the man. He wondered if this man knew his last name was Hamilton. *Is this guy talking about me? And who in the fuck is Frank? Could that be who is following me?* But, instead of asking all the questions running through his mind, Verdell simply stared at the Captain, waiting for him to continue.

The stare-off lasted a few seconds before Captain Logan whined, "You're not going to make me spell it out for you, are you?" sounding irritated.

This amused Verdell. Thinking quick on his feet, Verdell stated plainly, "Barry wants to make sure you know what you're doing since you've been so sloppy lately."

Verdell backhanded the Captain for good measure. He had no idea who the hell Barry was, but if playing on the Captain's fear of him is what he needed to do to get answers, Verdell would be all over it.

"Get your ass up!" Verdell ordered, standing over Stewart's body, who lay on the cracked asphalt paralyzed by fear and pain. Verdell took note of the fallen phone and the call still in progress before returning his attention to the Captain.

"Dhorian. Dhorian Hamilton." The Captain yelled.

Hearing his cousin's name gave Verdell pause. *What the fuck has Dhorian got his soft ass into? I bet it got something to do with one of his white-collar crime-committing clients at that lame-ass practice he works for. Damn.* Verdell never cared much for his cousin, but he did keep tabs on him. Verdell would figure out how to get word about the bounty on his head later.

Verdell saw Captain Logan sneaking to reach into his car out of the corner of his eye. Before he could come out with whatever he was getting, Verdell balled his fist and punched the Captain again. This time in his mouth.

Stewart Logan spat blood from his cut jaw and rose to swing. Verdell ducked and blocked as the Captain's fist went flying, desperate to connect. Tired of playing games, Verdell sidestepped and countered, punching Captain Logan in his torso, causing him to double over and vomit.

Verdell grabbed the Captain's collar and muttered through clenched teeth in the Captain's ear, "I know you're laundering money for MonClaire Pharma. All I want to know is who is funding you and what the fuck it has to do with me?"

The seconds that passed only infuriated Verdell more. He punched Captain Logan twice more in the face before demanding, "Start talking. Now!"

Verdell released his hold and drew his gun, pointing it at the Captain's forehead.

"Oh-oh-okay. Okay! Ju-just take it easy," Stewart stuttered, clearing his throat before continuing, "I seriously don't know who you are..." Verdell cocked the hammer on the pistol, "but, but it's, it's the Mellows."

"The Mellows?" Verdell asked more to himself to help recall a face than for further clarification from the Captain. However, to his benefit, Captain Stewart Logan spilled everything he needed to confirm Benji's intel.

"Yes, yes, the Mellows. They use local clinics to push their drugs before FDA approval and sometimes dabble in black market sales."

"Dabble in black market sales?" Verdell asked sarcastically. *This fool trying to get cute.* Verdell quickly fired two shots at the Captain's feet and pressed the gun's tip to his temple. Stewart Logan cried out as the heat from the smoking barrel sizzled on his skin.

"Details. I need details." Verdell stated plainly.

Now bawling, the Captain proceeded through his sniveling, "it's a front for organ sales. They've been doing it for years. First, the company advertises clinical trials. Then, the subjects sign up online and make an appointment to come in. When they arrive, they're tested for compatibility. Once they're finished, they're compensated for their time. And then…"

"Then what?" Verdell pressed, pushing the pistol further into the Captain's head.

"And the-then they're hunted. Hunted for their organs. Once they get the organs, they're sold to the highest bidder."

Damn, so it's true? Verdell thought. "The Mellows? Where can I find them?" he barked.

Stewart fell silent.

"Oh no, don't hold out on me now. You've already given me the good stuff. I'm sure when they find out that you gave me the entire operation, you're as good as dead anyway. Now, where can I find the Mellows?" Verdell demanded.

Captain Stewart Logan found his balls, maintaining his silence.

Tired of the games, Verdell wrapped his finger around the trigger, "Fuck it. I'll find out myself."

Before Verdell could squeeze the trigger, the Captain rushed him, knocking Verdell off balance and to the ground. Stewart Logan began fighting for his life. As much as Verdell could appreciate the effort, tonight would be the Captain's last amongst the living. Verdell bided his time, waiting for the Captain's wild punches to tire. As soon as Captain Logan stepped closer to connect, Verdell head-butted him, smashing his already fractured nose.

"Enough of this shit!" Verdell shouted as he snatched his

gun from the tar and cocked it. He kicked Stewart mercilessly, stomping the Captain until he could not move without a rattling moan to follow.

Captain Logan put his hands up in surrender, blubbering through swollen and bloody lips, "Wa-wait!"

Pow! Pow! Pow! Verdell blasted the man once in the stomach and twice in the head. The buzzing phone lying next to Captain Logan's dying body snapped Verdell out of his blood trance. The caller's name *B Mellow* glowed in the darkness. *I almost forgot.* Verdell picked up the phone, answering with silence.

"Logan! Where are you? I killed that lying motherfucker Frank, and it sounds like you will be next on my list. I can't hold the mayor off any longer. He's asking too many damn questions, and I'm sick of cleaning up your shit. So get here, now, or you know what will come next."

Verdell abruptly ended the call, cracked open the case's back, and removed the sim card. Pocketing the chip, he threw the cell to the ground and shot it twice. Back in his car Verdell sat, contemplating what to do next. He could not waste time chasing the organ thing. He only had three days max to blindside B Mellow, who he also assumed was Barry, before someone would find Captain Logan's body. Verdell texted dry cleaning to let them know about the mess and took off for the crosstown. Deep in thought about his next moves, Verdell passed a billboard. *Why didn't I think of that before?* He did not have the energy to dig into the story and expose it himself, but the woman on the billboard could. Verdell exited the expressway and drove into Palm River. The adrenaline running through him was suffocating in the car. Verdell needed fresh air, and he had to make a call.

Pulling over by the Maydell Bridge, Verdell got out of the car and took out his cell phone. "Benji? I know who is behind the killings. It's a wealthy family connected to the mayor."

"Wait. Wait. Slow down. Connected to the mayor?"

"Yes, the mayor."

"Well, that doesn't surprise me at all. You, of all people, should know how grimy politicians are. I mean, look at how your situation started."

Verdell inhaled deeply, "Benji, right now is not the time for a history lesson. I need you to listen. I got two assignments for you."

"Okay, okay." Benji groaned. "You take the fun out of everything. Give me the first one."

"I need you to contact Tiffany LaSalle at Channel 8 News and give her all the information you found on that Pharma company. Tell her the mayor and a B. Mellow are involved. Then, it'll be up to her to make sure the story lines up." Verdell instructed.

"I am pulling up her email now, zipping and encrypting," – Verdell could hear Benji's fingers typing furiously at the keys. - "adding a few niceties and done!" Benji announced excitedly.

Verdell pulled out his laptop and inserted the sim card.

"I'm sending you everything from Stewart Logan's phone. I

need you to send me his most frequented residential stops. Can you do that?"

"Why are you talking to me like this is my first rodeo, Vee? Of course, I can. Say less."

"See, that's your problem. If you did more working and less gloating, maybe you could start your own thing and stop moonlighting with me."

"Pssh. Excuse me." Benji sucked her teeth, offended. "I will have you know that you are not my only client, and my services are in high demand these days."

"What? Don't play games with me, Benji. I can't have no conflicts...."

"Yea, yea, yea." Benji cut Verdell off. "No worries from my end. I am very professional when it comes to my coin. I take the confidentiality of my clientele very seriously. So, you better start appreciating me and recognizing my skills, Vee."

Verdell winced at the gum popping, neck rolling, sister girl thing he imagined Benji doing on her side of the phone.

"Got it!" Benji shouted. "But you are not going to like it." Benji sighed.

"What? Never mind, just send it to me." Verdell barked, anxious to see for himself.

"Next time you call me, please lose the attitude. And your invoice is on its way." Benji snipped.

"My bad, I'm just..."

"Yea. Whatever." Benji dismissed before hanging up.

Verdell sighed. He felt bad. He did need to treat Benji better because she was very good at "tech-ing". She had not steered him wrong yet. Verdell transferred Benji twice the amount of her invoice with an accompanying note. I'm sorry. He'd apologize in person later.

Verdell looked at the addresses and immediately recognized two of the three on his screen. Benji was right. Verdell did not like what he saw. The Captain had been snooping around his dad and Tatiana. Verdell called Tatiana, but the phone went to voicemail. He tried again and a third time, and still, the phone did not ring. *Dammit, pick up the phone, Tatiana.* Verdell almost gave up when the thought crossed his mind. *Maybe it's just my number that's not going through. Fuck it. I'm going over there.*

*

Knock Knock Knock

Verdell lightly tapped on Tatiana's door to no response. Placing his ear to the door, Verdell heard soft music playing. He thought about knocking on the front door like a normal person would, but he did not want to wake Nanna. Hearing music coming from the side entrance leading to Tatiana's room seemed promising. He needed to see her.

Knock Knock Knock

Full of anxiety, Verdell pounded the door harder. The more time passed, the heavier his chest grew. Verdell would hate to start knocking like the police at 2:45 in the morning but laying eyes on Tatiana would make him feel better, knowing she was safe. Besides, they needed to address a few elephants.

Knock Knock Knock

"Who is it?" Verdell heard a soft voice answer, and his heart skipped.

Suddenly, his mouth grew dry, and Verdell could not find the words to announce himself.

"I said, who the hell is it?" the voice rose another octave.

Verdell stayed quiet and continued knocking. He knew Tatiana hated his playfulness, but it would feel good to see the irritated yet sexy look on her face. Or at least that is what Verdell thought. The swing of the Louisville Slugger overshadowed the look of irritation and sexiness on Tatiana's face as she answered the door.

"Tati, baby, it's me," Verdell yelled, hoping the announcement of his name would make her stop aiming for his head.

"Ooof!" Verdell groaned when Tatiana caught him in the stomach with the tip of the bat.

"What are you doing here, Verdell?" Tatiana asked hands on her hips.

She flicked on the porch light, and Verdell squinted at the brightness of the LEDs. When he finally focused his vision, Verdell noticed two things. The first, Tatiana's beauty. The second, Tatiana's belly. Tatiana must have felt his eyes roaming over her body because she grabbed her robe and clutched it tighter around her waist.

"Hello," Tatiana waved a hand in his face.

Damn. Tatiana is really pregnant. Tatiana's hand waving

snapped him out of his thoughts, but Verdell still could not find the words, so he simply stared.

"Why the fuck are you here, Verdell? What do you want? You've been MIA for almost two fucking months, and I hope you don't think you showing up here at," Tatiana looking down at her wristwatch, "at 2:48 in the morning is going to get you back into my good graces."

Lips pursed, bat positioned across her chest, the barrel part bouncing off her palm, Tatiana stood coldly.

"I just…I need you right now, okay? Verdell asked.

Tatiana's face remained hardened.

"My bad, Tati. I just been having a lot of shit going on. Too much shit."

"Everybody got shit going on, Verdell. That doesn't explain why I haven't so much as gotten a text from you. For all I know, you could've been dead."

Verdell ran his hands over his face in frustration. *Hell. She is right.*

Tatiana continued pressing, "For real, what's going on? I need to at least know if I should be worried or not. If somebody is chasing you, I need to prepare myself."

"Ain't nobody following me. And if they were, you know I'd protect you," Verdell stated matter of fact.

Verdell knew she deserved an explanation for his whereabouts but did not have one he thought would be good enough. Lifting his head for the first time since Tatiana snatched the door open, Verdell heard Tatiana gasp. *Damn, I forgot the Captain hit me.*

"Verdell, you have about five seconds to tell me what the hell happened to your face and why you decided to bring it here. What do you want?" and then a little less viciously, "Verdell, why are you here?"

Verdell knew he looked like shit. The Captain got in a couple of good shots before his blood spritzed Verdell's clothing.

"Tati, I just want you to bathe me." Verdell pleaded.

Tatiana took a step forward into the doorway, "What did you say?"

Verdell came closer, too, stepping into the light and stretching out his arms for Tatiana to see the full extent of his tattered and blood-spattered appearance.

Again, Verdell begged, "Tatiana. Tati. Could you please bathe me?"

Verdell was not surprised that Tatiana seemed taken aback by his request and beat-up appearance. He hoped that her anger would turn into sympathy as he took small steps toward her. She had to know the severity of the circumstances for him to show up after all this time.

To Verdell's benefit, his idea worked. Without asking any more questions, Tatiana took his hand and closed the door behind them. After locking the door, Tatiana directed Verdell to the bathroom like he had never been there before. Verdell could not blame her for treating him like a stranger. He disappeared at a time when she probably needed him most. Instead of being there for Tatiana, Verdell remained true to his nature and did what he knew best; he buried his feelings and became a ghost.

Verdell waited for Tatiana to say anything as he undressed in the bathroom. Instead, Tatiana moved around him, collecting his clothes, and running his bath as if he were not standing in the middle of the room. However, Verdell could see the wheels turning in her head. He welcomed the silence, though. They would talk when the time came. Right now, with all the darkness following him, Verdell only wanted to enjoy the smell of incense, bath salts, and acoustics of whatever soul artist Tatiana had crooning as he sat in a warm bath, with his lady washing his back.

Stepping into the clawfoot tub, water scorching his toes, Verdell thought, *damn, this water is hot. Her ass probably did this shit on purpose to punish me by burning my damn skin off. But I deserve it. This and a whole lot worse.* Verdell sat in the tub, face contorting as he hissed at the steaming water scorching his body. Tatiana sat on a stool by the tub, humming to the music as she ran her hand through the water. Verdell marveled at her face, unbothered by the temperature. The red hue of Tatiana's fingers, palm, and wrist let Verdell know she felt the heat even though her face did not show it. Verdell toyed with the idea that *maybe she's punishing herself too.*

When Verdell attempted to speak, Tatiana quickly put up her free hand to halt him. She took a loofah and smothered it in liquid black soap and began scrubbing his back. Verdell breathed in deeply. The sharp pains he felt from Tatiana rubbing on what he assumed were open cuts and bruises were calmed with each deep breath. The steam from the water, along with scents of lavender and coconut, relaxed him. Verdell slid further into the tub, submerging his face and hair. He stayed that way, contemplating the day's events. Verdell knew, at some point, he would have to tell Tatiana what had been going on and talk about the extra human that had taken refuge in her body. His lungs blazing, Verdell surfaced, gasping for air. The room felt different. The light was dimmer than he last remembered. Tatiana, no longer sitting on the chair, Verdell ran his hands over his face searching the room. The panic rising in his chest made him look for a sharp object to defend himself with. *Shit! I left my piece in the bag.*

"I thought you needed a moment to yourself," Tatiana cooed from the bathroom doorway.

Her open robe displaying full breasts, a rounded belly, wide hips, thick thighs, and a short curly mound made Verdell fumble through his response.

"Uh. Nah. I just uh, I wanted to umm, take it all in. It's been a while since I've been somewhere this, uh, peaceful."

"Well, I'm glad you came by. I was beginning to think I would never see you again. I missed you." She purred softly.

Tatiana posing like a bronze goddess waiting for her release, Verdell could not take his eyes away from hers. He recognized the hunger that sparked between them. Even though unexpected considering the circumstances, Verdell wanted his woman. Tatiana had never looked more inviting than she did at that moment. *My baby looks delicious as hell. Wonder how I could be so lucky?*

Beckoning Tatiana with his finger, he whispered sensually, "bring your sexy ass over here."

Without one word spoken, Tatiana let her robe drop to the checkered tile floor and let the warm water engulf her. It splashed over the sides of the basin as she straddled him. Their touching skin made beads of sweat drip from Verdell's temples. *I ain't even in it, and she feels this damn good. Shit, it's been too long.*

Tatiana began to position herself to take him into her center. Verdell wrapped one hand around her waist and outlined her lips with the fingers of his free hand. Then, holding her inches away from his throbbing shaft, it came to Verdell that he had never been with a pregnant woman before. He would not even have attempted something like it if it was not Tatiana, if it was not his baby. *But is it my baby?*

"Shhh. Shhh. It's okay." Tatiana whispered as she kissed his lips. "I'm okay." – Kiss. – "You're okay." – Kiss. – "We're okay." Kiss.

Verdell's lips were occupied with sweet kisses, and he could not respond even if he wanted to. No longer controlled by his thoughts, Verdell lowered Tatiana onto him. Her tightness sent a shiver down to his toes which he curled and uncurled to distract him from the moan trying to escape his throat. Verdell's eyes rolled to the back of his head as Tatiana's moans of pleasure echoed around the room. She rocked back and forth on his lap, creating a rhythm that made small underwater waves slap against his balls. They tingled as Tatiana squeezed her walls on his hardening shaft, the water intensifying the pleasure with each stroke. Verdell felt his climax coming too soon, and he lifted Tatiana up from his lap and positioned her on her knees inside the now half-filled tub. Her doe-shaped eyes gazed into his, ready and anxious for whatever came next.

"So, you missed me, huh?" Verdell asked quietly, positioning himself to enter Tatiana's moist slit from behind.

The water sloshed around Tatiana as she arched her back, preparing to receive Verdell's hardness. He noticed her maneuvering around her protruding belly, which looked a bit uncomfortable. But Verdell did not let that deter his mood. With the way she just rode him, he had confidence she could handle the *D*. Verdell could be patient. When Tatiana stopped moving about and looked over her shoulder to wink at him, Verdell thought, *I'm about to tear her ass up.*

Making her count each stroke, Verdell kneaded Tatiana's walls like dough. Before long, her legs were quaking as she whined, "Oh my God! Please don't stop. Do. Not. Stop. Shiiiit."

"That's right. You can take it." Verdell panted with every stroke.

He reveled in Tatiana's purrs of pleasure while he pounded her slow, giving her every bit of his shaft to the hilt. Verdell pulled at Tatiana's ponytail and sucked her tongue, kissing her deeply. Verdell's thighs grew weak, and he lost his rhythm when Tatiana's eyes began rolling to the back of her head in ecstasy.

He did not have time to apologize or readjust before Tatiana took control. Rolling her hips and rocking in sync with his motion, Verdell felt Tatiana squeezing her walls on his shaft. She reached back and began massaging his balls, and they contracted in her hand as she gently rubbed them.

"Fuuuuccckkk Tati!!!" Verdell screamed out in intermittent spurts, pulling out and spilling his seed on Tatiana's rear before collapsing back into the tub.

Verdell helped Tatiana from her position hanging over the side of the tub and kissed her neck and ears as she laid back on his chest. They laughed at the wet floor, playing with each other's fingers as warm water flowed from the faucet.

At the time when his mouth should have moved, Verdell's thoughts swirled. He wanted to let her know everything that had been going on, but only after they dealt with her little secrets first. Helping her out of the tub, Verdell wrapped a towel around Tatiana and another around his waist.

He pecked her gently on the lips, "I'll meet you in the room, okay?"

Tatiana nodded.

Anxiety filled the minute that passed before Tatiana emerged from the bathroom. Her body was still damp with the towel Verdell gave her wrapped tightly, accentuating her figure. He felt his manhood growing again, which he would make sure to address with her later. But first, business.

Verdell noticed her glow. *Tatiana is definitely pregnant.* Verdell counted her at about four or five months if he had to guess. *She could be further, but I need her to tell me something.* Deep down, he wanted the baby to be his. Verdell would go on the run with Tatiana, their baby, and Nanna if Tatiana wanted. Then, he could start over and build the family he always wanted. The family he could have had if things worked out differently for him.

Trying to mentally calculate the dates made Verdell dizzy. But his heart calculated Tatiana's willingness to sleep with him as confirmation that the baby had to be his. No matter what he did not know about her past, who Tatiana was to him over these last months made him trust her.

Verdell gazed at Tatiana, rubbing lotion on her still moist skin across the room. The silence choking them, Verdell had yet to provide a solid response on his whereabouts or the reason for his bloody appearance on arrival. Verdell did not know whether to start with an explanation or an apology first. *Of course, she won't believe me.* But, maybe, if he apologized. There was so much Verdell wanted to apologize for: abandoning her after the club shooting, not calling to check in, for his deceiving lifestyle. *Shit, I wouldn't believe it if I wasn't living it.*

He and Tatiana never spoke about their feelings or what it meant for their status, but Verdell knew they were in love.

"Tati, I..."

"Verdell, it's okay," she interrupted. "I understand. You think that if you tell me, it will change how I see you, and you would lose me."

Her coolness should have made him cool. Instead, it made him impatient.

"I know you're pregnant," he blurted out. Verdell was not

ready to address the Cairo secret. Especially so soon after making love to her. Instead, their baby seemed like the more pressing issue.

Tati's mouth attempted to play off what her face could not hide. "And what makes you think that?"

Verdell crossed the room and stood so close to her, he could feel her heart beating as if it were in his chest. Verdell looked down into Tatiana's eyes, caressing her face. He placed his hand on her stomach, and the baby kicked, surprising them both. Verdell gently kissed the tears streaming from Tatiana's closed eyes before wiping them away from her cheeks. He led her to the bed and sat down, moving her to stand in front of him.

Looking at her sternly, Verdell began, "Tati, if you knew you were pregnant, when were you going to tell me? You've had to know all this time, and you're acting like nothing's changed. Like you having my baby wouldn't change us. Is it mine?"

Avoiding his questions, Tatiana asked one of her own. "How did you know?"

Verdell noted that Tatiana had not been able to look him in the eye for longer than a few seconds at a time since his arrival. *So much for the baby being mine. If she wants to play this game, I can play it too.* Instead of taking the direct route and letting Tatiana know about Benji and how he found out about her pregnancy, he took a simpler way.

"I know pregnant when I see it. You're at least five months."

No response. Just a tight-lipped Tatiana. One arm folded

tightly across her chest as the other played with the key on her necklace.

Verdell looked slowly over her body until his eyes settled on her growing womb. "Have you been to the doctor? Are you getting the care you need? I can look into that. I mean...have you gotten anything for the baby? Do you know if it's a boy or girl?"

Verdell felt Tatiana's uneasiness as he shot off question after question.

"Well...I went to my first appointment to confirm, and that's been it, really. I haven't been back. I feel okay besides the back pain, but I'm good. In all honesty, I only found out two weeks ago. I mean, you ask me all these questions, and you don't even know if you should care that much. Besides, don't think I forgot that you did not answer my questions," she said slyly, slapping his hand off her stomach, face full of attitude.

"Listen, I've been MIA for the last month or so, but you've been pregnant. We can place blame all night, baby, but if you would've told me what was up that night at the club, maybe I would've taken you with me." Verdell said in a controlled tone.

"Maybe?" Tatiana huffed hands on her hips. "You just saying shit, Verdell," she finished before letting him respond. "You don't have to say things to make me feel better about what it is. I mean, we were only a hookup. I'm not your responsibility, and I'm not here to give you more responsibilities."

Verdell shook his head and laughed at her last comment. "Responsibility, Tati? Why do you think I'm here? I can help you with all of this." He spread his arms and gestured around the room. "I can put you up, I can pay your bills, I can buy your groceries, I can get you a brand-new wardrobe, AND I don't mind tapping your pockets every now and then without you asking. I know what responsibility is. I can take care of you and our baby."

Tatiana pouted in response. "So, why you never mentioned all this before? Me and Nanna were struggling before I got pregnant, and you never offered to help then."

Verdell chuckled, "You real proud, Tatiana. If I approached you with the "*I could change your world*" spiel, you never would have let me get close to you. Now stop all that ignorant shit, and let's start thinking of names for this baby. And don't worry about where I was. I was taking care of some business. Nothing you should be worried about. The only thing I need you thinking about is you, me, and this baby." Verdell smiled slyly up at her, wrapping his hand around her belly again.

Even with arms tightly folded across her chest, Tatiana's smirk told Verdell that her hard shell was melting.

"Please take care of our baby Tati." Verdell cupped her stomach with his broad hands, mushing his face where he felt the baby kick.

Tatiana bent down and passionately returned his kisses from his forehead to his chin and began removing her damp towel.

Verdell chuckled and grabbed the towel before it hit the floor. "Oh no, ma'am. Once is enough for you and little Peanut. Maybe tomorrow."

Tatiana slapped his shoulder playfully. Verdell, feigning hurt, pulled her down to the bed and wrapped them both in her blanket.

Tatiana fell asleep within minutes. The corners of Verdell's mouth turned up as he watched Tatiana sleep in the comfort of his arms. He closed his eyes and fantasized about all of their major life events; the birth of their child, walking her over the threshold of their new home, saying their vows. For the first time in a long time, Verdell considered what a real-life would look like, leaving his current existence behind and trading it in for peace and happiness.

*

A brightly lit screen and a pulsing phone woke Verdell up from his slumber. *Damn, when did I fall asleep?* He answered the phone groggily, "Hello?"

The other line hissed, "Yes, let me speak to the fucking idiot that handles personal problems."

The vaguely familiar voice popped Verdell up in bed, now fully awake. "Who the fuck is this?"

The voice, disregarding his question, snarled a statement of its own. "The girl is still alive."

"What girl?" Verdell asked, confused. "And you still didn't answer my question. So who the hell is this?"

"The dead girl that turns out to be an alive woman, no thanks to you."

Verdell's heart felt close to exploding. Confrontation was

not a new concept for Verdell, so he did not easily shake, but the anxiety building in his chest consumed his psyche. *What girl?* Verdell prided himself on always finishing the job. However, in his earlier years, there was one he did not technically complete. Verdell did not want to believe that this call could be about that assignment because he specifically told them to stay gone, to stay hidden. *Unless…. unless they didn't stay gone. Maybe they did for a while but returned. A lot can change in nearly ten years. And unless they had the means to leave town, they most likely never left the city.* Verdell thought a while longer. The little girl he spared would now be an adult. She was a pretty little girl, so Verdell did not doubt she would be an attractive woman. *Red hair, light brown skin, almond-shaped eyes, a scar above her right…*

Tatiana stirring in bed next to him grabbed his attention. She shifted in a way where the keloid skin above her right breast was exposed. Verdell's thoughts rushed past coincidence and went to his worst fear. *She would be…. She would be…. Oh my God! Shit. It can't be. She can't be.*

"Not only do we want our money back with interest, but we want the job finished, or we're going to stop giving you warning shots and make one of them connect."

At least Verdell now knew who had been following him and trying to kill him lately. "Look okay, okay, okay, okay, okay. If you kill me, you won't get your money. Let me check out your source to see if it's valid, and I'll take care of it for good this time." Verdell tried to calm the situation.

"Fine. Check your messages," the voice instructed.

Verdell saw the multimedia message come in and opened it. He stared at the side-by-side photos of Tatiana at twelve and her again at twenty-one. The similarities were uncanny. *How could I have not noticed it?* It explained why there was a certain familiarity about her that he could not put his finger on.

Recovering from his extended pause, Verdell quickly whispered, "Cool, I got it." And hung up.

Verdell leaned back and grabbed the Desert Eagle .44 from his bag. The past was back to haunt him, and terrified or not, Verdell needed to face it. He could not bear telling her the truth. Tatiana would never recover from finding out that he murdered her mother and almost killed her. *She would never forgive me.* The gun shook in his hands as he pushed it against Tatiana's temple. She remained sound asleep. *I wonder if she knows,* Verdell thought briefly.

Years ago, Verdell barely recovered from being accused of killing his first love and unborn child. Cocking the hammer, he knew going through with this would shatter him irrevocably. Verdell tried to fight falling in love with Tatiana, but how could he not? They were yoked. Fate aligned their paths when he decided to keep her alive and fake her death. Back then, Tatiana was a doe-eyed, red-headed, innocent twelve-year-old girl who did nothing to deserve the torture he helped inflict on her. At this moment, beads of sweat and tears mingling at the corners of his eyes, Verdell contemplated finishing the job he started close to a decade ago. He thought about the secrets

Benji uncovered, and they were minute compared to his past. Tatiana may not be as innocent these days. Nonetheless, she was his second chance at love, at a family, and the mother of his unborn child. Verdell rubbed the muzzle of the gun gently against the scar on her chest and winced as he remembered the pain and fear that swam in her eyes as he plunged the knife into her chest all those years ago. He tended to shy away from the jobs involving children after that.

Verdell moved the hair from her face. Tatiana was beautiful, and she was his. He fingered the scar again full of regret and touched her stomach, mourning the loss of yet another child he would never get to meet. "FUCK. I need to focus, and it'll all be over." He exhaled loudly.

Verdell adjusted his grip, placing the .44 at her forehead when Tatiana's eyes popped open. The piercing stare unnerved him. There was no scream like he expected. She did not ask, *"Verdell? Baby? What's going on? What are you doing? Please don't kill me."*

There were no questions and no pleading. Tatiana's wistful gaze held no accusations. Verdell only saw the pain of love in her swelling eyes and glare from the chrome-plated pistol that she pressed under his chin.

Tatiana cocked the hammer with ease while glaring down the barrel of death. To Verdell, her being quiet meant that his attempt on her life, even after the night they shared, was not surprising. Verdell could not tell if she knew he would pull the trigger or trusted him enough not to. Either way, Tatiana looked ready to blow his head off if it came down to it.

Tatiana spoke and broke Verdell's line of thought. "You weren't going to say goodbye?"

Out of all the questions Tatiana could have asked, Verdell had not been prepared for the one she did. Instead of answering Tatiana's simple question, Verdell spewed out his own emotional turmoil, "what I felt was too good to be true. I knew you from before. I know you would never love me or let me see my child if you knew the real me. It was in your eyes. I knew your stare. I remember all of my victim's stares."

Leaving the bed, Verdell did not fail to notice the compact Smith and Wesson M&P 22 that Tatiana kept aimed at his head as he moved around the room. When Verdell finished his rant, he locked eyes with Tatiana. Tears were spilling down her cheeks like thick syrup. The gun fell loosely from her grip. Inaudibly, Verdell sighed a breath of relief. He had never seen Tatiana use her gun, but the look in her eyes a few moments earlier let Verdell know she had the killer instinct. If he was going to have to leave this world someday, he rather it was at the hands of the woman he loved.

"Wha…what do you want me to say, Verdell?" Tatiana cried, sounding defeated.

"Tati I…I nearly ended your life years ago. This shit is…. it's too much for me right now. I got to go," Verdell got dressed and then hustled out the door with Tatiana's cries at his back. Walking away from Tatiana felt like murdering a piece of himself.

Verdell jumped in the car, slamming the door so hard his driver-side window shattered. Disregarding the broken shards of glass sprinkled on his lap, Verdell looked at his hands which had not stopped trembling since he received the phone call. Hot tears began flowing as Verdell choked on the pain and tightness in his throat from the breaking of his heart.

"What the hell is wrong with me? Why does this shit happen to me?" Verdell screamed aloud.

When Verdell considered the lousy hand he had been dealt, he had a hard time coming to terms with karma biting him in the ass when he thought himself innocent, to begin with. *Just when I think I'm past the fucking pity party. Of all the people I could have found and fallen in love with, why did it have to be her?* Verdell thought as he glanced at the side-by-side photos of Tatiana and her younger self.

Only hours before, he promised to protect her. He never thought who she had to be protected from would be himself.

Verdell looked at his watch to check the time, *4:35 a.m.* He had a few hours to burn before daylight. Convinced that happiness and peace would not be in his future anytime soon, Verdell's mind drifted to his current reality. He still needed to clear his name. He pulled himself together, wiping the moisture from his burning eyes, and pulling his phone out of his pocket. *Yo Benji, hit me up when you get this. You won't believe this shit.*

Epilogue

PAUL

"You think these campaigns pay for themselves? They don't! And there are some sick bastards in this world, and unfortunately, those are the ones willing to throw the most money. And their buy-in and support don't come cheap. So, we do what we have to do, what we've always done for the sake and the betterment of this family," Sandra shouted through her sobs while pacing the office floor.

Paul had been listening to her rant and rave for the past two hours non-stop. But he was okay with that. Her showing emotion meant that she was not leaving him, and after everything was said and done, she would help him with a resolution.

Sandra continued her tirade, "Something your selfish ass would know nothing about Paul. All you've ever done is look after your own ass while my brother, my family and I, have covered for you, hid your indiscretions, and made you appear to be some saint."

Paul's pride wanted to argue everything he had done for her family in return, but he knew better. Sandra rarely complained about putting up with his shit. Instead, she stood by his side when he was sick and made sure he had a second and third chance at a quality life. And getting more kidneys and finding an unorthodox surgeon to perform the procedures was not easy.

Sandra interjected with more of her fury, "Do you think your beloved city will follow you after they find out how many deaths you're responsible for? Do you think they would still vote for you after finding out that you're embarrassed to be BLACK! For Christ's sake, you're Black, Paul. Don't you think that is something that I should have known about? Our entire life together has been a lie! How could you not give me a choice?"

That last question stung. Despite having a mistress and a child outside of their marriage, Paul felt that he had been a great husband, father, and provider. Sandra nor Christina never wanted for anything. Even in all his good, Paul's worst fear had come to fruition. It was his Blackness that would stain his legacy. Paul was very tempted to play the race card here, but deep down, he understood his wife's pain and her sacrifice. Instead of letting her continue with her rhetorical attack, Paul dropped to his knees. He crawled on them until he was in front of her, head pressed into stomach and arms wrapped tightly around her.

"Sandra, please forgive me! Please forgive me for hurting you over and over. Forgive me for the damage that I've done to our family."

Paul mushed his tears into her white, freshly pressed blouse, making sure to rub his runny nose into it for extra effect. "Tell me how to make it right. I'm begging you. Tell me what to do. If you want me to go to your father and tell him what I've done, I will. If you want me to go to jail and be the scapegoat for the sake of the family, I will. If you want me to die in some unfortunate accident, I will."

Paul could tell that his words were eating away at Sandra's anger and decided that now was the time to put on the finishing touches of his apology. Squeezing her hands, Paul looked into Sandra's eyes and put on his best earnest voice, professing, "But I love you, Sandra. I love you like I have never loved another woman. If you can find it in your heart to forgive me, I promise that there will be no other woman, no other secret, no other betrayal, no other lie that would come between us. I am yours, and you are mine! We have created an empire. We have a beautiful family. So let me be the man you married and know me to be. I know I can make this right and make you happy again."

There was a moment of silence, and Paul did not dare break it. He figured at this moment, Sandra was trying to figure out how much of his bullshit to buy, and he would give her time to do so. It was the least Paul could do if she and her family were going to let him live. He was already at odds with Barry. Paul did not want to fight in his home too. At least not until he had an exit plan.

"Oh Paul," Sandra cried as she kissed him and wrapped her hands around his neck. Paul kissed Sandra back long and lovingly until she let out a moan.

It worked! Sandra's guard falling down was the best news Paul received in weeks. His ass was finally out of the hot seat, and with Sandra on his side, he could focus on his escape.

Epilogue

TIFFANY

"Tiffany? Tiffany LaSalle?" a voice yelled from across the room.

"Yes, over here," Tiffany shouted through the noisy newsroom while motioning the inquirer to come over.

Tiffany got straight to the point once they made it to her desk. "Yes, I'm Tiffany. How can I help you? I'm in the middle of a story."

"Actually, I'm here to help you," the woman responded confidently.

This piqued Tiffany's interest. She had not looked at the woman straight on until that moment. The woman's blotched skin intrigued her even more.

"Well, I have a few minutes. Follow me into the uh... conference room so we can talk privately."

Tiffany's wheels began spinning as she led the woman through the noisy building.

Once they were seated and the door closed, Tiffany asked, "Are you from South Africa? I thought I may have heard a bit of an accent."

"Actually, I am only here to discuss what I have to assist you."

"Umm, okay." Tiffany fidgeted. "So, I guess that means asking for your name is out of the question?"

The woman only answered Tiffany with a smile.

"Well, alrighty then. Let's get started. What do you have for me?" Tiffany asked, exasperated.

"I am here on behalf of my employer. He wanted to make sure that you received this information and the instructions on how to disseminate it."

"Instructions?" Tiffany questioned.

She was almost insulted until she began looking through the pages of the folder. It could not be a mere coincidence that damning information tying Mayor Paul Christen and his in-laws, the Mellows, to criminal activity landed in her lap.

"Is there something wrong?" the woman asked like she had not just dropped the atom bomb.

Rising up from the table, Tiffany exclaimed, "No, there is nothing wrong, but there is something quite fishy going on here. Who put you up to this? Is this some kind of expedition for a scapegoat? Because I will deny ever seeing these files."

The woman's lighthearted chuckle did not put Tiffany at

ease. Hyenas laughed before they attacked and ripped out hearts too.

"It's okay. Please sit down. I can promise that we are on the same side here."

Tiffany took a deep breath and, again, her seat.

"Now, all the information you would need to put down Paul Christen, his family, and even Barry Mellow is included in that file. All you have to do is agree to the terms."

"Are you sure that is *all* I have to do?" Tiffany asked suspiciously.

"Well, that and..."

"I knew it was something else." Tiffany barked.

The woman put her hand up to explain. "My employer would like for you to keep an eye on Tatiana Foster."

Now Tiffany knew it was not a coincidence. She had tried to stay away from Barry Mellow, Paul Christen, and anyone else close to that ordeal since her last run-in with Barry. Tiffany even ignored the numerous calls she received from Dhorian and Verdell regarding whatever information they had on him.

"Is your employer's name, Verdell?" Tiffany asked hesitantly, trying to link who would care enough to watch over Tatiana.

Disregarding her question, the woman rose from the table, "The instructions will be mailed to you along with payment. If you have any questions, please hold onto them until after the first set of instructions has been received."

And as quick as she had come, the South African woman with the blotched skin was gone.

Tiffany sat in the conference room, visibly shaken. She was tired of this feeling. Tired of being cornered and running scared. Tiffany settled that she would go along with Verdell's plan, but she would not do so without some protection of her own.

Epilogue

DHORIAN

Dhorian's hands trembled as he looked through the documents. It contained all the information he would ever want to know about Anne Marie Anderson. She gave birth to two boys on January 12, 1988, and gave one of them to her cousin to legally adopt not a day later. Dhorian assumed the man who raised him and who he was named after had no knowledge of the adoption because his name was nowhere on the paperwork. Even though Dhorian distinctly remembered having a funeral for his aunt, Anne Marie, when he was fifteen, there was a current address in Palm Beach. According to her background check, she was apparently doing well for herself. This made Dhorian livid at first. The woman he thought to be his dead aunt was actually his mother and happened to be alive and well.

After thousands of dollars and weeks in therapy, Dhorian

concluded that if Anne Marie had been gone this long, there was no need to bring up the past. He had no use for her. But maybe Verdell did. He and Verdell never saw eye to eye as cousins, and Dhorian was not sure they would do any better as siblings. *Twins at that.* Dhorian sealed the papers back in the envelope Christina gave him, wrote Verdell's name on it, and placed it in the family bible heirloom he received as a wedding gift earlier that morning. Getting married in the hospital's chapel was not his ideal wedding, but it was the least he could do before Christina gave birth to their baby girl.

Watching Christina and their newborn baby girl sleeping peacefully, Dhorian said a silent prayer of thanks. Christina gave Dhorian something he never thought he would find, closure. While it had been a hard pill to swallow and a lot to come to terms with, it made Dhorian realize that he had been too hard on her. All Christina wanted was for him to love her and for Dhorian to let her love him. Christina came through and helped to provide Dhorian with clarity when he could have been framed for murder. She gave him back his power, and to Dhorian, marrying Christina was his way of showing that he would not abandon her. Dhorian made sure Christina had the treatment and support she needed to beat her habit and stay clean for the sake of their baby.

At that moment, even though Dhorian did not want to be related to Paul no more than Paul wanted to be related to him, he was happy to have made an honest woman out of Christina. She deserved at least that. Dhorian vowed to take care of her and his child and give them a chance at a real family. One without all of the dysfunction.

Dhorian rotated the long-handled Q-tip in his daughter's drool, careful not to wake her or her mother, on whose chest she was sleeping. He kissed his daughter gently on the forehead and whispered, "Daddy is going to take good care of you and mommy just as soon as I know you're mine."

Epilogue

TATIANA

"It's like my life was destined to be fucked," Tatiana whined before continuing.

"Cairo is still out there. The man I love, and the father of my child is responsible for my mother's death and tried to kill me twice. My father says he is for his people but wants nothing to do with me – *his blood*. And Nanna can go any day now. So how am I supposed to be a good mother with all of this going on? Tatiana looked down at the sleeping pink bundle of patchy golden hair and green eyes on her chest.

"Well, I don't know who Cairo is, but from what you tell me of Verdell, he loves you. It may not seem like it now, but you'll see him again. And when you do, you'll either kiss him or kill him. Maybe both," Tiffany joked, trying to make light of the situation.

They both chuckled.

"Now your father is another subject. You let me deal with him. Your friend, Verdell, and other folks want to see him go down too, but it must be strategic. So, I don't want you worrying about him at all. I'm going to make sure he pays for what he did to you and your mother.

Playing with the baby's fingertips and wanting to change the subject, Tatiana asked, "Do you think she'll get darker? Nanna said that the dark part around her nail means she's going to get darker."

"I think she is going to be beautiful, just like her mother. No matter how her skin turns out." Tiffany gushed while cooing to the baby.

"You know that was a very *politically correct* white answer, right?" Tatiana scoffed playfully.

"Well, it doesn't matter if it's the truth," Tiffany laughed as she picked the baby up gently off Tatiana's chest and placed her in her crib.

Cool air replaced the warmth Tatiana felt from her baby's absence, and she covered her bare chest with the blanket.

Tiffany ran her hands through Tatiana's hair. It calmed Tatiana, if only for the moment. She had so many things going through her mind that Tatiana could not hear herself think. Even though she was glad Tiffany had kept her word and stayed around, Tatiana wanted to be alone with her thoughts.

Eyes still closed, Tatiana asked, "Can you please check on Nanna while you here? She should still be in the same room on the other side of the hospital."

"Of course. You know I will."

"Thank you for being here, Auntie Tiffany."

"No worries, Babygirl. I told you I got you. And while I'm over there, I'll see if her doctor will let Nanna come see the baby." Tiffany replied.

The idea of her grandmother being rolled into the room saddened her. Nanna had only seen her great-granddaughter once since Tatiana had her. Her grandmother's health was declining at a rapid pace, and Tatiana would soon, truly be on her own.

Tiffany cut in on Tatiana's thoughts, "I see that look on your face. Everything will be fine. I'll be back after I find out what time I can get Nanna over here and after I grab something to eat. You going to be okay while I'm out?"

Tatiana nodded her head.

"You sure? Because I can get Nurse Ratchet to take care of you while I'm gone." Tiffany joked.

"Seriously, I'm okay." Tatiana sighed.

Tiffany blew Tatiana and the baby kisses before leaving the room and gently shutting the door behind her.

Tatiana was happy to have a moment alone. When the motion sensor dimmed the room light, Tatiana reached under her pillow to feel for the handle of the Glock Tiffany left for her. Gripping the piece and having it close gave her the assurance she needed to close her eyes for the night. She knew Tiffany meant well, but she would not always be there. Tatiana had to look after herself and her baby, and there were too many enemies to leave their lives in someone else's hands.

Tatiana coddled her baby up from the crib beside her bed and placed her back on her chest. Her daughter cooed, and Tatiana gently rubbed her back and rocked while whispering, "I got us, Babygirl." until they both fell sound asleep.

Epilogue

VERDELL

Verdell was a wanted man. It never failed to surprise him how fast news traveled. Even thirteen hundred miles away, all radio stations, news broadcasts, and billboards flashed his face on a constant rotation.

K9s and armed security are at every checkpoint, and all major international airports are on red alert. Benji's text read.

I can see that. Verdell texted back.

You're here already? Where are you?

Verdell tapped Benji on her shoulder and said, "Right here," and she gasped loudly.

Grabbing her in what would appear to onlookers as an elderly father embracing his daughter, Verdell calmed Benji, whispering, "It's me. Chill on the screaming. You're going to blow my damn cover."

Benji stepped back from the embrace, taking in Verdell's appearance.

"It's only been four months, and you look like you've aged forty years." She said, circling him.

"Pretty good, huh? Prosthetics are the shit."

Playfully punching Verdell in the shoulder, Benji laughed, "Damn right!"

Verdell hunched over like the blow dislocated his shoulder.

"Are you okay?" Benji asked, concerned.

"Just playing the part," Verdell assured, looking up from under his bushy salt and pepper eyebrows with a grin.

They both chuckled.

"Seriously though, Vee. I'm glad you made it out of there. Things were hot for a couple months before I heard from you. I thought they got you."

"Well, I got a lot of *theys* after me, and *they* gone have to get in line. You got the stuff I asked for?"

"Yep," Benji said solemnly, passing him an attaché containing a passport, credit card, and other documents with his new identity.

Verdell handed Benji a tiny baby blue gift box from his duffle bag.

"What's this?" Benji asked, eyes wide.

"Well, it ain't me proposing to your ass. Open it up. And hurry up. My flight is getting ready to board."

Benji opened the box to find an even smaller sackcloth bag. "What is it, Vee?" She asked giddily.

Verdell snatched the bag and opened Benji's palm, pouring out five brilliantly flawless diamonds.

"Just my way of saying thank you for getting me out of the city, meeting me all the way out here, and putting up with my shit."

Still gazing at the stones in her hand, Benji scoffed, "No worries. My fee covered the extra costs."

A silence fell between them.

"So, this is goodbye for real?"

"I can't trust nobody right now, Benji. So, until I can figure all this shit out, nobody is safe near me."

Benji's eyes teared. Verdell could not remember Benji ever crying in all the time they knew each other. But he understood. His heart was heavy too. Verdell rather say goodbye now than be cornered and let a bullet say it for him later. He cared about Benji, but he would love no one else.

Verdell said his final farewell to Benji, leaving her standing at the departure gate. Boarding the plane, walking past all of the people who would never know there was a killer in their midst today. He took his seat by the window, watching as the other passengers mumbled and groaned at having to sit so close to others. *Benji was definitely on top of her shit to book all three seats in the row.* Verdell's worries would be focused on things less trivial than who was crowding his space at twenty thousand feet.

Verdell looked out the window as the plane took off, jealous of the clouds. They were free to come and go. They brought fear and shelter. That duality he had never been free to experience. *Maybe I can do the same.* Verdell would take this time off to regroup and to hunt. He never took his job personally, but nothing else could be just business after Tatiana. His death list was growing. The Camp had to be behind the phone call at Tatiana's that night. Paul Christen and whoever he had doing his muscle work made him damage any chance he had at love, and the Mellows had no idea who they were fucking with.

Verdell opened the attaché case to look over some of the documents, and a picture fell out. The baby was so beautiful that he could not help but smile. He flipped the photo over to the back.

Thought I'd include this so you would remember that you have a reason to come back." - Benji

Damn. This is my Babygirl. Verdell's cheeks grew hot, and he kissed the picture before putting it back in the case. He did not want to cry. They had all robbed him of his happiness. Maybe after he killed them all, he would be back to claim what was his.

ABOUT THE AUTHOR

Taveyah LaShay is an author residing in Brandon, Florida. She is behind the dramatic thriller trilogy, Requiem.

You can visit her online at *www.taveyahlashay.com* or on Facebook, Instagram, and Twitter (@ *TaveyahWrites*).

The first book in this series, *Requiem: Origins*, can be found on Amazon and Audible.

Made in the USA
Coppell, TX
23 April 2022

76925466R00226